THE GOD SPOT

THE GOD SPOT

by Dean Briggs

WORD PUBLISHING

NASHVILLE

A Thomas Nelson Company

THE GOD SPOT

Unless otherwise indicated, Scripture quotations are from the NEW AMERICAN STANDARD BIBLE®, © Copyright The Lockman Foundation 1960, 1962, 1963, 1968, 1971, 1972, 1973, 1975, 1977. Used by permission.

Scripture quotations noted KJV are from the KING JAMES VERSION of the Holy Bible.

Library of Congress Cataloging-in-Publication Data

Briggs, Dean, 1968–
    The God spot: a novel / by Dean Briggs.
        p. cm.
    ISBN 0-8499-3734-5 (trade paper)
    I. Title.
    PS3552.R4556G6 1999
    813'.54—dc21

                                                        99-12078
                                                        CIP

Printed in the United States of America
9 0 1 2 3 4 5 QPV 9 8 7 6 5

Acknowledgments

As with any work of this sort, special thanks are in order: first of all to my son, Hanson, for the joy of his name; to my mom and dad, Benny and Darlene Briggs, for faith; to early readers Todd Fuller, Paula Hubbert, Bobbie Cochran, and Vicki Miller (who says you can't have a great relationship with your mother-in-law, right, Vicki?); to such sages and encouragers as Warren Ripley and Rod Morris (thanks, Rod!), without whose advice I would have floundered; and to my dear friend and all-around-medical-guru, Dr. Thom Mohn, with additional medical input from Dr. James E. Thomas.

I also want to make special note of the University of Washington's Dr. John Medina, for his fluency in translating medical jargon into comprehensible terms. My thanks to *The Door Magazine* for an interview with Dr. Medina, which formed the basis of the fictional Dr. Remming's own communication skills.

Of course, I am indebted to the entire team at Word, in particular Joey Paul, who first believed in this project. Thanks for your "breezy professionalism," Joey.

Last, let the world know, I am ruined with love for Jesus. At the end of the day, all I really want is more of him. Thank you, Friend.

With great appreciation, I dedicate this book to
"Granny" Ruth Meils, who first filled my mind
with the wise and fanciful tales of
Mother Goose and Brothers Grimm.

And also to my wife, Amy.
We journey together or we do not journey at all.

If crime and disease are to be regarded as the same thing, it follows that any state of mind which our masters chose to call "disease" can be treated as a crime; and compulsorily cured.

—*C. S. Lewis*

Prologue

The camera zoomed in perfectly to capture the moment—an angry sign bobbing up and down. A sign that read, simply, "Kill 'em all and let God sort it out!"

The sign itself was nothing more than white painted cardboard duct-taped to an old broom handle. The man holding the sign was stocky and loud; his face was red from shouting. Around the perimeter, numerous groups of people pitched and yawed like ships at sea—some with the man, some against. And all the while, unseen, a voice whispered urgent directives into the cameraman's earpiece: "Zoom in! Hold. Get the clenched fist. Now . . . wide angle!"

Perfectly positioned in front of this crowd, an attractive black-haired woman with a microphone in one hand and a stack of media briefings in the other calmly gazed into the camera's glass eye. Her lips moved steadily, beaming her voice invisibly through the night into thousands, millions of homes, recording the event with a practiced melodrama for posterity and, hopefully, a thirty-eight percent market share. . . .

Dr. T. Samual Rosenburg grunted something in Yiddish as he flipped from channel nine to channel seven. Same thing. More people, more shouting, more prayers and luminescent candles. Rosenburg scratched his thin, scraggly beard.

The chain link grid and rolled barbed wire of the penitentiary were all too familiar by now. For the past week the only thing that ever changed on TV was the face of the commentator, from the attorney general to the victims' families to any number of social activists either praising the execution of noted serial killer Luther Sanchez as justice at work, or bemoaning the hypocrisy of state-sanctioned murder. Every story was eloquent and heart wrenching.

Rosenburg sipped his chilled Martin Brothers Moscato Allegro and watched with passing, disdainful interest.

". . . pending a surprise word from the governor, the man known as Bone Crusher will be put to death by lethal injection at the stroke of midnight in two short days, the first capital punishment in the state of Michigan since the new legislature stunned civil rights activists by overturning a law that has stood since 1847 . . ."

Rosenburg clicked the remote.

". . . so let's go live to Milan, where Karen van Meer is sitting with Luther Sanchez for a *NewsBeat* exclusive interview, which makes this the only interview Sanchez has granted in the five years since his incarceration. Karen?"

Rosenburg's interest was piqued, but he was careful not to show it. His wife was in the kitchen or upstairs somewhere. He glanced over his shoulder to find her, but it was not really her interest that concerned him. It was his own.

On screen, WDIV channel four's Karen van Meer was sitting in a folding chair near the bunk bed of Luther Sanchez. Karen was tall and slender, dressed in navy pants with a red jacket. Her bright-colored clothes stood out boldly against the flat tones of concrete and iron in Luther's cell. As the camera zoomed in through the heavy bars for effect, the tripods and lights and sound equipment stuffed into Luther's cell looked garish, like too many toys in a toy box. At the foot of Luther's bed, an iron crucifix hung from the wall, draped with the rosary.

Luther watched Karen with something between scorn and hunger. He was a rugged-looking man, mid- to late twenties, coal black hair slicked back in a tight little ponytail. Very Latin. Clean-shaven, with dark, pockmarked skin and smoldering eyes—not necessarily good-looking. His hands formed a tight, perfect triangle, the tip of which pulled at his lower lip.

"Mr. Sanchez," Karen began. "You are breaking a five-year vow of silence tonight. Why?"

Luther didn't answer at first. He seemed to be staring at a patch of concrete just to the right of Karen's face. A long stretch of dead air followed. Karen shifted in her chair.

"Mr. Sanchez," she stated again. "Now's your chance to tell *your* side."

Not so easy as that. Making people nervous was a game for Luther. His two forefingers tapped together; the fluorescent lights buzzed softly.

"Mr. Sanchez!" Karen demanded. "Why did you ask for this interview? Why break the vow of silence now?"

Luther neither smiled, nor frowned, nor moved his gaze from the spot on the wall. But as he spoke through the peak of his fingers, his heavy Latino accent brought a cool rhythm to the words. "I made no vow. I made nothing. I *was* made."

Karen van Meer was no rookie straight out of broadcasting school. She was a veteran field reporter for the NBC affiliate. But when Luther turned his face toward her, finally locked his dark brown eyes on her, so dark as to be opaque, the fierceness in them nearly made her flinch.

She tried another tack. "Mr. Sanchez . . . may I call you Luther?"

Luther shrugged. "*Me llamo* Luther Miguel Sanchez."

Karen knew enough Spanish to play his game. "Fine. Luther, what do you say to those who think your death is a symbol of society's right to protect itself against violent offenders?"

"I ain't got nothing to say to them. Society is a bunch of snakes biting each other, got it? Just a bunch of power brokers, all playing for their stake in the game. *My* stake in the game comes up in two days." He held up his index finger and thumb, then jabbed one of them into his arm like an IV. "Nothing but a needle and a drug that makes my heart stop pumping." He leaned into Karen's face so that she could smell the salt on his breath. "What's *your* stake, Miss van Meer?"

In his recliner at home, Rosenburg leaned forward, too, transfixed. A sort of guilt darkened his face. But Karen van Meer wasn't fazed.

"So you deny your own responsibility for the deaths of thirteen people?"

Luther laughed harshly. "I get it, I get it. You want to know what I deny, right? You wanna serve my soul on a platter for the little people out there in the Land of Oz—" He pointed to the camera lens, but his eyes never left Karen. The camera zoomed in, waiting for his reply.

It got one. Luther exploded, rising from his seat, jabbing his finger in Karen's face. "You want to know me, *señorita*? You want me to fess up like a child to his momma? Do I deny *this*, do I deny *that*? I'll tell you what I deny. I deny you the right to act like you give—" A flurry of expletives followed.

Professional or not, Karen could not hide her fear. Her skin paled. Even more, in that moment she realized the truth, that Luther granted this interview not for the chance to speak but to humiliate. Two prison guards shoved the criminal back into his chair. Luther spat. When Karen reassured the guards that she was fine, the interview continued.

"So, you want to live?" she demanded, brushing a fallen strand of hair out of her face.

Luther almost seemed caught off guard. He tilted his head sideways, his unblinking eyes considering the possibility as if for the first time.

"I was dead before I was born," he said finally. "The *man* made sure of that."

"The man? Who is the man?"

"Come on, *señorita*! Sugar Daddy. You know, 'Now I lay me down to sleep, Big Brother's got my soul to keep.'"

"You mean the government?"

Luther smiled, pleased. He asked, "Ever watch the movies?"

"Yes, of course."

"*Planet of the Apes?*"

Karen nodded. Luther grinned.

"You want a scandal, right? Listen—I'm the ape man."

Karen waited for more. Luther grew irritated at her slowness.

"In the movie, you know, the apes are like people. All the cats and dogs die, so humans start taking apes as pets, and pretty soon the apes are smarter than the people. And so there Charlton Heston is, running all around trying to survive, trying to fix what his own people screwed up years before . . . the ape man. Well, I'm him." Luther clenched his fist for the grand climax. "I was dead before my momma ever saw my face, *sí*? The man was there all along . . ."

"Where? What do you mean, Luther?"

"He was there—*in the womb.*"

T. Samual Rosenburg squirmed as he watched the television. He neither drank his wine, nor smiled, nor frowned. His face was grave. But he did not, could not, change the channel.

Luther sounded like a child picked on by the school bully. First he was afraid, then hurt, then the import of his own words began to boil inside. He lifted a shaking finger so Karen could see his torment and, by that act, somehow seemed to hold the inner forces of chaos at bay. His lips formed a tight, painful smile. "Day after tomorrow, the juice will stop this shouting, this noise"—he pointed to his head first, then to himself and to Karen—"but we are not so different as you think. You are me . . . could have been me. Can you hear me, Karen van Meer? You could have been me. Anyone could have been."

He rose to leave.

Karen started. "Just a few more questions, Luther—"

"Interview's over."

"Are you sorry for your crimes?"

"No more. Please. *Hasta luego,* Miss van Meer."

"Does that mean you're not sorry? You had no motive, no pattern. Why did you do it?"

"Enough!" Luther cried as chaos flooded back in. "Enough!" He lunged, pressing his flat, broad hand hard against the camera lens. The image on Rosenburg's television jostled and swerved hard to the floor as the camera tipped, slamming into the side wall.

. . . Static.

Rosenburg didn't move. At length he climbed to his feet, physically shook himself free of Luther's spell. He had other worries. Too many, in fact.

Besides, it was time to take his dog, Rachel, for her nightly walk.

1

The string of words flashing on-screen read more like an apology than a warning.

"Access denied. Inappropriate password."

Not *incorrect* password, or *wrong* password. No, such language would be far too derogatory to the casual hacker. Hank's guesses were merely "inappropriate."

Hank managed a placating smile. *Just tell me I'm wrong,* he thought. *Don't patronize.*

The politeness of the system rankled him more than it should. But Hank had a fair streak of paranoia running through him, thanks to the often strange ideas of his mother and the abundance of Teutonic genes donated from her side of the family. The very thought of a well-mannered computer fired a sort of Orwellian alarm in his head. Computers simply were not meant to nurture. They were meant to be rude with fact, another word for truth, which Hank knew to be scarce and highly prized, since all the wrong people were generally in control of it. Hank figured every period of history should offer mankind at least one bastion of cold, hard, unforgiving truth.

Modern man *did* have one, or at least used to. Computers made perfectly proud and unapologetic tyrants, and that's how Hank thought it should be. If a computer spat out a number or an answer that caused offense, well, you either changed your input or learned to deal with it. There was no coddling. No subtle attempts at pop psychology.

So much for progress, he decided, watching the fuzzy gray matrix of his laptop flicker in the morning's half-light. A politically correct computer, one that apologized for any contradiction of ideas, almost certainly pointed to larger woes. It meant that postmodern man's grip on truth had slipped into the shadowland of sappy TV sitcoms and "Hug Your Dirt" environmental campaigns. Hank hated environmental pandering.

He typed another random code and hit return. Same message. "Access denied. . . ."

This wasn't the first time he had stumbled onto a locked forum on the Net. Hank spent numerous hours online—was a junkie, really, whenever he had the time—but he was only a part-time hack at best. Though conspiratorial, Hank was rarely patient, which effectively ruled out the professional end of true hacking. And he was certainly no programmer. Instead, he had learned to gracefully yield to passwords and security codes a real pro might think scornfully bourgeois.

Too much on this highway to get waylaid by a stop sign was his usual excuse for giving up most of the time.

But the Net was tricky. Like a great, sprawling tree, where each leaf is a piece of information, and where each branch of leaves opens up to three more, the Internet was daunting to investigate, yet Edenic with possibility, knowledge. And thereby power. The Net was also about the most superfluous entity on the planet. One could not separate the two poles—both the abundance of information, and the abundance of junk—without doing damage to the whole. So as a matter of survival, anyone who spent more than twenty minutes online quickly learned the finer points of search engines such as Yahoo or Hotbots or WebCrawler to filter through the mounds of data that were just too useless or bizarre or narrowly focused to serve any purpose other than wasting time.

There was good stuff—a staggering amount, really—but most of the best remained closed to the public. Disciplined souls ignored web addresses that were guarded or appeared suspicious. Too many crazies out there; too many Big Brothers, cults of personality, corporate muscle, scam artists or wacko survivalists huddling together to risk getting caught in the dark side of the web when, in fact, all most people wanted was a cool screen shot, the latest stock quote, or a bit of research for a school project. For the more adventurous, however, a warning message wrapped around a juicy little piece of forbidden fruit was as good as an invitation laced with perfume.

Since the Net had grown around the notion that information should be exchanged freely and frequently, a site that prohibited casual access raised the hackles of purists. And nowhere does paranoia run more rampant than in the hearts of Net purists. Hank was not a purist, but he was somewhat mischievous. Despite his usually quick surrender, from time to time he could not resist that childlike pang of curiosity that strikes a person when he is told, without reason, "No, you can't."

So when the screen displayed its simple challenge: "Access denied. . . ." Hank could not help but wonder what was going on behind those closed doors. He took a few more halfhearted stabs at the password. Nothing. He didn't even know if the password was one, two, or three words. The message flashed again, in caps: "ACCESS DENIED."

Hank ran a slow finger over the surface of his trusty Macintosh as if the machine were Aladdin's magic lamp. Alas, no smoke, no genie. No silver key. He reached for the phone, dialed a number.

A sleepy voice greeted him on the other end.

"Kim, wake up, for crying out loud! It's ten o'clock already."

"Hank?"

"Yeah, yeah. Listen, I need some help. Kim . . . Are you there?"

A pause. Finally, "Can't this wait? I'm dead."

Hank ignored him. Kim Yu was perhaps the finest computer hacker at Columbia University and one of an underground group of national elites. As such, his identity was known only to a privileged few—his code name (all good hackers have one), to fewer still.

Kim Yu was the Wraith.

The Wraith wasn't one of those malicious anarchists known among the inner circles of cyberspace as Crackers and Spiders, who enjoy destruction as an end in itself. Kim was a bona fide Hacker. Simply put, he believed that information should be free flowing and readily accessible. He was not out to hurt anybody or anything, but if he had to do a little damage to an uncooperative system in the name of accessibility, well then, he was sure there was a good lesson in there against hoarding the wealth. Kim and Hank had formed a rough-and-tumble sort of friendship around two simple things: the Internet and jazz maestro Charlie "Bird" Parker, arguably the greatest improvisationalist in the history of the saxophone.

Hank said, "Do you remember that psycho e-mail I told you about a while back?"

Hank couldn't tell if Kim was thinking or sleeping.

"I think I do," Kim said at last. His voice was still thick and dry. "Three weeks ago? Four?"

"Something like that. So get this: A few days ago I was downloading my mail when I decided to do a little surfing . . . you know, the usual. I linked up with a couple of my Usenet groups, but not the one where I saw the first note. Anyway, another note shows up in my download. Didn't think a thing of it at the time. Until I read it."

"Uh-huh," Kim mumbled, sounding only slightly less bored than when he answered the phone. "What did it say?"

"Same as the last letter. Exact same! I can't remember the message verbatim, but it was really doomsday sort of stuff. Something about the 'final blasphemy' and how man 'has peered into the mind of God' or 'found the place of God in man.'"

"Hank, c'mon." Kim smirked. "That doesn't sound *that* unusual for the Net."

"Even for an academic forum?"

Kim's tone of voice changed ever so slightly. "Where were you?"

Hank grinned behind the phone receiver. He could see the little wheels in the mind of the Wraith beginning to turn. "I think it was sci.genetics or something," he said. "Definitely nothing alternative. Oh, and when I went back to the other site to check, the note was gone. All the other files were still there except that one. Isn't that a little weird?"

"Not really," Kim said. "The administrator may've let the note slide by on purpose. Maybe he thought it was funny at first, then changed his mind."

"And erased it? That one file? Nothing else?"

"Sure. No big deal."

"Maybe," Hank continued, sounding doubtful, "but the note also mentioned something called Club Cranium. Same as the last note."

"And?"

"And last night I found it. By accident, of course."

"Of course. Found what?"

"Well, see, I traced the mail's header file back to an address that seemed to be a home page. I checked it out, but it was blank."

"Blank?"

"Nothing there. Nothing. The address was legit, but it was just a blank white page. I checked it out again the next day. Same thing. Almost wrote it off right there, but then I remembered one of your tricks."

"You saved the code."

"Yep, the whole file. In HTML. Popped it open in my editor and bam!—there it was—another address, hiding like a vampire on Sunday. Can you believe it? What are the chances of me finding this thing only a few days after reading about it in this note?"

"What thing?"

Hank almost shouted. "Club Cranium! A classified mail thread and gopher site called Club Cranium. What are the chances?"

"About a zillion to one," Kim answered drily.

Hank's mouth was moist. "I need your help, Kim."

"Password?"

"Yup. I'm locked out."

Now the Wraith was wide awake. "Well, I guess we're just gonna have to find you a key, now aren't we, Hank?"

⚇ ⚇ ⚇

Halfway across the globe, Dr. Abu Hasim El-Saludin tended his garden with the meticulous eye and loving hand of a poet. The evening was late, but the warm glow of candles and pink-colored light spreading evenly through the glass arboretum made the darkness outside seem remote and thin.

The greenhouse was a menagerie of living delicacies: pale-colored evening primrose, hardy soapweed, desert bluebells, and gold-petaled brittlebush, just to name a few. Desert wildflowers were Dr. Saludin's private passion and they thrived under his patient care for a variety of reasons. The pink-colored light was not merely decorative. Saludin was testing a theory that pink light filtered down from heaven at the dawn of creation, when Allah, the One God, Blessed and Merciful, had formed the world with the breath of his mouth.

Regardless, the plants thrived.

Dr. Saludin examined the green leaf of a ghost flower, searching for mold or spores or bugs. He stared at the leaf for a long time, caught in a daze. No matter how hard he tried, he simply could not concentrate. Earlier this morning, a package had arrived from his associate in Detroit, Dr. T. Samual Rosenburg. Even though Rosenburg mailed the package via Federal Express, El-Saludin had refused to open the box all day. He had occupied himself at the university, with his family, and now in his garden, because he feared what Rosenburg's package contained.

He left the garden and walked past the open-air courtyard to the tiled portico where one great window faced east. Saludin lived in the nicer quarters of the city of Giza, which lay across the western banks of the Nile from ancient Cairo. Many wealthier Egyptians—politicians, artists, scientists—lived in Giza and worked in Cairo. El-Saludin gazed out the great window, eastward, past the city lights, past miles and miles of desert and water, to faraway Mecca. His heart filled with dread and hope as the last light of the evening fell away. Saludin was a man of peace and gentleness, a devout Muslim. But when he knelt on his prayer blanket, a beautiful rug stained with deep shades of crimson and blue, his prayers carried a richness of purpose born more of fear than faith.

After his prayers were done, he cast about for anything that might occupy him. When it seemed there was nothing left to do, no distractions to keep him from his duty, still, he lingered. At length, when a soft breeze touched his cheek, Saludin rose and entered his home. His beautiful wife and daughter greeted him with smiles. Saludin returned the gesture, but it lacked warmth.

"Abu," his wife said. "What's troubling you?"

Saludin touched her face. "Nothing. I'm sorry, nothing."

He entered his personal study and closed the door carefully behind him. Only a single lamp was on, the one sitting on the corner of his desk, so the room was dark and silent. Rosenburg's package lay on the neatly ordered desk exactly as Saludin had left it this morning. Behind his leather-backed chair were rows and rows of books of all kinds and shapes, arranged alphabetically and by topic. The thin Arab man lowered himself into the chair. The supple leather received him without protest.

Such a beautiful night, Saludin thought sadly. *Such a beautiful night . . .*

If Saludin had a vice—one that lay outside the provision of his faith—it was this: Occasionally he took great pleasure in a small tug on the pipe. He did so now, unhurried, methodical, to relax his nerves and ease his mind. Soon, blue smoke curled from the space between the pipe and his lips. He inhaled and stared into the darkness. The spice of the tobacco filled the air.

At length, he peeled back the corner of tape and opened the package. Someone, presumably Rosenburg himself, had stamped the word "Classified" in bright blue across every page. The first page was a personal letter from Rosenburg:

Esteemed colleague,

We have entered uncharted territory and I am beginning to feel more and more the dread of traveling without a compass. Please find enclosed the latest battery of test results on neurons and neuroglia found near the pineal gland. Compare these with related data from control groups 12-15. Do you see? Chromatin levels are elevated and the RNA code is unlike any I am familiar with. Also note the swollen synaptic vesicles on plates G and M. Astounding, yes? I say frightening. Cell tissue from this region shows extremely pronounced euchromatic stippling in the nucleus upon electron microscopic evaluation; the cells are literally bursting with smooth endoplasmic reticula, pronounced Golgi bodies, and exocytotic vesicles. Also, the cells seem to connect with pseudopodia-like dendritic mats to the surrounding tissue in a very invasive way. But at each synapse there is a cytoplasmic projection from a normal neural cell. In short, it looks like this structure is actually forming a functional neural network! As you will see, the data is rife with implications.

I am used to seeing destructive forces in the brain, not creative ones; but Abu, I am concerned where this research is leading. There are too many loose ends, too much we don't know to begin bragging about what we do. We must proceed with extreme caution.

Samual

Saludin leafed through the documents, feeling dread and fascination knot together in his stomach. There were about fifty pages of data, formulas, columns and columns of numbers—also color plates, drawings, and carefully labeled maps of the human genome.

The data was complex, but Abu Hasim El-Saludin was no intellectual lightweight. By any standard, this small brown-skinned man was an academic force to be reckoned with: an accomplished pharmacologist at the University of Cairo; Harvard educated; extremely influential in the field of neurotransmitters. He was not the kind of man who scared easily.

Nevertheless, as he read the documents from T. Samual Rosenburg, illuminated by the light of a single lamp, his fingers trembled.

※ ※ ※

If it wasn't one thing, it was another.

A tired cliché to be true, but not nearly so tired as Jessica O'Connel at this moment. She ran a finger through a tangle in her thick red hair and turned off the radio, leaving only the steady purr of the engine and wheels spinning over the pavement. All she wanted right now was a warm bath and lots of bubbles. And quiet. Yes, lots and lots of quiet. No jurists, no court clerks, no bailiffs or police or—

Telephones.

Her car phone was ringing. Jessica sighed. Cellular technology was, at best, a curse.

She was a beautiful woman, Jessica O'Connel. Not a dolled-up kind of beauty. And not merely pretty, or cute. Slender in the right spots, curved in the others, taller than average, kind of leggy: She had all the right mix. But it was the sparkle in her leaf green eyes and the way her hair caught a pumpkin-colored beam of light that caused most men to turn and look twice. Something about her skin—lightly dusted around her nose with pale pink freckles, smooth and natural and unashamed—captured an Albionic essence more than a tourism poster or Enya and a pint of ale ever could. She had just pulled out of the Multnomah County Courthouse after a grueling closed session with Judge Martha Shelby, an African-American woman of preponderous girth and generally foul mood. Judge Shelby, referred to by most of Jessica's colleagues as "Momma," had probably brought the novelty of prayer to more lawyers in Portland than Billy Graham ever could. Plain and simple, Momma scared all but the most grizzled lawyers silly, evoking that same quality of raw, primal fear generally reserved for chicken-killing pygmies in New Guinea when the sky thunders and the gods are angry. Of course, no one dared to call Judge Shelby her nickname to her face. But when the name was spoken—in small groups and with hushed voices—a great, unseen prayer usually followed, a mental genuflecting. For good measure.

Today, for some reason, the honorable judge had been merciful to Jessica. Her client had been granted a restraining order against her abusive husband and the kids were to be immediately removed from his custody pending further investigation.

But that was as good as the news would get. The bad news was that the restraining order wouldn't matter for another two weeks, since the judge had also fined the mother twenty-five hundred dollars for "wielding a weapon with the intent to harm," the weapon being a pair of needle-nose pliers aimed at her husband's privates.

No sooner had that meeting ended than Jessica got word from the county prosecutor that another one of her clients had jumped bail and was reportedly headed across the state line. This particular client was wrongly accused of incest by his adopted daughter. The daughter, a naive, lonely girl, belonged to some wacko cult called Lords of the Shining Path, one of dozens of New Age groups located in the Pacific Northwest, where cults reproduced like rabbits. The girl's claims were strong, but Jessica firmly believed in the father's innocence. With a fair bit of research she had discovered that this cult, whose leadership was strictly male, appeared to be funding their organization by encouraging their predominantly female acolytes to file sexual abuse charges against rich male relatives. It amazed Jessica that no one had ever noticed that the Lords almost exclusively chose blue bloods to follow them down their Shining Path. Jessica *had* noticed, and was *this close* to getting all charges dropped against her client. Apparently the father did not share her optimism.

The phone rang again. Jessica picked up the receiver.

"Hello?" she said, revealing just a hint of her leftover, lazy Southern drawl.

"Jess, I've got bad news." The voice was that of her secretary, Mandy. "Are you sitting down?"

For all her positive qualities, Mandy somehow managed to achieve both bad humor and worse timing. Of course Jessica was sitting down—Mandy had dialed her car phone. But all Jessica said was, "I'm on my way to the office right now. Can't this wait?"

"I don't think so. Julia's in the hospital."

Julia? Jessica's stomach dropped into the seat of her '67 Mustang. *Dear God . . .*

"Why?!" she gasped. "When?"

"Looks like a little warning from Smits."

Julia was a fifteen-year-old prostitute Jessica had recently befriended. Her adoring pimp, Smits, had kept one slippery step ahead of the law for years. Thanks to Julia, Smits now faced multiple counts of pandering and drug dealing. Julia broke the case wide open when she decided to turn state's witness last week, thanks in large part to Jessica's encouragement.

Jessica's heart sank as Mandy relayed the details. Cracked collarbone, two broken ribs, broken jaw.

So she can't talk.

"When?" she asked Mandy again.

"Last night. More like early this morning. She's OK, but she's pretty scared. Oh, and one more thing . . ."

Jessica could barely speak. "Go on."

"You probably already know this, but she has no money. Zero. St. Luke's can take her on Medicaid, but she may need some counseling before this is all over. Especially if you still want to try and put her on the stand."

Actually, Jessica was not the one putting her on the stand. She was a defense attorney and, in the strictest sense, had nothing to do with the case. But a good friend of hers, an assistant D.A., had offered Julia a plum deal in exchange for the testimony, so Jessica saw this as a real opportunity for Julia to get her life back on track. It was Jessica who had urged Julia to cut the deal, which took some doing; Julia was naturally terrified. But Jessica had reassured her, told Julia—how many times? beyond counting—that she would be safe. In the end, Julia trusted Jessica with almost childlike faith, even though they had known each other for less than two months. Jessica was the first person who had ever talked to Julia without shouting or hitting, who had given her a few dollars without expecting sex in return.

Jessica was the only friend Julia had ever had.

The image of that little girl lying in bed with a broken jaw stabbed Jessica's heart like a fireplace poker. Everything returned, everything she could not control, surfacing on cue. She hung up the phone, rubbing her eyes with the palm of her hand, as if that could hold the guilt at bay. She shouldn't have gotten involved and she knew it. She always knew it, crystal clear, about five minutes after the fact.

My fault, not hers. Mine.

Five minutes too late. Always five minutes too late. Now came the coping. This was how it started, how it always showed up, at times like this. She used to pretend she could handle it. If she was driving, like now, she would crank up the radio; if she was at home she would go jogging—anything to reschedule the burden. But the silence always returned. Night always arrived, velvet and suffocating. Guilt and loneliness, the two-faced demon, remained unquenched. That was how it began.

No, long ago. Longer, she thought. But it didn't really matter when. *Who this time?*

It was habit, a fail-safe, like a shot of whiskey to numb the pain. Jessica didn't balk or hesitate. Cursing, she thumbed through her purse, found a little book with numbers in it, picked up the phone, dialed. Waited. The other line rang three times.

Broken jaw, fifteen years old.

A lady answered the phone.

"Let me talk to, umm, Grady, please," Jessica murmured.

A minute later, a charming male voice answered. "Grady Jones here."

Jessica brightened, but it was as sudden as a light switch: too much, too soon. With one hand on the wheel and the other on the phone, her plaster-of-paris smile might as well have been a pink packet of tea sweetener. "Grady! Long time, no see!"

"Jessica?"

"Of course it's me, don't be silly! Where have you been hiding yourself?"

Reflexively, Grady distanced himself. "Jessica, what do you need? Is something wrong?"

Jessica swallowed hard, still smiling. "Why do you say that? Does something have to be wrong?"

Grady Jones could not see Jessica's face, the exaggeration of delight, the emptiness. He could only hear it in her voice.

"Something usually is," he replied.

Jessica laughed. Even though nervous, the sound of her laugh was beautiful, like a bell on a foggy morning. "You're going to make this hard on me, aren't you, Grady?" she said, pouting, coaxing, angling for control. "Going to make me beg? I don't mind," she whispered, "I'll beg."

"Jess—"

"Thought you'd like to see me, maybe. You know, for old times' sake. I've missed you."

"Jess—"

"Grady, don't tease me! How's tonight sound? I've got candles and wine . . ." She didn't. She would have to buy them. ". . . Mother Nature can do the rest. Remember?"

"You don't understand, Jess. It's been a long time. I'm different."

Jessica whispered, near desperation, "Let me help you remember."

"I don't want to! All I want to do is forget! It doesn't have to be this way, Jessica. It can be better. I know that for a fact."

"Grady?"

"Listen, I've got to go. I'm sorry—"

Click.

The line was dead. Alone in her car, skimming the pavement at sixty-five miles per hour, Jessica felt the blood rise to her face, a deep and angry hue, the color of humiliation. She thumbed through her book, hand trembling, looking for another number. Any number. She did not want to be alone tonight. Her father had left her alone once, long ago, forever. One day he was there, the next he was gone.

She did not want to be alone.

Julia lay in a hospital bed, the victim of Jessica's legal pimping. That was the plain truth of it. There was no difference. The state of Oregon had solicited favors from a child who did not wish to give them, in exchange for promises of security and hope, with *her* help. Her encouragement. Jessica felt her stomach roll. It *was* her fault. *God, no* . . . Jessica couldn't stand the silence, not like this, not when her heart was broken. The relentless voices in her head demanded justice— for her, for Julia. For the world. She dialed the phone.

Busy . . . Not there . . . Busy.

She cursed, pressed the accelerator, hit the wheel. Then the tears began.

A fiery redheaded Irish girl, Jessica O'Connel was a junior member of the small Portland law firm of Kirkland, Stubing, and Minsk. The star recruit of Cornell's law school class of '94, she possessed a brilliant legal mind, was tenacious, cunning in litigation, and could offer the jury a smile that either froze their toes or warmed their hearts. Jessica possessed a beguiling, potent mix of acerbic wit and Southern charm from her early years in North Carolina. After only three short years, she had proved herself to be the firm's brightest talent. Brightest and, to the senior partners, somewhat frustrating as well. Jessica had a penchant for taking on the most hopeless long-shot cases. Her tender heart bled seven different shades of purple, and every shade brought in poorer and poorer clients. The generally prudish Kirkland, Stubing, and Minsk tolerated her generosity in the hopes that hers was a fading innocence, a fad—the aspirations of youth that still believed the world could be changed with a legal briefing and a passion for justice. What they were beginning to understand was that hers was no ordinary passion. No, mind you, passion for Jessica O'Connel was spelled with a capital *P.* Jessica was stubborn, bullheaded, and altruistically narrow-minded to a fault.

In truth, all the senior partners (especially Minsk) began their legal careers with a measure of the social sentiment that throbbed in Jessica's veins. So when they looked at her, though one eye scolded, the other eye saw a small part of himself living still, like a forgotten shadow or the memory of a better self—a truer code of honor—and that part always silenced whatever protest was about to be spoken. Now in its thirty-fourth year, Kirkland, Stubing, and Minsk had developed quite a prestigious reputation.

With Jessica O'Connel, they had heart once again.

Having peaked and sufficiently burned off the twin rivers' morning mist, the sun began its lazy southward arc through the blue Oregon sky. Outside the air was fresh and mild, which was good, because Jessica had been stuck in traffic for the last twenty minutes.

Finally free of the slow-moving train of steel and rubber, Jessica's day got bumped another couple of notches in the form of a policeman and a speedometer pushing eighty right down the middle of Interstate 5. Lights flashed and a siren blared and Jessica pulled over to the shoulder, wiping her eyes. Black-colored thoughts formed in her head.

When it rains, it . . . .

A pouchy-faced man in a familiar blue uniform tapped on her window. Jessica rolled down the glass. Her lips were set in a tight non-smile, her eyes straight ahead.

"Hello," she said. Her voice was resigned, weary. She had reached Tony right before she heard the siren. Tony What's-His-Face. He was coming over tonight . . . in fact, seemed quite eager. She dreaded it.

The officer bent down, bored, perturbed. Over his shoulder, way off in the east, Jessica glimpsed the majestic snowcap of Mount Hood rising from the Cascades like a mighty tower. It stood so tall and still, so impervious to the pettiness of day-to-day affairs . . . and so far away. For a moment Jessica allowed herself the sweet pleasure of imagining she was there, in a cabin on the mountain, all alone—anywhere instead of here. But her vacation was still five long weeks away. And Tony was tonight. . . .

The officer, an average-looking run-of-the-mill cop with an aging Chicago accent, was looking at her as if waiting for a reply. Jessica realized he must have given an impressive speech, but she had not heard a word he said.

"Look, I'm sorry. I was speeding. I deserve a ticket."

Both eyebrows lifted slightly. From the moment he turned on his siren, the officer had begun bracing himself for any one of ten classic excuses. Cops get so tired of excuses.

"Umm . . ."

"I was speeding, I was speeding. Probably seventy. Seventy-five, maybe? You're just doing your job. Let's hurry it up. I'm late for a meeting."

Classic Jessica. This was no show, no put-on. Even when the penalties came out of her own pocket, Jessica O'Connel knew the difference between right and wrong, usually in terms so clearly defined, so black and white, they'd likely choke an otherwise moral man. She could tolerate the thought of leniency for others. Even Tony. Or Grady. Just guys looking for a free ride, right? But not her. She knew the game. It wasn't their fault she begged for sex to keep the pain in her head from exploding. So like a good marine she asked for nothing, neither favor nor reprieve, just saluted and waited to hear how many push-ups this one would cost.

The officer fumbled with his ticket pad, reached for the pen in his pocket, dropped it. When he bent to retrieve the pen, he bumped his head on Jessica's car door. Jessica leaned out the car window, said nothing. Poor shmuck was having as bad of a day as she was.

When he rose, the policeman looked her in the eye.

"I've been doing this for twelve years now, ma'am. You're only the second person I've ever pulled over who owned up to it. The other was a nun back in Chicago. So . . . well, just be careful. And lighten up with that right foot. You might break that gas pedal if you're not careful."

Not wanting to give him the chance to reconsider, Jessica hit her blinker and slowly accelerated onto the freeway. After crossing the Willamette River, she headed south, away from downtown. Barely had she set foot inside the offices of Kirkland, Stubing, and Minsk than her loyal secretary flagged her down.

"Been one of those days, huh?" Mandy whispered upon seeing her. Cradling the telephone to her ear and busily scratching notes on bright pink paper, Mandy made a wiping motion with her finger underneath her eyes, a signal; her lips moved: *"Mascara."*

Jessica nodded, brushed her cheeks with a tissue, said nothing. When the call was done, Mandy thumbed through a stack of papers—people for Jessica to call, appointments, court schedules. She smiled pleasantly, gave her the stack, and shuffled her off like a mother hen herding a stray chick.

Jessica stopped, said, "I'll need the—"

"Shining Path file. It's on your desk."

"Thanks. I was thinking about visiting Julia, too."

"The hospital number's written at the top there." Mandy pointed to one of the notes. "And I've already rescheduled your four o'clock just in case. . . ."

Jessica couldn't help but smile. Whatever personality quirks Mandy possessed—and there were quite a few—she was the one force powerful enough to keep Jessica's life organized. It was ironic that a woman of Jessica's stripe, who possessed such precise mental faculties, could live her life surrounded by persistent chaos. Her office was never truly clean, always cluttered with massive legal tomes earmarked at a half dozen precedents; papers seemed to appear *ex nihilo,* as did newspaper clippings. Home was no refuge. Her clothes lay here and there, wherever they dropped; lipstick and eyeliner on the coffee table or (how was it possible?) in the refrigerator; overdue movie rentals, etc. But through Mandy, though the externals fell into disarray, Jessica's daily schedule remained intact.

Everybody needs an obsessive-compulsive secretary, Jessica had often thought in the past, and she did so again as she headed toward her office, shaking her head. Once inside, she eased into her comfortable leather chair and slipped off her shoes. If there was one good thing about women's shoes, it was taking them off after a long day. Jessica just sat there for a moment, eyes closed, stretching her nylons with her toes.

When she opened her eyes again, the cult file was on top of all her other desk clutter, right where Mandy said it would be. Jessica glanced over the many notes, each one representing an obligation, a commitment, a portion of time. She sighed.

Vacation could come none too soon.

Outside, sitting in a black Volvo parked across the street from the red-brick offices of Kirkland, Stubing, and Minsk, a strikingly beautiful woman with platinum blonde hair watched the firm's solid oak double doors with unusual attentiveness, as if expecting something. Or someone.

On the floor beneath the passenger seat of her car, a small reel-to-reel tape recorder rolled smoothly. The unit had a single small antenna. Strapped around her wrist was a tiny wireless microphone, and tucked behind her right ear was a flesh-colored, nearly invisible earpiece. She was wearing dark, stylish sunglasses and had the look of vodka and ice, cool and lethal. Even though the weather was mild, her hands were wrapped in a pair of sleek Isotoners. She listened intently to the headset. There was a long patch of static—had been for about half an hour, broken only by the occasional ringing of a phone or the rustle of papers shuffling. Suddenly the muffled sound of human voices broke through.

"Are you coming back to the office afterward?"

"Maybe. I don't know. I may just head home."

More papers shuffling.

"Well, have a good one."

"You too. See you in the morning if not before."

A sound like a purse opening . . . shutting. Keys jingled. The face of the woman sitting in the Volvo formed a mask of calm anticipation.

It was 3:41 when Jessica emerged from the brass-trimmed double doors of the firm. The woman in the Volvo put her mouth to her wrist and spoke in low tones, never taking her eyes off of Jessica.

"Tuesday, April 4. Number Seventeen calls it a day at"—she glanced at her watch—"3:42 p.m. I'm guessing she's going to the hospital to visit the girl her secretary was talking about. She's right on pace so far, showing all the classic signs. And I mean classic. Extreme personality traits, severe moral inconsistency. The girl's nothing less than an angel, except when she's a whore." She said the last part like a little sneeze, with scorn. "Will maintain surveillance—"

Suddenly the woman reached up and lowered her sun visor. Jessica was walking straight toward her. She didn't flinch, didn't do anything, just sat there, unperturbed, staring straight ahead. When it appeared that Jessica might actually be watching her, she casually raised a gloved hand to cover the left side of her face. Still, Jessica drew closer, closer . . . then all of a sudden angled away, seemingly unaware, heading for her own car two spaces down. Within minutes Jessica was edging her banana yellow Mustang into the street and charging off to the hospital. The blonde waited a moment or two, breathing evenly, before turning the ignition key. The engine whispered to life. She reached over and switched off the recorder, pulled out the earpiece, was about to pull into traffic when her cellular rang.

"Yes?"

"Where are you, Decker?" The voice was male, relatively agreeable, but obviously accustomed to quick answers all the same.

"Downtown Portland," the woman known as Decker said, tightening her lips into thin lines as she watched Jessica's car melting into traffic. Her voice matched her face: sharp, angular, just a little bit sexy if you're into condescension. And about five degrees cooler than room temperature. "I'm following Seventeen at the moment. Or at least I was. Can this wait?"

"Sorry, no. How is she?"

"You'll get my report."

"Sure. Listen, Susan, there's been a diversion."

So Susan listened as the man on the other end of the line laid out all the details.

"What about Jessica?" she asked when he finished.

"She'll be fine for a few days. Nothing's changed. But this situation in Detroit is potentially embarrassing. The agency wants zero publicity, got it?"

"Got it. When do I fly?"

"Tomorrow."

"Tomorrow!" Susan Decker cursed under her breath. "You always do this to me, Nix."

"Hey, give it a rest, Decker. I could have sent you tonight. After six years you'd think you'd change your attitude a little bit."

Susan drew each word out slowly. "I like to stay focused. One thing at a time. It's what makes me good."

"That's a nice story, Decker. But the perks never seem to bother you, now do they? Just make sure you're in line at the airport tomorrow morning. Your tickets are waiting for you. As usual."

Susan bit her lip, cursing again. This time only in her head.

"Fine. I'm there. What's the game?"

"You'll find out when you arrive. Oh, and Susan?"

He waited for her to respond. She waited for him to give up. He won.

"What?" she muttered angrily.

The answer was syrupy sweet. "I'm *so* looking forward to your report."

8 8 8

Hank downed a chocolate malt and wiped his mouth, sort of jogging-skipping-walking on his way to the intensive care wing of the medical complex at Presbyterian Hospital on the campus of the College of Physicians and Surgeons at Columbia. Presbyterian Hospital and Columbia University were both venerable and stalwart institutions, and the permanent alliance of their names and resources only made them more so. CPMC, the Columbia-Presbyterian Medical Center, was the banner name under which the numerous departments and research centers of the mega medical complex found their identity. Situated between Broadway and Fort Washington Avenue, the seventeen-story building of the College of Physicians and Surgeons connected at every level with the wards and services of the Presbyterian. Hank's boss, Jay Remming, had his office in the adjacent William Black Medical Research Building, an attractive brick high-rise containing research laboratories for the faculty members of the College of Physicians and Surgeons.

Having been a Dartmouth undergrad, Hank had never actually lived on or been a part of the university's campus proper, known as Morningside, situated in Upper Manhattan between Harlem and the Hudson River. Instead he had roomed in the infamous Bard Hall his first year, on the twenty-acre campus of CPMC located about two miles north of the Morningside campus. Now he lived in his own apartment a little farther north in the historic Washington Heights neighborhood. Surrounded by such opulence, Hank realized early on that the taste and flavor of money had their rewards, especially compared to the windswept Kansas farmland of his childhood. His apartment complex on West 166th Street overlooked a cozy bend of the

Hudson River near the George Washington Bridge; and when the city lights were bright and a crescent moon hung low in the sky, it wasn't hard for him to imagine that all the world was a dream.

But for now, all he could do was pick up his pace. As late as he was, he might as well have been dreaming. His little chat with Kim had taken too long. Hank was on his way to join Remming for a quick circuit through ICU and radiology.

At least, it *could* be quick. If not for the trailing gaggle of interns.

Hank mumbled something under his breath, a sour bit of humor, thinking of the white-coated flock of interns that would soon be ogling Remming like adoring teenagers at their first rock concert. Since Hank was Remming's senior resident, the students might even pander to him for a moment or two. Usually a couple of the female students tried to flirt. Hank had a Steve McQueen look and charm about him, rough and undomesticated by the lab coat he wore. But Remming's good graces were what the students prized. He was god here, which made the irony of Remming's probable absence even richer to Hank. Remming rarely showed up for rounds. Why should he? His advanced residents could do the job of herding the cattle just fine. Remming cared little for the whims and pubescent fawning of anyone lower than a first-year resident. And what a disappointment that was for the little teenyboppers! They would almost drag their heels and pout when Hank took them on rounds alone. Remming's name always appeared on the schedule, just in case. And so they came.

Nothing personal, their eyes would say to him. *We just want the Nobel prize winner. . . .*

Hank was long past taking offense. After all, during his first couple of semesters he had been struck with the same sort of childlike wonder. The students would learn, just as he did: Jay Remming, M.D., Ph.D., Nobel prize laureate, and one of the most respected African-American scientists in America, if not the world, was a *very* busy man.

Hank was a fourth-year resident at Columbia, one short year away from a prestigious fellowship in California and, after that, a glorious piece of lambskin certifying him as a neurosurgeon. In this much, he was a purist. Nothing got Hank's dander up more than those silver-spooned prep-school brats whose rich fathers predestined them from

the birth canal on to be either lawyers or doctors and who, upon entering either field, immediately began whining without a smidgen of self-
respect about how hard their program was. No, Hank was the product
of blue-collar parents who respected a good education and sacrificed
proudly, like a monk at vespers, to give Hank his shot. Hank was not
among the upper crust of intelligence, but he was very bright—a fair
mix of academics salted nicely with a street kid's wit. He had known
since his seventh-grade biology class that medicine was for him. As a
senior in high school, he had narrowed it down to the neural sciences,
settling quite eagerly on neurosurgery his sophomore year at
Dartmouth. The rest was history. If he was somewhat lackadaisical in
other areas—and, most assuredly, he was—Hank could at least rest
secure knowing he had worked his tail off every step of the way for his
first and deepest love—medicine.

Specifically, the brain.

"Hank" was just a nickname. His real name was Hanson. Hanson
Nathaniel Blackaby. While he liked the name Hanson quite a bit, his
friends took to calling him Hank early on, said it seemed to fit his personality a little better. Hank didn't mind too much. A name is a name
is a name as far as he was concerned. But he figured his future wife,
wherever she was, probably would want him to use his real name for
professional reasons—Dr. Hanson Blackaby sounded distinguished,
authoritative, un-"Hankish"—and that was fine with him, too.

Rounding the corner to radiology, with the last of his malt wiped
across the back of his hand, Hank nearly smashed into the chief radi-
ologist. After a quick apology he moved on, rounded another corner,
finally coming face-to-face with a sea of hopeful faces.

The hopefulness quickly turned to disappointment.

"Again?" one of the braver young female interns asked. "It's been
almost two weeks."

Hank adjusted his lab coat.

"Good to see you, too, Daphne. Let's go!"

2

The phone rang at 6:13 a.m. Jessica lay sprawled on her bed in a long T-shirt, legs and arms poking out from underneath the sheets like a box of spilled matches. Her body felt so heavy as to be embedded in the mattress, a piece of lead dropped into fresh, thick clay. Drunk with sleep, she rolled over on the fourth ring, hit snooze on her alarm clock, and rolled back over. The ringing sound continued. One eye cracked open, then another. Mechanically, she picked up the phone.

Her voice was dry. "Hello?"

"Jess, is that you?"

Jessica had to think for a minute. "Yeah, it's me."

"You sound funny. Aren't you up yet?" the caller asked.

"Elizabeth?"

"Jess, you've got to wake up. Sit up in bed." Elizabeth waited on the line for Jessica to obey. She was Jessica's sister, older by four years, and was used to telling Jessica what to do. Jessica didn't move, however. She just forced herself to come awake. On the nightstand beside her was a note:

> *Thought I'd get out early.*
> *It was great last night. I'll call you.*
> *Tony*

Jessica felt her stomach turn. She had hoped it was all a dream—would have settled even for a nightmare. She wanted a shower. "What is it, Elizabeth? It's a quarter after six here."

"Well, I wasn't going to call at all, but then just this morning . . ."

Jessica waited. Finally, "What about this morning?"

The voice in her ear trembled. "Jess, Mom's not doing so good."

It took a minute for the words to sink in, for her sleepy brain to catch up with her ears, but her heart immediately began thumping hard in her chest. She jerked into a sitting position, fumbled for the lamp beside her bed. A soft halo of yellow light swelled outward, causing her to squint and wipe the hair from her face.

"What do you mean?" she said.

"I mean she's taken a turn for the worse. Much worse."

The air began squeezing from Jessica's lungs; yet the words coming from her mouth sounded surprisingly calm. "Ellie, what are you talking about? Last I knew, Mom had a bad case of arthritis and the flu."

"I know, I know."

"Have you taken her to the doctor?"

"Yes, of course."

"And?"

Elizabeth was obviously stressed. She grew defensive. "And what? The doctor doesn't know any more than we do!"

None of this made sense, at least not this early in the morning. Maybe not at all. So Jessica asked her next question very slowly, for herself and Elizabeth. "Talk to me, Ellie—what is going on?"

Her sister didn't know how to answer. She told Jessica the symptoms: shortness of breath, disorientation, nausea, numbness in the extremities, muscle spasms. She described how it all just seemed to come out of nowhere, about a week ago; how this new illness slowly sort of replaced the flu and the arthritis. It was so gradual neither Ellie nor her mother thought anything of it at first. In fact, they hardly even noticed. But the symptoms kept getting worse; now it was bad enough that Jessica's mom was quite frightened. Elizabeth, too.

"I think you should come early," Elizabeth said in her ear. "Like today."

Jessica immediately withdrew. "Are you sure? I mean, it can't be that serious, can it? Couldn't you just be—"

"Overreacting?" Elizabeth sounded tired. "Some things never change, do they, Jess?"

"I'm sorry, I'm sorry. It's just that I've already made plans and all, and this has come up all of a sudden."

"Well, I've been with her for the last two weeks and if I were in your shoes I would be on the next flight out of Portland. I'm scared, Jess. I mean it. Really scared."

No doubt true—obvious even—but Jessica couldn't help rolling her eyes. Elizabeth was always scared about something. Nevertheless, all she said was, "I'll see what I can do at the office and call you back."

The line went dead. Jessica rubbed her face, feeling the residue of sleep, sweet and gentle, fade into wakefulness. With everything she had to do, she found herself just sitting for a while—a long while actually—thinking of her mom and pushing back the feeling that, somehow, everything was about to unravel.

8 8 8

Inside the thick concrete walls of the Federal Correctional Institute in Milan, Michigan, the grayish pall of death drained the color from the lights, from the low chatter of voices, from the faces of the guards.

Outside, social reformers of every stripe maintained their steady vigil, but an unspoken, unnegotiated truce of sorts had taken place. Everyone could feel the air tightening, like the relentless turn of the screw, minute by minute, hour upon hour. It was a painfully human scenario. Very little time for shouting or dogmatics at the moment, though more would surely erupt before it was over. Now was the time of waiting; of praying or dreading, hoping or weeping. Breathless anticipation abounded. It was 8:27 p.m. A cool, brisk Wednesday.

And Luther Sanchez was about to die.

In a small antechamber near the warden's office, at a table covered with deep blue cloth, the muscled young Latino sat hunched over his last meal like a caged eagle. His eyes darted around the room—to the warden, who stood like a pillar, taking long, slow draughts on a hand-rolled Dunhill, and to the three guards, who watched him with eyes of apathy and loathing, and only a hint of pity. Their hands never left their holsters.

Luther sat alone, dressed in blue jeans and a plain white T-shirt.

Around his neck hung a small chain with a cross on the end. In his shirt pocket, rosary beads. He was freshly shaven and smelled of cheap cologne.

He was alone.

� ❊ ❊

"Excuse me, sir!" a squat, obtrusive woman barked, standing near the penitentiary gate. In a well-rehearsed motion she whipped out a small pad of paper and a ballpoint pen from her overcoat. "Missy Jenkins, *Detroit Sentinel.* I'm wondering if you have any comment on the case involving Luther Sanchez?"

Waving her pen excitedly, Missy tucked a thick strand of mop-water-colored hair behind her ear. She was one of many media hounds swarming the entrance to the prison: radio, television, newspaper—even a magazine or two—mostly state or local affairs. CNN was there, too, but channels seven and four from Detroit were the big boys here. Missy had been riding this case off and on for the *Sentinel* for more than four years. Now everything had come to this. Final call.

At last.

She focused on the man before her. He looked to be fiftyish, gray hair and warm eyes. He held a single white candle in front of his face, flame-tipped, so his eyes sparkled in the darkness. On his jacket was a tag that read "Americans for Compassionate Justice."

Missy almost smirked. She needed a scoop in a big way and these special-interest groups were suckers for five minutes of spotlight, especially the liberal ones, the ones with mottos like, "Love your criminals, don't kill them." But that ground had been covered a dozen times already. Nothing left for her but grunt work and eighteen column inches.

Surprisingly, the man brushed away her invitation as easily as a child squashes a bug.

"I have no comment," he said.

Missy was persistent. "Sir"—she peered closer at his name tag—"Mr. Barnes . . . what has your organization done to secure a stay of execution for Luther Sanchez, and why do you feel it is merited, considering his heinous crimes?"

The man offered her a polite, thoroughly unamused smile. "You're looking for a story. I understand. It's your job. But the time for stories has passed. There's nothing left to do but pray."

She waited for more, but that was it. That completely unaffecting soliloquy was the sum total of her scoop for tomorrow morning's issue. The man disengaged himself from Missy's presence and started to wander off, still holding his candle. Missy doggedly followed.

"So you don't have much confidence in Luther's attorneys, is that what you're saying? Will you go on record with that?"

The man paused, turned, shoulders slumping. He rubbed his eyes. "I have been in contact with Mr. Sanchez's attorneys. They are doing everything they can. One of them is at the governor's mansion right now with new evidence."

"But—"

"But what? Time is running out."

"Is or has run out?" Missy asked.

"Mr. Sanchez is the only one who can really answer that. I daresay his battle is lost, but we must keep up our hope. Life and death are decided in seconds, not hours."

Missy put pen to paper, said, "May I quote you?"

The man shook his head. Missy pressed forward, afraid to lose him. "Has the justice system failed Luther Sanchez?"

That little sound bite grabbed him for some reason. He paused, looked from her to the candle to the crowd. When he spoke, his voice was low. "No more than the rest of us, I would imagine."

He turned and walked away.

❁ ❁ ❁

The table before Luther was lavish enough for royalty, candlelit, laden with fine stemware and silver platters—but not of smoked pheasant, lobster tail, or juicy cuts of prime rib as one might expect. These were the usual fare for last-meal requests—when a prisoner tried to live like a rich man for once, or maybe stick the state with a high-priced dinner tab—so the warden had been surprised when Luther asked for simple things: real Mexican tamales, chili, spiced corn, jalapeños and beans. And tequila, one glass. Worm and all.

It was the meal his mother used to fix for him when he was a child. All except for the tequila, of course. And the silver platters. And the stifling awareness of death.

But as Luther stared at the food before him, smelled the sweet, crunchy tamale husks and the pleasant burn of the hot peppers in his nose, the silence of the room turned strangely hollow. He lifted his crystal goblet, turned it in his hand and set it down, like a gift for a friend. When he pinged the rim of it with a spoon, the sound rang out high and clear, then blossomed, impossibly, into absolute clarity. Life itself became acute, almost luminescent. The blue tablecloth deepened into a shade of fathomless purple. The soft air grew softer, the guards more wary.

Luther smiled.

☗ ☗ ☗

Outside, at 8:30 p.m., a black sedan edged its way into the swirl of lights and cameras and milling people outside the prison. The crowd parted, eager, curious, as the gates swung open to allow the vehicle entrance. Although the windows were tinted black, there were obviously two people in the car—a driver and a passenger.

A name went up, like a whisper on fire.

"Ravelo. Father Ravelo."

Missy was fortunate enough to be at the early end of this gossip line. She leaped at the car as it slinked by, tapping hard on the passenger window. The man inside *was* a priest. She could tell that by his collar. He glanced at her briefly, startled at her sudden appearance, then waved her away as kindly as possible. He did not roll down his window. The car angled toward the gate.

"Father!" Missy shouted through the glass. And like a meaty bone pitched to a pack of hungry wolves, a clamor ignited around that one single word. Reporters and microphones and bright lights all jammed toward the passenger window. Flashes popped in sequence. Missy was almost thrown against the car by the rush of bodies. But she held her ground.

"Father Ravelo! Is that you?" she called, tapping on the glass. The car inched forward through the press of bodies. Missy had to glide along with it, her face flat against the window. "Have you come for Luther's last rites? Do you have anything to say? How do you expect him to feel? To look? What will you tell him? How long have you known him?"

About a hundred questions were asked in the space of a single breath, by Missy and everyone else. It quickly turned into a shouting match. Whoever could say their question the loudest would win. Then, almost on cue, the car broke free of its human restraint. It was inside the gate. Father Ravelo turned once to look at Missy. His face was blank, grave. The car accelerated down the long drive and disappeared.

8 8 8

Luther was a killer. He was nicknamed "Bone Crusher" because that was exactly how he killed his victims. He crushed their skulls with a blunt instrument. All thirteen of them. At the present moment, however, sitting at the table staring at a plateful of hot tamales, he could have been an altar boy.

No antics. No madness. Nothing.

Ironically, some prisoners grew defiant at times like this. They shouted and cursed and started fights for no reason, almost in desperation, as if to prove to the grave and to the Keeper of Graves that they possessed a virility of soul too potent to claim just yet.

Those few were the exception. Most men grew somber. Even in the holding blocks, where the day went on like any other day, the imminent death of Luther Sanchez had a gripping effect. It was no easy thing to confront the scope of life and death from behind a row of vertical gray bars. That's why the phrase "doing time" was such a misnomer. "Remembering time" was more accurate, for all a criminal sentence meant in the end was that a person had plenty of time to remember exactly where things began to go wrong. Those with hard hearts didn't care to think or remember, which was a kind of blessing. But for those who did—who dared to remember the past—the death of a comrade formed a window into their own mortality, and a commentary on the wasted time that would mark its coming.

Luther Sanchez had no more wasted time. In less than four hours, the state of Michigan would inject into his veins a chemical that would cause his heart to fail. In less than four hours.

He reached for a fork and cut into his unshelled tamale.

§ § §

The evening had been splendid.

Dr. T. Samual Rosenburg and his wife had enjoyed a leisurely dinner with friends at an exquisite little Greek restaurant along the river overlooking the dark beauty of the Detroit skyline. They dined on lentil stew, brusqueta, braised mutton, spicy cabbage rolls, and baklava, all tempered with a lovely French Bordeaux that Rosenburg could still taste on the tip of his tongue. Mrs. Rosenburg was a board member of the Detroit Philharmonic and their friends were doctors and writers, so they chatted at length on the state of science, politics, and the arts. It was exactly the sort of evening the upper strata of American society considered normal.

Unfortunately, the joy was short-lived. After bidding their friends good night, the Rosenburgs headed home with little fanfare or conversation, climbing the steps to their town house feeling quite satisfied. When they unlocked the door, Mrs. Rosenburg took off her coat and called for the maid to put a pot of tea on the stove. Samual retired to his library and clicked on his private TV.

All fine so far.

But there, plastered monotonously across every station, flashed picture after picture of the dramatic Luther Sanchez story, replete with up-to-date shots of the penitentiary, the protesters, the death chamber, the attorneys—even mugs of the killer himself, as if anybody within a three-hundred-mile radius didn't know exactly what he looked like.

Rosenburg found it all quite discomfiting, as he had since the story broke several months ago. He checked his watch. It was about time to walk the dog anyway.

He rose and donned his light overcoat and hat, called for their little poodle, Rachel, named after the bride of Jacob—which was about as close to orthodoxy as Rosenburg had come in the last twenty years—and headed for the door. A little fresh air would do him and Rachel good.

T. Samual Rosenburg lived with his wife south of Highland Park in an ornate, two-story townhouse fashioned after older Victorian estates. The area was fairly wealthy. Small parks were frequent and well maintained along the boulevard, as were the immaculate connecting streets and the wide cobblestone sidewalks. Streetlights in the area looked like old gas lamps. Traffic was light. The area was designed for modern opulence with an old-world charm and it worked just dandy. Rachel pulled Rosenburg along on her little leash, tongue wagging in a perfectly proper fashion, but her little tail bobbed gaily.

The streetlights had kicked on about an hour ago, glowing like giant lollipops along the tailored sidewalk. Rosenburg glanced at his wrist, but he had removed his watch after arriving at home. He guessed the hour to be late, about ten-thirty or so.

Only an hour and a half. Ninety short minutes. Then midnight.

With each step Rosenburg grew increasingly disturbed about the imminent execution of Sanchez. Although this walk was intended to clear his mind, the opposite happened: The farther he walked, the faster his steps, the more confused and angry he became. A seed of dread grew deep in his belly, turning his thoughts dark.

Vastly unaccustomed to the moral qualms and indecisiveness generally attributed to lesser breeds of men, Rosenburg was not the kind of man to be trifled with, nor was he used to feeling uncomfortable. As a noted pharmacologist at Sinai Hospital, he was a figure of some importance—the kind of man a variety of organizations relied on for counsel. He tended to be gruff, blunt, showing little concern for diplomacy or political maneuvering, but he possessed a decided measure of brilliance within his field. From this curious combination of virtue and vice he had garnished a sheetful of positions, titles, and the accompanying prestige, which he navigated with aplomb, the cumulative effect being a tidy little slice of power for himself at the end of the day. He was, loosely phrased, a medical philosopher for the Institute of Global Relations, a Detroit think tank with international muscle. He also served on a number of boards for charities and medical groups, even a national pharmaceutical manufacturer. And he carried fairly high security clearance with the CIA, presumably a requirement for placement with IGR.

But power breeds in men of conscience an equally weighted sense of responsibility, which is what Rosenburg now wrestled with. He had reason to know of Luther Sanchez's past. And given the strings he *could* pull—the governor was an old friend—he wondered about the moral complications of a decision either way. Despite his devout Jewish upbringing, guilt and all, the idea of moral certainty was one he had long ago abandoned. Rosenburg fancied himself an enlightened Jew, meaning humanistic, with only a vague devotion to the god of the past, whose chief virtue, in his opinion, lay in the rituals and myths necessary for the perpetuation of community among a people.

So what of Sanchez? In all fairness to himself, Rosenburg *had* called the governor once on Luther's behalf, about two months ago. It was a halfhearted call for clemency, true, but who was he to single-handedly malign the prudence of twelve jurors and an honest judge? Sanchez was an admitted murderer! The state had a right—no, an obligation—to protect society from further aggression. . . .

Rosenburg rounded the corner of the block. The arguments were as tired as he was and he knew it. He was invested. Luther was not a random event. A few more strides placed him squarely before the steps of his town house. The air was a little chilly for this late into spring, but he didn't mind. The bracing wind offered him a kind of resolution, since he could muster none on his own. He faced his home, blank faced, powerless to move. Rachel barked once. He quieted her; slowly raised one foot, then another, until all the steps were climbed. Inside, his wife had finished her tea and sat on the sofa reading the *Atlantic Monthly*. Rosenburg slipped past her with a quick greeting, releasing Rachel to her care.

Once inside his study, he closed the door, feeling the burden of his decision root him in place as tangibly as if he wore lead shoes. Luther was a killer, for heaven's sake! He could not change that fact, could change nothing at this point! But had that always been true?

To talk would be a breach of confidence, he knew. But to remain silent would be a breach of soul. Besides, the governor could be trusted—of that he had no doubt. In the end, Rosenburg wondered if he really had a choice. For just a moment, a brief moment, he pondered the intricate trickle-down effect of consequence upon consequence that a single wrong decision can take.

Then he opened his phone book of private numbers and reached for the phone.

☗ ☗ ☗

Jessica had hoped for a more relaxing vacation than a rushed flight and sick mother were bound to provide. She had hoped to catch a few plays on- and off-Broadway, to lie out on the beach, to sleep in. Fat chance of any of that now.

But these were selfish thoughts she knew, leaving her torn between honesty and the familiar guilt that followed it. In an effort to escape these mental gymnastics she had thrown herself into a hard day's work. The senior partners all agreed that her mother was a priority, so taking off work earlier than scheduled was no problem. And Mandy, champ that she was, had already lined up the cheapest flight out of Portland by the time she got to work, since Jessica called her first to tell her the news.

So the day passed fairly quickly, which was a sort of bright spot considering how poorly it had begun. Jessica hoped her mother was all right. She just didn't know why she had to go and get sick now.

After work she returned home, packed enough clothes and shoes and accessories for four women, set her house in order—a polite and vaguely accurate description of what Jessica considered to be real cleaning—and finally made ready to leave. She threw on an old pair of sweats and popped her hair into a ponytail. Might as well be comfortable on a flight this long.

It would have been a good idea to clean out the refrigerator before departing, but Jessica didn't have the heart to get rid of any of the stuff yet, especially since it had survived so bravely up to this point. So she grabbed a soda and the only piece of fruit that happened to be the right color, which was an apple, and began munching. Last thing she did was forward her home phone to the office. Mandy had volunteered to be her social secretary while she was away, but Jessica declined.

It was early evening by the time Jessica made it to the airport. She was late, as usual. After checking her baggage and tickets at the ticket claim, she made a quick visit to the ladies' room. A few things are universal to women: one of them is hatred for the little toilet closets people are forced to use when stranded thirty thousand feet in the air.

When Jessica emerged from the rest room, passengers had begun boarding her flight, so she stepped in line and inched forward. It looked to be a crowded flight, but within minutes she was thumping down the little connecting ramp to the plane with a small handbag under each arm.

Standing outside the security zone near Gate 29 was a man, mid-thirties, wearing a light gray trench coat and opaque sunglasses. He held up a magazine so that his face was mostly buried, but his eyes flicked back and forth between Jessica and the monitor overhead announcing destinations, departures, and arrivals. He watched until Jessica boarded the flight, until the plane itself taxied down the runway and lifted into the air, before reaching for the airphone next to him. He was perfectly nonchalant in every motion, every twist of limb and lip. Just a businessman waiting for his flight.

He dialed a number. A man's voice answered.

"Nix here."

The man on the airphone sounded a little tired. He wasted no time. "Seventeen is gone. Flight 459 to La Guardia."

"Carrier?"

"Northwest. She's scheduled to arrive at 6:47."

"Good, good. Nice work. Continue surveillance of Twelve and Nineteen. Are you mobile?"

"Got the tickets in my hand. Everything cool with Decker?"

"Everything's smooth. We'll keep you informed."

The line went dead.

8 8 8

The only illumination in the bedroom of Hank's dark apartment was the light bleeding from his Macintosh Powerbook. It was an older model, a little slower than some, but he loved it. Besides, he didn't have the money to upgrade. He sat transfixed in front of it; suddenly inspired, he would jerk into a quick burst of typing, then fall back, puzzled, searching, followed by another quick burst, then repeat. He looked neither mad nor brilliant, only very confused, except for when he rapped on the table with his knuckles or the palm of his hand, at which time he looked irritated as well.

"Blast!" he muttered, making a gun out of his thumb and forefinger and aiming it right at the middle of the screen.

. . . *Bang.*

Another round of failed password guesses. Each time Hank tried—and missed—he swore the computer received some sort of electronic surge in its processor that was the silicon equivalent of sadism.

"Inappropriate password," the computer would say, almost laughing.

So Hank amused himself by talking back, saying something tough and Dirty Harryish, like, "Pass this word, buddy," or "One flick of the switch and *your* access is fried." The computer stoically disregarded these juvenile insults, returning the same message every time.

"Access denied."

Which riled Hank even more.

He was about to resort to insulting the computer's questionable lineage when his pager buzzed from the clip on his belt. Mildly annoyed, he yanked it off and peered at the little panel of glowing numbers. The call was from Nursing. He dialed the number quickly.

"Nurses' station."

"Hi, Peg. This is Hank."

Peg sounded apologetic. "Dr. Remming needs you to check in on Mr. Kagey."

"Now?"

"I think so."

Hank smacked his leg with his fist. Remming had already left word on his answering machine reminding him to pick up the latest battery of test results from the Center for NMR Spectroscopy, which chafed Hank more than a little. True, the center was one of a handful of the delicious privileges associated with a $30,000-a-year Ivy League medical degree, housing three Brukers for biological applications of high-resolution NMR spectroscopy, including structural studies of proteins and nucleic acids. And although the specific research capabilities of the facility were designed for the clinical study of genetics, biochemistry, and neurology more than the practical—such as Hank's field of surgery—his mouth still watered every time he walked in the doors: proton field strengths of 300 MHz, 400 MHz, and 500 MHz; equipped for three-channel operations of triple-resonance experiments; basically, some of the most powerful equipment of its kind in the country.

Toyland, as far as Hank was concerned.

In a sense, he realized this. Hank knew he was fortunate to be even remotely associated with Remming on these projects. He even felt that Remming was grooming him for a position at his side, maybe on the Columbia faculty. But sometimes Remming was so secretive, so elusive, that Hank felt he might as well be working blindfolded. On top of that, he hated feeling like the bat boy at the community softball games, serving as gopher for this and that, never really playing in the game.

And now, Mr. Kagey.

"Do me a favor, will you, Peg? Call Johnston. See if he can do it. I'm kind of busy. If you can't reach him, call me back."

"I'll try."

"Thanks."

The password . . . the password. Kim was supposed to have blown this whole thing wide open by now. Tonight was going to be their big crackerjack night, he and Hank, but the notorious hacker had left a message on Hank's answering machine saying he had some "absolutely critical" thesis research that should have been completed about three days ago and couldn't wait any longer.

Yeah, right.

So that left Hank to crack the code alone, which was a farce by any standard. Hank knew the bare necessities: A password is like a door, an access point, and that if you don't have the key to that door, then you have to walk around the house and find an unlocked window or screen porch. If you can find one—which a good hacker always can—you slip inside and sneak up to the front door, where the password is, jam a little bit of code into the gears and watch the password grind to an inoperable halt. Then you walk back outside to find the front door wide open.

No password needed that way.

The Wraith could do this sort of stuff in his sleep. Kim had found hacking to be profitable in many ways, not the least of which were certain social advantages. For instance, if Kim saw an attractive woman on campus, he wouldn't bother to get her name. He just jotted down her license plate number and broke into the license bureau files later that night to find out more information about her. No embarrassing introductions or stupid male *faux pas*. Easy as cake.

For Kim, at least. What Hank needed was a password.

On a whim, he decided to check his hard drive to see if he still had that anonymous note. Luckily, he did. Not erased yet. He opened, read, and printed the note, but there was little to make sense of:

> *To him who has ears to hear: the final blasphemy is upon us. Modern science, guided by perversity, ignores divinely appropriated boundaries. Fools! Man peers deep enough into the mind of God to find the place of God in man, but has not the sense to fear. I am not blind to their schemes. I fear! But my voice is small. So they mock (powermongers!), the Club of Cranium, fraternity of fools, brilliant in their ignorance, they mock the divine with voyeuristic crimes and a bit of gray matter and label it a medical miracle. I fear this message comes too late. The press releases have been prepared. The stage is set. It is all madness. Curse us all . . . we should know better.*

Hank didn't have a clue what any of that rambling meant. But it sounded cool, like some crazy street-corner prophet with a long beard and a sign that read "The End Is Near!" As far as Hank was concerned, whoever that old man was, he probably told a truer story than the six o'clock news ever would. Anyway, if there was a password in the note, Hank didn't know how to find it.

But he wanted so badly to break in!

Thesis or no, he decided to give Kim a call. Before Kim could even greet him, Hank said, "Kim! You gotta help!"

Kim let out a striking and imaginative string of curses over the phone, behind which Hank heard the sound of Parker's "Confirmation" blowing smoothly in the background. Hank smiled. Kim at least knew how to study with style.

"Hank, I told you, man, I'm busy. I'm sorry, but—"

"I know, I know," Hank broke in. "You've got this thesis to do and all. I just want some tips to get me off the starting blocks, OK? Where does a hacker begin?"

"Another time, all right? This weekend, maybe. I should be free."

Hank pulled his trump card. "Fine, sure. I guess you're right. Say, how's Madeline?"

A long silence followed. Hank had been saving this card for just such an occasion and he played it now beautifully. He had sprinted down a side street for Kim about a month ago to get Madeline's as-of-yet unknown license plate number. Kim followed up with a bit of hacking and liked what he saw. Three or four dates later, things were still going smoothly.

Kim sighed. "Fine. Five minutes. What do you want to know?"

Hank grinned. "Just a few simple tricks."

"I'm listening."

"OK. Where do you start when you're trying to nail a password?"

Now it was Kim's turn. "Where do I start? *Where do I start?*" He smirked. "Should I begin with creation?"

"Don't make me bring up Madeline again."

"That charm works once, my friend. Are you past the log-in?"

"No problem. 'XXAdmin.' I've seen you do it hundreds of times."

"Not bad. Still, if this forum has any sort of security at all, a generic log-in like that might only get you partial access. There's likely to be higher-level log-in codes."

"I'll take my chances. What about the password?"

Kim grew serious, deliberate. The master craftsman was about to pass on his mantle to a young apprentice and he wanted Hank to fully absorb the weight of his next few words. With great meaning, he said, *"The easiest route possible is the easiest route possible."*

Hank waited for more. Finally, "Uh, right. That's good. Could we talk about computers now?"

"I'm very serious. Forget Hollywood. The one great flaw of computer security is that the same people who program the systems are the ones who either *used* to hack or *will* hack sometime in the future. It's a completely inbred society. Get it?"

Not really. But Hank made a valiant effort at following this convolution to enlightenment. "Only a certain kind of person likes to stare at a computer all day?" he ventured.

"Exactly. So most passwords and security codes are drawn from a similar pool of people. Generally the same age, same mentality, same interests—"

"Computer geeks," Hank pitched in. "Techno-weenies."

"Watch it, I'm one of them," Kim said. "But stereotypically speaking, yes. Anyway, these people tend to gravitate to certain things. Don't ask me why, I don't know. You're the brain man."

"OK, like what?"

"The older generation draws pretty heavily on mythology, typically Greek or Roman. Serious crackers prefer Norse. I know it sounds weird, and I have zero psychological studies to back me up on this, but the typical hack thinks Poseidon and the Valkyrie are just pretty darn cool. I've never met one that doesn't. Younger hacks might be drawn to comic-book characters or big-time military hardware, like the F-16 or the Apache. It's an inner-circle mentality."

Hank groaned. "This could take forever."

"*Au contraire*, things are looking up, my friend! Before I *ever* go to the trouble of breaking in a back door, I spend a couple hours running through a list like this. You'd be surprised, Hank. It's rarely as fancy as you'd think."

"Well, just the same, you'd better keep your weekend open, OK? I have a feeling I'm not going to get far."

"I'm telling you, Hank, most systems have a pitiful veneer of protection. Laughable. But it keeps ninety-nine percent of the population out, because those people don't know where to start. I've given you the place to start. Honest, you know half my secrets right now. Even a password as generic as 'God' has gotten me into places that should have known better."

Despite Kim's encouragement, Hank felt his momentum seriously deflating. He said, "I'll give it a whirl. Thanks for the help," then started to hang up the phone.

Kim called to him. "Hank?"

"Yep?"

The satisfaction in his friend's voice was obvious. "We're even," he said. The line clicked before Hank could respond.

"Not if you marry her," Hank muttered under his breath.

He looked down at his desktop. The computer stared at him in abject defiance. Hank placed his fingers on the keyboard, trying to recall all the mythology he could remember from his sixth-grade social studies class.

"Zeus," he typed, feeling a little embarrassed that he couldn't remember anything better to begin with.

The computer denied him.

"Thor," he tried.

Nothing.

"Apollo" . . . "Vulcan" . . . "Neptune."

Nothing.

Hank scrambled for more words. His fingers clattered on the keys. "Loki," he typed, feeling pretty proud for pulling that one out of his Norse hat. The computer remained unimpressed.

"Access denied. Inappropriate password."

Hank went wild: Mohammed, Jesus Christ, Buddha, Valhalla, Venus, Jupiter, F-15 Eagle, Apache attack chopper, Stealth Bomber; heck, he even typed in "Great Spirit," just in case a Native American had configured the system. Over the course of the next half-hour, his guesses veered farther and farther from Kim's instructions. What did it matter? He could hardly remember any more mythology, and besides, this was kind of fun, this stream-of-conscious approach to hacking. Anything was fair game: Moses, Mother Teresa, Mussolini, Aunt Jemimah, Erik the Red, Styx, Debby Boone, Olympus—

The computer flashed a new message. Hank's heart stopped.

"Please verify the password."

The new line ended with a blinking cursor, a prompting for more. Hank scrambled to remember which word he had typed last. Mussolini? No, no . . .

His fingers moved very carefully.

O-l-y-m-p-u-s.

He held his breath, blinked, hit return. The screen changed colors, a doorway swinging wide; a box appeared in the middle of the screen that read simply, "Club Cranium Data Exchange." Hank let out a whoop of triumph and almost fell out of his chair. He clicked a button on his computer and a list of four options appeared: "Send. Receive. Read. View Directory."

What a rush!

Any of the subtle moral implications of actually breaking in where he had not been invited were completely lost (or abandoned) between the thrill of the moment and the etherlike vagaries of cyber property. His mind raced faster than his fingers could follow. His hands were sweating. Slowly, he guided his pointer to the fourth option: "View Directory." He double-clicked.

Another box flashed on-screen. Inside were dozens of files, mostly message postings by the looks of it. The "Receive" and "Read" options were still here, too. Hank skimmed the contents. All the filenames were nondescript, arranged chronologically. One of them caught his eye, a file called "MerdthIn." He guided the cursor over, clicked on it, thought of reading it first, but then, with a certain giddy thrill, started clicking on several files, anything that sparked his interest. He figured it was best to get in and out like a cat pouncing rather than hang around and get snagged, since a lot of programs can list who's connected at any given moment. With about twenty or more files selected, he chose "Receive" from the options listed.

The screen flashed: "Restricted access code. Limited receive command clearance. Do you wish to cancel download or continue with available files?"

Hank clicked "Continue."

"Downloading 9 of 23 files. Please wait. Approximate time: 2 minutes."

His heart raced. He couldn't help but grin. Plundering the goods like pirates of old was an intoxication as powerful as any liquor, any aphrodisiac. Hank understood in that moment the great seduction of hacking, the repartee of mind versus machine and man against man. Each campaign against a fortified computer stronghold was a chess match of wit and skill.

"Checkmate," Hank said, feeling quite the scoundrel. What he actually wanted to do was leap up on his chair and shout, "Avast, ye scurvy dogs!" but that would have been a bit too rowdy for his apartment complex. And besides, about five seconds after shouting it, he would only feel silly, not triumphant.

The computer beeped a new message: "Download complete."

Hank exited the program, logged off the Internet, and began printing the files he had downloaded to his hard drive. His cavalier attitude quickly turned to intrigue as the first page rolled out of the printer. First he felt confused, then fearful, then fascinated. An odd sense of incongruity sprouted like a weed in his brain as he skimmed the address headers of the first file; it was the kind of feeling that takes a while to sink in and make sense. Every electronic message transferred between computers over the Internet automatically registers the geographical location of both the sender and the receiver of the file.

Club Cranium was located at Columbia University.

And his supervisor, the noted Dr. Jay Remming, was one of the members.

3

"H e can get violent in a hurry, so be careful."
       The guard's warning was neither ominous nor dramatic, but rather as flat with fact as pointing to the sun and saying "hot." It was also the only words the man had uttered since the long walk down the long concrete hall toward Luther's maximum-security cell. As Father Ravelo was ushered inside, he noted the same unapproachable cynicism on the faces of all the guards he passed. Five of them waited outside the cell in case anything should go wrong. One of them, the one who had offered his half-spoken warning, accompanied Ravelo inside.

The heavily barred door rattled shut behind them. Ravelo heard the locking mechanism drop in place with a finality that nearly caused him to flinch. Ravelo was a perfectly average-looking man: medium height, horn-rimmed glasses, tending to stoop; a potbellied scoop of vanilla in both presence and bearing, so much so that the cloth and collar of his vocation appeared a little too highbrow for his grasp. Yet Ravelo had been a priest of the Roman Catholic Church for nearly twenty years. Twenty going on fifty, it felt at times. But no matter how tiresome the hierarchy could become, he had found a certain joy there also, a richness of experience, thanks largely to the love and sense of community generated by his small parish in Detroit, the Church of the Ascension, which had received the bulk of his service during the last seventeen years.

Luther did not rise to greet the priest; in fact, the condemned hardly acknowledged Ravelo's presence. He sat on the floor in the corner across from his bed with his legs folded underneath him and a loose sort of smile on his face. Ravelo thought the expression a bit odd, a mark more of precision than pleasure, judging by the set of Luther's eyes.

A calculation, maybe? He couldn't be certain.

Nonetheless, the air in the room was heavy with the musky odor of perspiration and fear—so much that Ravelo felt his soul shrivel upon entering. He held a crucifix and a small black Bible pressed against his body, made no sudden moves, just watched the criminal with a keen eye. Luther simultaneously seemed to focus on nothing, everything, having the hope of both on his face and the knowledge of neither.

"I did not expect you to come," Luther said, turning to the priest. "You surprise me."

Ravelo noted the rhythmic flow of his words, the rolling r's. Luther's speech was a smooth mixture of staccato chops and long, sliding vowels.

"Why?" the priest asked.

Luther did not answer him. "Did you know I asked for you by name?" he said.

"Yes, they told me so. The warden. When he called."

"Do you remember us meeting?"

"No."

Luther kind of laughed. "That's good, Preacher. I wouldn't have believed any other answer."

"When did we meet, Luther?" Ravelo asked, intrigued.

"Four years ago. It was Easter. You told me every soul can have a resurrection."

Ravelo pondered that memory; not his own, for he had none, but Luther's. There was something to the warp and weft of the prisoner's words that urged Ravelo to look, gently, deeper, beneath the dark reflective surface, as of waters passing by. It was not an unusual occurrence. The priest traversed through the barnacles of this physical world guided chiefly by whispered voices from another, namely that of intuition. And if intuition was first, then reason trailed a distant third in Ravelo's summary of personal motivation, though he had not yet surmised what might rank as second.

He was an oddity, this priest of God. If Ravelo supplied anything to the office, any sliver of self that spoke not with the voice of mundane virtue—those are qualities easily associated with holy men—but rather with transcendence, it would surely be his profound feel for the heart of a man. He wore this gift as naturally as a lady wears a fine leather glove and slipped it on quite comfortably now with Luther; he had, in fact, been gravely attuned to Luther since first entering the prisoner's cell.

He said softly, "What did you do when I told you that, Luther?"

The prisoner laughed. "I cursed you to your face."

"And what did I do in return?"

Luther sucked his bottom lip. Tentatively, as if entering unexpected territory, his mouth opened to speak, then closed again. "You reached out and grabbed me . . . tight, you know . . . real tight. Like a bear hug. I couldn't even get away. I think I cursed you again. Louder."

Ravelo smiled as the memory finally returned. But his voice was low and firm when he spoke. It sounded like wind in autumn.

"Luther, you're about to die. And you need Jesus."

By all outward appearance, Luther must not have heard the priest. He continued to stare, blankly, yet not so blank as to reveal dullness.

"You shouldn't have come, Father," he said at last.

"Not true. This is exactly where I should be. With you. Now." Ravelo bent down so that he could look Luther in the eye. Luther shied from his touch. His voice began to take on a familiar edge: precarious, gulping at both madness and sanity. As Ravelo watched, rubber-stretched tension began to build in the muscles of Luther's face, his body, in the cell itself. Still, Ravelo moved closer. Luther backed away angrily.

"You should *not* have come, Father!"

Ravelo said soothingly, "My son, the truth remains true: Every soul needs a resurrection. Will you receive yours? Will you take last rites before you die?"

The rubber band of Luther's mind snapped like a whip tail. He squinted so that only thin slits of white and brown could be seen in his eyes. They were devil's eyes.

"I have no soul to save!" Luther cried. Thoughts and rage came faster than his mouth could speak them. "Jack-in-the-box . . . the clown! When you least expect it—boom!—out I come, *sí*?" He thumped himself hard on the chest. "I kill! I could kill you, now! Do you want that?"

Ravelo said, "No."

"I don't want to hurt you, Father. But if you turn my crank, I have no control. This madness—all here." He pointed to his head. "It's more than me."

Ravelo frowned. "What are you talking about, Luther?"

Luther made a sort of howling sound, a sound of pain that surged up from some inner threshold full of knowledge too deep for words. He pushed to his feet so that his back scraped against the wall, holding his hands out in front of him like a boxer fending blows from three opponents. As quickly as the terror rose within him, it left again. He sank down, deflated. "I don't have any soul for you to resurrect," he mumbled. "No soul. You should go." He reached out and touched the priest. "Please don't go."

"I'm not. I won't."

Luther nodded. Ravelo said, "I can see how it tortures you."

Luther reached out and pulled the priest's neck closer so that their faces were only inches apart. "You believe in original sin, right?"

Ravelo nodded.

Luther said, "Me too. Ain't that funny?" His face and voice contorted into a sort of low chuckle, as if he really did find it funny. "But my sin is chemistry, man. Magic! Mine was *put* there."

The approaching clatter of high heels on the smooth concrete floors echoed loudly, suddenly, into Luther's cell. A slim blonde knockout appeared beside the five guards outside. One of the men whistled and the others chuckled like wolves until they saw the warden and Luther's attorney rounding the corner behind her, heading their way. Susan Decker regarded the men before her with equal parts boredom and condescension. The guards fell silent, not so much because of her, but because of the dour expression on the warden's face. He was obviously not happy.

Susan didn't care why the guards had shut up; she was just glad they had. After two different flight delays, rental car trouble, and a throbbing headache, Decker was in no mood for another hassle, especially lowbrow locker-room humor from adolescent men. Behind her, the warden's frown deepened with every hard step he took, but Susan didn't even glance over her shoulder or acknowledge him. She peered quickly into Luther's cell, surmised the situation, flashed a badge that Ravelo could not make out, and demanded entrance from the guards. Ravelo sensed that something was amiss and quickly began offering Luther his last rites.

Luther, too, seemed gratefully ready. He saw the woman, Ravelo knew, for his face fell into a sort of doglike territorial anger. Spurred on by the sight of Decker, sanity was his to claim for a few brief seconds. He received from Ravelo such comfort and penance as the priest could offer, though Ravelo was unsure whether he received out of spite—toward the woman, the world itself—or madness or sincerity. Still, for a moment, he became a child:

"If you tell me I am free, then I will believe," he said.

Ravelo held up a crucifix, which Luther kissed awkwardly. "The truth is that Jesus died for murderers and madmen. That truth can set you free."

"No. Nothing can."

"Yes."

Luther began to shake with the effort of concentration. Voices in his head demanded death. Anybody's. His own. The priest's. The guards'. He pulled at his hair. "I have nothing left in me. No goodness, no faith."

"Nor do I," Ravelo said, and his words were like a rag dipped in cool water on Luther's mind. "No one asks you to believe completely. Believe as much as you can."

The prisoner almost wept. "It is not enough."

"It is. You must trust me. Grace and mercy will supply the difference."

The guard inside the cell, quietly scoffing at Luther's tears and Ravelo's softhearted spiritual talk, turned to face the commotion with the woman, who now argued loudly with the other guards, none of whom seemed inclined to grant her entrance, badge or no, without the warden's say-so. Then the warden finally caught up to them, stepping into the middle of it all, demanding an explanation—for what Ravelo could not hear, nor did he try too hard (though he could tell that the woman's attitude was haughty)—and so the argument came full circle to begin all over again.

Ravelo glanced at his watch. Twenty to midnight.

Susan Decker was talking. "Either you give me full and undiluted access to the prisoner from this point until his execution or—"

"Or what?" the warden snorted, cutting her short. "You'll have my head on a platter?" The guards all snickered. Warden Pinkerton was that rare type of man blessed with a career that required little more personality than a steel-toed boot might possess. He cared very little for anyone who tried to interfere with *his* prison or *his* prisoners, even scum like Luther Sanchez.

Susan Decker arched one eyebrow high above her left eye. The more intense the pressure became, the more softly she spoke. "No platter, Warden. Too kind, too quick for my taste. I rather think I'll have the entire federal penal system bury you in so much paperwork you'll only wish you had been fired."

She stepped closer to the warden, so close that he could feel her body, the warmth, the hint of curves; she was beautiful and terrifying. The warden chomped his cigar between his teeth, unimpressed, but Luther's lawyer, watching, swallowed hard. Susan said, "Now, *lose* the priest, got it? And all but two guards. I want minimal external contact. From this point on, I'm Luther's shadow and you are my bag boy. I'm with Luther until he dies."

Luther heard every word she said. Ravelo saw the loathing, the rage, return to the prisoner's face. He almost seemed to recognize the woman. Quietly, his lips moved, making words but no sound. He reached out to his bed, grabbed an envelope, and tore a strip of paper from the flap, but, of course, had nothing to write with. Prisoners were forbidden to possess pens or other potentially dangerous objects without supervision. Luther's eyes darted around the small, blank cell.

"Are you looking for this?" Ravelo whispered, catching on to the game. He produced a small black pen from the flap of his Bible and handed it over. "Who is she, Luther?" he asked.

Luther shrugged him away. His eyes blinked back and forth, back and forth, from Susan to the paper. He took the pen from Ravelo's hand and scribbled something almost unreadable on the paper before folding it in half and half again, so that only a little knot of white could be seen.

"Killers die," he muttered, stuffing the wad of paper into the priest's open hand. "This is how one was born. I—"

He stopped short. A high-pitched sound rang out all of a sudden—the muffled beeping of a cellular phone. Rang again. All the contending voices ground to a halt as the sound lingered in the air. Luther's attorney opened his briefcase and pulled the antenna.

"Yeah?" he said, taking a step or two away from the cluster of bodies. There was a long pause. Then, "Uh-huh. I see."

Everybody held their breath. Everyone except Susan Decker. She took the time to glare through the iron bars the way a cat stalks prey. Not at Luther, mind you. Susan watched Ravelo. The priest smiled casually, having the presence of mind to do nothing—absolutely nothing—with the crumpled note in his fist. He picked up the crucifix and began the remaining portions of Luther's last rites. Susan's eyes never left him. As the guards and warden whispered together, Luther's attorney continued his long string of curt replies, never really asking any questions, but apparently receiving answers just the same. At length, he hung up the phone. The air was completely still. The silence was deep. The attorney took three steps forward, pushing past Susan and the guards, so that his face could touch the bars and his eyes could meet with Luther's. His voice choked with emotion.

"Luther, my friend. I'm sorry. The governor has denied any clemency. All our appeals have been denied. There's nothing more we can do. I'm so sorry."

Luther said nothing. The warden and guards watched him, prepared for any reaction, but with those words he faded into further emptiness. Ravelo had no idea of the condition of Luther's soul. Only that he was a violent, evil man. And that for a moment he had seemed to want more. Luther's face reflected a mirror image of peacefulness—dark, tranquil, frightening but calm—and that was close enough. If that state of mind could hold for another fifteen minutes or so, then a lot of misery would come to an end for many people, including Luther, at least in this life's reckoning.

"Let me in," Susan demanded quietly. "Let me in now."

The warden was scratching something on a clipboard. He didn't even look at her. "Ms. Decker, I'm going to speak to you one more time before you leave and that time is now, so listen real careful." He pulled the cigar out of his mouth and pointed it vaguely in her direction. "I don't give a flying flip that you're a spook for the CIA. You could be my dear, sweet grandma and I wouldn't pay any more attention to you. The mood I'm in right now, I wouldn't give a nickel to see God ride up on a Honda."

He smiled patronizingly before continuing. "But because you seem to have a reason to be here, and because I'm such a likable fellow, I'm gonna let you stand *outside* this cell, where you can watch and fuss and fume and primp your hair or whatever you want to do. I'll even let you sit in the room when we push the button in a few minutes. But until he's dead, my prisoner is *my* prisoner. And you're nothing more than a visitor with a nice pair of legs."

The warden turned and stumped away.

"Boys!" he called behind him, glancing at his watch. "I want Sanchez marching my way in . . . twelve minutes! We got a job to do. Bring the badge with you if she's done pouting in time."

Decker flushed red, said nothing. Ravelo made ready to leave. He took his crucifix and Bible in hand and stepped over to where Luther stood. Luther's eyes were vacant, his jaw clenched hard, but Ravelo wrapped the criminal in a fierce and unexpected embrace that surprised even the guards. Luther's body turned stiff and unyielding. He did not return the embrace; neither did he resist it.

Ravelo released him. Luther said flatly, "It was a lot like that."

"I remember now," replied the priest. He turned to go.

"Father," Luther said. "I don't know where you're heading. Some waiting room or something, maybe, but I don't want you to watch me die, *sí*? I know that's what you're supposed to do, or at least that's what they told me. But I'd rather you just left."

Ravelo nodded.

"Good-bye, Luther. May God have mercy on your soul."

Luther sat down on the bed. One of the guards opened the cell door and Ravelo slipped through. He did not glance behind him.

Susan Decker laid a firm hand on his arm as he passed by, following him to a safe distance away from the others.

"You probably noticed that Luther is a fairly unique pathological study," she said sweetly. But her grip did not slacken. "That's why I'm here. Did he act funny? Or say anything unusual? It would really help me out quite a bit."

Ravelo kindly but firmly removed his arm from her grasp. "He said the same things most men say when they are about to die." Then he asked, "Who are you?" In truth he already knew her name. He had heard the warden say it a couple of times. But he just wanted to hear her response.

Decker brushed past his query. She was all business. "Listen, I'm sure you understand—umm, Father—?"

"Ravelo. Michael Ravelo. And you are—"

"Anyway, I don't really have time to sit and chat. What I would like to know is what Luther was telling you when I walked up. He seemed so intent."

"He is an intense man," Ravelo agreed, but he could not avoid the sarcasm. "He killed thirteen people, you know."

Susan Decker did not laugh. Her eyes narrowed.

"And I *am* a priest. So there is the matter of his soul."

Decker tried hard to keep a sweet disposition, but she had such limited reserves. "You seemed to be talking about *more* than just the afterlife. That is my chief concern."

Ravelo blinked. "I'm sorry, really, but no."

"No?"

"No," Ravelo repeated, this time more slowly. "I feel it is precisely *none* of your concern."

Of the many advantages of celibate life, Ravelo decided right then that one would surely be the absence of angry women in his life. Susan Decker showed Ravelo her teeth, perfectly straight, pearl white. Her red lips were moist. It was not a pleasant smile. "Luther Sanchez is a court-certified paranoid schizophrenic and a ruthless sociopath. He's crazy. *Nothing* he might have said to you matters."

Ravelo nodded agreeably. "He did sound pretty crazy."

Decker relaxed a little, very little, even kind of laughed. "Mad as a hatter!"

"Crazy," Ravelo repeated. "So why are you here again, *Ms. Decker?*"

The smile faded. Decker knew Ravelo was wise to her act, so she cut to the chase. "Luther's the kind of prisoner we don't like to take chances with. Too scary. We just want to make sure nothing goes wrong."

"We? Who is—"

He never got the chance to finish his sentence. Susan Decker had wheeled around in one fluid twist and was already striding away, heels clattering on the flat concrete.

"I'll be in touch if necessary, Father Ravelo. Believe me, I'll be in touch."

§ § §

Early the next morning—and Jessica knew it to be *very* early by the exhaustion she felt—Jessica's plane landed at La Guardia International Airport in New York City. If she had had a reason to know it, she might have mourned the death of one Luther Sanchez in a Michigan penitentiary several hours earlier. But she did not know and did not mourn. All she knew was the pain of many stiff joints cramped in a small space for a large amount of time.

Elizabeth was there to greet her with an equally tired smile.

"Jess, it's good to see you!" she said warmly, wrapping her arms around her sister's neck. Elizabeth was attractive in her own right, but not with anything approaching Jessica's beauty. She was dark haired and lean for a mother of three, but her body could not hide the natural wear and tear of birthing. Her features were similar to Jessica's: high cheekbones, full lips, soft complexion. But where Jessica's personality ignited her graceful features into a piercing white fire, Elizabeth's nature tempered her beauty, making it comfortable, accessible—lovely just the same, though not as sweeping.

Jessica returned the hug. "This was the only flight available," she said. "Sorry it's so early."

"Nonsense, you're the one that must be tired. Come on, I'll help you with your bags."

They made for the baggage claim, shuffling along in silence. Even though it was quite early, the airport was packed and buzzing in a dozen languages with business travelers from around the globe. La Guardia was always packed. Jessica looked out the great panes of glass into the warming gray morning and felt the familiarity of home soak into her bones like hot chocolate in winter. It was a while yet before the New England states would truly feel the heat of summer, and even then the heat would be mild, but spring had definitely arrived. Fog was on the ground like a field of gray cotton. The air was wet. Pigeons cooed and pecked the ground. Soon the flowers would bloom. Outside the airport all Jessica could see were huge jet engines and steel-barreled planes, riding on long stretches of black asphalt and yellow stripes. But she could see the other things in her mind, well-remembered pieces of her youth that sprang to life so easily with just a little tug, which somehow the airport provided. She looked forward to Hamden and to the low ridges of the Connecticut shores.

"How's Mom?" she asked finally, and both wondered why they had waited so long to broach the subject.

"Not much change, at least for the better. But not much worse either. She can't wait to see you."

"Good. Great, really . . . about her health, I mean." Jessica fumbled for words, despising her own clumsiness. "I mean it's good she wants to see me, too, because I want to see her, but I just . . ." She hesitated at the last, cautious with hope. "Does she really? Want to see me?"

Elizabeth reached out and grabbed Jessica's hand. "Of course she does. It's been a long time, you know."

"I know. Too long. I hope she's doing well. Is she able to get around at all?"

"Not easily," Elizabeth sighed. "She's lost a lot of feeling in her fingers and toes. It's spread to her hands and feet and arms now. She's very weak."

"I was thinking about her on the plane," Jessica said. "Tell me more."

"There's not a lot more to tell. Just that lately even simple things are too much for her, like brushing her teeth or peeling potatoes—"

"Or dialing the telephone?" Jessica asked.

"Exactly."

"Sounds like ALS to me."

Elizabeth was blank faced.

"Lou Gehrig's disease," Jessica replied. "A client of mine had it last year. Oh, I hope that's not it."

Elizabeth said nothing. The baggage relay began belching out luggage. Jessica's was among the first to come out. Together, they gathered the bags and headed for Elizabeth's car.

"How long have you been with her?" Jessica asked.

"Three weeks now. I really can't stay much longer."

They exited the airport through sliding glass doors and headed out into the chill gray morning. "You must be absolutely drained," Jessica said. "I'll take over from here. You need rest."

Her sister shook her head, but her eyes turned down. "I'm all right."

"Did you drive or fly?"

"John drove me up here from North Carolina. He had business to take care of in Buffalo. I'm flying back, though."

"How are he and the kids?"

"Fine. I miss them terribly, of course. They tell me Maple Hill just isn't the same without an O'Connel girl there."

Jessica smiled. "John is the only guy who would even remember. He's the last of a dying breed, that man of yours."

Elizabeth stopped suddenly, looked at Jessica with long, sad eyes. "I wish you lived closer, Jess. Oregon is such a long way away."

Jessica knew she shouldn't feel defensive. "For all practical purposes you are *just* as far from Mom as I am, Elizabeth. I see no difference between Maple Hill and Portland."

"There is a difference! Maple Hill was home for all of us once."

Jessica looked away. They started walking again. Elizabeth glided along silently beside her, unresponsive. Her black woolen trench coat flapped in the gusty air, reminding Jessica that she was a little cold herself. She had bruised Elizabeth's feelings, she knew that. Somehow, she always managed to say the wrong thing. Elizabeth's feelings bruised way too easily—she knew that, too—but Jessica excelled at hurting her sister. She nudged Elizabeth with an elbow.

"You know how I am, Ellie. I just need a little space. Besides,

Maple Hill hasn't been my home for years. I hardly even remember the place. Hamden is as close to home as I have on the east coast."

"Well, I don't know why you got so bent out of shape," Elizabeth said, pouting. "I wasn't even talking about Mom; I was talking about me. I miss you, too, you know. And besides, it hasn't been *that* long."

Half to herself, Jessica whispered, "Seems like it to me." But then she changed the subject. "We should take Mom to the hospital. Tomorrow, I think."

"Tomorrow," Elizabeth agreed.

░ ░ ░

When Hank was five years old—the memory was as clear as if it were formed of crystal—he and his mother had visited the park one golden afternoon so that little Hanson could play on the jungle gym, which didn't happen often. Trees were jungle gyms out in the country where Hank's family lived in their double-wide on three hundred and sixty-five acres of wheat fields. Shiny *metal* jungle gyms were a treat.

Anyway, Hank had played and played and worked up quite a sweat, showing off for his mom and the other kids, already proving himself to be quite an athlete. Wherever Hank was, if other kids were playing, Hank became the point man. It was his natural role. Gifted children develop confidence quickly. He had the gift, knew it, and used it.

Afterward, sitting on a bench drinking lemonade with his mother, Hank had noticed another mother and child at play. The other boy was roughly his own age, maybe a couple of years older. Hank watched him try to run and climb, but his movements were jerky and stiff. He fell quite often, but rarely cried. His mother, smiling, would just come over and dust him off, and back they went. He couldn't do the monkey bars or anything like that because he wasn't coordinated enough. But he played and played just the same. Hank's mother told him the little boy was what they called a mongoloid. Down's syndrome. Hank watched, fascinated. He had a tender heart. He knew he could do things that little boy could not.

When it was time for the little boy and his mother to go, they passed by where Hank and his mother were sitting. The little boy's eyes were unusual, puffy. Hank had never seen anything like that before. His nose was stubby, but his mouth was wide with a toothy smile.

And then it happened.

The little boy glanced at Hank and stopped, pulling his hand free from his mother's grip. He stared at Hank, at Hank's face and hands; last, at a small scratch on Hank's leg that had left a trail of thin, dark blood down his shin. No big deal. Hank hardly even noticed that sort of thing anymore.

The little boy waddled over, arms swinging with exaggerated determination. Hank remembered feeling nervous. The boy was even stranger looking up close. He squatted, looked at Hank's leg. Didn't touch it, just looked; then at Hank's mom, then at Hank. Though his thick tongue wagged a little, slurring the words, Hank understood just fine. How could he not?

"Mommy says Jeeshus loves YOU!" he declared loudly, pointing his finger right at Hanson's nose.

Out of nowhere, just like that! Hank was stunned; he even felt upset. Beside him, his mother nodded politely, a pitiful smile on her face. No "Hi" or "Bye"; mail delivered. Boom! The little boy turned and left. He didn't say another word.

Something had happened that day. When he got home, Hank cried for three hours straight. He didn't know why. His mother tried to console him, but she didn't understand. No one in the family did, not his dad or his brother or sister. But something happened. A seed was planted and made alive within him, almost without his permission or consent, but alive nonetheless. The seed had a name: Jesus. Named by a little retarded boy.

Hank never saw the boy again, but the memory of that day often appeared in his dreams. It had somehow become a defining moment for his life.

He needed all the definition he could get.

In his hands, the Club Cranium documents were creased and smeared. He had printed them last night, had stared at them for hours since—last night and this morning—trying to piece together what he could. Little of it made any sense.

The initial surge of adrenaline had long ago subsided. Hank wasn't even sure what had sparked his interest in the first place. After all, who cared if Remming was a member of some organization Hank had never heard of? The world was full of private little clubs, the adult equivalent of backyard tea parties and "No Girls Allowed!" tree houses. So what? No crime there.

But that rambling little note had seemed so urgent, so . . . important. *"The final blasphemy is upon us."* Anonymous, true, which screamed of a prank. And nonsensical—another strike. But even with rational arguments to the contrary, the message had stuck to him like a cocklebur. So Remming was a member of Club Cranium? And Club Cranium, whatever that may be, was located on the campus of Columbia (or at least it maintained a forum on Columbia's mainframe where postings and other files could be exchanged)?

All in all, no big hairy deal.

That was almost what Hank thought until he started thumbing through the papers. A couple of them were encrypted and read like gobbledygook, which was maddening in its own right. But a few of the postings were clear and easy to read, messages exchanged between Remming and, it appeared, three other doctors: a T. Samual Rosenburg in Detroit, a pharmacologist; Selma Volgaard, a bioengineer from Sweden; and someone named Abu El-Saludin, another pharmacologist from Egypt. Hank had heard of Rosenburg—who hadn't?—and Dr. Saludin sounded vaguely familiar, too. Volgaard, not at all.

A fifth person seemed to be in the loop, on the fringe, with brief and sporadic communiqués (Hank counted only two out of the twenty or thirty he had downloaded). Both of the messages strongly alluded to money—no dollar amounts attached and nothing too specific, but the tone of the messages sounded like a donor addressing his charity of choice. *More like a bookie slipping a Franklin under the table in the shadowed corner of a diner,* Hank thought. And oddly enough, although there were clearly four scientists at work, the messages were directed exclusively to Remming.

"Allocation of funds conditional on progress as scheduled," said one message. *"Official liaisons will be provided for support as necessary. Frequent correspondence is essential; secrecy, more so."*

The person in these messages called himself Monitor Nine, whatever the heck that was. Hank wasn't even sure if the person was male or female, but he—or it—seemed to be an ambassador for something called the Merideth Institute.

Nothing there to suggest criminal activity by any means, but it was quite odd just the same, and it left Hank feeling queasy in his stomach—nervous, as if he had just slipped a cookie from the cookie jar and found a razor inside. It wasn't that he worried about stealing the cookie so much as he wondered what to do with the cookie now that he had it.

So he kept reading, reading until his blue eyes blurred. And the more he read, the less he liked: crazy stuff, piecemeal, nothing cohesive. Just a bunch of little puzzle scraps all thrown in together about a new project or research effort that the four scientists were collaborating on. Something big. Something secretive. And very low-key. Each member seemed to have an assigned task and—

Bingo.

Hank almost thumped himself on the head. It didn't take a brain surgeon to figure out that the four scientists, surely, formed the backbone, if not the whole, of Club Cranium. But that was a minor triumph. He scanned for more.

It was slow going. Trying to make sense of the fragments was like trying to figure out the plot of a movie after arriving an hour late and leaving twenty minutes early, with half the dialogue missing. The encrypted files were no doubt the key, but Hank didn't have a prayer of making sense out of them. He suspected that the majority of files in the forum were encrypted, especially those files that demanded higher-level access to download. Probably a mistake that he got the encrypted files he did. So all that was left to examine were the postings, which Hank could follow well enough at least in terms of the vocabulary, but he had no framework for the messages themselves, no map legend with an *X* to mark the spot. So he plodded along, cursing himself for only downloading a small handful of messages, but fearing to return to the forum too soon on the heels of his last entry.

The tone of the correspondence left little to the imagination. There was too much hesitation, even anger and fear, in Rosenburg's and Saludin's messages, and too much sense of thrill in Volgaard's, to mistake this as routine research. Remming played the role of mediator and diplomat, which was his forte. He seemed to Hank to be the driving force behind the effort. But *what* effort? That was the killer, and no matter how hard he tried, Hank couldn't quite get a grip on it.

There were commonalities. The pineal gland, a small lobe at the center of the brain, seemed to be the focal point of the research. Or maybe a region very near it; Hank couldn't be sure. Something also called "serotoxomiasin potentiated tissue."

Hank tugged at the skin of his jaw. *Serotoxomiasin?*

That word, that phrase in fact, was repeated several times, abbreviated to SPoT by Remming and Volgaard but spelled in full by Rosenburg and El-Saludin. Whatever it was, serotoxomiasin—coded as "STM-55" in the files—also seemed a focal point. And a lightning rod for some rather harsh editorials by Rosenburg.

"We are proceeding down a path that presumes to answer in one fell swoop questions that have resounded for thousands of years," read one of Rosenburg's messages, dated November of last year. It ended with a warning: *"Our findings could bring tremors to the landscape of our society more deadly than a hundred earthquakes. Beware, my friends, the arrogance of science."*

Volgaard curtly replied in a subsequent message that the "arrogance of science is of minor consequence compared to the weakness and stagnation of fear." Hank flinched. Hardly a subtle scolding.

But he could not help smiling when he read Remming's final response, full of soothing, diplomatic words, urging the members to stay focused and impartial to the preliminary data, no matter how "far-reaching the implications seem at this stage."

The grandiose language and sense of self-importance confused Hank. He didn't know what to make of it. This wasn't the A-bomb, for crying out loud, or Columbus and the New World. This was a little bit of brain chemistry.

Or was it?

Fortunately, most of the messages merely discussed chemical composition—or rather theorized it—because the details seemed sketchy. All Hank knew was that he had never heard of SPoT before, although serotoxomiasin did sound similar to serotonin, which was a critical neurotransmitter in the brain. According to the papers, serotoxomiasin seemed to come from a cluster of nerve tissue near the pineal.

But not all the time.

". . . extremely limited success replicating SPoT outside the central control groups," wrote Volgaard in a paper dated January 12, the last of Hank's papers and the most recent of all those he had downloaded. "All efforts to pin down the nature, saturation, and possibilities of the pineal body nerve aberration and serotoxomiasin have been thwarted."

So maybe time was not the issue after all. The random factors mentioned in Volgaard's message made Hank think that the presence or absence of this SPoT thing was more related to certain groups of people than anything else. And what was with Volgaard's militaristic language?

Thwarted? For a research project? Hardly the dispassionate voice of pure academics.

It all added up to something fishy, Hank thought, shaking his head and reviewing the papers again. Yet the sum total of his efforts last night and this morning amounted only to more questions and fewer answers. If only he had downloaded from the bottom of the Club Cranium pile instead of the top, he would have much more recent data to go on. The files were almost certainly organized chronologically, meaning he had grabbed the oldest of the bunch, dating back as far as a year ago, maybe two. He sat back in his swivel chair and breathed deeply. His eyes and back ached.

What did it all mean? Hank folded his fingers together and stretched his arms, making his knuckles crack like a semiautomatic rifle. He hated dishonesty, especially in those he admired. He figured it went back to his inherited impulse for truth.

If there was an answer to find, he wanted to be the one to find it. And if there was one man who would know the answer, it would be Remming.

Let's hope all this is just a huge misunderstanding on my part, he thought. *Let's hope Club Cranium is benign. And let's hope Remming . . .* He let the thought linger unspoken in his mind. There was nothing concrete on anyone, or anything yet to arouse suspicion. This should have made him feel hopeful, optimistic. It did not.

Don't disappoint me, Remming. I've invested too much in you.

SPoT was obviously the key. The pineal gland region was the source. And Hank, at least, was the self-appointed hero for the moment. Which meant there was only one thing left to do:

Confront Remming.

4

Hank would get his chance sooner than he realized. As it happened, he was supposed to drive Jay Remming to the airport later that afternoon. Dr. Remming viewed his residents as personal valets as much as understudies and always had at least one on hand (usually Hank) to ferry him around or to guard his automobile—a sizable commitment since Remming was always flying somewhere or another. To his credit, however, Remming usually provided the car, his own, a classy little BMW, which meant that Hank had the privilege of driving it back; this also meant that if Hank was feeling particularly brave that day, a detour down a scenic little piece of empty road might follow. Hank owned his own vehicle, the same car he had in high school, a virtually mufflerless '68 Duster. After sitting two years unused in a barn, the trek to the Big Apple was probably the vehicle's last long road trip, but it was fine for occasional city travel. Like most New Yorkers, Hank quickly learned that cabs and subways, or a bicycle even, made more sense than trying to fight the traffic and other cabbies. He kept the car now more for sentimental value than anything.

As for the BMW, alas! In four years Hank had only felt brave enough to solo once.

On this occasion, Remming was scheduled to speak in Geneva at an international consortium sponsored by the World Health Organization. Remming frequently worked with WHO as a consultant, mediator, and technical adviser for various policy considerations, information dissemination, and educational forums. The man had a knack for making the complexities of his science readily accessible to laymen and political figures, without patronizing or sacrificing depth—a real boon for conferences of this nature. In fact, Remming served as an adviser to several organizations of national or global significance, including the National Institute of Health and, of course, WHO.

That much, Hank knew.

What he didn't know was that Remming also advised the Office of Medical Intelligence, a still-classified spin-off of the CIA secretly established by Eisenhower in the fifties. At the time of its creation, the OMI was chiefly dedicated to processing intelligence gathered on the chemical warfare capabilities of the Russians. Instead of being abandoned, or at least pared back at the conclusion of the Cold War, the OMI manifest blossomed significantly, so much so that by the time Remming was asked to serve six years ago, nearly $700 million and some change was being funneled through the budget to fund the "research efforts" OMI deemed worthy.

Nor did Hank realize that Remming and four other scientists had served during Desert Storm on an advisory board hastily assembled by the National Security Council. The NSC was in something of a bind at the time. Just weeks before the first air strike was to commence, the council got skittish about Iraq's biological war machine and whether or not the military's standard issue could or would do the job against a full biological assault. President Bush had already drawn his "line in the sand," so the political pressures were high to press forward, but the council was receiving conflicting intelligence reports on Iraqi scientists creating a powerful new strain of neurological bacteria that the protective gear could neither detect nor safely filter. Since Bush did not want to go head-to-head with a Third World country and lose, or even be partially embarrassed, Remming and his colleagues were given the nearly impossible task of engineering—in a matter of weeks!—some sort of genetically induced natural defense mechanisms that would give the American soldiers an extra boost should their hardware prove insufficient.

They failed, of course—simply not enough time. But if Hank had known any of this, he might have reconsidered his decision to challenge

Remming on the still-nebulous secret affairs of Club Cranium and the various questions of ethical duplicity. *Unproven* duplicity, he reminded himself. Even so, the tension between Rosenburg and Volgaard was obvious; equally obvious, in spite of the secrecy, were the tones of wonder and mystery regarding this *thing* near the pineal gland. And serotoxomiasin. What in the world was that?

All he knew was that Johnston, the poor soul he stuck with the call from Nursing last night, had decided to return the favor (it had been *his* turn to drive) by sticking Hank with chauffeuring Remming to the airport. Remming hated parking his car in public lots. The good doctor wasn't really concerned about the safety of his Beamer, since airport security was decent. The issue was money, pure and simple. Remming was as wealthy as a man needed to be, but a miser to the last. This, of course, annoyed Hank, but a lowly resident does not tell a Nobel recipient that he is foolish. No, he just smiles, tips his hat if he's wearing one, and asks, "Where to, sir?"

So there they were, together, on their way to JFK International. Remming had been dictating notes to his tiny microcassette ever since they left, not an uncommon event at all. In fact, the image of Remming—robotlike, arm crooked to his face, straight backed, walking the campus (the only time he seemed less than graceful)—was a running joke among the med students, especially since Remming required all his students to own a recorder as well. That way, no one ever had an excuse for lost notes; more important, a single tape from Remming could be distributed to many students, thus decreasing by severalfold the need for direct human interaction.

Efficient, systematic, impersonal. One hundred percent Remming. Hank, out of rebellion, hardly ever used his recorder, though he did own one.

So conversation was sparse. For some reason, Remming had opted to drive this time, so Hank rode dutifully beside him. A few more minutes passed. When at length Remming put away his recorder, it seemed the time for confrontation had arrived, yet Hank hated the very thought of it. Should he be bold and blunt? Cool and conniving? Subtle? Should he confront at all? The answer seemed obvious. A full frontal assault was not only foolish but wildly presumptuous! What did he expect Remming to do? Break down, blubbering, and own up to something Hank could not even define? Hardly.

Let's see your evidence, Hanson. . . .

That would be Remming's first demand. He would be so calm. So collected. So *cutting.*

Well, you see, I don't have any. I just got this feeling deep in my gut. . . .

And that's really all it was. A feeling. Zero evidence of anything actually wrong, just a few loose, fishy ends. Hank's heart sank. Maybe he had been a bit overzealous last night.

No. He was his mother's son. The truth was what mattered. He ventured out, snakelike.

"You've been out of town a lot here recently," he began casually. That much wasn't hard, since Remming had been absent much of late.

Jay Remming smiled. Fortyish, plus a little, his short black hair had already begun to gray at the temples, but this only lent greater dignity to his persona. He was not your stereotypical calculator-brained, lab-coat-wearing scientist. As a proud African-American, Remming was a man of regal bearing: crisp, aristocratic, comfortable with exposure, commanding that rare flavor of presence and speech that marks a figure for the history books. When Hank first met him five years ago he had been reminded of an old picture of some great African clan chief: lean and firm, slender face, with a long, flat nose and caramel brown eyes. Remming was generally quiet, not at all flashy, but he had a predatory wit, as if he always knew something you didn't, and a biting sense of humor.

Listening to the man could be a simultaneously humiliating and spellbinding experience.

"The premeds giving you fits?" he asked, the corners of his lips tugging upward.

"As always," Hank said. Then the nervousness hit. "So what's the big topic for Geneva?"

"Oh, let's see . . . I believe the title given to my speech is 'Brave New World: Genetics and the Great Unfolding of the Human Paradigm.'"

"Sounds like a hoot," Hank said, adjusting his seat belt. *Hoot?*

"Actually, no," Remming answered drily. Hank knew better than to believe him. Remming loved to pretend at aloofness when the world begged for his services. Driving the car with one lazy hand draped over the wheel, Remming spoke again. "I thought I gave you a memo on this?"

"No."

"Well, I meant to. You know I petitioned the chancellor for extra funds so that you could accompany me to Geneva."

Hank's eyes widened with surprise.

"Obviously, no luck," Remming stated, then to soften the blow, added, "It's just as well, really. You would have been bored. The conference is a sort of a 'State of the Body Address' for the various Secretaries of Health and other medical officials. Most are from member nations of the UN, but few of them are actually scientists or physicians. Happens annually."

"Hmm. So what's the point?"

"Point?"

"For the conference, I mean."

Remming shrugged. "These people are the policy makers of health for the whole world. They need to stay abreast of what's happening."

It was as good an opportunity as he would get. Hank took the plunge. "And just what *is* happening? What's new? What's on the cutting edge?"

Remming almost chuckled. Hank had spoken a little too forcefully. "Where did *that* come from?"

"Just making conversation," Hank said, holding his ground. "You're on the front lines and I haven't had the chance to catch up lately."

"Catch up? You have more time to read the journals than I, Hanson."

Only two people in the world still called him Hanson: Remming and Hank's mother, the latter of which nearly broke out in hives when a nickname was used in her presence. Remming, on the other hand, used Hank's real name for purely professional reasons, which translated, meant maintaining appropriate distance between student and teacher. He was *not* Hank's buddy, never would be, and wanted to make that perfectly clear as often as possible. Even so, from time to time Hank suspected a certain level of affection—half begrudged and certainly well masked—leaking from the older man, affection he did not allow other students. If ever asked, Remming would deny it to the last.

"I'm tired of reading the journals!" Hank snorted. "Besides, you know the politics of those things. You're the one who taught me. Everything's filtered."

"Such a cynic!" Remming laughed.

"A realist, I'd say."

"Regardless, I don't have much to tell. I haven't done anything exciting in I don't know how long."

Liar, Hank thought instinctively. But the roundabout game was getting him nowhere and he knew it. *What to do?* His palms grew sweaty.

"Do you know why I got into neurology?" Hank asked rhetorically. "All my life I've wanted to know a big secret, you know? A really big secret. That's what I love about this field, *our* field . . . we get the chance to listen to the secrets of the brain. But I want to know more. I want to know what's out there! You can understand that, can't you?"

It was a potentially meaningful moment. Hank even surprised himself at the seriousness of his own voice. Yet no sooner were the words out of his mouth than he saw, in his mind, a pitiful picture of a young stand-up comic onstage for the first time. Got the well-rehearsed routine. Got his big opener—a sure thing if there ever was one—huge laughs, right around the corner. Then, for some reason, the young comic begins describing to the audience how a toilet works. The crowd of faces watches him from the darkness, very confused.

Such was Remming's response.

The conversation fell to silence. Hank began to rail against himself. *Great! Now we're both too confused to even speak. The man has a freezer for a soul! And you just offered an unsolicited confession of nearly Catholic proportions!*

He had hoped his talk of secrets and all might be a hint to Remming, a spring, a lynchpin. Anything. But that was based on the enormous assumption that Remming could read his mind and knew in advance what he aimed for. Even more, that once Remming got there, he would care!

Nevertheless, Hank had drawn on fairly deep reserves for those feelings, so his words, however random, at least sounded sincere. He stared silently out the passenger window, waiting for a reply, feeling more and more like a Judas for even attempting to catch Remming's hand in the cookie jar, but not knowing how to let the matter go. The heater in the car, on low, and the steady hum of tires and asphalt were the only sounds. Remming turned to look at him. Inwardly, Hank braced himself for a snide commentary on inappropriate personal divulgence. Probably melt the glass in front of his nose if he knew the man at all. Instead, Remming made a rare gesture of personal grace. "Hanson, I don't know what you're driving at. Literally *everything* we're doing at this stage is on the cutting edge. We're in uncharted territory. You know that. We're pioneers. Everything is a big secret."

Yes, but some are bigger than others, Hank thought. Actually, he was relieved.

They were approaching the airport. Traffic had been heavy to begin with, then thinned out for a while. Now it was heavy again. The drive from Upper Manhattan to Lower Queens was long and monotonous, but the noon sun was bright and the heat it offered made the day more cheery than it rightly should have been. As they drew near, Hank watched the steady stream of planes floating skyward and descending almost nonstop; great gray birds, several tons of steel, hanging from the clouds as if on a string. For a moment he felt as though he were back on the flatlands sitting on the barkless stump of a fallen tree, late in the afternoon, with the sky wide and empty and three lonely hawks tracing nearly perfect circles around and around and around. One of the hawks let out a loud, lusty cry . . .

Which sounded remarkably like a car horn.

Hank's reverie broke; a couple of cars ahead, some nameless driver was shaking his fist at another car and lying on the horn.

"Simpleton," Remming muttered.

Then another car swerved and cut him short so that he had to slam on the brakes. Remming's hands gripped the wheel so hard that veins bulged and bone lines protruded. Yet he did not curse. Hank knew he would not. Remming was probably a godless man; Hank did not know for sure. Maybe he was many things, in fact, but he had never uttered a curse word in all the time Hank had known him. Remming thought cursing to be the only wit available to intellectual inferiors. He simply refused to be a part.

The moment passed. Traffic in New York City was a contact sport and everyone wore black and white stripes; it was a fact of life. So they kept moving. The silence returned. Navigating through the taxis and motel shuttles and assorted other vehicles made for slow going, but in time they found themselves approaching the British Airways concourse. Remming was lucky enough to grab a shoulder parking space right off the terminal entrance. Almost as an afterthought he reached into his inner coat pocket and withdrew a piece of paper.

"Here's the itinerary. I'll be back on Sunday, so look sharp." He glanced at Hank, then, eyes suddenly keen and focused, asked, "You know the spot?"

That word, the way Remming said it, made Hank's heart drop to the floor. He faltered for a moment. "The spot?"

"Where to pick me up?"

"Oh yeah, sure. Same as always."

Remming left the keys in the car and the engine running. He popped the trunk and started to get out. Unthinking, Hank reached out, almost groped for Remming's sleeve, wisely choosing not to at the very last. Instead he spoke loudly. Artificial. Nervous.

"I don't know as much about the spot as I would like to!"

It could not have sounded more brash and assuming. A professional boundary was breached. Yet as disapproving as Remming normally might have been, now he seemed perplexed. He bent down, allowing a tone of genuine concern. "Are you feeling well, Hanson? You've been acting strange all morning."

"I'm fine," Hank said. "I just wonder what makes one *spot* more interesting than another." He tried not to lay too much emphasis on the word. Just enough to ring Remming's bell.

The doctor's face was blank.

"I'm really not sure what you mean."

Something made Hank think he did know. Something in his voice. And so it came to this. Summoning all his courage, Hank arched one doubting eyebrow, said, "Don't you?"

He couldn't be certain whether Remming understood or not. At the very least, the older man's paternal concern had long since disappeared. Now he was saccharin sweet and impatient. "All I know is that I've got a plane to catch. And you're making me late. I don't like to be late."

"Why don't I pick you up at a new spot?" Hank said daringly. "I'm sure there are all kinds of new spots to explore."

Remming sat very still and very quiet.

"You and me. Together," Hank said. "Or is your team already full?"

The doctor pulled back and eyed Hank warily. He was no fool. The mask of mild charm he wore so casually fell from his face like a gate closing. His voice slipped into low gear as he stared hard at Hank.

"I'm not sure the tone of this conversation is entirely to my liking, Hanson."

Hank smiled innocently. "Just trying to make sure there's not a better place to pick you up. I guess the same spot will have to do."

Remming glanced from Hank to the splotchy windshield and back again. His face was dark but subdued. "I guess it will." Both men exited the car. Hank headed for the driver's side. Dr. Remming grabbed two bags of luggage and aimed for the sliding glass doors of the terminal. He did not glance back.

"Dr. Remming!" Hank called out. Remming did not stop, did not turn, but his eyes were lucid, catlike. "You've got nothing to worry about, really. I'll keep your spot safe while you're gone."

Remming slipped through the doors and disappeared. Luggage or no, Hank knew well enough to notice that his stride was more jerky than normal.

"See you Sunday," he breathed, heart pounding. "After I've done a little more research."

5

The assembly of some five hundred persons was a rich global mix of the many tribes of humanity. Looking out from the head table, Jay Remming noted the texture of the crowd, the many skin colors, clothes, and customs. Emissaries from the dissolved Soviet Union were there—Kazakhstan, Lithuania, Russia, Ukraine, and Belarus—wearing earphones for translation; numerous Arabs; Europeans of every stripe; a large consort from the Far East, especially Japan and China, a smaller one from India and Singapore; Israel, also, small but mighty; only a few African nations; and of course America, Canada, and a handful of the more powerful Latin American nations. Far too many countries to identify completely, but Remming was pleased at the number attending.

Pleased as possible, anyway.

His irritation was not with Geneva; that much was sure. The city was, as always, ancient and lovely, nestled on the southern banks of Lake Geneva near the slow blue waters of the Rhône River. In the Old City, south of the Rhône, where the streets were narrow and winding and little gardens sprouted here and there, the rough, worn stonework of the buildings was more quaint than any postcard could capture. Geneva was an international haven of peace and the central office to a number of global operations. North of the river, in the newest section of the city, lay the European headquarters of the United Nations, the National Council of Churches, the Red Cross, and various international financial institutions.

But it was the sight of the distant, rugged Alps, wearing her bright cape of snow so tight about her shoulders, that should have cheered Remming the most. He was born in Colorado. Mountains were near to his heart and Geneva boasted a stunning view of the Mont Blanc massif. For anyone's imagination, such a sight should have been sufficient.

But Remming couldn't relax. He was nearly driven to distraction by his last exchange with Hank. A little voice in the back of his head kept nagging him, saying Hank, somehow, had tapped *in*. Or had been leaked information. But by whom? Maybe it was all just coincidence and misinterpretation—a farce of missed cues and poor humor. Maybe. But Remming suspected the worst. Having tried to bury his suspicion, forget it, rationalize it—even after fifteen hours of airtime and a couple of fine Swiss meals—he remained restless. His sleep last night had been troubled and unsatisfying.

That was, however, last night. Today, he was the keynote speaker and needed to concentrate. Glancing up at the massive marble headstone at the rear of the chamber, he read a simple, engraved claim, that the World Health Organization had been established as an arm of the United Nations in 1948 for *"the attainment by all the peoples of the highest possible level of health."*

A noble goal. Remming rolled his eyes. Too noble for its own good.

If the world was full of cynics, Jay Remming was surely their unsung king. And with good reason. In spite of his success, beneath the glossy externals, the doctor's life was far from pristine. Divorced, a casualty of war from the sexual revolution, Remming's dysfunction would have been fully evinced for public display were it not for the force of personality laid atop it. He suffered that vague sense of rootlessness—subtle, incalculable—which plagued most of the Boomer generation. Not that he would own up to any such affliction, much less even recognize it. In fact, if accused of anything so weak as an occasional spat of existential angst, Remming would first probably scoff, perhaps too loudly, feeling justified, second, in his habit of blaming nearly all modern ailments on psychoanalytic double-talk (a curious dichotomy for a man of science). Indeed, Remming's armor was brighter and bolder on a bad day than most at the peak of their lives; but there were chinks, for those who cared to look, and all the posing and detachment were, as irony would have it, illumined markers, bread crumbs dropped by the subconscious, pointing to one simple fact:

Remming was a guilty man.

Again, it didn't take a rocket scientist to figure out why. His oldest son, Joshua, whom Remming had loved fiercely, died of a cerebral hemorrhage on the operating table under his own knife. That was seven years ago. At the time, proud and unpliable, Remming went away on sabbatical and shut himself off from everyone for a period of six months to grieve. When he returned—collected, calm, sane—he informed his wife, Anna, that she was no longer necessary in his life and no longer loved. Devastated, she moved back to her home in Atlanta, taking the remaining three children with her. Remming saw them once a year, most often at Christmas, but he rarely spoke of them or his wife.

Then, almost a year to the day after Josh's death, Jay Remming won his first Nobel prize.

Few knew the details of the divorce. Most of Columbia's faculty knew only what they read in the papers at the time. Colleagues and peers were generally uninformed and Remming had but a few confidants. By default, his students were almost unanimously excluded from such privileged, personal information. Only Hank had taken the time to find out even this much, which, though sketchy at best, placed him squarely in Remming's inner circle. This, too, spoke volumes of Remming's opinion of Hank, however distant the method of their relationship. Remming trusted no one. But he trusted Hank. To think that Hank would betray that trust was . . . well, distracting.

Usually Remming knew most of the other speakers on the agenda. This time he only knew one or two. And since he had bothered neither to read the day's program nor introduce himself to any unfamiliar faces last night at the reception dinner, he still only knew one or two. He was up next. The conference moderator, another man he didn't know, was rattling off his introduction like an all-points bulletin. Remming only half listened. It took forever. Finally:

". . . a brilliant mind at a most critical juncture in the history of man and science, please welcome Dr. Jay Remming."

Polite applause rose from the crowd. Remming stepped to the podium—no notes, no papers—scanned the audience, and calmly announced, "Not long ago, a group of researchers dropped a single gene into a female mouse and turned that mouse into a male."

It was an almost effortless seizing of the reins. He let those words and the silence that followed sink in and squirm around for a few seconds before continuing. Within the space of twenty words, the audience was hooked. He opened his mouth, more boldly:

"You did not hear me wrong. This was a full-scale masculine conversion, complete with testes, sperm-producing cells, and the mouse equivalent of an ego. An amazing feat, I'm sure you realize, but the most puzzling and beautiful fact was not so much the conversion itself, but the fact that the conversion was accomplished with one *single* gene. Imagine parachuting an admiral onto a battleship and having the change in command turn the boat into an airplane. This is the power of modern genetics."

Remming took a half step back from the podium, letting his eyes rest on the smooth grain of the wood, pondering his next words. He did not have to think long.

"Honored assembly, leaders of the nations, I stand before you today with a simple declaration: The world is about to change. Forever. Worldwide, scientists have embarked on a mission that will soon lead us to the very threshold of existence. Today, I will be your guide.

"So bear with me for a moment. If I were a theologian I would tell you that, over the course of my work, I have put my face against the face of God. If I were an artist, I would say that I have been given a small pocket flashlight and been placed inside the Louvre in the dead of night; I would say that I wander here and there, purposefully but blind, shining my little light on the most infinitesimal masterpieces of creation, and as I look I record each one, as do others like me, so that the next time we pass this way we are not so blind. But I am not an artist. And I am certainly no theologian.

"My declaration, then, is this: I am a molecular neurobiologist. And my task is simple: to understand man; to decode man; with your help, to remake man."

No one spoke. No one even coughed. Remming continued.

"The Industrial Revolution powered the nineteenth century, affecting national and world economies, social structures, and the political climate. In the early twentieth century, mechanical science gave way to physics and chemistry. The atom was split. The theory of relativity was born. In the mid- to late twentieth century, astronomy put men on the moon and brought the stars to our doorstep. So what is left? Not an outward quest, but inward. The next revolution in science will be biological. Genetics, in particular. And mark my words, the coming advances in genetic engineering will dwarf the remarkable achievements of previous decades, with proportionately greater global impact on all cultures and peoples.

"For all our many differences—religion, clothing, customs, history, whatever—humans share one remarkable truth. We all have forty-six chromosomes. Twenty-three from our mother and twenty-three from our father. These forty-six contain the sum total of genetic data available to all humankind. Yet if you were to type out all the data contained on those tiny forty-six chromosomes, you would create an encyclopedia approximately 500 volumes in length, with about 300 pages per volume. Every single cell possesses this tremendous amount of information. Yet fully ten million chromosomes—over 200,000 times that contained in you or me—could fit comfortably in a period at the end of a sentence typed on an ordinary piece of paper."

Remming spread his hands out on the podium frame. He was relaxed, but he also understood the power he possessed. He was in his element.

"Many of you know some of the basics, but as I move into the deeper material later on it will benefit each of us to share some sort of common language, so bear with me. A gene is nothing more than a specific sequence of four chemicals—only four—signified by the letters A, G, T, and C. The arrangement of these four chemicals along the DNA strand forms a specific definition for every human trait just like a dictionary defines words by assembling other words together. Considering the number of traits available to humans, a single gene sequence can be very lengthy, even if it does nothing more than specify that your chin is supposed to have a cleft in it. And all this data is packed into every cell.

"It might help to imagine that a cell is like an egg. The yoke would be the nucleus and the white part is called the cytoplasm. The cytoplasm possesses most of the molecular factories which make the various biochemicals necessary for human existence. The nucleus is the command and control center that directs the manufacturing processes of the cytoplasm. The nucleus is sort of like the 'brain' of the cell because DNA is stored there—an amazing amount of DNA, actually. A typical nucleus possesses almost 1.8 meters of DNA, yet that DNA fits in a space not much more than six microns in length. That's like stuffing thirty miles of spaghetti into a blueberry.

"Obviously, there is a lot of data stored in a very compact space. The human body is a very efficient archive. But our exploratory tools are getting better and better. Science is becoming more and more adept at identifying and localizing the specific traits and locations of genes within the body. We have discovered tiny molecular scissors called 'restriction enzymes' that allow us to clip and trim DNA at very specific places. We have also discovered molecular spot glues, called 'ligases,' which allow us to paste foreign genes together. We have learned how to transport new genetic sequences from one cell to another—such as in the case of the female-to-male mouse conversion. We can dress up an otherwise foreign gene with the equivalent of romantic perfume so that it becomes irresistible to a potential host. We can hijack and reprogram unwanted viruses, neutralize them, contaminate them with a desired gene, and shuttle them off to infect a cell for us. We can inject a gene into a cell with tiny syringes, like a flu shot. Scientists have placed the luminescent gene of a firefly in a tobacco leaf and do you know what happened? That same leaf glowed in the dark like a light bulb! My point is this: Whatever boundaries exist for genetics would be a matter of pure speculation at the present because no real boundaries are anywhere in sight.

"Genes in a cell are like light switches in a room. You can have a thousand switches in one room—or one cell in this case—but until one particular switch is thrown the lights won't come on. Geneticists now believe there are what we call 'master genes.' When these genes are turned on, they incite a hierarchy of other genes to cascade, turning on or off, affecting multiple reactions simultaneously. This is what takes place at conception. There is a master gene called 'Mio D1.' You can stick it into a fat cell and turn that fat cell into a skeletal muscle. There is another gene that can turn cells into nerve cells, cartilage cells, etc. These genes are invaders in one sense, but in another they are merely forcing a different switch to be thrown, turning on a different part of the developmental program.

"There is a tumor called 'teratocarcinoma.' This tumor is the focus of significant research efforts around the world right now. It looks like your garden-variety tumor with a mass of semidifferentiated cells. But when you dissect a teratocarcinoma you find a strange thing inside— bits of bone, eye tissue, muscles and fat, and skin that has hair on it. There is even a documented case of a researcher finding a fully formed finger inside a teratocarcinoma. It is as if this thing is trying to become human but something has gone drastically wrong. What could cause such an aberration? Right now we aren't sure. But we feel certain this tumor will soon yield important clues on the nature of master genes."

Remming took a deep breath and a sip of water. The sea of faces before him remained focused. A few were bored, but not many.

"In my particular specialty," he continued, "which is the brain, genetics has a particular bearing on all functions: Intelligence. Disposition. Temperament. Creativity. Even things that were once considered virtues or vices are now yielding to genetic explanations. We have localized genes related to aggression and alcoholism. We have strong genetic evidence for homosexuality as a birth trait. We have found that nearly one in five babies may be predisposed to shyness because a part of their brain known as the amygdala is hypersensitive. Severe depression is being treated with Prozac. How many of you have heard of Prozac?"

He raised his own hand and waited for the audience to respond. Participation was important. Gradually, nearly everyone raised their hand.

"Prozac is nothing new," he continued. "It is simply a synthesized version of a chemical the brain already produces called serotonin. Serotonin is one of many critical messengers in the brain called neuro-transmitters. These 'messengers' are produced by specific nerve clusters hundreds of thousands of times a day, and they follow specific pathways throughout the many regions of the brain, with the specific purpose being either to inhibit or excite a particular response, behavior, or emotion. Prozac works because chronic depression often results from low levels of serotonin in the limbic system.

"But that's only the beginning! New neurotransmitters are being discovered daily. Some, admittedly, are of only minor significance, but others are proving monumental. And it doesn't take a rocket scientist to understand that the delicate balance of the brain is a critical factor in the health of the human condition."

Remming's inflection began to change. He was reaching a critical juncture in his speech.

"This leads us to an interesting predicament, because we all have unique personalities. As human beings, we hold certain values dear. Our sense of individuality is one of them, maybe the most important one. Yet I must ask because science now forces the question: How many cherished elements of the 'self' will eventually prove to be concrete manifestations of neurobiology, rather than the subtle shading of some amorphous, pseudospiritual idea known as 'the human soul'? The answer? Countless, I assure you. Maybe the whole thing. Our entire psychology breaks down to a molecular level. Personality is no longer just psychology; it is chemistry. Are you angry or patient? Do you have a penchant for wild, anonymous sex, or are you content with celibacy? These are real questions, but the answers are not so multiplicitous as we once believed. More and more, the common denominator is genetics."

Here it was, at last—the big payoff:

"Ministers of science, secretaries of health, leaders of the nations, you would do well to prepare for the coming earthquake of neurobiology. Because in the end the simple truth is that very little of your personality, of anyone's personality, may be truly theirs to claim, either the good or the bad of it. We are *all,* honorable and evil, victims of our genetic inheritance."

For those who understood, it was a breathtaking assertion. Most did not, at least not entirely. Yet everyone took notice and a low murmur arose. Remming caught the wave.

"The moral ramifications of that fact are sweeping! The implications for government, for laws, for the most fundamental orderings of society will be significant, even colossal. So the question is rightly posed: As science unravels bits of personality, does personal account-ability unravel with it? But that is a question for the ethicists and politicians. If morality is at stake, it is your issue, sirs and madams, not mine."

So Remming spoke, leading the assembly like a child down the halls of genetics and neural science. His task was to create interest and to paint with a broad brush, to give an overview, so he discussed the radical importance of molecular studies to combat the growing tide of drug-resistant bacterial disease and superviruses. He offered com-pelling genetic evidence for a number of maladies worldwide and urged the assembly to press their governments for expanded research funds. He made every fact he shared simple to comprehend but, in characteristic manner, no less easy to bear. Jay Remming refused to compromise the burden of his knowledge with easy explanations and cheap sentiment. He spoke in panoramic word pictures of the coming millennium; he made references to Aldous Huxley's *Brave New World;* he spoke mainly of the promise and hope of these bold new frontiers, but briefly touched also on the dark side of knowledge—the shadow world of black-market genetics and the very real threat of extreme human devaluation. These were minor concerns to him, but to men-tion them was of political value. There was a need for vigilance, true, but for Remming the quest for knowledge was a pure thing, a Platonic ideal, and any threat to the contrary was probably made either by a fool or a coward.

He spoke for three hours. Tomorrow he would speak again for half that amount before flying back to New York. When he finished on both occasions the applause would change in tone, would be more than polite, more appreciative than when he had begun his speech. It always was. Remming, with full awareness of the irony, connected easily to the same people he generally scorned. His fluency with them was one more sampling of his power over them. And the people, almost without fail, clapped their hands and begged for more. Even world leaders.

Soon, Remming thought, listening to the applause, smiling, wav-ing politely, *soon I will offer you the key to your very souls. I will hand it to you on a platter of genes, clean and new, like the soul of a baby. Sooner than you know. . . .*

After the presentation, Remming was approached by a well-dressed man who identified himself as Stewart Newman, head of the Special Projects Division for Genetics Advancement at the World Health Organization. Remming had never heard of Newman before, much less met him, even though Newman said he had followed Remming's work for years.

"Finally got the chance to meet you and didn't want to pass it up," Newman said in a crisp, pleasant British accent.

Remming's smile was distant. He glanced over Newman's shoulder to the crowd behind, looking for Selma Volgaard. They were supposed to rendezvous after his speech.

"I'm surprised we haven't met before," Remming said, only half interested. "I've been a guest here in Geneva several times."

"Oh, I rarely get the chance to attend one of these meetings. My work is very hands-on. I'm always somewhere or another. Hardly ever in one spot."

Not looking, Remming reached out, took hold of Newman's hand. "Well, nice to meet you . . . ," he said, pumping the hand a couple of times before attempting to slip away.

"Actually," Newman said, not quite releasing his grip, "we *have* met once before. It was at a symposium in Tokyo—1983, I believe. You wouldn't remember, of course."

"I'm sorry, no."

Newman let go and stepped back. "Well, you're a busy man. Just wanted to say hello is all. Maybe my department will be able to assist you someday on a project. Something to benefit the world. How's that sound?"

"The whole world?"

Newman grinned broadly. "I like to think big."

"Hmm. Me too." Remming checked his watch. *Where is Selma?* "I really should be on my way."

"Of course, of course. Sorry to have kept you so long." Newman patted him on the shoulder, sending him off. "I'll just keep admiring your work from a distance if that's all right."

"How can I say no?"

"You can't."

Odd. Remming stopped midstride, glanced over his shoulder. "Does that mean something?"

"Nothing at all. It's part of my job."

Remming stared quietly, left the question mark open on his face.

"Keeping tabs," Newman said just as pleasantly as he had said hello. "On people like you." Not even a hint of a threat. Remming thought it sounded like a warning just the same.

"Good day," he said, turning on his heel.

Stewart Newman watched him disappear into the crowd.

That night Remming met with Selma Volgaard. She greeted him at the door of his suite with a professional, hurried smile and entered without a word. In her left hand she held a leather binder stuffed with papers that hung from the edges like sausage. She held up the binder as if it were evidence for a jury.

"I have brought many documents for our review tonight."

"Excellent," Remming answered. "I'm sorry we missed each other earlier today."

"We did not miss," Volgaard said. Since her English was not good, she kept her dialogues short and forceful. "I was there. You were busy. After the conference you talked with a man. I did not want to interrupt."

"Stewart Newman. He's one of the directors here at WHO. Have you heard of him?"

"No," Volgaard said, "but nice speech." She offered Remming an enigmatic smile. "You do that well."

Remming gratefully inclined his head toward her and then motioned to the table behind him. Together they took their seats. The dining room was separated from the kitchen by a fully stocked wet bar and Remming had coffee percolating; he poured a cup of coffee for himself and a glass of wine for his colleague. The suite was large and rich: three bedrooms, a loft, open rafters, and two huge bay windows that overlooked the frosty blue sky of the Alpine ridge line. Tonight, with the moon burning cold and pale and the snow melting like milk down the mountainsides, Remming thought heaven and earth looked near enough to scrape each other. Far off, a long procession of skiers with torches made their slow, winding way down the slopes. Inside, it was warm. The furnishings were plush, but comfortable; the decor rustic, trimmed in mahogany and copper and handblown glass. Remming had stayed at this same lodge for as many years as he could remember, all compliments of WHO.

On the table beside him sat a white conference phone. Volgaard began spreading out her papers in a haphazard manner that immediately annoyed Remming's sense of order. He said nothing. Instead he reached for his own files, neatly organized, withdrew them from his leather attaché, and glanced at his watch. He took a sip of coffee. It was bitter strong.

10:56 p.m.

"Did you bring the tissue samples from Runwell?"

Volgaard shook her head. "Rail service to Wickford has been closed many days."

Remming smiled politely. "You told me you had them already. Two weeks ago, when we talked."

"How do you say? Anticipation? I will have them soon."

She buried her nose in her papers again, simple as that. As a woman, she possessed none of the raw physical presence so characteristic of her Viking heritage. She was, in fact, the antithesis of the Nordic ideal, being neither handsome nor tall, with weak, drooping shoulders and a receding chin. Diminutive and wiry, she drew further attention to that fact with a tight little bun of hair balanced precariously on the back of her head like a bagel, pulling the loose skin of her cheeks with it, so that she always seemed to be emerging from a wind tunnel or a new bout of plastic surgery.

Once upon a time—three years ago? whenever they first met—her stark features had bothered Remming. Even now he could not help but feel himself grow tense at the kinetic energy of her body, the tight compression, like a spring, and the wolfish gray eyes. But having spent a fair amount of time with her, Remming knew Dr. Selma Volgaard to be a woman of formidable intellect and tenacity. She did not merely walk or speak: She cut like a laser and thundered.

10:58. Neither spoke, just shuffled through their papers silently, sifting through layers and layers of data, sharing a document with each other at times, maybe a word or two of explanation, then processing and more processing.

The phone rang at 10:59. Remming answered, said hello. The deep, rich voice of Dr. Rosenburg hailed out so loudly that even Volgaard could hear. After a few pleasantries, Remming switched the phone over to conference call and put Rosenburg on the loudspeaker.

"Greetings, Dr. Volgaard!" Rosenburg exclaimed. "What new seeds of destruction will you have us plant in the heart of society tonight?"

The older man's tone, at least, was light. Volgaard forced herself to chuckle. Remming adjusted the position of the phone speakers for optimal clarity.

"Dr. Saludin will be joining us soon," he told Rosenburg. "We're probably interrupting your dinner, Samual, so I'll try to keep this short."

"Don't worry about me. This is needful."

It was obvious he wanted to say more by the emphasis he put on *needful*—obvious, too, that Volgaard felt the same. She opened her mouth as if to respond, closed it, then opened and closed it again. Restraint was a difficult virtue for her. She was by far the youngest of the team, being in her early thirties. Staring at Remming from across the table, she noted again how smooth-skinned he was, nearly hairless, almost feminine. A *severe* fault, in her opinion, which was worth noting, since Volgaard was a faithful and meticulous chronicler of the faults of mankind. In her estimation, a certain expected ruggedness precedes a man of Remming's reputation. Where she expected stone and iron, Remming was illusive and cunning, a vague shape of purple satin blowing in the wind at night. He was a *black* black man; but even she could not deny, he was all the more compelling for it—graceful and feline, like a black cat slipping through shadows.

No one said a word. Rosenburg had left behind an uncomfortable silence and everyone knew it. Done intentionally, no doubt. Volgaard watched Remming tap his pencil on the tabletop and took pleasure in knowing that he was more uncomfortable than she. In the background of the phone, in Detroit, Rosenburg's chair squeaked. Mercifully, at about that time, a new beep rang out: Dr. Saludin, having just returned from meditating in his garden. A quick round of formalities followed; then Remming called the meeting to order.

"My friends, we stand at a juxtaposition in our research."

Rosenburg loudly echoed his agreement.

Remming continued. "We have reached a stalemate of sorts, not amongst ourselves, but between the progress of our efforts and the facts as we know them. I submit to you that further progress is impossible without forming some sort of reasonable hypothesis to build upon and guide us."

Volgaard nodded her head curtly. "I am agreeing with you."

Rosenburg balked. "We don't need conjecture; we need facts! The truth of our findings will declare itself at the proper time."

"You are wrong," Volgaard said. "Dr. Remming is right."

Rosenburg barely stifled a flurry of curses. Instead, he poured himself a glass of wine and began to sip very loudly. The smooth flavor calmed him. When he spoke again his words were vague and full of doom. "None of you survived the Holocaust. In Hitler's hands anything—anything—could be used as a weapon."

"We are not Hitler," Remming said gently. "And this is anything but a holocaust."

"Not yet! Not to you or me. But we're talking about power and government! We are tampering with forces of far greater consequence than anything Hitler ever possessed."

"You're overreacting."

"No. You are *under*reacting! You do not see the things I see. Do you know why I fear power and abuse? Because I have felt them both. I've told you before of Fort Detrick, eh? And Lejeune? Yes, I have. And I say our task should be only to reveal, not define."

"But facts *are* facts," Volgaard said.

"What facts? What do we know?"

"Many things in part," Abu said quietly, speaking for the first time. "But none *beyond doubt.*"

"That's not quite true. We know a few things for certain. We remain unsure on others," said Remming. "We don't know the why or how. We do know the location near the pineal gland and the messenger, serotoxomiasin. And we know it only affects a certain group—"

"So far!" Rosenburg added.

"No," Remming said, drawing the word out slowly. "We have

done broad tests. It may be uncomfortable for all of us, but the question of who is affected remains unchallenged. I would stake my reputation on it."

A brief pause. No one wanted to speak next or knew what to say. Saludin made the first attempt.

"The French philosopher Descartes believed the pineal to be the seat of the soul," he said, as if he were tossing out a kernel of corn for the others to chew on. "Horphilos of Alexandria said much the same thing in 300 B.C."

"This isn't the pineal body," Rosenburg answered. "It is only near it. And Descartes died nearly four hundred years ago."

"What of that?" Abu continued thoughtfully. "Leonardo da Vinci drew plans for a helicopter long before Descartes was even born." His voice softened. "I don't like this any more than you, my friend. But that doesn't mean it is wrong."

"What about Gage?" Rosenburg said irritably. "Somebody tell me how he fits into the picture? How do you account for him and those like him?"

Volgaard: "We don't have to. Gage is one of a handful of cases. Remarkable but incomplete."

Rosenburg: "The evidence that rational, moral processes originate in the command center of the prefrontal cortex is incontrovertible!"

Remming: "And far too specific to be possible. The prefrontal cortex alone could not support the sheer number of variables of moral choice, not only from one problem to the next, but even the subtle shadings of any single decision. Ethical dilemmas are much too complex for the cortex alone. It's just too specific, Samual."

"Too specific?" Rosenburg cried. "What is this nerve cluster near the pineal we are all investigating? What is SPoT? What is serotoxomiasin? Are they not specifics?"

"In location only. The process and mechanism are far more sophisticated."

"Word games, Dr. Remming!" Rosenburg cried in exasperation. "Word games!"

"Not at all, just bear with me: If the prefrontal cortex functions at all for the purpose of moral reason, it is only because it is a part of a broad and complex pathway, probably the most far-reaching network in the entire brain. I think what we are discovering is that this pathway begins in the SPoT region with the production of STM-55. The prefrontal cortex *does* appear to allow humans to apply reason to complex social situations, and that *does* have a certain moral function. However, serotoxomiasin seems to be much more sophisticated and exert much more influence, while still tapping into the powers of other latent moral cores. Think of it this way: A large river is fed by many smaller supporting streams. Now reverse that flow. STM-55 is the large river, but *it is both feeding and directing the smaller streams.* STM-55, serotoxomiasin, undiscovered until now, is running the show, the director of an epic movie in which he himself stars. We've assumed for a long time that these other isolated regions and individual subnetworks were the stars, but they're really just the supporting cast."

"Bah!" Rosenburg muttered.

"Don't dismiss me yet, Samual! We must make a leap here, but it is not a great leap. Even your prefrontal cortex is well known to be reciprocally connected to other regions and networks: subcortical nuclei in the limbic system—the hypothalamus, the thalamus, the amygdala. These areas process emotion, regulate basic biological functions, and affect social cognition and behavior, all of which contribute something to moral choice. But they seem to comprise a severely limited solution when isolated from the broader control of serotoxomiasin as it is manufactured by the nerve cluster near the pineal. So the question is not what does the prefrontal do, but *how* does it do it? It is not the key player. Phineas Gage is a fascinating historical case—yes, a railroad spike did puncture his prefrontal cortex; yes, he did survive; yes, his personality was drastically and suddenly altered from upstanding citizen to cursing degenerate—but it is a misleading case for our purposes. We would be wrong to focus there."

Volgaard agreed. "The prefrontal cortex does not act alone. It is not sovereign. At the very least we know of high concentrations of Serotonin R_2 receptors in the prefrontal."

El-Saludin chose that moment to speak again and his voice was full of dread. He had feared this moment since before the conversation began. "There is more," he whispered. "More about serotoxomiasin."

Remming strained to hear him, eyes widening. Volgaard leaned forward to the phone like a hawk swooping on field mice.

"What did you say?"

"Many, many receptors for STM-55 in the prefrontal cortex," Saludin continued. "More dense than the serotonin by a factor of three. Suspiciously dense. I analyzed the final test results myself yesterday afternoon. I don't know what it means."

"Are you certain?" Remming asked.

A pause. "Absolutely certain. And there is more"—he inhaled deeply—"the *receptors* are present in *every* group tested. And in multiple expressions and locations. In fact, I have not yet found a cellular type or physiological region that does not contain receptors."

A great silent gush of breath exhaled from all four members, a sound of wonder and fear. Even Rosenburg was silenced for a time.

"Impossible!"

"Every group? Every cell type? You're telling me that *everyone* has receptors for STM-55?"

Volgaard pushed in ferociously. "We have them, the four of us? Are you sure?"

"As of yet, no group is excluded. No region appears untouched, at least from receptors. It appears only that the presence of SPoT itself is group specific."

"Amazing!"

"No," Abu said sadly. "It is dreadful. It is as if something is missing in the rest of us."

Remming hardly heard him. "How is it activated? Or inactivated, for that matter?"

"I don't know. I just don't know. We're dealing with a substance that has a molecular mass two and half times greater than that of serotonin and fully twice that of GABA or noradrenaline. The amino acid chain is too complex to say yet."

"Any positive binding on the DNA probes?"

"Two of them. One partial. One very significant. I think that one is the key."

"Activation!" Rosenburg roared. "How? Transmitter re-uptake?"

"Doubtful."

"Enzymatic degradation."

"Not a chance."

Volgaard gave voice to what each of them was thinking. She tossed her thought out like a grenade, watched it fall and explode. "Maybe it doesn't shut down at all."

Abu fell into an even deeper silence, but Rosenburg went ballistic. "Have you gone mad, woman! A constant stream of a neurotransmitter as potent as serotoxomiasin would short-circuit the brain!"

"Maybe. Maybe not."

Remming waved his finger in front of his face, thinking. "She may be right, Samual. These people claim to have been touched by God. Maybe the constant flow—"

"You are ruling out three-fourths of the world's population!" Rosenburg shouted. "Three-fourths! Entire cultures! Every major religion."

"Except one," Volgaard said.

Remming echoed her with awe. "Except one."

In Egypt, Dr. Saludin sighed, bowed his head, said nothing. But Rosenburg roared louder, like a frustrated old lion. "This is blasphemy! I am not even a practicing Jew and I am deeply offended!"

"Get ahold of yourself, Dr. Rosenburg," Volgaard said. "Human morality is certainly not a factor, much less the divine. We are dealing with extremely selective genetic mutations, nothing more."

The old man's voice dropped to a lethal whisper. "You know good and well, Selma, that genetic mutations are random and unpredictable. They don't line up into a definable category."

"You may be partly right," she mused, glancing at Remming. "But try a different angle. Maybe this anomaly does not—how do you say?—'manifest' randomly in this category of people. Maybe it is *creating* the category. Maybe we have discovered a biological explanation for what Christians mistakenly call salvation."

"Or correctly call it," Remming said. "In which case we have stumbled onto the most explosive finding in the history of science."

Abu moaned, "It is a God SPoT."

Rosenburg scoffed at the notion. Volgaard said, "Don't be foolish, Dr. Saludin! We are scientists. We should know better."

"I am Muslim," Abu replied simply. "Are you saying my belief in Allah is foolish?"

"Of course she's not," Remming answered quickly. "Only that we must be careful. This is only the beginning—"

"For whom? For Christians?"

"For all of us."

"Who do we tell first?" Volgaard asked. "We should report our findings."

"No! Tell no one. Not yet. Agreed? This is simply off the charts, way too much more we must learn. I can't imagine the politics of trying to announce this without incontrovertible data. Got it? No leaks. None."

Everyone agreed. Of course, Remming did not tell them he had been reporting their findings to federal agents for some time now, that the next meeting was with Special Agent Susan Decker on Monday, their fourth such meeting in the last year. Nor did he tell them she was CIA; that, although the funding for this project was strictly private, the donor foundation in question had specifically requested oversight from the government for the purposes of accountability—presumably his own, which chafed Remming to no end—and so lacking better alternatives for such a sensitive project, the oversight boiled down to CIA liaisons. He told them none of this, partly because he disliked Susan Decker intensely, but mainly because of his great disdain for the many strings—"necessary review, minimal intervention" was how Decker described it—that came with government involvement of any kind. And he certainly did not tell them that Decker had been briefed on everything up to this point.

Almost everything, anyway. Remming knew how to play the game to his advantage.

"So our hypothesis is?" Volgaard asked. "This is what we are trying to have, is it not? To help me say, 'syn-thesis' of thought?"

Remming nodded quietly. A trace of static hummed over the phone. Remming summarized: "First of all, Dr. Saludin, get me the code of that successful probe. I need it immediately. Beyond that, our guiding hypothesis is this: Christians, defined as those who tangibly espouse the Christian faith, and Christians *only*—or at least those who call themselves such—possess a cluster of nerves near the pineal body that produce a specific, powerful, and otherwise unknown neurotransmitter, which we have dubbed serotoxomiasin, STM-55 . . . a chemical that appears to have a genuine, profound, and lasting effect on their behavior."

"Dear God, have mercy," Rosenburg muttered, and then he hung up the phone.

6

Monday morning, Missy Jenkins got it in her head to give Father Ravelo a call, so a little after ten o'clock she phoned him at the parish. An older lady answered, pleasant enough, but sounding very rushed:

"Church of the Ascension, may I help you?"

Missy heard papers shuffling and file drawers opening and closing. She offered only the basics, since her early impression of Father Ravelo included words like "guarded" and "inward." The less the secretary knew the more likely she was to get through, or so she figured; besides, polite silence was pretty much standard practice for any reporter on a first call. If the other party wanted to play hardball, Missy felt plenty comfortable flexing a little media muscle. Even with a church secretary.

Fortunately, she didn't have to. Mrs. Huggins, the secretary, was gabby as a magpie, jotting down her name and asking if Missy was related to a fellow in the church whose last name was Jennkins. Two n's. No, no, said Missy. Just one. No relation. She played this game for a good bit, then asked again about Father Ravelo. Mrs. Huggins laughed, began to explain that the father was out for a few minutes— she never volunteered exactly where, since most people did not take lightly to a priest spending his free time in the local bar—when Ravelo came rolling through the front door with an easy glide and a smile on his face. The secretary covered the phone with her hand and whispered gaily, "Did you win?"

"Afraid not," Ravelo said. "Jack embarrassed me pretty good. But I'm heading back for lunch. Giving him plenty of line before I bury the hook." He made a casting-and-reeling motion with his arm, then winked and headed for his office.

Mrs. Huggins turned her attention back to Missy. "Well, you're in luck! He just walked in. Yes, yes . . . hold please." She called for Ravelo before he disappeared around the corner. "Missy Jenkins, Father?"

The priest frowned, thinking. "Jenkins, Jenkins. Do I know a Missy Jenkins?"

The secretary shrugged.

"Send her through. I'll pick it up inside."

The secretary transferred the call, then went to fetch the priest his morning cup of coffee. Ravelo picked up the phone in his office.

"Father Ravelo? Missy Jenkins, *Detroit Sentinel.* We met last week at the execution—"

"Ah, yes! I remember now, Ms. Jenkins. I had a hard time placing the name at first. But believe me, your face is etched in my memory. Forever."

Missy laughed nervously, then fell quiet.

Ravelo said, "What can I do for you?" He heard Missy scribbling furiously on a pad of paper; what, he could not imagine.

Then, all in a rush, Missy began: "The paper is doing a feature spread on capital punishment. You know, a human-interest piece."

Ravelo started to cut her off right there, but Missy didn't give him the chance.

"It's gonna be neutral, neither pro nor con, so you don't have anything to worry about, really. No politics. What we're trying to do is explore the tragedy of an execution from all sides: the criminals, their victims, their families. You get the idea. Not so much the legal question of capital punishment as the ramifications of it in human terms for society. . . ."

She spoke like a machine gun—little finesse, plenty of volume and speed. Father Ravelo listened—what choice did he have?—but with a jaded ear. He had no intention of committing to an interview with the *Detroit Sentinel* and would have told Missy as much if she had given him half the chance.

She did not. So he sat and listened. After his secretary brought him his morning cup of coffee, the priest nodded his thanks, blew at a curl of steam, took a sip.

And listened some more.

Missy could put as much spin on a story as a politician, which made for a dreadfully dull conversation—if one person talking a lot and the other hardly listening could be called conversation—but she seemed earnest and decent, so he tried to be polite, which meant little more than saying the phone was next to his ear.

Missy made her sales pitch not once, but three times, with little variation of theme. Ravelo thought she sounded a tad too desperate. At length, when there seemed to be no end in sight to her monologue, the priest did what he always did in a situation like this: notched the phone on his shoulder and reached for the guitar by his desk, a classic Washburn six-string. It held a place of honor in his otherwise humble office. As soon as he touched the smooth nylon strings he smiled.

Missy sure could talk!

Music was one of the few unadulterated pleasures in Ravelo's life. At one time it had been his only pleasure, his only anything, really. But the accompanying excess and vice had made a cruel master. The cliché was tired, to be sure: sex, drugs, rock 'n' roll. Been there, done that. Mixed memories, mostly painful. Ravelo regretted nothing but the loss of the music. He ran the tip of his finger over the polished wooden surface and began scratching out a decent cover of Zeppelin's "Stairway to Heaven," a tune that apparently every would-be guitar virtuoso adores.

But a priest?

At long last, Missy began to wrap up her prolonged and melodramatic explanation of exactly why he *must* participate in the planned feature. ". . . and so I think a few quotes from you would really provide the depth and balance I'm looking for in this piece. Anything Luther said to you during those last few hours would be perfect. Anything on the last rite. Your thoughts on the spirituality of death. Anything."

"I really don't think so, Ms. Jenkins. But thanks for calling—"

"Father Ravelo, listen . . . I understand your reluctance, but you have a real opportunity here. You could make quite a statement for all the churches of Detroit."

"And you could get quite a story."

"Maybe. I hope so. But that's not the point."

"Ms. Jenkins, you undoubtedly want to put together a moving tribute to man's inhumanity to man and maybe you have the best of intentions—I don't know. But I'm afraid my participation in your feature would constitute an irony I simply don't feel comfortable with. My answer is still no."

Missy said nothing and the phone fell quiet. She seemed to be listening. "Is that you playing the guitar?" she asked carefully. For the first time, her tone sounded intrigued, genuine.

Ravelo felt a little as if he had been caught with his hand in the cookie jar. He stopped for a moment, then started playing again, more softly. "I dabble a bit, yes."

"'Stairway to Heaven'?"

"Right again."

Missy smirked. "And you want me to believe you have a problem with irony, Father?"

Ravelo smiled. "Touché. My answer is still no."

"How long have you been playing? Or may I ask?"

Ravelo sighed. He should have just hung up. "I was in a rock-and-roll band in the early seventies. Nothing big. No label. We made a name for ourselves around Detroit, Chicago, St. Louis. That's about it."

Missy let out a long, slow whistle. "I guess there are a few surprises left in the world."

"Believe me, you're exaggerating the novelty," Ravelo said.

"Maybe. But a priest with a past? Sounds like a story in itself."

Ravelo stopped strumming, put down his guitar. He sat in silence for a moment, watching the plastered cracks crawl up from the floorboard of the dusty cream walls like veins. He reached into the top drawer of his desk and pulled out a wadded piece of paper. At first he just held it, unthinking. In the corner another relic from his former life rolled up and down in a ceaseless dance, slow and thick like honey. Amazingly, the lava lamp still worked; in front of it two little orange fish swam in tired circles around their rounded fishbowl home, pausing only to watch the lava ball rise and fall. Their bulbous eyes blinked at Father Ravelo from a distance.

"I suppose I do have something of a checkered past," he agreed thoughtfully.

"Don't we all," Missy said, noting the pathos in his voice. "Luther Sanchez had a checkered past, too, but he never escaped. He never got the chances you and I have had. Help him tell his story, Father. Give Detroit a new perspective."

Ravelo was unmoved. "No thanks, Ms. Jenkins."

"Please, Father! I need a break. I *need* this story. Help me out."

"I'm sorry. Good-bye."

He hung up the phone. The fish jawed at the glass and little bubbles leaked from their lipless mouths. Their fins were like a train of silk unraveling in the water.

Ravelo looked again at the piece of paper he held. Luther's last message to him was scrawled across the yellow skin in shaky, almost incoherent letters. The spacing was erratic, difficult to follow, but it looked like "mustbe102354."

Those words, that number, had haunted Ravelo in the days since Luther had died. Luther had obviously thought they meant something. Or had found meaning in them. Or maybe the scrap of paper was nothing more than the final delusion of a very troubled soul. Ravelo had no idea.

Must be 102354.

The priest sighed, picked up his guitar again. All he knew for sure was that he had to find out.

At half past noon, Ravelo headed back to the Silver Star, his favorite local joint, located just three blocks from the church, below street level and tucked under the belly of an aging shopping center. One part diner, two parts pool hall, three parts tavern, the Silver Star was one of the last fading icons of the glory of post-Depression Detroit.

The owner—his name was Chubs—had done little to restore the place, even though the Silver Star had an eclectic history: home to bootleggers, hideout of "Pretty Boy" Floyd before the Kansas City Massacre, even visited more than once by Ransom Olds, the pioneer of the automobile. Still, Ravelo knew the thought of restoration was the last thing on Chubs' mind. All the big man wanted was to keep the lights low and the money moving. He was a gruff stump of a man, built like the leg of an elephant; on his massive left arm, tattooed in green, a seminaked hula dancer twitched whenever he made a fist. Chubs was a patriot of sorts, having served in Korea, returning with a limp and a bad temper, which was better than the one he had left with. What he mostly wanted now was to be left alone; or at least that's what he grumbled about whenever someone began to get too friendly with him about their problems.

So this was the Silver Star—"Chubs' Place" most called it—home to bikers and small-time thugs, dealers and bookies and drifters. There were decent folk, too—Joe Sixpacks, men with loud voices, dirty jeans, and sun-browned skin. The common denominator was that Chubs made sure they all felt welcome, or at least safe. True, he didn't particularly favor his job as unofficial patriarch to this part of the city. But he never seemed in a hurry to abdicate the role, either.

Ravelo, fascinated as usual, observed all of these group dynamics with a clever eye, and without interruption, even though he himself had become a part of the dynamic, an outsider with a ticket to the local dance. The priest knew the labels, knew who was "good" and who was "bad." But he also knew nothing was ever *that* simple. Many of the bikers volunteered with the Salvation Army at Christmastime. Many of the thugs had daughters and wives. Many of the Joes slept with everybody *but* their wives. And one of the dealers gave lavishly to charity—to ease his conscience, he told Ravelo once.

It was a mishmash of humanity—the priest thought it a grand place to hang out. Every day he stopped by for a morning cup of coffee and most days he visited again for lunch. The familiar pale blue neon sign had become a welcome sight to him, hanging over the corner of the street, flickering on and off; a blue star with the lower arm nearly doubled in length, pointing like an arrow to the foot of the worn wooden steps leading down. Ravelo had asked Chubs once, "Why blue? Why not silver?"

"Got a great deal" was all Chubs would say, as if that much were obvious. But he had offered Ravelo a rare grin and the priest figured that was answer enough.

Although his presence had been viewed with suspicion at first—a suspicion bordering on hostility—Ravelo had carefully made himself a part of this ragamuffin band at Chubs' Place, adapting to their ways, their vernacular. He played pool under the solitary light of the hanging lamps with whomever he pleased; he told Catholic jokes; he ate heartily and listened often; he talked of life and politics and, very often, God. He was "one of the boys" now, for the most part. They didn't mind his collar; he didn't mind their tattoos and foul language.

It worked.

Today he was welcomed with a heavy slap on the back and a friendly epithet or two by the same man he had lost a game of pool to earlier in the morning. The scrap of paper left him by Luther Sanchez still lay heavy on his heart. He pushed the burden aside for the time.

"Think you can take me twice, Jack?" Ravelo asked.

"Doubtful," Jack answered, flat faced. Ravelo knew he was lying.

He ordered a plate of corned-beef hash. Chubs fixed a mean plate of hash, not to mention his personal specialty, kielbasa and kraut. A half dozen tankards littered the long bar, left casually by people who languished under the filtered cones of light around the pool tables, cue sticks in hand, their slouching postures and sweaty T-shirts marking them as either very drunk or very tired; trails of purple smoke from their cigarettes curled into the lights so thickly that a layer of haze cloistered the air at about eye level. Only a handful of people were here at this hour, which was not unusual, since Ravelo had gotten tied up at the parish longer than he had planned. He looked at his watch; it was nearly half past one.

"Beer, Padre?"

Chubs always offered the priest a beer. Ravelo always politely refused. "No thanks. Gives me bad breath."

Chubs laughed. Just about everyone at the Silver Star drank beer—a whole lot of beer, actually—but rarely anything harder. He handed Ravelo a sloppy plateful of lunch and the priest laid in with a vengeance. Behind him, the crack of a clean rack of billiard balls sounded out, followed by a couple of quick ball drops and a muffled curse.

Jack was already leading.

"Hey, Father . . . ," a half-spoken voice murmured from beside him, a greeting, not a request. The owner of the voice took a seat at the bar two spaces down and ordered some sort of imported Italian beer. Ricky Carletti wore black, all black, from his leather pants and spit-shined boots to his tailored silk shirt and fedora. He took off his hat and nodded indifferently to the priest; beneath, his hair was slicked back, his eyes were wide and dark, and a little wisp of mustache clung to his upper lip like mildew on shower tiles. A toothpick dangled from his mouth.

Ricky thought he was a cool cat.

"Hello, Ricky."

"How's business, Father?" Ricky asked smugly, trying hard not to smile. Ricky thought he had a corker's wit.

"Souls going to heaven every day," Ravelo answered.

Most good Catholics would have already genuflected by now. Ricky just grunted, half proud. "Not mine."

Ravelo put down his fork, watched, waiting.

"Come on now, Father," Ricky said, half mocking, as if the priest's feelings might be hurt. "Don't act surprised"—in truth, Ravelo could not have been less surprised if someone had amazingly informed him that the pope was Polish—"we've had this talk before. I've thought about everything you've told me. But you know what I think? Hell can't be too bad, you know? I mean, after all—"

"You'll be with friends?"

Ricky was mildly surprised. "Yeah, right. *All* my friends."

"Heard it before, Ricky. It's old. I need something new, something creative. Show some originality, for crying out loud."

Ravelo turned back to his plate and resumed eating. Chubs, if he listened at all, did not seem interested. He refilled a couple of tankards and eventually wandered back to the kitchen. But Ravelo had intentionally raised his voice. His insult lingered in the air.

Ricky's face flushed. A mobster doesn't just take an insult, however small, on the chin. He reached down to his boot, eyes darting around the room, and withdrew a small polished knife, which he firmly planted in the bar. Jack and a couple of other men looked up suspiciously. Very few people liked Ricky.

"This is all the originality I'll ever need."

"You don't have to impress me," Ravelo answered, waving at the same time to Jack, as if to say, *not a problem.* "I know you're tough."

Ricky traced the edge of the knife with his index finger. The blade was extremely sharp and a thin line of red blood sprang immediately to the surface of his skin, but he showed no evidence of pain—just licked his finger and smiled at the priest. Ravelo had no idea what this particular display was all about, only that Ricky usually attempted extravagant games of confidence, like a peacock fanning his feathers, when he desperately needed to mate himself to someone else's fear.

The only problem was, for all the people who actively disliked him, hardly anyone feared him.

And that, for Ricky at least, was a *real* problem. When you aspire to be a major player in one of Detroit's big-time crime syndicates, you need at least one of several qualities: panache, looks, instinct, or presence. Above all, cruelty. Ravelo knew this because Ricky frequently bragged about his exploits, even though he had none of those "qualities." He was a muscular youth—twenty, twenty-one—but small and, unfortunately, possessing all the failings of a short man's complex. Ravelo knew Ricky wouldn't hurt him—he was Italian, he didn't have the guts to hit a priest—but to let Ricky know that he knew would have been disastrous.

"How many people have you killed, Ricky?" Ravelo asked suddenly, surprising even himself. This was generally not the kind of territory he liked to explore.

"Plenty," Ricky said, uninterested.

"One? Five? Thirteen?"

"Too many to count."

Ravelo took a sip of tea. "C'mon, talk to me."

Doglike, Ricky's face fell into anger, which puzzled Ravelo, since this was an unusually ripe opportunity for Ricky to gloat. Assault, robbery, grand larceny, arson: These were Ricky's pride and joy. He often bragged about how he had learned remarkably efficient assassination techniques from his cousin, a former Navy Seal. Now, however, Ricky glanced furtively over both shoulders, as if someone might be listening. "I kill people all the time. I lose track."

It just didn't seem likely. Ravelo had never before pressed Ricky for details of this nature, mainly because he didn't want to hear them and he still didn't. But something important seemed to lie on the other side. Ricky obviously felt awkward. For once he could not hide it, which Ravelo took to be a good sign. That reaction urged the priest on.

"How many, Ricky? Take a guess."

"Lots," the young man whispered. "I took a score on a girl just last night. It's my job."

Ravelo noticed that Ricky was sweating.

"Do you like it, Ricky? The killing?"

"Sure, man! Why the questions?" Ricky swore at the priest, made a cracking motion with the flat of his hand against his wrist.

And then Ravelo understood: Ricky had never killed anybody in his life. He smiled; as if it were a random thought, said, *"It would be interesting to know what men are most afraid of. Taking a new step, uttering a new word . . ."*

The mafia man's back was slouched, trying to appear casual, but there was a stiffness in his jaw that betrayed him. Nevertheless, if he heard at all, he did not comprehend the priest's meaning. He said nothing.

He didn't need to.

Having glimpsed the thin possibility of connecting with Ricky, on whatever level, Ravelo was not about to be dissuaded by male pomposity, however angry and foolish—and dangerous—the lad was. He pushed his empty plate aside and slid over to the seat next to Ricky.

"That was Dostoevsky. *Crime and Punishment,*" he explained, uncomfortably close to Ricky's face.

Ricky shrugged. "Am I supposed to be impressed or something?"

"Not impressed."

"Then quit looking at me that way!"

"All right." Ravelo rose and circled round to where Jack was racking a new game.

"You ready to take a stab, Father?" Jack asked. "I whupped you pretty good this morning, you know."

Ravelo's face grew dramatically mournful. "Jack, by the time I'm finished with you there's gonna be nothing but a puddle of half-digested beer and a pool cue right where you're standing."

Jack laughed. "Break 'em, Padre!"

So Ravelo broke and the game began. At last, geographically distant, Ricky visibly relaxed. Between shots Ravelo tugged at the lad for answers. He was predictably reluctant to give them but seemed even more reluctant to leave. Ricky acted the gamut: distant, scornful, angry. But he never moved. Ravello had never maintained a conversation of this length with him. The priest was pleased . . .

"Ten bucks you choke, Father—"

. . . *plunk;* even more so with his snooker game, presently strong enough to command an appreciative expletive or two from cool Ricky. The boy didn't know how to simply compliment someone; nevertheless, he couldn't help but admire Ravelo's last shot. And all at poor Jack's expense, who was less than amused, being down two straight.

"Where'd all this come from?" Jack muttered as the final ball dropped.

"Connections," Ravelo said, winking.

There was a lull. Jack started to rack again, but Ravelo bowed out. "Won all I need to today. Don't want to push my luck, you know."

Jack cursed again, mildly enough. He had his own special vocabulary, it seemed.

Doubtful, Ricky said, "You really think you got connections? I mean, real connections? None of this Hollywood stuff."

Ravelo laid his cue stick on the thin green turf of an empty table. "I can only tell you this, Ricky. In a place that you can't touch, I've got hope."

Ricky snorted. Ravelo's face was solemn. "Laugh if you want, but can you say the same?"

The boy—for that is really all he was—only laughed louder in response. It was a hoarse, vain sound. He cursed the priest, then as if the thought of blasphemy just occurred to him, traced a quick cross on his chest. He made no apology.

"We all need hope."

"I don't need nothing!" Ricky snapped. "Got that? N-O-T-H-I-N-G. All I need is this knife"—he pointed to his boot—"and my .45. Maybe one of the pretty things down on Michigan Avenue occasionally. Or Eight Mile. Right, Jack?"

Jack didn't reply.

"Then why did you make the sign of the cross?" Ravelo asked.

"Habit. I can also make this sign." He extended his middle finger to the priest indifferently. "Same habit. No big deal."

"I guess not," Ravelo said, turning away. "Wanna give me a lift, Jack?"

"Sure, Padre. See you, Chubs."

Chubs waved and that was the end of it. Ravelo turned to Ricky before they left. "The more you think you've got it all under control, the less you know about anything."

Ricky flipped him off again, as casually as waving good-bye. Ravelo closed the door. Soon, they were off. The drive back to the church wasn't long. Jack, feeling quite sociable with a beer or two in his belly, talked a bit about their game and Ravelo's smashing victories; Ravelo smiled, but did little more than stare out the windshield, unhearing, watching the signs and fading buildings pass by as though they were nothing more than heaps of brick and light: a nearly famous old sub shop called Daddy Jakes . . . a couple, three more used car lots, not quite so famous . . . a Chinese carryout restaurant . . . a heavily secured branch (bravely misplaced in this part of town) of the great Michigan United Savings and Trust . . . another bar . . . and then, around the corner, was the sprawling yellow stone face of the Church of the Ascension.

The church had only a modest steeple, but a beautiful stained glass depicting Christ rising to heaven from the Mount of Olives dominated the curved area above the front doors, which were newly painted deep purple, the color of wild orchids.

The Church of the Ascension was an urban outreach community, for many reasons probably—location being a prime factor—but mainly because that's how Ravelo liked it. The doors were always open, and on Wednesdays and Saturdays, the soup kitchen easily served upward of five hundred meals each day; for many people it would be the only meal they would eat for several days. Large signs on each side of the front door, almost embarrassingly bold, welcomed young and old to gather.

Ravelo got out of the car and waved as Jack drove away. As he headed for the front door, he felt much less chipper than earlier in the morning, his mind still on Ricky. That one was going to fight him every step of the way to Jesus. Scratching his balding head, Ravelo climbed the stairs, one free hand in his pocket the way it had been most of the day, still clutching the wrinkled scrap of Luther Sanchez's last troubled message.

8 8 8

"We really have no idea," the doctor said, plopping down in his chair, letting the clipboard in his hand clatter onto the surface of his desk. He appeared drained and unashamedly frustrated. "Not even a theory."

Jessica rolled her eyes. She and Elizabeth and her mother had spent the last fourteen hours at Hamden's community hospital—since about five o'clock last night, when Jessica's mother passed a significant amount of blood in her stool. In that span of time her mother had endured repeated blood tests—three total—a CAT scan, X-rays, the works. Each time the doctors felt sure something would turn up. Each time, blank faced, they returned answerless.

Now the three O'Connel women sat together in the office of the chief of staff with two other Hamden physicians, pondering the dwindling possibilities of an illness without description. Though by no means a large hospital, Hamden Memorial was reputable, well equipped, and surprisingly well staffed. Right now, for the conference, a pathologist and internist had joined Dr. Marshall, the presiding chief, to brainstorm. The three of them and several colleagues had followed Mrs. O'Connel's case closely for the better part of a week.

"You're sure that ALS is out of the question?" Jessica asked.

Dr. Marshall held up empty hands. "As sure as we can be. Every test we've run has come back negative."

Jessica's mother sat beside her, unmoving, except for the occasional twitch of an arm or a leg or the corner of her mouth. She did not show emotion, though Jessica could tell she was terribly frightened. Elizabeth just looked tired.

"What about the twitching, the loss of muscle control? Aren't those classic symptoms?"

"Yes . . . and no. They're also symptomatic of Parkinson's, muscular dystrophy, and other diseases."

"And those don't work either?"

"I'm afraid not."

The pathologist cut in. "You're on the right track, though, Ms. O'Connel. This looks so close to ALS on the outside that it would fool a lot of people. It even looks remarkably similar to ALS on the inside. Her nervous system is degenerating at a systemic level, including the spinal cord and brain stem. The motor neurons in these regions are not responding to drug treatment. We've even tried electrical stimulation. Nothing. That sounds like ALS." He paused, frowning. "The only problem is that it is *not* ALS."

"There is an unusual amount of hemorrhaging in the upper colon and uterus," said the internist. "Even a little bit in the spleen. Almost random, but not quite. It just doesn't make sense."

"Why does there have to be a connection? Couldn't we be looking at two problems?"

"We have already gone over that—"

"Then go over it again!"

Elizabeth touched Jessica's arm, calmed her, said, "So we don't know for sure what it is. There are still steps we can take, right? I mean, just because we don't know the specifics doesn't mean we have to just sit on our hands and wait for the worst."

Mrs. O'Connel's head twitched; her hands danced in her lap. But her eyes were unwaveringly fixed on the doctor. If it was a matter of courage, she could summon it. What she needed was a little reassurance.

Dr. Marshall was an honest man. "I don't think that would be wise, really. A shotgun approach to the kind of therapies we might recommend could have devastating effects in other areas and still do nothing to halt the progress of this disease."

"Besides," said the internist, a little defensive, "we've already tried most of the drugs that could possibly help."

"But only in limited doses," Jessica countered.

"Of course."

"So how about more aggressive treatments?"

"Larger doses? Combined drugs? I have to concur with Dr. Marshall there—"

"Surgery, then!" Jessica said, her voice rising. "What about surgery?"

Dr. Marshall's soothing voice resumed command of the discussion.

"I'm beginning to think the best approach at this point may be a genetic or neurological solution."

All three O'Connel women sat very still, a little unsure of what the doctor was suggesting. So he told them. He said he was trying to think "Big Picture," that there was a possibility—a pretty good one in his opinion—that Mrs. O'Connel's ailment was the result of some sort of genetic malfunction.

"Defective genetic structures often show up at birth," he explained. "Down's syndrome, for example. The effects are immediately apparent. But we're discovering that many other diseases—"

"Maladies," said the pathologist.

"Ailments, whatever . . . can lie dormant for several years. Then all of a sudden, one day, boom! We don't know why or how, but we do know it happens. The body begins to fall apart in very specific, genetically defined ways."

Mrs. O'Connel placed a shaking hand to her breast. Her voice was thin. "And you . . . think this may be me?"

Dr. Marshall removed his horn-rimmed glasses and stared her right in the face. "All I know for certain is that twenty years ago we would be at a dead end right now. Today, we at least have one more outlet."

The shaking hand lifted. Mrs. O'Connel touched it to her open mouth. No words. It sounded like more of a death sentence than a genuine alternative.

"There really are no guarantees," said the pathologist kindly. "Most genetic treatments are experimental. Still, there are real possibilities."

"There are a number of genetic specialists in New York City," Dr. Marshall said. "I wish we could help you more, but we just aren't equipped for this sort of thing. We aren't geneticists."

For Jessica, it was too much all at once. She felt as if she were falling down a hole, watching as the hole at the top grew smaller and smaller. She could only imagine how her mother felt. It all began as a common cold, for crying out loud! Then arthritis. Now this. The pathologist was describing a couple of "very qualified" research centers. Dr. Marshall did the same. She barely listened. The three physicians drew up papers. Almost offhandedly the internist said he was friends with a Dr. Jay Remming, said he was a Nobel prize–winning neurosurgeon and geneticist doing experimental research at Columbia University. Jessica hardly heard.

"A brilliant man," the internist told her mother. "I went to school with him at Harvard. No one better in the world. And if it makes you feel any better, Columbia is part of the Human Genome Project, a global genetics research effort."

But it did not make Mrs. O'Connel feel better. Nor Jessica. Nor Elizabeth.

"I know how difficult this must be for you, Mrs. O'Connel—" Dr. Marshall began.

"No," she said, managing to smile in spite of herself. "You don't."

"I wish we could do more, believe me. But hope is not lost. You have nothing to lose and everything to gain. I hope you consider our counsel very seriously."

The internist's voice was grave. "If anyone can help you, Mrs. O'Connel, it's Jay Remming."

7

Abu Hasim El-Saludin was having a bad day. Not unusual, of late, though this day seemed particularly bad. Last night Club Cranium had convened over the cloistered safety of international phone lines and, in the space of a few moments, begun the unraveling of his life. He awoke this morning to prayers, fasting and, most regrettably, a self-pity the likes of which he had never felt before. Anger, too. Deep and throttling.

Though his family made every effort, nothing could pacify him on a day like today. His daughter brought him a sweet cold nectar, hand squeezed. His sons recited perfectly a long passage from the Koran they had been struggling with for some time. He tended his garden with vigor while the special rose-colored filters filled the place with pink light. But though the soil was rich and black and the foliage green and the soapweed and brittlebush fairly glowing with health, his heart simply was not in it. There was peace all around—peace and beauty— but none for him. So he walked to the market in Giza, saw children playing; he watched an old beggar—lame or blind, he could not tell— sitting on the corner; watched him for a long time, the little details, how he took money and gave thanks. So genuine. No self-pity. Abu felt ashamed.

Finally, at home again, his wife sat with him in silence, touched his face, kissed him, and then, knowing him like no one else, left him alone. Abu could not speak his fears; he had no voice for the words.

Only a dim comprehension of his life like a bridge spanning a vast chasm, and of a coming earthquake, and of collapse.

El-Saludin's wife kept a home that was full of windows and light and breezeways that smelled of lavender. From outside, the spilling sun laid wide beams of light over the window ledges, then pooled them together in the courtyard beyond the living area. Abu sat on the sofa, feeling the purity of the light and the cool breeze, but remaining stubbornly unaffected by their cheer. At length he rose and entered his study, where it was dark and pristine and ordered, smelling of old paper and leather.

There were two sounds, both soft: one, the throatless purr of his wife's Persian cat, chiding him for interrupting her nap; and two, the almost imperceptible whir of the fax machine. On the latter, the green front panel LCD confirmed two arrivals for the day. Abu stared at the fax machine from a distance, nearly sightless in the dark. The door behind him was ajar so that the light from the living area fell flat on his feet, as if unwilling to go farther. His eyes darted back and forth from the fax machine to the wastebasket beside it. Back and forth, back and forth.

At length he moved, surprisingly quick. Within three strides he was at the wastebasket, stooping down—irritated all the while—snatching out a handful of half-wadded papers, unfolding them against his chest; with three more great strides he was out the door, pounding toward the glass arboretum, anger growing in him with every step, and yet bleeding away quicker than it could coalesce. El-Saludin knew truth to be the enemy of no man, only of a man's false ideas. But this particular "truth"—if truth at all—was such a dangerous beast! Grown to full measure, he knew it would not be kind, least of all to him.

The pages from the wastebasket were from Rosenburg mostly. One from Volgaard, too. Hers was full of reckless youth: scientific bravado masquerading as wisdom, demanding this and that. Abu disliked her. More to the point, he did not trust her. She was too . . . *something*. Brilliant, but undisciplined, maybe, though her clinical scholarship was beyond dispute.

There are other kinds of discipline, Abu thought. He entered the arboretum and a sort of tranquillity seized him for the first time that day, quite in spite of himself. The heat brought little balls of sweat surfacing to his skin. He sat down on a small bench near the back, all hazy with colored light, patting his forehead with a handkerchief. As he skimmed the first couple of pages from Rosenburg he felt distracted at first, then a little foolish for discarding them as he had. Then, at length, the words began to sink in.

Rosenburg had been angry when he wrote the message. It was obvious in his writing, the shape of the letters: deep, gouging pen marks, like hammer and chisel on stone.

My dear El-Saludin,
*   You must delay the progress of our research! I am beginning to suspect that my government, and maybe others, are cooperating partners in this effort. I dare not say more, knowing my words sound tantamount to mutiny. But at the very least we must agree that our colleagues have run well ahead of the available information into wild speculation. . . .*

The letter continued. More data, passionate editorializing. Rosenburg, it seemed, had begun to test the effects of a synthetic approximation of serotoxomiasin on field mice. The tests were premature, and so done in secret, not having been sanctioned by Remming or the group as a whole. Rosenburg would only say that the results were inconclusive, blaming the lack of something more concrete on the elusive composition of STM-55. But El-Saludin knew that his team in Cairo had reached a fairly exact coding for serotoxomiasin; Rosenburg possessed that sequence. The letter abruptly closed:

*   I believe neither in a supreme god, nor a personal one, but rather in the immutable laws of science and reason, and in the struggle for human decency. Yet I respect a man of faith such as yourself. You and I must serve as anchors if the project is to realize anything of value. Use whatever devices seem appropriate. My hands are tied, but not for long. . . .*

Abu put the letter away.
Allah, save me, he thought. *Save us all.*

Monday, 11:09 a.m. Hank tried to appear nonchalant. Not an easy thing to do when you're illegally breaking and entering.

And throwing your whole career away in the process . . .

He was seated at Jay Remming's office desk, staring at the computer monitor. The large screen was full of blank, flat black. As he stared at the cryptic "C>" in the top left corner, dark thoughts formed in his head.

How many times have I told Remming to spring for a Mac?

OK, back up. He wasn't breaking and entering in the most technical sense. After all, as Remming's senior resident, Hank had been entrusted with several demanding responsibilities and, consequently, wide access to Remming's world. He possessed one of only two copies of the key to Remming's office—the other belonging to Environmental Services. Hank was largely responsible for reviewing all patient referrals, requests for special assistance, etc., then narrowing down that list to a manageable handful; not entirely manageable, as Hank well knew, since Remming prized the unique and unknown above the merely manageable. And so a large part of his job was making sure any untreatable human failings that bore the unmistakable scent of genetic or neurological distress did not fall between the cracks. He was responsible, too, for screening the medical journals for new findings; for handling patient follow-ups in many cases; and, of course, there were numerous surgeries and, increasingly, experimental procedures to perform on a whole host of candidates: brain-cancer patients, severe epileptics, victims of Alzheimer's, Parkinson's, and a number of more exotic psychological diseases, such as schizophrenia or autism or even bulimia. Sometimes, since Remming was a master of dual disciplines, he would combine neurological surgery with gene therapy. In those cases, more and more, Hank was given full rein in OR.

All in all, he figured he was averaging about twenty-five hours of sleep a week. Easier to gauge it that way than by the day. But Hank loved it. This was the life he wanted to live, all except for the criminal activity he was currently engaged in. It wasn't the invasion of literal, physical space that troubled him. Remming's office was wide open to

him—had been for about a year and half now. And with the exception
of a couple of drawers, Hank had been through Remming's file cabinets
a hundred times. He had a genial (his perspective), semi-flirtatious
(hers) sibling rivalry sort of relationship with Remming's secretary,
who was not much older than he. He even had full access to
Remming's computer. Sort of.

On the downside, Hank had never had a reason to snoop around
before. And he had never used an opportunity when Remming was
away to look for anything incriminatory. Never knew he needed to. So
even though no criminal act had yet been committed, his conscience
said he was breaking and entering just the same. He tried to argue with
his guilt. But since he kept glancing up at the slightest sound, he figured his conscience was right.

He should have been grateful for small things. A conscience of *any*
kind was hard to maintain in New York City, harder still at med school
and beyond. Sometimes it was easy, sometimes not. Though thoroughly converted as a child, he had done little to cultivate an active
expression of faith in adulthood and it was starting to show, like balding knees on a pair of old jeans. Hank knew Jesus was real and for a
while in middle school and high school he had pursued the understanding of everything that meant with a freshness that still made him
ache to recall it. Now, however, he found the rigors of faith largely
unappealing, which left him coasting on spiritual fumes—making
right choices, keeping up appearances, but colorless.

Three years ago at Christmastime he had returned home and,
wonder of wonders, his family wanted to go to the special services at
the local Methodist church. Fresh from the pounding cynicism of his
college education and medical degree, Hank had nonetheless dutifully
responded. They sat together in the candlelit service breathing hymns,
thinking of snow, feeling warm and fuzzy. His mom and dad were
good people, but they didn't know an apostle from an epistle. When
the pastor got up and began to speak of the Incarnation, he said that
throughout history many men had wished to be, tried to be, gods, and
many gods had appeared as men in myth, but that only one God had
ever been willing to *become* a man. He said that in the simple act of
the Incarnation, Jesus had demonstrated the fundamental reversal of

the entire value system of man . . . to become *less* in order that others may become more. What king would choose such a humiliating birth? Only the King of all kings, he said. . . .

It was a simple message, but it had re-ignited Hank with the simplicity and awe of that little boy with swollen eyes in the park. Briefly, his faith was real again.

The very next year, after thirty-some years of marriage, his mother up and left his dad, said she hadn't loved him in years, was tired of being treated like a slave by a slob. Said she was even more tired of pretending now that Hank was on his own. She still loved Hank, of course. Just not Hank's daddy.

So much for warm and fuzzy.

Hank wiggled his fingers above the keyboard. Remming's office was nice and big and bright. Two huge windows, one facing north and the other east, filled the room with speckled green and yellow light as it poured down through the canopy of trees just outside. There were two fashionable navy blue chairs seated opposite the expansive solid oak desk. The walls were painted pine green, trimmed in navy and oak, accented here and there with vibrant African art and pottery. A wall of filing cabinets to the south and another wall of elaborate shelving filled with expensive-looking medical books—as well as Remming's prized collection of first-edition William Blake poetry—made a mundane point lavishly obvious: Dr. Jay Remming was handsomely compensated for gracing Columbia University with his presence and reputation.

The outer door spilled into the secretary's office, where there were a coatrack and a water cooler and a few other sparse accommodations. The hallway beyond led to a handful of other offices, mainly for department chairs and upper-level faculty, so traffic was minimal and generally quiet. Hank heard Mrs. Sassanelli, the secretary, softly clicking away at the keyboard.

He typed a command on Remming's computer, hit return. The directory of files on Remming's computer scrolled up faster than he could read. Hundreds of files. What was he even looking for? He felt pretty safe that Remming would not return anytime soon, since his schedule was pretty full on Mondays and Tuesdays with patient referrals.

Hank hit the directory again, stopping and starting, scanning the file-names as quickly as he could manage, but they were all MS-DOS abbreviations with weird suffixes, archaic and nonsensical to anyone but the actual user who had named them. Remming had an elaborate computer setup. Fast processor, laser printer, high-speed modem, local-area network. Hank scrolled some more. More. More. Bit his lip. This would take forever. He wanted something to leap off the screen and land in his lap. Big, bold letters, reading, "EVILPLOT.TXT." Something. Anything. He kept scrolling.

Nothing.

His hands were sweaty. Hank saw all kinds of familiar filenames: student evaluations, department memos, faculty advisements, general correspondence, research notes. Nothing, though, looked even vaguely related to serotoxomiasin, Club Cranium, Merideth Institute, or that crazy Monitor Nine thing. Nothing mentioned the pineal gland.

He changed tactics. What about a password that would allow deeper-level access to the Internet forum? Or better yet, maybe Remming had stashed the encryption algorithm somewhere around here. Hank could use that formula to transform the gibberish of the encrypted files into readable text. He started opening drawers and thumbing through pages, being careful not to disrupt the orderly appearance of the desk. He opened the middle drawer last, rifling through the pens and note pads and staples—

He glanced up again. Remming's monitor had faded to black. Hank's stomach hit the floor. *What the—?* At about the same time the modem came suddenly to life and began belching and squeaking loud, raucous sounds. Startled, Hank pushed nervously away from the desk.

What had he done? He had never seen this happen before!

Unless I triggered something . . .

No. No, that wasn't it. The computer seemed to have automati-cally launched some sort of communications program, probably sig-naled by the modem call.

But who's calling?

Words appeared, then a picture, then more words. The picture was a simple logo. Beneath, it read:

The Merideth Institute

Dedicated to the promulgation of creative scientific discovery for the global benefit of a united humankind.

Other stuff. Too much to absorb at once. Then everything disappeared and a blank white page appeared. At the top, three words began to flash: "Achtung! Unscheduled communiqué!"

Hank had no idea what purpose the German-English mix was for, but he began to feel very uncomfortable just the same. He glanced up nervously. Mrs. Sassanelli was standing at the cooler sipping water from a little paper cup. Her back was to Hank; he prayed it would stay that way. He glanced down. The screen began to fill with words. He tried to read some but they came too fast. Something about deadlines and new resources being made available.

Mrs. Sassanelli turned. Hank tried not to look at her. The words flowed. She waved pleasantly from the other room. Hank acted surprised, waved back, watching out of the corner of his eye as she wadded up her little cup and threw it in the trash can. One eye on the screen, one eye on her. One eye on the screen, one eye on her. Not too obvious. He hoped. She sauntered a bit, doing nothing really . . . showing off her figure; flirting, for anyone who cared. Mrs. Sassanelli was a young, pretty thing with an unhappy marriage.

Luckily, her phone rang. Hank heard the light, fluttering electronic beep. It sounded like music. She leaned over to answer it.

Thank God . . .

"Hello?" Pause. "Uh-huh, yes. Certainly. Right away." Her voice was faint. Not faint enough. Too close.

Hank heard her hang up, pick up the phone again, make a call. He focused his attention on the screen, back to the beginning, scanning quickly. A single word in the opening paragraph caught his eye:

SPoT.

"Urgent! New deadline established for download of SPoT sequencing trials . . . 2300-08-05-99 . . . adjust all other target dates accordingly . . ."

Hank thought a moment. *Five weeks, five weeks. What's in five weeks . . . ?*

" . . . as incentive . . . significant additional resources have been allocated for future research . . . to be determined by . . . supervisor's personal pleasure . . ."

Mrs. Sassanelli hung up the phone. The modem continued to squawk and bark. The message wasn't *that* long, but it was full of directives and scientific jargon, so it was slow going. All the same, Hank was astonished at the tone of the letter. So official. So . . . insistent. Mrs. Sassanelli pulled a file from one of two filing cabinets in her office. This time, Hank didn't even glance her direction. Like a bad dream, he simply wished she would go away.

Instead, file retrieved, she started walking toward him.

"Find what you're looking for?" she asked, standing just inside the doorway. Hank jumped. Mrs. Sassanelli giggled.

"Sorry, silly! I didn't mean to scare you."

"No, no," Hank said, wiping his brow. "That's all right. I was just all wrapped up in this." He pointed as absently as he could at the glowing screen. The computer was positioned so that it would be impossible for her to actually see what was happening on-screen without standing almost directly beside Hank, which was a good thing, since he had no idea what he would do if she tried to move closer.

Mrs. Sassanelli glanced toward the modem. "That thing has been going off *a lot* recently." She rolled her eyes and began to inspect her red-painted fingernails for flaws. "Really annoying. Such an awful noise!"

On-screen, the message seemed to be concluding. And there, at the bottom, like the signature on a love note—except that the letters were not the flowering handwritten script of a young lover, but rather a blocky sans serif computer font—was the name of the sender:

"Monitor Nine."

Hank just stared, open-mouthed, feeling his heart hammer like a tom-tom. *Monitor Nine.* That was all. No personal name. No address. No other information at all. Apparently, the stamp of that name was self-possessing of authority.

"Yoo-hoo? Dr. Blackaby? Everything OK?" Mrs. Sassanelli said, concerned.

Hank nodded apologetically. "Sorry. No big deal. Just double-checking some possible scheduling conflicts. You know. Same old thing. I thought I saw something really wrong, but it's nothing."

Finally, the modem went silent. The program collapsed without a trace, except for a little blinking asterisk in the lower right-hand corner.

Some sort of on-screen verifier, Hank figured. The room was quiet for a moment. Perfectly calm everywhere, except inside, where Hank was exploding, wondering what to do next.

No evidence! Need evidence . . .

Mrs. Sassanelli said, "You ought to save yourself some steps and double-check with Dr. Remming."

Acting purely on instinct, Hank made a rather dangerous decision. With his right hand, he guided the arrow of Remming's mouse to the little asterisk and clicked once, twice. . . . The verifier sprang to life. In seconds, the full message was back on-screen. Mrs. Sassanelli moved closer.

"Dr. Blackaby, you're acting kind of strange. Have you heard a word I've said?"

Hank held up his index finger, semipatronizing. "Sure, sure."

Mrs. Sassanelli now stood directly across the desk from where Hank was sitting. She leaned over, arms on the desk, intentionally allowing her V-neck blouse to fall slightly. Hank couldn't have cared less.

Command: Print. Wait. Wait.

". . . Sure I heard you. Double-check with Remming." Hank knew he must look as though he were sitting on a bed of hot coals. His armpits were wet and his face was flushed. "It's just easier to do it myself since Dr. Remming is tied up solid with appointments today and tomorrow."

Mrs. Sassanelli let out a soft little laugh. "See? You should talk to me more. Dr. Remming is on his way down *right now* for a quick lunch. He phoned just a minute ago to have me order a bagel sandwich delivery."

To her great delight, Mrs. Sassanelli now commanded Hank's undiluted attention.

"Now!" he almost shouted.

She smiled happily. "Right this very moment. See all the trouble I've saved you?"

Hank groaned. *I'm in so much trouble. . . .*

"Why now?" he barked. "What about his appointments?"

The secretary shrugged. This was the most focused attention she had received from Hank in a good long while—since, well, before

Hank found out she was married. "I don't know. He said something about a fax he received this morning from a . . . Hamden? Some local hospital. Does that ring a bell?"

Hank offered her a weak, nervous, quivering-lips smile and shook his head. He stared frantically at the very quiet laser printer, focusing all his attention there for the sake of clarity. Anytime now, anytime. He knew, because he heard the motion of her voice, that Mrs. Sassanelli was still talking. But he just stared at the printer, waiting, biting his tongue; stared at the front panel until, in utter horror, he saw the power light—

Was not flashing.

Hank's arm shot out from his side, punched the power button, returned to the screen, to the mouse, all in a hurry. His legs were bouncing up and down underneath the desk.

Command: Print! Again. Wait. More wait! No time to wait!

". . . so you ought to just check with him when he gets here, don't you think? That would be the easiest."

As if from a great distance, Hank heard himself say, "Later. As soon as this prints I've got to run."

Fast and very far . . .

He closed the program. The blinking asterisk returned. Out of the corner of his eye he saw, through Mrs. Sassanelli's office, the door to the hallway begin to open. Hank saw the arm of Remming's white lab coat, the coal black skin of his hand on the doorknob . . .

Print, print, print!

And it did. Slowly. Hank heard the printer engine calibrate itself, then whir to a low buzz; the toner drum began to roll; the first sheet of paper was seized from the paper tray and began its methodical course through the guts of the machine. Outside, where Remming stood, the door opened halfway and stopped. Hank heard the doctor's muted voice conversing with someone, probably another faculty member.

One page . . .

Remming sounded a little irritated; or maybe that was Hank's imagination. Either way, time began to crawl.

Two pages . . .

The door started to open wider. The conversation was finished. No way to stop the print cycle now.

Three pages! Done!

"There he is right now," Hank said a little too loudly, pointing, as he grabbed the pages and made for the door, the only door, which meant passing right by Remming. He folded the pages as he went, stuffed them in his jeans pocket, wiped his face with his sleeve, and tried to breathe deep.

"Thanks, Mrs. Sassanelli. Thanks a lot. I'll just talk to Dr. Remming on my way out. You were a big help. Big help. I'll just talk to him right now, maybe. Thanks. Bye."

He did not wait for her to respond. Remming turned and was closing the door behind him right about the time Hank met up with him.

"Hello," Hank said as calmly as possible, brushing past Remming. "Just heading out."

"Hanson?"

Hank stopped midstride, wishing like anything his sweat glands would dry up. He felt pretty confident he could pass for rushed, rather than marathon runner, if only his heart rate would drop below 250. All the same, when Remming glanced up from the half dozen pages in his left hand, he looked Hank up and down rather doubtfully.

"Why were you in my office at this hour?"

Hank played the part well: blank faced, innocent. "You know I come in every now and then when you're taking appointments."

It seemed to work. Actually, Remming had made the conscious decision while in Geneva to give Hanson the full benefit of the doubt; to assume that Hanson's little word games on the trip to the airport were just that: a silly, contrived, coincidental attempt at humor that crossed wires. Better to assume the best, Remming reasoned, than to act out of paranoia and, in the process of trying to safeguard the research, reveal himself when there was no real suspicion on Hanson's part to begin with. Hanson seemed in a hurry, that was all. Besides, what could he find? Remming had taken every precaution. . . .

"Of course," Remming said. He visibly relaxed. As did Hank.

"By the way, there's a couple of scheduling conflicts we need to work out, but that can happen later."

Remming thrust his handful of papers into Hank's face. "Take a look at this."

Hank read through the documents quickly: woman from Connecticut, suffering increasingly severe symptoms, unknown illness. ALS had been ruled out, but her disease seemed strikingly similar. Biopsy results of tissue samples were included in the fax. The Hamden physicians seemed to feel the only avenue left to explore was that of the genetic level.

"She'll be here in half an hour," Remming said. "Her daughter is bringing her. I'll probably want to be with them for the rest of the day, so I want you to clear all other appointments that are not absolutely necessary."

"Yes, sir," Hank said. And then he was gone. He did not even reach for the papers in his back pocket until he was several blocks away, safely hidden away in his apartment.

Remming waited patiently through a few moments of static silence.

"Special Agent Decker," came the cool, inquisitive voice on the other end of the line.

"It's me," he said at last, deadpan. "What do you want to know?" He abhorred these conversations and no longer felt the need to hide that fact.

Susan Decker was back in New York. Remming, with the door to his office safely closed behind him, had called her at the CIA offices in Lower Manhattan. It was 11:30 a.m. on the dot.

"Such extraordinary punctuality, Dr. Remming! I'm pleasantly surprised. You must really be—what is that little colloquialism?— 'taking a shine' to me after all."

"Ms. Decker! What do I need to report?"

Susan Decker slipped off her heels and made herself comfortable in her overstuffed leather chair. Balancing the receiver between cheek and shoulder, she said, "Oh, everything."

So Remming told her about the teleconference with the other members. He told her about Dr. Saludin's findings: that, for whatever reason, *receptors* for STM-55 were present in everyone and across multiple brain regions. Briefly—taking great delight in his use of intellectually condescending tones—he detailed why those findings were monumental, elaborating for her the working hypothesis everyone agreed upon

(Decker was completely unfazed) that only Christians possessed the SPoT and hence were the only group affected by STM-55. He admitted that his team did not yet understand the evolutionary implications, whether the anomaly was present *before* or *after* birth, much less any relationship to claimed "religious" experiences. Decker hypothesized the primitive need for social order, which amused Remming—an astute observation, possibly, but inadequate for such a complex phenomenon. He also mentioned the delay in Dr. Volgaard's retrieval of brain samples from Runwell and shared many other findings, the sum total of current research on several fronts, being careful all the while not to betray either the direction or the results of his *private* efforts, which amounted at present to only a trickle of information, but could yet bear significantly on the project as a whole. His secret file was the shrill voice of his brilliance demanding freedom; it was his ace in the hole, the one small token of his refusal to completely capitulate to bureaucracies that insisted on interfering in efforts they neither truly understood nor cared about.

Decker did not interrupt the conversation once. When Remming finished, she asked a single question. "Any problems with the staff?"

Remming hesitated, but mentioned Rosenburg's increasingly volatile attitude toward the project.

"Is it a concern?"

Remming considered carefully. "Not yet. Dr. Rosenburg sees the dark side. He has lived the dark side. You know his history. He's cautious."

"But is *he* a problem?"

"He could be, but not yet."

"Anything else?"

"That's all."

"Thank you for your cooperation, Doctor. I'll be checking in again soon."

The first thing Remming saw when he grabbed the computer mouse—after the screen saver blinked off—was the flashing asterisk.

The first thing he thought was *Hanson Blackaby. . . .*

Not five minutes ago, when Decker hung up and the line went dead, Remming had been too irritated to achieve true anger. So he had taken another look at the fax from Hamden Community Hospital.

Something about this case, something about the mixed signals on Mrs. O'Connel's data sheets . . . In the back of his mind, an ache began, a memory, an itch. So he had reached for the mouse to pull up previous files, to try to find any related histories.

And there was the asterisk.

Dr. Jay Remming had rarely, if ever, felt the sinking nausea that comes from the shadowed underbelly of personal fear. He felt that fear now. He clicked on the asterisk—boom! the program opened—didn't even bother reading the message, not yet at least; he knew it was from Monitor Nine. What he wanted to know was when the transmission had occurred. He had not been expecting anything! Those fools! He checked his watch, scrolled through the text, mentally reviewing: call to Decker at 11:30 sharp; so Hanson had been in his office at least as early as 11:25, maybe even before. . . .

There! At the bottom, in smaller letters, the program automatically provided a time and date stamp. Transmission: 11:18 a.m.

The beeper on his phone rang.

Remming answered quickly, calmly. "Yes, Mrs. Sassanelli?"

"Your bagel sandwich is here, sir."

"Bring it in please."

The door opened moments later and Mrs. Sassanelli strolled in carrying a clear plastic container. Inside was a plump brown bagel, split in two, stuffed with peppered turkey breast, mayonnaise, tomato and bean sprouts; also, homemade potato chips and a kosher dill, on the side.

"Thank you," he said, faking a smile, taking the sandwich and setting it aside. The secretary turned to go. "Umm, Mrs. Sassanelli, I try to keep a log every now and then and I was wondering if you could remember when Hanson arrived today? Or approximately how long he was in my office? It would be useful for his evaluation."

Mrs. Sassanelli touched her finger to her lips.

"I don't recall exactly because I had to run down the hall earlier this morning. But he had been here ten or fifteen minutes by the time you called me. I'd say he arrived shortly after 11:00."

Under the desk, Dr. Remming clenched his fist.

"Thank you, Mrs. Sassanelli."

Four seconds later the phone rang. Expecting Hank, Remming grabbed the receiver, a low growl ready in his throat. Instead a nurse spoke in his ear, her voice shrill with fear.

"The case from Hamden just arrived!"

"Where?"

"ER. You'd better get over here, quick . . ."

The line went dead. Remming hung up the phone and aimed for the door.

"Don't let anyone in my office while I'm out," he told Mrs. Sassanelli. The young lady shrugged agreement.

From Remming's office, it was a pretty good hoof to Emergency Services, but the doctor's long strides were nearly twice that of shorter men. He wore his white lab coat, shirt and tie underneath; a little pin on his coat pocket announced with minimal fanfare: "Jay Remming, M.D." Although he knew the situation was urgent, he did not quite run (for that was a rather inelegant form of motion) but rather purposefully moved with speed. Nobody greeted him or waved as he passed by—you don't "wave" at Jay Remming—except Alberta Pickwick, one of the janitorial staff, and she waved only because she was the nicest, most simple lady God had ever made.

When Remming arrived at the lobby of Emergency Services, a nurse quickly escorted him through the swinging doors to a frenzied room of people and noise. Standing calmly at the back near the double doors, he listened with a critical ear to the various commands flung about the room like darts, the loud cacophony of medical call-and-response jargon ordered by one-half of the people and obeyed by the other half. Everyone scurried here and there like ants, the queen of their attention being Mrs. O'Connel's frail, thrashing form. Three nurses and several residents bent over the bed where she lay; a couple of them intubated her with a long corkscrewed hose, threading it roughly down her throat. Her flowered blouse was open and half a dozen electrodes dotted her chest and neck. Monitors lined the bedside, blinking and beeping loudly underneath the halogen lamps.

Mrs. O'Connel was clearly unconscious, but her body shook violently on the table. The chief resident shouted, "Give me 200 milligrams of Diazepam! We've got to get her under control!"

Just then the attending physician broke through the double doors. "Have you got the tube in?" she demanded, pushing past Remming to the table.

"In!" shouted the chief resident.

Another nurse started rattling off vitals: "Sixty-two-year-old female. Collapsed in the vehicle driven by her daughter. Difficulty breathing. Pressure 90 over 50. Heart rate 130. Pulse is weak."

"Stroke?" another resident suggested.

The doctor ignored him, took one glance at Mrs. O'Connel, said, "I want 7,000 units Epinephrin. Now!"

One of the nurses reached for the crash cart and filled the syringe to seven. She squirted a bit out and handed it to the doctor.

"She looks cyanotic," another nurse said. Remming agreed. She did appear bluish.

Respiratory failure . . .

In the corner—almost hidden from view if that was possible—stood a striking redhead, one hand clasped over her mouth, silent, horrified. Remming saw her as an afterthought, absorbing all of this in an instant. He glanced up at the EKG monitor. The thin green line peaked and valleyed erratically.

She's going V-Tach, he thought. The emergency physician seemed to read his brain. She, too, had just glanced at the monitor.

"I want 120 milligrams Lidocaine!" the doctor ordered, thumbing Mrs. O'Connel's eyes open and peering at her pupils.

The other nurse promptly supplied the needle. The physician

injected the drug into the catheter imbedded in Mrs. O'Connel's right cephalic vein.

"She's flatlined once," said the nurse with Remming. "Outside."

Remming glanced at the blood pressure monitors: 80 over 50 and falling. Then 75 over 40. Not good.

"I want to speak with the daughter. Is that her?" He motioned to Jessica.

The nurse nodded. "I'll get her for you."

"And all charts."

"Of course. Right away."

Remming withdrew to the hallway and waited. Soon the nurse reappeared with a clipboard and bleary-eyed Jessica in tow. Remming took the chart wordlessly, studied it for a while, not bothering to introduce himself. As if his silence were a judgment demanding explanation, Jessica started to babble. "She was doing fine . . . not good, really, but no different than she has been all week." Her tongue was thick and sticky from crying. "Then about fifteen minutes before we got here she just sort of fell apart."

The charts Remming held revealed little more than the fax he had already received: loss of muscle control, difficulty breathing, nausea, intense pain in the lower abdomen.

Jessica continued, " . . . I'm her daughter. Jessica."

At last Remming looked up. "I'm Dr. Remming. I'll be handling your mother's case from this point."

The sounds of the struggle for Mrs. O'Connel's life could still be heard behind them. Jessica breathed deeply, then did it again to better focus on Remming. "I want to know what is happening to my mother."

Remming wiped his chin as if there were a goatee. "That is a difficult question at this point. You said she just fell apart. How? How do you mean?"

Jessica pointed to the room where her mother still lay. "What do you mean how? That's how! She just started shaking and convulsing and then she couldn't breathe."

Remming made a note in the chart. "Can you tell me anything about her lifestyle that might be relevant?"

Bewildered, Jessica said, "Lifestyle?"

"Anything from her past? Anything recent? Any particular medications that might not be listed here? Any comments she might have made?"

Jessica shook her head. "I'm telling you, this came out of *nowhere*. Her entire illness . . . it's like it just appeared. Someone flipped a switch and there it was. A month ago she was fine."

Remming looked at the chart again. For an uncomfortably long time he seemed to be weighing two unattractive options, preferring neither. Finally: "It says here your family is originally from Maple Hill, North Carolina."

Jessica disregarded the observation. "What do you propose to do once my mother is stabilized?"

"*If* she is stabilized, I have a full battery of genetic tests I will want to perform. Few of them will be painful for her. Combined, they will help us isolate—"

"Wait, wait, wait. What do you mean, 'few'?" Jessica interrupted. "How many tests are there? What kind of pain are we talking about?"

Remming tried to be diplomatic. His sincere desire was to see Mrs. O'Connel's health restored. "Madam, let me assure you, we will go to extraordinary measures to make your mother comfortable. Each of my staff knows they are personally accountable to me for my patients' well-being."

"What tests are we talking about here?" Jessica insisted. "What will be painful? I thought genetic sampling was basically blood work and math."

"I would really prefer not to discuss those details at the present moment. You are under significant stress and—"

"I don't care about the stress! If my mom is going to be poked full of needles and drugs for what may well be an incurable disease you know nothing about, then she—and I—might prefer other alternatives. Less painful alternatives."

"Madam, you are not thinking clearly. Your mother might die without treatment."

"She might die *from* treatment! Or with treatment! She's not a random guinea pig!"

Remming's jaw tightened. He wanted to be reasonable. He needed to be reasonable. In his opinion, Jessica O'Connel was *not* being reasonable.

"I will probably request an MRI—"

"Magnetic Resonance Imaging."

Remming smiled patronizingly. "You've done your homework."

Jessica decided it might be useful to make a point. "Not really for my mother's case," she said acerbically. "I'm a lawyer."

Fresh appreciation flickered through the doctor's eyes, or so Jessica thought. But it would take more than a legal title to impress a man of Remming's stature. "It's difficult to answer your question with the sort of textbook precision you seem to want. You see, at Columbia we believe in a multidisciplinary problem-based approach rather than technique-based. In that respect, every case is treated as a unique case. Nevertheless, I shall endeavor to be 'square' with you." He held up his fingers like little quotation marks, then began rattling off procedures in monotone. "I will probably request a systems-level analysis of your mother's nervous-system functions to determine, among other things, receptor breakdown, poor signal recognition, ion conduction, etc. I would not rule out glandular malfunction at all, so I will want to do structural studies of your mother's entire endocrine system, her proteins, mineral concentrations, nucleic acids, plasma, and immune system. I will want to perform a complete battery of nonroutine chemical and biological assays, and, with your permission, bone, nerve, and muscle biopsies. To all these ends I shall most likely employ crystallography, electrophysiology, high-resolution spectroscopy, and a host of other really fancy doodads. Now, have I sufficiently answered your questions so that we may move on to weightier matters?"

Patronizing, indeed. But it was the kind of information Jessica wanted. She nodded.

Remming said, "I would like to admit her to the Irving Center for Clinical Studies as soon as possible. We can monitor her more closely there, make her more comfortable. You might also like to know that by the end of the day your mother's case will be logged on to CPMC's central computer, after which I will request immediate attention from my chief colleagues at our various centers of study. We have a program for molecular neurobiology, the Center for Molecular Recognition, and the Center for Neurobiology and Behavior, all of which may contribute a piece to this puzzle. Hopefully the tests I have already described will help us 'pick up the scent' of her illness, if you don't mind such a crude metaphor. And if the illness appears to be systemic, we can begin to formulate a biogenetic response. Hopefully. The larger issue is the time frame we have to work with, which, by the looks of it, is narrowing rapidly."

One of the nurses emerged from Mrs. O'Connel's room and motioned to Jessica. "She's stabilized," the nurse said. "She's very weak, but she's alive."

Jessica rushed into the room. Remming followed. Mrs. O'Connel was unconscious, but the air bag attached to her mouth expanded and wrinkled shut with regularity.

"BP 110 over 50," a nurse said. "Heart rate is level."

The attending physician was removing her gloves over the sink. The blue mask covering her nose and mouth pooched out slightly when she spoke, but her voice was calm.

"Maintain Lidocaine drip and fluids. Monitor respiration. And add 400 milligrams Dopamine and 250 milliliters of D5W."

"I want her in ICU as soon as possible," said Remming, making his presence known for the first time.

The physician, likewise, regarded Dr. Remming for the first time.

"Is she yours?" she asked.

"Yes."

"Keep her here another half-hour, then move her upstairs," the doctor ordered her staff. Then she left the room.

Remming guided Jessica back out into the hall. He stood close and talked low. "Tell me more about your mother. How many children does she have?"

"Just me and my older sister," she answered quietly. "Why?"

"Did your mother ever say she wanted more children?"

An odd question. "Not very often. She had some medical problems two or three years after I was born that eventually led to infertility. She didn't like to talk about it."

"What kind of problems?"

"Female problems, I suppose. Gynecological. I don't know any more than that."

"Who treated her?"

Jessica vigorously began rubbing her temples. "I don't know. How in the world would I know? Dad was a military officer. They received free medical care at Camp Lejeune. That's all I know. I was just a baby. What does any of this have to do with my mom now?"

Remming said nothing, just scribbled in his personal note pad, which Jessica failed to notice. Nevertheless, she was beginning to grow weary of the doctor's continued veil of silence. Everything about Remming seemed to guard against intrusion—his infrequent hand gestures, the detached expression on his face; he was emotionless, like a heap of ashes, save the severity of his eyes, which never left Jessica's face.

"Has your mother ever experienced temporary blindness or blind spots, sort of dark holes that just show up in the middle of her field of vision?"

Amazingly, she had. "Twice that I know of," Jessica answered, somewhat taken aback. "It's been years now. Lasted for a day or so and then just went away. Scared her to death. Elizabeth told me about it."

"Elizabeth . . . your sister."

Quick nod.

"What about blackouts?"

"No. Never. At least nothing was ever mentioned to me about blackouts."

"Abdominal spasms?"

Jessica drew out the answer long and slow. "Yes. But those were years ago. Nothing has happened recently. I'm telling you, Mom's been the picture of health. Good diet. Walks a mile every day. Just had a physical last year and passed with flying colors. All that information should be in her files."

"Did anything seem to precipitate the numbness in her extremities? Anything at all?"

They were going in circles. "I told you, this came from nowhere."

Remming started to speak again, maybe another question, but Jessica planted her feet. "Am I being interrogated? Because if I am, I'm having a hard time finding the relevance of your questions."

"You are not being—"

"Well then maybe before the twenty questions continue, you could tell me what *you* think is going on? What do two blind spots have to do with my mother's present condition? What is going on here?"

Remming took a step back and sort of summed up Jessica with those simmering brown eyes. They faced each other in a low-traffic area, at least according to a hospital map, but in an emergency unit there is no such thing as low traffic. Nurses and doctors passed by, patient beds rolled in and out, people cried or worried . . . there were blood and bandages . . . had been for the entire span of their conversation thus far. So it struck Jessica, as Remming watched her, what a magnificent cocoon he had formed around both of them, quite apart from her consent or even knowledge. By sheer force of will, he had placed his own silence around them both. But with his eyes now on her from a distance, she knew that Remming wasn't giving her the lookover that a guy gives a girl walking down the street. It was a calculation of worth and formidability.

"When you are dealing with something as nebulous as the human genetic blueprint," he replied, "—and that is what I believe we are dealing with, a malfunction in that blueprint—everything must be traced and verified first, *then* processed or eliminated from consideration. You are a lawyer. It is not so different for you."

Jessica did not reply—just watched him watch her. For all the grandiosity, his answer was as generic as a plumber's business card and she knew it. He was playing cat-and-mouse with the facts. She did follow similar investigative procedures with her clients, so she knew how to spot an angle on a question. There was definitely an angle here. She just couldn't figure out what. So she made herself plain.

"My mother's life is at stake here, so I'll gladly tell you whatever you want to know. But don't dangle carrots in front of me if you aren't going to let me eat. Remember, she's only your patient. You have nothing to lose. But she's my mother."

Remming smiled politely, making sure the smile was genuine. People who questioned his authority, expertise, or methods immediately earned his highest levels of scorn. But not twenty seconds prior he had determined that Jessica O'Connel would need to be finessed, not manhandled. Her mother's illness was part of a much bigger picture that demanded, at the very least, a delicate touch. If he wasn't careful, things could get sticky, personally and professionally. So carrots had to be dangled. If only he could have dangled them in front of someone else, he felt certain things would have gone so much smoother. A part of him truly regretted it had to be this way.

Jessica took a deep breath. "Listen, I know you're just doing your job, but you've got to understand, I want to make sure this is done right. It's important to me. It's how I'm wired."

Remming said, "You just want to feel like the communication is going both ways?"

"That's right."

A good move on Remming's part. "I don't do *that* very well," he explained. "It's how *I'm* wired. You see, I'm good at what I do and I expect other people to follow my lead. But I will try to rise to the occasion with you. So let me begin by saying this. CPMC is a profoundly advanced medical system. I may not impress you with my personality. But if your mother can be cured, this is the place where it will happen."

Jessica relaxed, nodded. "It's been a very stressful day. I'm sorry."

"Not at all!" Remming cocked his head to one side. "By the way, how old are you, Miss O'Connel?"

"Twenty-nine."

Remming seemed to be doing the math. Something like a light bulb went off in the expression on his face, but it quickly passed. "We'll talk again later. I won't do anything without your consent, but I will have more questions. For now you should get some rest."

Rest? Hardly.

She had *tried* to sleep, of course, was practical enough to go get a hotel room and at least make an effort, but it didn't work. So a little after noon she grabbed a book from her luggage and headed back to the hospital to sit with her mother in ICU. Nobody from the hospital had called her, so she figured her mom was still unconscious, but Jessica decided she would rather sit in a hospital room with her mom than in a hotel room without her.

Sure enough, her mom was unconscious, but the heart monitor beeped a steady rhythm and, as far as Jessica could tell, the crooked green line crawling east on the screen looked solid. Jessica was amazed at how peaceful her mom seemed. Gravity had begun to work its wonders, smoothing the wrinkles in her face and hands. Her posture was relaxed and natural. The IV drip gave her face an almost glowing fullness. She appeared to have lost ten years.

She was almost beautiful again, but it made Jessica sad to see her so. Neither woman had spoken more than twenty minutes total to the other in the last five years. Or was it six now? Jessica didn't know. Too long, that was all. Mrs. O'Connel had not been able to forgive Jessica for leaving the east coast, just as Jessica had not been able to forgive her father for dying an early death, which forced the whole family to leave Maple Hill in the first place and return to Connecticut where Mrs. O'Connel had family. Of course Elizabeth never really had to leave, at least not for long. Within the year she had returned to North Carolina to marry her high school sweetheart. And although she was a little young for marrying at the time, John was a good man and Maple Hill was a good place to start a family. That left Jessica and her mom alone in Connecticut. And young Jessica, full of emotion, was thrown into another culture, another school, another life, with little more than anger at her father for leaving the family behind.

There were times when all she wanted to do was crawl into a hole and die. She felt alone, isolated, unable to express. Her mother had an Easterner's sensibilities and a Yankee's warmth, which meant she was one of those people who was stuffed full of love, just not very good at loving. Jessica's father had always been the one to dole out hugs. She had grown up craving her father's affection, and getting it. And then he was gone.

What was there to fall back on? Neither of her parents had ever been particularly religious people. They did the normal stuff, went to church regularly, worked hard, believed the Ten Commandments were as good as law or better—were in fact really decent people—but not much more.

All Jessica had was the love of truth.

Peculiar, to word it like that, to think in those terms at such a young age. But not to Jessica. Truth had been with her from the beginning, as early as she could remember. It was how she survived those years. In transition, unsure of herself or much of anything else, the intuitive pursuit of Truth—big Truth—became an anchor, a focal point for her life. It was not easy; the compulsion was divisive. Her friends didn't understand and her family thought it strange. It separated her from her peers. But, ever present, unwilled, innate and, yes, compulsory, the idea of truth—the longing for epiphany—provided both the hope of resolution and the means to achieving it after her father's death. It led her to law school. She learned to be angry at her dad, angry at Elizabeth, but not full of hatred, because in truth the questions had not yet been answered, and as long as there were questions there was hope. If the truth was out there, somewhere, then she only had to be patient enough to find it—or let it find her.

Unfortunately, her patience never included her mother's pain.

Prodded by the thought, she reached out and stroked the older lady's cheek with the back of her hand. The unfamiliarity of the touch felt shameful.

"Why has it been so hard for us?" she whispered.

The issues were complicated. *Everything is complicated,* she thought. In agreement, the voices in her head rose up to accuse her, demanding satisfaction. Where was justice for herself, her mother? Broken relationships, no time to mend.

Now death.

Maybe that was justice. Maybe God was punishing her. The thought had landed Jessica in more beds than she cared to count. If she weren't so tired she would probably have been in one now, trapped naked between the sheets with a stranger beside her, cursing the stars for shining.

So complicated.

On her side, Jessica had been too wrapped up with her own difficulties—trying to forgive her dad and Elizabeth—to realize that she was blindly punishing her mother for the unfairness of life. At the time it made sense, like being tied up and slapped around, then given a stick, set free and told to hit something. When a person reaches that point, what or who they hit is not so urgent as the simple need to strike out. Psychologists call it projection. Death and geography were two things Jessica could not surmount, but she still had this stick—an emotional stick—and her mom, who always seemed to be saying the wrong thing or enforcing the wrong rules, had been readily available for beating.

Such was the past, full of ready memories, which Jessica chewed on from time to time like a piece of molded cheese. Now, as she looked at her mom, the past simply didn't seem to matter. So she sat down in one of the padded vinyl chairs near the bed where her mother lay, pulled out her book—a collection of poetry—and read. After a couple of hours she rose to get a soda from the machine in the waiting area outside. She came back with a couple of magazines, read some more, talked briefly with the nurses, then back to the poetry. Quite apart from any effort, she fell asleep about fifteen minutes later, slumped over in the chair, red hair falling about her shoulders like a basket of rose petals. She fell asleep, and she dreamed . . .

The voice of her mother woke her. "What are you reading, Jess?"

Jessica jerked out of the chair and found herself staring straight into her mother's open eyes. In an instant, the haze of sleep fell away. A watery blue film clouded the surface of Mrs. O'Connel's eyeballs, but Jessica could tell she was trying hard to focus.

"Mom? How do you feel?"

Bravely, a ghost of a smile crept into the corners of the older woman's lips. "I'm all right. Actually"—she reached toward her IV tube—"they must have a dozen different drugs in me because I feel quite nice. What happened?"

Jessica saw no reason not to tell her. By the end of the tale, Mrs. O'Connel's brave smile had grown dim. The life just drained out of her. Jessica tried to reassure her.

"Dr. Remming is one of the best doctors in the world. Everything's going to be OK."

Mrs. O'Connel didn't act as though she'd heard. She asked to sit up a little in bed, so Jessica tucked another pillow behind her head and elevated the unit. Activity was mercy to them both. It prevented silence. But when the pillows were in place and the silence came again, the two just sat there staring at the walls, at the folds of the sheets, hungry for words.

"Have you talked to Elizabeth?" Mrs. O'Connel asked finally.

Jessica nodded. "I called her earlier today. She wanted to come, but I told her not to."

"I guess she needs to be at home with her family."

Jessica could tell her mother was a little hurt. "Actually," she replied, growing nervous all over again. "I did it for selfish reasons." She looked outside the window, bright white, and her voice dropped into her throat. "I kind of wanted you all to myself for a while."

Those words were like medicine to Mrs. O'Connel. Everything about her seemed to grow stronger. Still they sat there, fidgeting.

"Why don't you read me a poem," the older lady said timidly. Jessica thought it a marvelous idea. She reached down to her book, thumbing through the pages.

"I don't really know what you like," she said, clearing her throat. "But here's one by Robert Browning."

> *Just when we're safest, there's a sunset-touch,*
> *A fancy from a flower-bell, someone's death,*
> *A chorus-ending from Euripides,—*
> *And that's enough for fifty hopes and fears*
> *As old and new at once as nature's self,*
> *To rap and knock and enter in our soul,*
> *Take hands and dance there, a fantastic ring,*
> *Round the ancient idol, on his base again,—*
> *The grand Perhaps.*

No sooner had the reading ended than Jessica felt witheringly self-conscious. *Someone's death?* . . . "I just thought you might like that one," she whispered.

Mrs. O'Connel had closed her eyes. "It was lovely! I have no idea what it means, but it was lovely. The 'grand Perhaps'! Do you have another?"

Pages flipped. Jessica awkwardly searched for something more appropriate. When she found it, she drew a deep breath to calm herself and let her voice slip into a slow, rolling cadence:

> *There is a pleasure in the pathless woods,*
> *There is a rapture on the lonely shore,*
> *There is society, where none intrudes,*
> *By the deep sea and music in its roar:*

I love not man the less, but Nature more,
From these our interviews, in which I steal
From all I may be, or have been before—

Suddenly, a sleek male voice took over.

—To mingle with the Universe, and feel,
What I can never express, yet cannot all conceal.

Jessica turned, startled. Dr. Remming stood in the doorframe like a shadow-drenched statue, arms folded in front, clutching a clipboard.

"You must be Dr. Remming," Mrs. O'Connel said.

"I am," he replied. "And you are looking quite a bit better than last I saw, if you don't mind me saying so." He turned to Jessica. "Lord Byron is a marvelous poet, but I prefer Blake myself."

Jessica raised an eyebrow. "A spiritual poet for a man of science?"

Remming showed his teeth in a smile that felt more like a cool breeze than a show of pleasure. "I could care less about Blake's theology. What I like is his vision, his scope. When our mythology could no longer satisfy his metaphorical needs, he went and created a whole new mythology. Brilliant! That is what I like."

And so Remming showed that side of himself normally reserved for political leaders and power players . . . anyone, really, with large enough purse strings. True, he wasn't accustomed to—how could it be said?—backward compatibility—but this situation demanded care. And besides, Jessica intrigued him.

"I'll be back in a few minutes to speak with you both." He turned and left the room.

Mrs. O'Connel watched him leave. Her eyes stayed on the door, fixed on the outline of the shape, the light from the hallway beyond. Her watery eyes had not grown clear, but her words were full of memory. "You know, Jessica, when you were a little girl, I didn't mind working two jobs. I really didn't. I didn't mind any of it. Even our arguments."

In nine years, the subject had never been broached. Jessica felt a cold sweat spring to the surface of her skin. Her heart began to pound. She tried to laugh. "You're just being polite now, Mom."

"Am I?"

There was no escape. "I remember fighting like cats and dogs! We didn't argue. We went to war."

"Jessica, *you* went to war."

The daughter ducked her head. "I know."

"What I'm trying to say is that it didn't matter. None of it did. I could take it all as long as you were with me. But when you left— when you *wanted* to leave—"

"I know. I'm sorry."

Mrs. O'Connel reached out, found Jessica's hand lying on the bed beside hers. She squeezed it tight. "Don't be. I was wrong. From the moment you were born there was something different about you. I couldn't keep you any more than I could keep your father."

Jessica remembered. All too well. She remembered writing letters to heaven about her father, letter after letter, hoping someone would read them.

"Something in you burns, Jess," her mother continued. "After all these years, I still can't put my finger on it. But something in you is lit like a fire."

Her mother used to joke that the doctor had never slapped her fanny because he knew Jessica would have argued the fairness of such an act. Jessica had never cared whether all the dots connected as long as the final picture made sense *morally*. Whenever the world offered her a spaghetti sandwich, Jessica's craving for a semblance of moral order would inevitably force her to tuck in all the loose pieces, but not to make the sandwich less messy.

Only to make it feel right, to feel *true*.

"Get some rest, Mom," Jessica said, reaching out, touching the older woman's brow. Something here did not *feel* right. "I'll be here when you wake up."

9

Later that same evening, about six o'clock, just as the western sun began to draw out the long shadows of New York's skyline and turn the greening park leaves to flame, Hank decided to drop by Kim Yu's apartment to see if he could persuade the Wraith to do a little more . . . wraithing.

Hank didn't bother knocking, just barged in and headed for the fridge, a task far easier said than done. Since the guts of Kim's apartment always lay somewhere on that continuum between street riot and a New Madrid earthquake, "heading for the fridge" could, roughly speaking, draw fair comparison to a dangerous mission through a demilitarized zone—the kind of thing a fellow could proudly recount to his grandkids years later.

Brilliant—maybe—was an apt description for Kim Yu. Tidy, no way. He was eccentric, sloppy, and possessed by varying degrees of madness. He was also several times more paranoid than Hank would ever be. (Further to the contrary of the stereotypically thin, spectacled Oriental, Kim was actually a little heavyset with perfect vision.)

So Hank began picking his way around, over numerous wires and cables draped across the floor like thick weeds of spaghetti; past boxes and books and stereo equipment and computer disks; past at least three different computers; over furniture, chairs, even paintings, some of which Kim just never bothered to hang. When he reached that heap in the middle of the room Hank knew to be the sofa, Hank lifted the corner of a pile of blankets that lay on top of the heap. There was Kim, underneath, catnapping. Hank grinned devilishly and immediately set about making enough noise to raise the dead.

He clanked jars, slammed the fridge, opened it, slammed it again, and made as many purely annoying noises as he could with a couple of crusty pots and pans and some four-day-old unwashed silverware.

"Knock it off in there!" Kim finally bellowed, pulling a cushion over his ears. "Didn't your mom ever tell you not to wake a sleeping genius?"

Indeed, enough to raise the dead. *Even a wraith* . . .

"Oh, did I wake you?" Hank said. "Gosh, I'm sorry."

Kim rubbed his eyes, stood groggily, lumbered into the kitchen. "Let's talk plain. How much would I have to pay you to leave?"

"Not nearly enough money in your bank account, my friend."

To that, Kim raised a "So-you-doubt-my-powers?" eyebrow, as if bank accounts were no more trouble for him to inflate than a balloon. Hank kept laughing. Kim did not. Hank stopped laughing.

"You remember that thing I've been telling you about?" he asked. "The forum on the Internet?"

Kim shrugged, popped a can of Coke, and listened to the fizz before hoisting the can to his mouth. "Sounds to me like an intranet."

"A what?"

Kim rolled his eyes, as if this sort of thing should be common knowledge to all but the most criminally insane. "An *intranet.* A series of machines linked together through the Net, but still protected from uninvited users. A sort of private mini-Internet within the bigger, public structure."

"By a password?"

"More than that. We call it a firewall . . . an unlisted destination with a password security system at the other end for good measure. Probably like the one you bumped into, though, yes."

"Bumped *through,* you mean. I'm quite the hacker myself now, you know." Hank seemed quite proud.

Kim snorted. "Believe me, if you did it, it was an accident."

"Accident? Serendipity? Fortuitous alignments of the stars? These things are more complicated than your limited faculties can comprehend."

"Uh-huh."

Hank chose the moment to segue. "*Despite* all that, I have sort of reached the end of my expertise, vast as it probably appears to you. So I came here to ask a question."

Kim folded his arms, leaned back against the cabinet, and waited. Hank had hoped he would play along just a little more, make the game a little more fun, but no. Do gods play the games of men? Kim fully intended to make him beg. Hank shamelessly complied, taking on the voice of a schoolboy.

"Can the Wraith come out and play tonight?"

Kim smiled.

About twenty minutes later both of them were sinking into the worn-out cushions of the booths at Marvin's, a hole-in-the-wall on 14th Street, a stone's throw north of Greenwich Village. Being a small-town farm boy, Hank never ceased to be amazed at the variety of experiences and culture found within a few short miles north and south through the heart of Manhattan. Some of the voices and images were sweet and subtle and begged for his attention: the old gypsy woman selling fresh-cut flowers on the corner; joggers and children in one of the small, greening parks; the patio cafes with couples and business-people sipping iced cappuccino and herbal teas; dirty back alleys struggling for hope.

Other voices, the more common voices, were not usually so acquiescent in their bid for attention. And so, too, there was plenty of the typical and base: the decadence of Times Square; the garish evidence of money, fame, power, cruelty, elitism—snobby art, emotionally disconnected and disenfranchised masses. But also the goodness of a soul, of many souls, evidenced in eclipsical moments: a glimpse of transcendent architecture, or even a juicy bite of thick New York pizza. Whatever the denominator, high or low, Manhattan's seven square miles of real estate were thoroughly inebriated with the lusty stuff of life: from the Baroque splendor of the Ansonia apartments, shelter to the rising stars of tomorrow's Metropolitan Opera, to the dreamy, new-rock charm of hippie poetry and cigarettes at the Knitting Factory, to the onetime hotbed of abstract expressionism—Cedar Tavern—to the frenetic pace of speed chess and sidewalk art in Washington Square, the perpetually awake American city was most vibrant, *most* awake, along the jostling sidewalks of her most famous street, Broadway. Here, the grand conglomeration of New York City's disparate elements were relished in all their glory. Along Broadway lay the richness and history of Manhattan: north of Marvin's, Times Square and Lincoln Center, the elegant Upper West Side and Columbia's Morningside district; farther south, Bowling Green, the Wall Street high-rises, Staten Island, the Statue of Liberty . . .

All of which made Marvin's a great place to be at just about any time of the day. Kim had discovered the little prize of a restaurant about six months ago while trying to sober up from a night of recklessness. Like most of the city's eateries, Marvin's made a great cup of joe.

Now, sitting across from each other, the two friends laughed (read: Hank laughed. Kim rarely split his lips), ordered burgers and fries, and conspired together on how to crash Club Cranium's party. Hank could hardly keep away from the edge of his seat.

"I can smell Remming's nervousness," he said, only mildly disturbed that he now found himself so excited by the possibility of Remming's corruption.

"Does he know you're onto him?" Kim asked.

"I don't know, I don't know. I kinda think so, but something's there, I'm just sure of it. Here, take a look at this."

Hank produced the folded copy of the message from Monitor Nine. Kim scanned it:

"*. . . New schedule . . . additional funds available upon review of product. Information produced, tested, and authoritatively concluded by . . .*"

"What's this all about? What *product*? Didn't you say this was a bunch of scientists working on some sort of brain something-or-other?"

"So I thought."

Kim kept reading. "Mmm, sounds heavy," he murmured. The further he read the more his face fell. Before he even finished he put the letter down and looked Hank squarely in the eyes. "I'm beginning to think you should not get involved."

"C'mon, what do you mean? I want to get to the bottom of this."

"All I'm saying is that I think you ought to back off. . . ."

Hank was flabbergasted. "There's a smelly fish at the bottom of this barrel and Remming's name is on it! Now if my career is built on the fortunes of this man, I want to know whether or not it's time to bail."

"I'm not stupid, Hank. You want to play spy and we both know it. If you were *really* interested in your career, you'd forget all about this."

Hank was getting angry. "You don't know anything, Kim. My father worked two jobs for thirteen years to save up money for me to go to medical school. Did you know that? I can remember my mother standing in a store, looking at dress after dress, but never buying, because she wanted to save the money for me. Ever since I was a kid, all I talked about was being a doctor. I dissected anything I could get my hands on. Don't tell me why I'm doing this. You don't have a clue why I'm doing this. Got that? Now, can you do anything to help or not?"

"Well, that all depends. Are you committed?"

"Yes!"

Kim regarded him skeptically for about three seconds; then he hunkered down in the seat and got a hungry look in his eyes. "For a project of this size, I need a few assurances from the other end of the line before I'm willing to draw a circle on my head for a target. Nothing personal, you understand."

"Of course. A man's got to draw the line somewhere. Hey, I know. Maybe you should *tattoo* the line. Have you considered a tattoo of a circle? Like a big red halo, right here." Hank drew an imaginary circle around the top of his head. "That way you would only have to do it once. Might be rather fetching."

Kim cut him short with a withering glare.

"No? OK, fine. So what are we going to do about all this?"

"I don't know," Kim mumbled, scanning the document further. "There's probably some big-time encryption involved here."

"I think so," Hank agreed. "I don't really understand encryption, but I did get a couple of files that were all a jumbled mess. And there were a bunch more files the system wouldn't even allow me to download. Said I didn't have high enough access or something."

"No telling how deep their firewall runs. In all seriousness I'm pretty surprised you got through period."

"Hello! Is anybody home that I recognize? What happened to the Wraith? Don't you have some sort of blood oath to the god of anarchy? Is this more than you can handle? Is that what you're saying?"

Hank stoked the fires well. The very thought of a system that might be uncrackable made any cracker worth his weight in hard drives want to crack it or die. Kim said nothing, just sort of snarled, his face intent upon the letter. Impatiently, Hank said, "All right, all right, skip to the bottom. Have you read that yet? What's all that stuff about?"

Kim read aloud, quickly, softly:

"Effective immediately . . . new protocols established for all scheduled transmissions. Possible leaks preclude conventional methods . . . random mobile transference necessary for security purposes . . . current scramble number: 555-1837."

"Sounds like the key to the castle!" Hank said triumphantly.

"More like Pandora's box," Kim answered drily, sucking on his bottom lip. But he, too, was eager. "Still, it's definitely a break. Does he know you have this?" He waved the paper.

"Maybe."

"Once upon a time we could've just traced the call through Mama Bell. But she ain't so polite about who she lets into her bed as she used to be."

"It doesn't sound like we have much time. Five weeks according to the letter."

"Until . . . ?"

Hank spread his empty hands. "Don't know."

Kim folded the paper and slid it across the table to Hank. Hank waited expectantly for more. "What? What?"

"Nothing. I have ideas," Kim replied matter-of-factly. "But not now. The important thing for now is—are you willing to take risks? This won't be easy."

"Yes."

"Then that's enough. All work and no play makes Hank a dull boy. Besides this place is too noisy. We'll talk about it later." He glanced furtively around the room. "What you need right now is a woman! You do remember what those are, don't you?"

"Long hair. Curves. I think so. Where's yours?"

"Hey, how should I know? I'm a free agent."

Hank scoffed. "Just click your heels together and come back to reality, tough guy. You're like a little puppy dog. Did she go out of town or something?"

"Headed to Buffalo to see her sister. Be back in a few days."

"A few days? You're not fooling me."

Kim grinned. "Seventy-three hours and"—he checked his watch—"fourteen minutes, to be exact. Now can we get back to your miserable life? When was the last time you had a date?"

"Lock up your arrows, cupid. I'm not a project."

"How about that one right over there?"

As smoothly as he might, Hank tried to follow the line of Kim's not-so-subtle gesturing. If his finger had been a magic gun, the bullet would have landed on a booth around the corner of the building where a cheerleader-cute blonde sat alone, early twenties, reading a book and sipping on a glass of iced tea among a crumpled handful of opened sugar packets.

"She's reading," Hank mused. "She has a brain. You're getting better, Kim."

Kim reached over and popped him lightly on the head, tousling his mop of sandy locks. "Open your eyes, man! It's not her brain I'm looking at! Just go say 'hi' for crying out loud."

"And then what?"

"Talk. Tell her the truth."

"Which is?"

Kim shook his head at the obviousness of the answer. "That you haven't had a date in, what? Five years? C'mon man, don't be too proud to beg."

"Kim, give it a rest. This isn't a singles bar and I'm not a swinger. You know that."

But Kim would not give it a rest; Hank knew the sooner he got it over with, the sooner his friend would shut up. So he rose, strolled casually to the young lady's table. Kim watched carefully but could only see the head and shoulders of the girl over Hank's backside. He saw her look startled at first, then puzzled, then glance his way. Kim smiled, kept watching. Her lips moved. Then she waved . . . at Kim

. . . and started giggling. Kim waved back, confused. Hank turned on one heel and headed back.

"I think you should be very pleased with me," he said happily, sitting down again.

"What?" Kim grinned. "What'd you say?"

"Let's just say, in some romantic sort of way . . . I made her laugh."

"C'mon. What happened?"

Hank grinned devilishly. "I simply told her you were a poor Korean immigrant who just moved to the States and couldn't speak any English except 'Need rest room,' 'Coke, please?' and 'I love Markie Post.' I told her you thought she *was* Markie Post, that you were terrified and embarrassed and in love because you were the Markie Post Fan Club president of your village in Moong Si, where your family was the only family with a television and it only got one low-bandwidth channel of all *Night Court* reruns. She was flattered, believe me. Did you see her wave?"

Kim laid his head back, groaning. Out of the corner of his eye, he glanced at the girl again. She still watched him, with a sweet, pitiful expression, as if he were a child or a lost puppy. She waved again.

Baleful eyes turned toward Hank. "Moong Si?"

Hank chuckled as he climbed out of his seat. "China, Korea, Vietnam. It's gotta be over there somewhere."

"I could have helped you tonight. You would have thanked me. You blew it."

"Exactly. I blew it off. Let's grab a movie."

Kim left a decent tip on the table and both men headed for the door. "I gotta say though, I would want a Coke as quick as possible. That part was good."

"Back to reality, Kim. Here we go. The movie for the evening is . . . ?"

Kim smiled. "*Hackers,* of course."

❁ ❁ ❁

That same evening, a couple hundred miles away, Missy Jenkins sat at her desk, nearly buried beneath the jumbled mass of papers and files and microwave popcorn strewn all about. All the lights in the office were out except hers and two others, one belonging to her boss. She had pored over file after file in the Luther Sanchez case, looking for some angle, some crack in the dam.

Nothing.

Ravelo was unwilling to talk. Still. Luther had been dead for almost a week now. Buried two days ago. The news was over. But something deep inside her belly said the *story* was not. Some hunch—that hunch she had learned to trust over the years—stuck in her like a bur in tube socks on the Oklahoma brush. Over her head and on the side wall, three rows of journalism awards proved her hunches had been good in the past.

But were they still?

Missy no longer had the confidence to answer that question. She was tired and frustrated. The tepid halo of light spreading across her desk from the fluorescent desk lamp was beginning to cast weird shadows and shapes between the cracks and crevasses of the layered papers. She looked up, rubbed her eyes, and sighed. Ahead of her, another set of lights flicked off, deepening the darkness around her. Emerging from those shadows, her boss strolled past with one finger hooked over his shoulder, slinging his jacket behind him.

"You're not getting any younger, Missy," he said. "Time to go home."

"Yeah, Jack. Pretty soon."

"Whatcha working on?"

Missy wanted to dodge, but in the fog of her mind she couldn't imagine how. Softly, she said, "Sanchez."

The boss frowned; he was senior news editor. "The story's dead, Missy. Dead as Luther."

"I don't think so. Something's up."

"No—"

"C'mon, Jack, you saw the interview with Karen van Meer. Luther was hypnotic! He knew something. He was trying to say something. To tell us something."

"Charles Manson is hypnotic, Missy. He's also deranged out of his gourd—"

"What about that guard I told you about? He said some spook from Central Intelligence was there hovering over Luther like a hawk the last few hours. Father Ravelo was there. He saw it all."

Jack sighed. He wanted to give Missy a break. He really did. She had been good once. "Will the guard go on record?" he asked.

"Of course not. He's afraid for his job."

"Will the priest?"

Missy looked down. "No."

"Then the story's dead. You've got no leads."

"But I might be able—"

"Kill it! End of discussion. Now I want you downtown tomorrow ripping the lid off the can of Councilman Licking's kickbacks. I want worms everywhere. Got it?"

She nodded. Jack turned sharply and disappeared out the side door. Missy pushed angrily away from her desk, extending her legs and arms into a wide X-shape, stretching, then deflating. A sharp pain flared in her neck from the effort. She rubbed it and groaned. Before her, the shapes of all the letters of the alphabet forming words on her pages and pages of notes blurred into one big gray, goopy haze. Weeks of effort.

This was her big break. The life and death of Luther Sanchez.

Gone.

She stuck a pencil between her lips and stared at nothing for a full five minutes. The artificial buttery smell of the popcorn lingered in the air, turning her stomach. At length she rose, grabbed her purse and note pad, reached for her coat, and hit the switch on the light. Instantly, darkness. Far behind her desk, one dim office light held steady. Otherwise, the red, glowing "Exit" over the door Jack had gone through was all she could see.

The phone rang. She thought about ignoring it. It was late.

"Jenkins," she said, picking up the receiver. Silence on the other end. Then a cough. Then a calm, reassuring voice.

"Ms. Jenkins, this is Father Michael Ravelo."

8 8 8

"Code Blue! Intensive Care! Code Blue! Intensive Care!"

The urgency of the words thumped in Jessica's mind like the steady beat of tom-toms before war, to the rhythm of her own legs pumping for more speed as she flew upstairs, not waiting for the elevator, heart racing. *Code Blue!* Bitterly, it occurred to her how accustomed she had become to the calls over the intercom system.

This one had jolted her.

With every footfall, the voice pounded at her brain: *Code Blue, Code Blue . . .*

So detached that voice, so professional. Infused with a metallic quality by the ceiling speakers, the announcer—whoever she was— probably sat in some remote corner of the hospital, well insulated from the pain of her own messages. Jessica ran.

Not ten seconds earlier she had been sitting in the hospital cafeteria blowing steam from a scalding mug of hot chocolate. It was Wednesday morning. Her mother's condition had changed little over the last three days. Dr. Remming remained determinedly aloof.

As she ran, taking two steps at a time, the intercom kicked on again.

"Dr. Jay Remming to ICU. Dr. Jay Remming to ICU . . ."

She ran faster. From nowhere, hot tears sprang to her eyes.

Dear God, please . . . , she thought. *I'll do anything.*

It seemed to take forever to get there. *They should make the cafeteria more central!* she argued angrily. Then, *Mom, don't let go . . .*

At last she burst through the doors into ICU. A fleet of nurses and physicians already swarmed her mother's room. Jessica couldn't even get in, but she could see through the window. The physicians were pounding on her mother's slack body, trying forcefully to resuscitate her. They were performing CPR. They were shocking her chest, so that her small frame lurched upward and her back arched violently. Still, her mother's arms dangled lifelessly off the side of the bed. The green line was flat.

Jessica looked around in horror, absolute horror. She wanted to scream or shake someone; she could do neither. Instead, she just stood there like a statue, perfectly calm, no tears, beholding the passing of her mother, feeling it in her bowels as if they were being wrenched from her stomach. A sickening wave of guilt or shame or despair—something—maybe just sadness, knotted up deep inside, way deep, beneath her rib cage and lungs. Still she stood, watching. She couldn't even look away.

It was then that she noticed Dr. Remming huddled in the corner with a clipboard between his folded arms. He was speaking in low tones with another white-coated physician, probably part of the team working on her mother. He was nodding his head, staring intently through another window into Mrs. O'Connel's room, regarding his dying patient with a certain sadness, though there seemed to be little actual feeling behind it. A clinical sadness. Jessica wasn't sure if he even knew she was present. But she saw that he had not even lifted a finger to save her mother's life. Maybe he could have done nothing. Maybe it was not his field. But he didn't even seem to care to try.

She did not trust him from that moment on.

Inside her mother's room, the doctors and nurses no longer struggled to revive her mother. One of them shut off her monitor. Another looked up at the clock and scrawled the time in her chart. Another covered her face with the bedsheet. Jessica heard their voices as if from a great distance. For a moment, she thought she might slip into another world.

We were just beginning again . . .

"Ms. O'Connel?" a voice said. A young, fresh-faced doctor stood before her. "I'm sorry, but your mother is dead."

🞘 🞘 🞘

Dr. Remming was staring at his computer when Hank walked in. It was about three o'clock, so the sun had already found enough of an angle on the slightly western north window to slink inside and lay a swath of amber and honey across a patch of carpet and books. Blake's *Age of Innocence* lay open on the desk. The air smelled of jasmine. Hank had no idea why.

"Hello, Dr. Remming," he said, rapping lightly on the door.

Remming looked up, motioned to Hank. "Come in."

The older man looked a little haggard, Hank thought; the complexion of his skin seemed darker. "I stopped by to see if you wanted to work out those scheduling conflicts," Hank offered.

"The what?"

As casually as he could, Hank began shuffling closer to the east window. "The scheduling conflicts I mentioned to you the other day. Nothing much. I can probably take care of it myself if you'd rather."

"Sure, sure. Fine." Remming returned to the computer but did nothing. "The case from Hamden died," he continued in a flat voice, cheek resting against his closed fist. "In ICU, earlier today. I won't need you on that, if that helps the scheduling."

Hank had seen this vacuum of emotion before in Remming. In the most human sense he did occasionally grieve. Most of all, however, he mourned the loss of knowledge a patient's death represented. Especially when the illness in question framed a really good neurological or genetic puzzle.

A brain twister, no pun intended.

So most of his sadness lacked pathos. Still, in this instance, Hank thought he heard more. "Are you going to do an autopsy?"

"Probably not. I don't think the daughter will allow it. I'm going to ask, though."

Hank stood by the window now, looking outside pensively, as if all of a sudden he intensely appreciated nature. Remming caught his eye. The tenor of his voice changed.

"We have some things to discuss, Hanson."

There went lunch. Hank swallowed, tried to remain calm, leaning his shoulder against the window. His face felt flush.

But Remming was not on the hunt. Apparently he thought it wiser to proactively confess and thereby diffuse further suspicion. Angling for position, he said, "I know you probably saw a message on my computer the other day that might not make sense. And I understand now your earlier comments. But it's really nothing extraordinary. I'm just doing some extra research with a team of scientists I have dealt with before. This sort of collaboration is nothing unusual."

Caught off guard, Hank replied, "I don't remember any message."

Remming mistook his answer for compliance. "Well then, we have nothing to worry about. You have a bright future, Hanson. A bright future, indeed. I would hate to see you mess that up by jumping to some wrong conclusions. I say that only because you've acted a little strange of late. Everything all right?"

Hank nodded. "Yes, fine, just fine. I—we just haven't had the chance to talk shop in a while."

Remming leaned back in his chair. It was more comfortable to be suave and controlling when you were relaxed. "Makes perfect sense! I figured as much really. You see, I have learned that it is always best to assume the best—about other people, I mean."

Hank thought, *But it's not human nature.* He didn't say that, though; he only smiled, said, "I agree."

Remming glanced away. Just for a second. It was enough.

Click.

The latch on the window slipped open. Easy as pie. Hank's arms had been folded as he leaned against the window; over the course of the conversation he had snaked his left hand up through the crook of his arm to the latch. To Remming, it would have looked like a nervous self-hug at best.

Remming placed a pair of reading glasses on the tip of his nose and started pecking on the keyboard. He was all business again. Easy as pie.

"Will that be all, Hanson?"

Hank moved to the center of the room. "Yes, sir. That's all."

He left, closing the door behind him, greeting Mrs. Sassanelli with a barely restrained devil of a grin. *All I need to nail you to the wall.*

10

I forbid you to press for an autopsy!" Rosenburg nearly shouted, his face suddenly bulging and red.

Remming, on the other end of the line, remained calm. In fact, the angrier Rosenburg became, the cooler Remming got. All had been fine in the conversation to this point—at least as fine as it could be with a cantankerous old soul like T. Samual Rosenburg.

"I only said I wanted to *request* the procedure, not demand it."

Rosenburg lowered his voice. "The girl. What's her name?"

"Jessica. She will almost certainly deny the request, anyway."

"I don't even want you to ask."

"Samual," Remming purred. "This is a marvelous opportunity to trace the effects, long-term. None of the other cases came *to us* for assistance. Mrs. O'Connel's body is available to us."

The older man was unfazed. Over the phone, Remming could hear a wine glass clinking as Rosenburg poured himself another half glass.

"Kosher wine, no doubt?" Remming asked.

"Ha!"

"Samual, you know we can obtain valuable data."

"We have records on all of them already," Rosenburg grumbled. "We don't need more. Not now."

"Those records are old. Secondhand reports from second-class scientists."

"Good enough! I don't want anything remembered that has long been forgotten. We were young and stupid then."

"You were brilliant," Remming declared.

"No! We were foolish. We played with life. It is like what you are doing with this wretched God Spot. Only *you* are not so young."

"But don't you see? An autopsy here could help us be more precise in serotoxomiasin research. You laid the foundation thirty years ago. Please, let us build on it."

Remming had pushed too far. Those were the worst possible words he could have spoken. Rosenburg snorted derisively. "You insult me, Dr. Remming. You and your silver tongue. Am I so easily persuaded, like all the others who adore you? You say the two are linked, the present and the past? Good. Then both shall pass with the death of this woman. No autopsy!"

He slammed down the receiver. Sweat trickled down the trembling skin of his forehead and into his thin, gray-flecked beard. Cursing, he removed the handkerchief from his back pocket and patted his brow. A swallow full of almond-colored wine was all that remained in his glass, warm and supple; he downed it in one shot and licked his lips.

After all these years. Everything can still fall apart.

Rosenburg did not truly trust Jay Remming. Respected him, yes. Who didn't? But when push came to shove, Rosenburg had yet to see any sort of guiding ethos in the man's soul.

Hoisting himself and his thick, rounding belly out of the seat, he called for Rachel. Outside his study in the living room, his wife sat on the sofa watching television. As the poodle came prancing around the corner, all fluff and cotton, Rosenburg said, "I'll take Rachel for her walk now."

He didn't wait for a response.

Across the street, two men dressed in black from head to toe sat in a black Honda hatchback. They wore black winter caps and black gloves. One of them was passive, detached, the other fidgety. Both smoked.

"Been a while since I been to Highland Park," said the fidgety one.

"Yeah," said the other. His cigarettes were long and slim, with filters in the tip. The other guy smoked Marlboros. Both of them watched the door to Rosenburg's town house with a dread sense of anticipation.

"There he is," the nervous one whispered as Rosenburg emerged from the double doors wearing a light overcoat, breathing heavily.

"You sure that's the one?"

"Got the address right here," he said and slapped the piece of paper he was holding as proof. From where they sat hidden in their car, the two men could see the fog of Rosenburg's breath billowing into the night air from the light of the old-fashioned streetlamps. The short, potbellied man started to walk down the street, past the car. Dancing proudly at the end of a long leash was a fancy white poodle.

The one behind the wheel, the calm one, scraped his seven o'clock shadow with the back of his fingernails. Turning to his companion, he said, "You're the man." But Ricky Carletti didn't move. He just watched Rosenburg walk, saw the heaviness in the old man's gait, listened to the soft clatter of his feet on the red cobblestone.

He didn't want to kill the man.

The thought made him feel weak and foolish, so he tried to get rude with himself. *Every virgin has a honeymoon,* he sneered. *Every fool has his day.*

"I'm gonna pop him good," he whispered to his friend, running a hand over his plastered coif of black hair. The thin little strip of post-adolescent fuzz under his nose twitched. "You watch me."

The one with the long, slim cigarettes grinned. His teeth formed perfect rows of polished ivory. He sounded thirsty. "I'm watching."

Quietly, Ricky got out of the car, his heart thumping more fiercely than an approaching helicopter. Inside his black leather gloves, Ricky's hands were wet.

Just another job, he thought. *No big thing.*

On the other side of the street, Rosenburg's parallel path brought him even with the car. A few more steps and the old man's wide, slightly hunched back began to show. Ricky thought he heard Rosenburg mumbling to himself, sounding angry. Maybe he was just talking to the dog. Regardless, he seemed oblivious to Ricky's presence along the empty street.

Ricky moved.

With surprising agility and speed he dashed around the front of the Honda, his feet barely disturbing the dust on the ground. First he made a wide sweep of the street in the opposite direction as Rosenburg, swinging beyond his victim's field of vision, then doubling back and lining up behind him maybe ten, twenty paces. With each step every shred of hope that remained in his soul—hope for a good life—cried out, *Stop! It's not too late! Stop!*

Ricky did not stop. This was to be a double killing: of the old man *and* his own nagging conscience. He had carried a crippling sense of empathy in his brain too long. Tonight, Ricky would become a killer. He had asked the boss for this task specifically, knowing one good rub was all he needed to advance. He *wanted* to be hard, tough. He wanted everyone—including that priest—to know that you don't mess with Ricky Carletti. Tonight would prove it. There would be pride. And then promotions, and with each one, power.

Stop!

Ricky did not stop. He quickened his pace, grew angry. With each advancing step, the voice in his brain grew quieter. *No, no . . .*

The silencing of the voice forced a rush of power through his veins. It felt good, cool, numbing. He was almost upon Rosenburg now; the old man was close. Ricky reached out.

Something crackled underneath him. He had stepped on something, a branch maybe. Rosenburg's head whipped around. Ricky lunged.

Too late—

Pure, furious instinct siezed him: quick, extended arm, hand around the old man's mouth, a flash of polished steel. Rosenburg collapsed, gurgling, clenching both hands around the soft, fleshy tissue of his neck. The cut was clumsy but sufficient. Under the pale light of moon and streetlamps, the sidewalk bled.

Rachel began barking furiously. Panicking, Ricky reached down to quiet her; she bit him. He howled, cursed, grabbed her neck with his other hand and twisted. Instantly, her body slackened. Ricky turned. Rosenburg had stopped thrashing by now. His dead body lay in a heap—half on the manicured grass, half on the sidewalk. Quickly, Ricky removed the old man's fat wallet and Rolex, yanking last on his fancy gold rings. He roughed Rosenburg up a little bit, too—his clothes, his face. The appearance of a struggle was necessary. The boss had been specific: Make it look like a robbery.

So there he was, in his moment of triumph, pummeling a dead man.

He wanted to scream. This was his moment! This was his! Instead he gagged, tasting bile. Finally, as everything dimmed, a harsh voice sounded from behind him. He stopped, turned. His friend was hanging out the window of their car.

"Geez, enough, man! You can't kill him any more. Come on."

Ricky pushed away. He did not see Rosenburg. He did not see the dog. He did not see anything. A milky red haze covered his eyes. All he did was grab his knife, rise, and stumble toward the car.

This was his moment.

Inside, the cool guy started the engine and peeled out.

"What came over you, man?" he asked, eyes wide.

Ricky said nothing. He hardly understood the question.

"For crying out loud! You started pounding that old man like he was a side of beef. You pig! Look at you. It was a clean hit and now you're a mess." Sure enough, blood was splattered on Ricky's face and hands. He glanced at his still-clenched fists—at the swollen, bruised knuckles—with surprise; he felt nothing, no pain.

Something was in his left hand, something thick and doughy. At first he didn't care, didn't know; then he willed his hand to open. It refused, as if it were not his own but belonged to another body. His brain had no control. He dropped the knife from his other hand and pried his fist open.

Rosenburg's severed index finger rested in the palm of his hand.

"I mean, it was cool and all . . . ," his friend was saying, puffing once, twice, on his cigarette. The man's expression could not have been more vacuous. "I just don't know why you had to kill the dog."

Ricky vomited.

⊕ ⊕ ⊕

The game, Kim Yu said, was all about patience.

Together, Hank and Kim—or rather, Kim, with Hank watching—tried to break through the personal password on Remming's PC. The evening was late. The movie was over. The time was right. The two men hunched over Kim's computer as the hack plucked away at the keys, attempting to connect by modem. Zero luck. Kim couldn't break the password. None of Hank's suggestions helped.

The game, Kim said, was also about perseverance.

So they tried logging on to Columbia's mainframe, hoping to find something there; possibly a side door into Remming's system through the mainframe. After three or four hours of failed attempts, Kim said their best chance of progress was to get ahold of the decryption code.

The game, he said, now involved risk. Translation: danger.

Hank waited until 11:30, the time of shadows in a sleepless neon city. With the pewter night darkening the skies and hiding the winking stars over the Big Apple, he returned to the scene of the crime. Remming's office was ground floor, overlooking a beautiful stretch of trees and grass, which, in a few hours, would be filled again with reclining, book-nosed students. Now the shade of those trees, purple and green on the black evening grass, formed a marvelous connecting web of darkness for Hank to burrow under. He had altogether skirted campus security, wearing gloves, blue jeans, and a dark, mottled sweater the color of river rocks. Around him the air was chilled and still, the moon, gratefully, hidden behind a wide bank of clouds blown in from the ocean. He felt relatively calm.

Strangely, the actual morality of breaking and entering never crossed his mind, so much as the nagging sense of disloyalty. After all, what he was doing was really just a minor extension of his regular work-hours' access. After-dark privileges, that was all. Even so, the sense of betrayal could not be so easily quelled.

Hank reached the window. Glancing left and right, he held his breath . . . lifted. The window slid open easily—a minor feat, but still a triumph considering it had been a full two days since he'd unlatched Remming's window in the first place.

Can't believe . . . no one's noticed.

It was like playing spy, a game he had loved to play as a kid. Back then, on the Kansas flatlands, the problem was a profound lack of good cover and hardly anyone to play with. Except for little Megan Rourke, the youngest daughter of the Blackabys' nearest neighbors.

Crow-haired Megan was a year younger than Hank and had always been as cute as a button. For years, he had a crush on her, had always imagined her to be the one he would marry one day. He told her so quite often, would even go so far as to make her promise to marry him in return. At the time it seemed like the heroic thing to do to ensure their happiness. After all, they were in the third grade! With a grin, Hank recalled the most humiliating spanking he ever got was when Megan's older brother caught the two of them kissing underneath a shade tree down by the little stream that separated his daddy's property from the Rourkes' farm, and tattled to his mom about them. It wasn't a hard spanking—he thought his mom was amused, actually—just embarrassing.

Of course, a little ingenuity can turn a bad deed into a good opportunity. Hank was not about to let Megan's brother slow down their torrid love affair. After the exposé, the only way he and Megan could kiss was if they were in a dark place—or so Hank had confidently declared—so he made up the game of spy to cover their tracks. Hank had always been something of a lady's man. *Wonder what my mom's doing down in the kitchen? Let's go spy in the closet!* Of course, most of the time, Hank was too nervous to kiss her, even though he knew, in her girlish way, that she wanted him to. They would just crouch down together or stand chest to chest, innocent and giggly, peering through a crack in the wall or from behind a door or underneath the bed or whatever. Just being *close* . . . that was the thrill.

Amazingly, they never got caught again. By the fifth or sixth grade both were off to bigger and better things, new loves, new kisses. Who would have thought such harmless romantic encounters would be the beginnings of his criminal career in research theft?

Just one more time. Avoid getting caught again . . . just one more time.

This wasn't childish sport. The open window lay before him. Climbing inside, he glanced over his shoulder to make sure no one had noticed. The campus was nearly barren. An occasional student passed by on the sidewalk about ten yards from the window, but Kim had already patched through to the security and facility management mainframe and scheduled a couple of important banks of lights to shut down for about an hour. Along this stretch of campus, all was dark.

Remming's office lay ripe for plundering, like a small unprotected village along the roaring path of Vikings. Hank pulled a small flashlight out of his pocket and turned it on. The rudeness of the beam in the otherwise dark room nearly startled him, made him feel vulnerable, discoverable. He tried to soften the light, then thought better of it, realizing speed was a better security measure than absolute stealth. So he began rifling through files. In Remming's file cabinet. In his desk drawers. Along the rows and rows of books. Anything for a clue.

Nothing.

The bottom cabinet drawer was locked, always had been. Hank knew the contents of the other drawers, but knew of no way to break into the locked drawer without actually vandalizing the property, and that would certainly be foolish.

He quickly came to a dead end, which kicked his brain into overdrive. What to do? He reached for the phone, fumbling over the number pads.

"Yep?" Kim answered after a single ring.

"I can't find anything," Hank whispered. "Nothing. What should I do?"

"You're sure? No notes or anything?"

"Zip."

Kim thought a moment. "Is Remming's computer live?"

"Sure, it's always on. But there's passwords for certain sections. I only have access to his schedules and stuff."

"He's partitioned the hard drive. Makes sense." Kim thought some more. "What about his applications? Surely he doesn't have his telecom software protected."

"You mean like his modem stuff?"

"Yeah, the software that establishes the link over the phone lines."

"I'll look."

Hank sat down in the seat and skimmed the screen for information. The computer was in sleep mode, so it took it a second or two to wake up.

"Got it," Hank said. "What're you thinking?"

"No time, just dial me up," Kim replied. Hank felt comfortable with an application of this sort. With only a little help from Kim he had the phone number plugged in and the parameters set in about half a minute. Even so, it felt like ten. He began to feel his nerves straining.

"Hit it!" Kim said, his voice peppered with revolutionary zeal. He loved this stuff.

Hank clicked the mouse. The lights on the modem starting blinking, the computer started squelching like a CB radio. Then . . .

"Welcome to the Love Palace," Kim breathed.

Hank saw the link confirmed on the monitor: *"Connection established: 31,200, ARQ, V34 LAPM, V42BIS. Host System ID: J.Remming. Link: Unknown."*

Kim began to explain. "Just about every encryption code is based on the universal PGP standard. PGP revolves around public access keys that can be customized with an individual's private access key. Encryption algorithms jumble a message, a picture—just about any form of data, really—by funneling every letter or pixel through this algorithm. The result is gibberish . . . no discernible pattern or meaning. That's on the output end. On the input level, however, the key is actually very simple."

"Unless you don't know it," Hank drolled, growing more and more nervous. How long before security drifted by? Blast! The flashlight was still on. He turned it off. Now the only light in the room was the glowing phosphor blue of Remming's monitor.

"Fortunately, I visited Amsterdam this year," Kim was saying. "Remember?"

"Yeah, yeah, yeah. The big international hackers' convention. The one the FBI tapped, right?"

Kim's voice swelled with pride. "The same. Anyway, I hit it off with this dude, a brilliant Hungarian programmer. He's into all kinds of cool stuff . . . stuff beyond cutting edge, way beyond. Just freaking godlike, really."

Hank realized his twitching fingers had begun to steadily drum the desktop. "Umm, Kim, you know I'm sitting here in the dark. Illegally. Get the picture?"

Kim sounded mildly offended. "Chill, man! I'm moving as fast as I can! I've already searched the main partition. Now I'm digging for a secondary."

On his end, Hank heard Remming's hard drive chugging and scratching quietly, controlled by Kim's unseen hand. The monitor, however, revealed nothing.

Kim was muttering. "Uh-huh, uh-huh. Fat chance . . ." Then he said, "What was the password you used to access the Internet forum?"

"Olympus."

"Home of the gods," Kim mused. Hank heard him typing. "Nope. Doesn't work here. Give me something else. Something simple. Remming's birthday. His wife's name. His kids. Anything."

"Brain," Hank said, feeling an ache beginning to throb in his own, spreading from his temples to his eyes. "Blake, maybe. His wife's name is Anna. I can't remember his. . . ."

"There it is!" Kim shouted, so loud that Hank jerked the phone from his ear. "Oh, boy! The motherlode. You're a master, Hank. It was 'brain.' How banal can you get?"

Hank felt his pulse accelerate. "We're set, right? Can I get the blazes out of here now?"

"No, no! Not yet! Hold on . . ."

Hank waited. About a minute later Kim announced, "I can't do anything with this stuff."

"What do you mean?"

"Well, I just tried to copy a file or two to my hard drive and it wouldn't let me, just as I expected. This is top-secret stuff, you know. There's probably some copy protection underneath this whole partition."

"Translate, please!"

"Unless I use the proper software or the approved downloading methods, we've got nothing. Worse-case scenario: We could cause the data to self-delete off of Remming's system."

Hank groaned. "We're chasing phantoms."

"No, it's all real. We just have to play by the rules." Kim drifted off into silence. Hank could hear his gears turning. "That message you got the other day, the automatic download—do you remember the software it came in on?"

"You've got to be joking. Of course not."

"Try."

"I can't remember! MasterCom, maybe? That's what I'm using now."

Hank glanced at his watch. It was a quarter after midnight. He had been in Remming's office for almost forty-five minutes. Too long. Too long. Something could go wrong at any moment. He was not safe here. In and out, that was the plan. . . .

"I want to get out of here, Kim. . . ."

"Stay put. I'm searching."

An interminably long pause. Finally, sounding altogether uninspired, Kim mumbled, "Maybe this is it."

"Maybe?"

"Maybe."

"Maybe! Maybe! What does that mean, 'maybe'?"

"It means we really don't have a—"

"Shhh!" Hank sputtered, cutting Kim short. His fingers locked viselike over the lip of the desk. "I think I hear something!"

He hunkered down in his chair. Every cell on the surface of his skin began to tingle. At first he heard nothing. Then, not too far away, nearly far enough to be subconscious, the clatter of hard heels sounded on the concrete flooring outside Remming's office in the hall. The clatter first—then harsh, angry voices.

One of them was Remming.

At some level, right then, Hank felt the marrow in his spine calcify, as if his whole body had just been dipped into liquid hydrogen.

He choked on the phone. "I've got to—it's Remming! Got to . . . Go! Disconnect!"

He slammed down the receiver. Through the window of Remming's office, Hank could see into the darkness of Mrs. Sassanelli's reception area. Beyond that, he heard a key fumbling in a lock. With the hypersensitivity of nearly primal fear, Hank felt every tumbler in the lock fall into place inside his rib cage. On the glass of the door, warbled light reflected red and white, dimly, but enough for Hank to know the door was opening. He sat paralyzed. Suddenly the light to Mrs. Sassanelli's office flared, pouring into Remming's purple-black office. Hank heard the voices more clearly now, saw the hem of an overcoat flapping. Remming was almost shouting.

"He was a friend! Do you hear me! A friend, a colleague! He was brilliant!"

A woman's voice, sounding like velvet and frost, replied, "We needed a solution. You said he was a problem."

Remming's arms flailed, almost as if he wanted to strike the woman. Hank had never heard him so angry, so out of control. He saw the dark silhouette of the man's arm reach for the office door. Petrified, Hank's eyes devoured the room, darting here and yon, finally to the open window. Could he make it? No time, no time. . . . There were no corners in this room! No place to hide!

A sound. A sound! The key in the door . . .

Hank scrambled, rose, turned a discombobulated circle, then hunkered down, stricken.

Doorknob turning . . .

Hank gasped, dived under the desk, pulled his knees to his chest, buried his face in his lap.

Door twisting open . . . loud voices . . .

Oh no, the monitor!

Hank's hand shot out from underneath the desk, fumbled for the monitor's power button. The screen's blue light spilled into the room like a leaking faucet. It would be noticed for sure. The button! Where?! Couldn't find it, couldn't reach . . .

The door swung wide. Hank leaned, stretched; found it!

Thwick.

His hand darted back under the desk. Remming and the woman stepped into the office as the lights came on. The static electricity on the blue screen crackled softly, then the whole thing faded to black. Hank prayed and prayed. They seemed unaware—of Hank all scrunched up beneath the desk and of the slightly ajar window. They were too caught up in rage. Hank could feel the energy in the room, the indignation burning in Remming.

"I never said I wanted him killed! This is unthinkable!" Remming shouted, so loud his voice echoed off the walls. Hank swallowed hard.

Killed?

Remming continued to rant. ". . . Death is not a solution. It's finality! Do you call that a solution? Is that how your organization manages complications?"

"A crisis," the woman corrected calmly. "The Company considered it a crisis." Hank was amazed at the sureness of her voice. It was hard for him to concentrate. Claustrophobia began to constrict his chest.

"There was no crisis! No crisis. Do you even know what a crisis is? A crisis is the resurrection of Hitler. A crisis is a global outbreak of Ebola. A crisis is finding out that every third person on the earth is a man-eating alien. Do you get me at all, Ms—?"

"Susan," the lady interrupted, saccharin sweet. "Please, call me Susan. No need for formalities at this point in our relationship."

Remming exploded. "Does that pitiful little brain of yours even register what I'm saying?"

The woman known as Susan laughed softly. "You're angry. It will pass. You said we needed a solution. The Company gave you an executive action. You should be flattered, really, the power you have."

Oh, please! Hank thought, as the peril he was in began to slowly take root. *Someone's been . . . did he say? . . . oh please, God!*

Remming grabbed the sides of his head and began to twist in sheer agony. "Solution! Is that the most creative solution you can imagine? This is completely out of control. It's ludicrous! I want all ties severed—"

"Sit down, Dr. Remming."

Decker motioned to one of Remming's two luxurious guest chairs, then seated herself leisurely in the opposite chair. She curled the fingers on her left hand and began to survey her fingernails. "I think it's time you and I had a frank discussion. That's why I called you here tonight."

Remming remained standing, but calmed himself, at least for the time being. In reality, everything sort of folded up inside him like a sleeper sofa; Hank could feel the veneer of civility between his mentor and the woman wearing thin. He became even more nervous, knowing that if this woman, Susan—whoever she was—merely rustled a cushion or two of Remming's proverbial sleeper, the whole spring-loaded contraption would pop. Big time.

Still, Hank didn't budge, didn't make a peep, even though his severely constricted muscles ached for movement. He hardly dared to breathe. It was rapidly becoming clear to him that more than his career lay on the line. It could mean his life.

"You were about to request a complete severance of federal oversight for this project," Susan said. She thought a moment. "This is your answer, so follow me carefully here: Your request is unequivocally, arbitrarily, and categorically denied. Outright. Absolutely. No appeals. No higher authority. No 'Suggestion Box' for you to drop your complaint into. As for Rosenburg, this project couldn't afford the kind of liability he'd become. We did what we thought was necessary—"

Hank gulped. *The Samual Rosenburg?*

"—And as for the immediate and foreseeable future of this relationship, it's very simple: You do the science. You make the whizbang discoveries. You get the glory, but you report everything—everything— to me. I don't call the shots any more than you do. But I follow every single protocol. You will do the same." She glanced up from her fingernails, full red lips savoring each delicious word. "Now, can that great, magnificent, genius mind of yours understand what *I'm* saying? Or shall I start over? Believe me, I'll enjoy it even more the second time around."

Remming didn't move, just stood there, seething, arms dangling helplessly at his sides; he saw nothing but malevolent shades of red. Decker, all blonde and curves, adjusted her position in the chair, crossing her legs so that her miniskirt hiked a little bit higher on her thigh. She folded her arms suggestively. It wasn't a come-on; it was a tease. She wanted Remming to feel angry *and* uncomfortable, hate and desire; it was a neutering of control that transferred any remaining power he possessed into her hands, a tactic she had honed to perfection over the years.

Hank saw none of this: neither Remming nor Susan, nor the prescient sexual politics. The front of Remming's desk went all the way to the floor and Hank was immensely grateful that it did. But the long silence that followed nearly gagged him. The woman's presence was like a black hole, or a January breeze off Lake Erie, sucking at the warmth in the room, allowing nothing to escape. And Remming? Surely he had reached the end of his rather short leash. Hank almost cringed, expecting the Big Bang at any moment . . . the unbridled Remming, in all his fury. But when he finally spoke there was such terrible defeat in his voice, a sound like Hank had never heard—never thought to hear or even to vaguely associate with Remming. The effect was crippling. Remming's flat, monotone response rose from his chest and passed through his lips as if through prison bars.

"I just barely spoke with the man this evening."

Decker was unsympathetic. "You've got more important things to concentrate on. Forget about it. Move on."

Remming looked away for a moment, his eyes scanning the room. "I suppose you already know about Mrs. O'Connel?"

"Of course I know about Mrs. O'Connel. She finally kicked off a couple of days ago in ICU, right?"

Remming's lips curled, but he refused to look Decker in the face. "She died in a lot of pain. She did not 'kick off.'"

"Yes, well, whatever you say. You're the doctor. We'll need to discuss her case sometime soon. Not now, but soon."

Then, for some reason, silence followed, injected almost unnaturally into the conversation. Something about the silence felt creepy, as if there was a new awareness in the room. Hank's pulse exploded. Had they found him? Somehow? Felt his presence? How? Nothing had changed. Nothing! He was just as hidden as before. He had made no sound. *Oh please, God.* Every muscle tensed, ready to spring, leap, run, fight, whatever; and yet simultaneously he strained to grow more quiet . . . not even to breathe.

Calm, calm.

Patiently, wanting to scream, feeling as if he sat naked on a barrel in a crowded theater, he waited for another exchange between Remming and the woman. Anything, please! He wanted nothing more than to dig a hole in the floor and crawl away. For all he knew, one of them had a gun drawn and pointed at the desk!

Why the silence?!

Another three or four seconds passed. Eternity, really. Then all of a sudden, Remming firmly announced, "Well, if that's all you have for me tonight, then I think this conversation is over."

"Susan," for that was all Hank knew her as, seemed surprised. "Nothing more to say?"

"It can be said tomorrow. Let's go."

Decker didn't argue, just rose and walked away. Hank heard the light switch flip. Everything fell to darkness. The color of night felt like mercy to his eyes, his brain. After the door closed and locked, Hank listened carefully, making sure it wasn't a trap or that they weren't still in Mrs. Sassanelli's office. Slowly, he crawled out, almost gasping for breath but afraid to make noise. Anything he did—movement, noise, his pounding heart—felt like a flare in the darkness, drawing attention. So he just lay on the floor, nearly sobbing but too nauseated to even know how. Rosenburg, dead? He was a part of this Club Cranium thing. Now he was dead. Hank felt completely numb.

After a while he rose, called Kim. He should have fled and never glanced back, and he knew it. But now more than ever he knew something was horribly wrong. The authorities would laugh in his face without some sort of concrete evidence to back him up.

Kim answered the phone cautiously. "Hello?"

"It's me. I'm all right."

"Holy Mary, Hank! What the heck is going on! I've been sitting here for the last half—"

"I know, I know! I'll explain later. I just want to get out of here."

Kim calmed down. "Yeah, right. OK. So what's next?"

"Tell me how to get this stuff off of his hard drive. Say it in plain English, really slow."

So Kim told him. Just a few steps on Hank's end, not too hard to follow: Find and open MasterCom (the software Remming used) . . . go to the setup menu, probably Alt-S . . . signal the Timed Execution Facility . . . double-check the automatic callout and download schedule to match the time and cellular number from Hank's stolen message. Only one thing to change. Set "Redial" to at least two. That about did it. It wasn't a sure thing, but at this point it was the only chance they had. Without understanding the importance of any of it, Hank followed the instructions to the last letter. Then:

"Anything else?"

"That's it," Kim answered. "Now get out of there."

"Are you sure this will work?"

"Trust me. Leave, now. Good-bye."

The line went dead. Hank turned off the monitor with a trembling finger, grabbed his flashlight, opened the window wide enough to scramble out, and then disappeared into the crisp spring night.

8 8 8

More time, they said. More time.

Jessica lay in bed at the Hotel Columbian, exhausted, weary, but with the sort of overstimulated brain buzz that kept her wide-eyed when she desperately would have enjoyed sleep.

More time.

That's what Remming told her, and a handful of other physicians related to her mother's case. Whenever she tried to skirt one to get information from another, the whole group sort of closed ranks and began mouthing the same push-button response: We're baffled. We don't understand. We need more time.

They had asked to do an autopsy, of course, especially Remming. Surprisingly, Jessica found herself willing, but she refused to grant consent until Elizabeth had been suitably informed and felt comfortable with the idea, which had not yet occurred. Jessica had tried to reach her at least a half dozen times, but the line was always dead, kept giving her that hypernasal "If you would like to make a call, please hang up and try your call again" message. Since she couldn't reach her now, the autopsy was stalled, even though Remming kept saying that the longer they waited, the less chance they'd have of finding anything conclusive. Maybe not the way she wanted it, but that's the way it was. Besides, he seemed just a little *too* eager.

So here it was, almost one o'clock in the morning, and she still couldn't sleep. Events from the last three days gyrated through her mind with unceasing persistence. If ever she began to drift or relax, some random thought or feeling would pop out like a jack-in-the-box and work her up all over again. Most of it, she knew, was the rigorous and unforgiving requirements of her own guilt. Like a raw spot, or a sunburn on her back right between her shoulder blades, the ache remained too hard to reach but impossible to ignore. She had no epiphanies, reached no resolutions, either about her mom's life or her death. All she had were memories, most of them disappointing. And this, too, was her fault, not her mom's.

So what remained? Exhaustion, yes. Sleeplessness, yes. Grief? Yes, of course; but strange and remote, as if altogether removed from the actual substance of the pain. Jessica felt so detached from her mother's life as a whole that the tears—when they came—came unannounced, like total strangers, and with a ferocity of soul that left Jessica nothing but a shell for hours after the fact. When she was able, she rationalized all of this as penance, the necessary residue of the incongruities of her relationship with her mother.

Lying in bed with her eyes wide open, staring at the ceiling, free of tears, mind racing as usual, Jessica finally found solace in a single thought, the gentleness and clarity of which soothed her troubled mind:

What remains? What remains? Mom is gone. What remains?

Only one thing: the truth.

With that thought, Jessica was asleep.

8 8 8

About a quarter after one, Hank stumbled into Kim's apartment, looking pale and worn. At the kitchen counter stood his friend, bent over some small black rectangular object with tiny screwdrivers and tweezers and other such tools. Kim glanced up, face flat, cracked a can of soda and gave it to him wordlessly. Hank cleared off as much space as he could, plopped down on Kim's sofa and drank.

"That was scary stuff," Kim whispered. "You all right?"

Hank tried to smile. "Just your average med-school breaking-and-entering scam." He motioned to the kitchen. "What's up?"

"This is how we're going to secure the data from Remming's system. You programmed the automatic download, right? Everything was correct?"

Hank nodded but said, "I still don't get it."

Kim reached for the black object on the counter, which Hank now recognized as a cellular phone. "A little-known fact of cellular technology, my friend! It is surprisingly easy to manually change your own phone number. Just pop open the cover, do a little tweaking, and voilà! My phone now has your number. Or in this case, 555-1837, the new download number so graciously supplied by your friend Monitor Nine, whoever the heck that is."

Hank frowned. "It can't be *that* easy." He rose, took the cellular phone from Kim and studied it.

"See? There and there." Kim pointed. "Piece of cake. It would have been a reasonable security measure if you hadn't intercepted the message."

"We reroute the call to your modem."

"Nope, not even that. We simply receive the call they are already making as if it were *their* modem. The only trick is to get in first. Their modem will be set to receive and that's sort of a problem, except it'll just think it missed on the first try and will reset and wait for a redial. On our end, I've hacked a piece of scrambling code that will confuse Remming's modem at disconnect to make it think the whole transfer failed. Which means it will try again. Their modem answers—fine, happy to oblige—Remming's call log shows no other connect or transfer, in and out, bam! We've got the goods."

"Ain't life full of irony?" Hank mused. "So if I had a cell phone and you wanted to listen in, all you'd have to do is switch your phone to my number?"

"Nifty, huh? Speaking of which, if all your ducks are in a row, we're set to receive here in about"—he glanced at his watch—"T-minus eight minutes and counting. I'd better hurry!"

Kim snatched the phone from Hank, tweaked a little more here and there, then called the cell phone with his apartment phone to test the number's integrity.

Sure enough, it rang.

"Where'd you get the cellular?" Hank asked as Kim plugged the new phone into his modem and disconnected the wall jack.

"A friend. He needs it back by tomorrow. Handy way for the evidence to disappear, don't you think?" He stared Hank full in the face, suddenly serious. "Just a little over two minutes, Hank. You sure you want to go through with this? Now's the time to turn around and walk away."

Hank twisted his neck so that his spine crackled. "Nope. I want to do this."

Kim couldn't help but grin. Both men turned their attention to Kim's computer screen. He had a big system—big with a capital B. Two systems actually, one a Macintosh, the other a PC, but the bigger of the two was darn near gargantuan. 466 MHz PowerPC G4 chip, 256 meg of RAM, 18-gigabyte hard drive, 21-inch monitor, all the extras.

A techno-weenie's dream machine.

The countdown continued. Two minutes . . . minute and a half . . . one minute . . .

"What do we do after we get it?" Hank asked. "It will still be all garbled."

"Not for long," Kim murmured, with all the solemnity of swearing on his mother's grave.

Thirty seconds. Fifteen. Five. Hank inhaled, closed his eyes, crossed his fingers. If this didn't work . . .

The cell phone rang. Instantly, the modem lit up in response. On-screen, the connection played out.

"Transferring: 429 files. Approximate time remaining: 12 minutes."

Hank let out a whoop and holler. Kim, the stoic one, puffed out his chest, nodded his head, and strutted a little circle around the victory site.

"So tell me how we're going to make sense of this stuff," Hank said.

"We don't need to," Kim replied. "My brilliant Hungarian friend already has. Sort of."

Of course, Hank was clueless, so Kim briefed him in the most generic terms he possibly could. Something about this programmer he'd met in Amsterdam—Hank couldn't even pronounce the guy's name—who had developed a three-tiered "deductive compiler," or so Kim called it. Apparently this little piece of software had already gained something of a cult following in the swirling underground of the hacker subculture. Among the inner circles of that movement, the software was code-named Rosetta. Rosetta was designed to do one thing: analyze an otherwise nonsensical schematic and make sense of it. Such an undertaking, while simple enough in theory, required immense horsepower in practice, horsepower that simply was not available even three or four years ago, except on a mainframe.

Now the horsepower sat in Kim's own living room. So, in a situation involving encrypted text, for example, Rosetta's three tiers worked thusly: First, Rosetta contained a simple key-generating engine. PGP encryption involved a public key—represented by a certain number of characters, usually somewhere from five to eight, like A4JK98MZ—which corresponded to a private key, also composed of a certain number of characters. The public key was used to encrypt a document. The private key was used to decrypt, or translate. Public keys were distributed freely. Private keys were fiercely guarded.

So what the first tier—the key generator—did was painstakingly examine every possible combination, and there were a bunch of them. About 255 to the eighth power. Hank didn't know what that totaled, but Kim said it was a number with about twenty-six zeros behind it. Literally, trillions of possibilities. How could any sense be made out of such random variables? Hank began to despair. The private key sounded like the proverbial needle in a haystack, only worse.

Enter tier two: Rosetta took each newly generated private key possibility and combined it with the known public key, then dumped both—along with the original, encrypted file—into an alternate PGP coding environment. Finally, tier three employed a complex neural network to analyze the structural integrity of the decrypted message. The neural net was like your basic high school English teacher on steroids: capable of analyzing in almost human terms the context and meaning of combined words and sentences, checking for spelling, and critiquing the document's grammar and syntax. Rosetta then kept a log of the ten keys with the highest hit ratios.

"But if these files have intense medical jargon and complex formulas, the neural net phase will have a much harder time. The spelling alone will give it fits, much less the context. We may have to widen the parameters. For speed, I've configured my computers to process in parallel."

Hank was just glad the explanation was over. He didn't really care how it worked as long as it worked. Still, the theoretical power of Rosetta boggled his mind.

Twelve minutes were up. The blinking modem lights dimmed and the computer beeped twice. A message on-screen read, "Download complete. Connection terminated."

Kim turned to Hank, his face eager. "So let's have it. We're ready to rock 'n' roll!"

"What do you mean?"

"The public key. Where is it? We need it."

Hank's face fell. Suddenly, he was very tired. "I don't have any public key! I didn't even know I was supposed to have one until now!"

Kim thought a moment, bit his lip, said, "OK, OK. No problem. You remember the address and password for that Internet forum?"

"Club Cranium? Yeah, sure. Olympus."

"That's where the public key will be. We can download it from there."

So Kim took the captain's chair in front of the glowing computer screen and logged on. Sure enough, there it was. In and out and he had it. Hank was surprised. Kim explained that a public key needs no security. It's worthless in and of itself. The whole point of the public key was to give *other* individuals a way to send secured messages to *you*. Without the public key they simply couldn't do that, so nobody who valued secrecy tried to hide his or her particular public key. The private key was what mattered; the public was incidental.

"Except that without the public key and Rosetta you couldn't work backwards to figure out the private," Hank mumbled, leaning against Kim's shoulder. His eyes had begun to grow extremely heavy.

Kim was delighted. "Quite right! There's a sort of Machiavellian irony to it, isn't there? Ah, the advance of technology!"

"If this is true," Hank said, beginning to grasp the big picture despite the haze in his mind, "you're telling me that hacks all over the world have almost routine access to whatever they want? Government documents, the global stock exchange, military secrets . . ."

Kim swiveled in his chair and stared Hank straight in the face. "You're beginning to grow afraid, aren't you, Hank?"

Hank pursed his lips, wisely pondering a suitable response. Subconsciously, he lifted his eyes, noticed all over again the big poster stretched on the wall right over the computer in front of him. He had seen it a thousand times before—bold, stark letters, black on white, declaring: "Anarchy Now!"

Hank laughed. Kind of. It was all he could do. He closed his eyes, turned on one heel and drunkenly staggered to the couch. His weary body felt like lead. "Don't go and launch Armageddon on me, all right, Kim? All I want is Remming's files."

"Got it under control, my friend. We're in Rosetta right now."

Hours passed. Then: "Hank, wake up! I think we've got a match!"

Hank had no recollection of falling asleep. Total elapsed time felt like five minutes, tops. He roused slowly, struggling to his feet. Kim had shoved a handful of papers in his face. Bleary-eyed, he took them, glancing at the clock on the wall.

4:45 a.m.

"No Armageddon, right?" he asked through a pasty-toothed half smile.

Kim's voice was grave. "I'm not so sure. Take a look at that stuff. I glanced over it and it looked like quality to me, but I don't have a clue what I'm looking for. All I know is that it sounded scary."

He didn't have to instruct. Hank was already reading, had already read enough to know that Rosetta had done its job. Masterfully. The entire Club Cranium files lay in his hands.

*De*crypted.

The more he read, the more he, too, became afraid.

"Drop this on a disk for me, will you, Kim?" he whispered. "Make that three disks. Three copies."

Kim handed him the disks. Dimly, Hank noticed that Kim didn't look tired at all. He was in his element. He was the Wraith.

"Hey, Hank. Don't worry. Only a handful of hacks around the world have access to what I've got here. A few hundred maybe. Most of them are OK."

Hank hardly cared at this point. He was still skimming the documents. Hundreds of pages. Kim must have been printing for quite a while.

"Keep one of these copies for yourself and hide it someplace here, would you?" he asked.

"Sure," Kim gravely replied, taking the disk.

Hank grabbed an armful of everything, disks and papers, and headed for the door.

"Lay low. I'm not sure we're safe."

11

H ank stayed up the remainder of the night reading. His exhausted body protested in the most dramatic terms, but Hank remained absolutely fixated on the Club Cranium files. He didn't make it through all the hundreds of pages, not even close, but he made it far enough to know what all the fuss was about.

And oh my, what a fuss.

The weight of the data seemed to suggest that those people who called themselves Christians, who, more important, claimed a legitimate "conversion" experience, like Hank—and *only* those who called themselves Christians—possessed a biologically unique characteristic: a tiny cluster of ganglial tissue near the pineal body. What's more, this nerve cluster secreted a previously unregistered neurotransmitter called serotoxomiasin, or STM-55, which apparently controlled a vast array of beneficial physiological and psychological brain functions. Hank felt relieved to finally understand the context and meaning of words he had puzzled over for so long from the postings. But the implications were staggering.

In the simplest human terms, the research in his hands scientifically proved the unfathomable: basically, that Christians were right. Or at the very least, they were unique. Even more amazing, this SPoT—called a God Spot in some of the files by Doctors El-Saludin and Volgaard—was no theoretical abstraction, no working hypothesis. The stage of nebulous ideas had long since passed. The data Hank had been examining—for hours now—was hard data, tangible. This God Spot was nuts-and-bolts science.

In other words, what had once been debatable in the absence of absolute proof—namely the theological notions of faith and salvation—now appeared to be as concrete as any other scientific reality, whether that be gravity or solar energy or the molecular composition of water. Hank could hardly believe his eyes. What did it mean? Was it all some sort of hoax? Hank immediately dismissed the idea. For one thing, apparently Dr. Rosenburg had been murdered. As in, dead. In fact, the tone of everything up to this point—especially between that lady and Remming last night—had been gravely serious. No, this was no hoax. So, what then? And who was "the Company" she had referred to? Could that be the Merideth Institute? All Hank could do was continue reading, perpetually stunned. The information in his hands held the capacity to become, simultaneously, the most jolting scientific, sociological, and theological find of the last two thousand years.

Too big, too much. You're in over your head, Hank. Way over.

Precisely. In *too* deep was the problem. The time for backing down was, oh . . . about twelve hours ago. The only road left open was straight ahead. Plain and simple, he had stolen top-secret research data from his own boss. Highly inflammatory research, to say the least. If Remming played with fire and got burned, Hank's career could get burned, too.

You didn't know that at the time, he had to admit. *You didn't have to go snooping.*

"Plausible denial." That was the phrase public officials applied to purposeful ignorance. "Bliss" was the cliché. Fine for some. Never worked that way for Hank, though. Hank's realism and paranoia insisted on facing something square on, not with head in sand. He *had* snooped; snooping seemed wise at first, especially since his future *was* largely wrapped up in Remming's. That's just the way it worked at this level. Not only does the captain go down with the ship, but the ship and the passengers go down with the captain. Crimes and misdemeanors aside, though, with the data in hand, the stakes were now much higher. Not only Hank's career was on the line, but the faith of millions. Possibly the fate of the faith. His faith. In his hands.

What is this research all about? What's really happening here?

In real terms, the watershed of an alleged God Spot was nothing less than the validation of a single religion above all others. In this Hank took surprisingly fierce pleasure, bordering on patriotic. He had grown up hearing the stories. You couldn't help but hear them in the Midwest. How America was God's country. Jesus Christ's country is what they meant. In his hometown, with a church on virtually every street corner and a Southern Baptist university right in the dead center of the city proper, the stories were everywhere. Stories of the faith. Of the church. Of the Bible. He had heard the stories a million times.

Then came that day when he made the leap from hearing to believing. That day in the park, the reality of which had been a quiet process ever since. His parents were plainspoken folks—good people but not religious. They knew a few of the stories but didn't understand. Besides, faith was supposed to be a personal thing.

Now this, the most outlandish of all, that those stories might be scientifically viable. If faith was now the purview of science, might it not also become a matter of public record? What then? Hank rubbed his eyes. Within the text, the four researchers themselves seemed deeply divided—some aggressive, some cautious, some shouting outright blasphemy. Hank understood so much now, so much of what the postings could only hint at. Too much to absorb at once. Too tired to absorb anything else . . .

And then the last note, a journal entry from Remming. Something about parallel research he was doing. Something the others didn't know about. A key to the whole thing. No specifics. The last thing he remembered reading was the smeared red numbers on his alarm clock. 7:53 a.m.

At precisely 9:30 the phone rang. Hank stirred at the fourth ring but didn't bother to answer. He didn't really want to talk to anyone and, if the truth be told, felt more than a little afraid. With the heady rush of piracy now grown several hours old and the cold reality of his loot feeling more and more like a burden than a prize, Hank woke with a familiar sense of apprehension. Now, paranoia never feels like paranoia to the paranoid. It feels like wisdom. In this case it felt particularly so, since distance almost always yields a certain objectivity, which, coupled with his internal misgivings, fairly shouted, "Proceed with extreme caution!"

So Hank lay in bed. On the fifth ring, the answering machine kicked in. Hank could hear his own recorded voice mixed with static.

"It's pretty simple, folks. Name, number and any other relevant data. The name's Hank in case you've called the wrong number, but if you're a beautiful Swedish girl named Nina, then this is the right number for sure. Medical emergencies can reach my pager at 555-7526."

Two short beeps, followed by an unmistakable voice:

"Hanson, pick up the phone."

Hank jerked upright in bed, stricken. It was Remming! He didn't dare move. Remming waited a few seconds before speaking again.

"I don't know if you are there or not, Hanson, but we must talk. This is very serious. Meet me under the Triborough Bridge on the west side at 11:00 a.m. sharp. That's an hour and a half from now. Don't disappoint me, Hanson."

Click.

☸ ☸ ☸

The first thing Missy Jenkins noticed as she stepped through the heavy oak doors of the Church of the Ascension was the simple decor of the sanctuary. The usually ample supply of heavily embellished icons and statues seemed strangely absent to a nominally faithful Catholic girl like herself. Missy hadn't been to church in years, but she was raised by as devout a pair of followers as the pope was likely to find on any one continent. She knew the rituals and liturgies and rosaries and such. And she knew all too well that guilt-ridden, heavy, mystical feeling a good Catholic Mass can imbue.

But when she stepped into Father Ravelo's parish hall, she felt absolutely none of those elements, the absence of which made her even more uncomfortable. It was not a big church, not at all, but the sanctuary was full of light, with both the eastern and western walls ablaze with simple stained-glass portraits of Christ from the four Gospels, in succession, leading up to the Crucifixion. And then, over the northern wall, behind the platform and podium, shone the loveliest window of all, a simple rendering of Jesus' ascension from the Mount of Olives into heaven, with angels all around and people below, looking on with wonder and joy. To Missy's immediate right and left were rows and rows of candles, most of them burning, silent prayers for the dead. Beyond the candles, in each corner, were the confessionals. The walls were cedar, polished but otherwise unadorned; the floor, marble. And high above, the vaulted ceiling flowed symmetrically toward a rounded glass dome, like tributaries into a river, through which even more sunlight fell. All in all, Missy decided it wasn't so different from the churches she had attended as a child.

But something *felt* different. Good different. Uncomfortably different.

Midweek Mass had already begun, so Missy tried to make her way to a pew as carefully and quietly as possible. The Mass was in English, not Latin, and Ravelo's voice filled the hall with clarity and vigor.

"The mind of Christ," he was saying, "is the mind of the Father. For what did Christ say? He said that he did nothing of his own initiative. In John chapter five we see Christ revealing his absolute submission to the Father. Listen to the words of Jesus: 'Truly, truly, I say to you, the Son can do nothing of Himself, unless it is something He sees the Father doing; for whatever the Father does, these things the Son also does in like manner. For the Father loves the Son, and shows Him all things that He Himself is doing; and greater works than these will He show Him, that you may marvel. . . . I can do nothing on My own initiative. As I hear, I judge; and My judgment is just, because I do not seek My own will, but the will of Him who sent Me.'"

Ravelo glanced eagerly around the room. "Brothers and sisters, do you see? Here is Jesus, God in the flesh, abdicating his eternally held rights of omniscience to the will of Father God! Do you perceive the scope of his sacrifice? Amazing! How much more should we seek to renew our minds—why?—so that like Jesus himself we may 'prove what the will of God is, that which is good and acceptable and perfect.' We have all been given the mind of Christ. And Christ was given the mind of God. What a glory to our spirits! What a hope for the redemption of our flesh! . . ."

When the time came to rise and partake of the Eucharist, Missy found herself falling in line with everybody else. Ravelo, draped in ecclesiastical cloth, held the cup and the bread in his hands; an unexpected delight crinkled the wrinkles around his eyes when he saw her. Missy found herself smiling, too.

Then Ravelo asked an odd question. "This is the body and blood of our Lord, Ms. Jenkins," he said. "I would love to share it with you. Is Christ the shepherd of your soul?"

Missy's smile faded. In fact, she blushed. When she tried to frame an answer she stumbled over the words. Finally she said, "I'll just wait for you in the back," and made haste to duck out of sight as quickly as possible, which was actually next to *im*possible in the large, well-lit open spaces of the Church of the Ascension.

❂ ❂ ❂

"Hello, Ms. Jenkins!" Ravelo said pleasantly.

"Hello, Father," Missy answered, still a little embarrassed. Internally, she kicked herself. Shyness would not do! Not now. She hated the bashfulness that had crept into her work of late, knowing it was the natural course of falling confidence. Once she had been as hard-nosed as the rest of them. Now, without any sign of a husband or kids to blame, her "come hell or high water" approach to journalism had reached new levels of domesticity.

Sometimes she overcompensated. Like now.

"What do you say we get right to it!" she declared. The effort sounded so contrived that it struck both her and Ravelo as a snatch of dialogue from a bad TV show.

"How about if we just talk a bit," Ravelo said. "Neither of us is very comfortable right now. Let's go to my office."

Again, Missy blushed. She hated blushing! "OK, fine. Your office. I like that."

"I'm reluctant to do this, to participate in anything that capitalizes on the life and death of anyone, even a killer like Luther Sanchez."

Missy nodded, mentally laboring over her next move. She had come this far, but intuitive interpersonal skills and finesse were not her forte, unless you consider a bulldog intuitive. She was that kind of unfortunate soul whose thin layer of engaging personality was deeply buried beneath a thick layer of pure annoyance. As far as the wrapping went, Missy was not necessarily an attractive woman, with thin lips and even thinner dirty brown hair cut in a straight bob with her long bangs peeled back from the middle of her forehead and tucked behind both ears. She was slightly overweight—not plump really, just substantial. But oh, could she write! Missy possessed an astounding gift with the written word and had a keen mind for laying siege to an issue until the walls collapsed and its secrets were revealed. She read voraciously. There was hardly a topic brought to conversation to which Missy didn't contribute some completely nonessential tidbit.

"We can work something out," she said, trying to sound reasonable. Father Ravelo did not take it so.

"I'm not interested in working things out, Ms. Jenkins. I'm not interested in the commercial profitability of this story for your newspaper, or even the profitability of a story like this for your career."

"Feel free to speak your mind, Father." Missy snorted, mostly joking, sort of not.

Ravelo folded his hands together and smiled. "Please understand. I don't mean to offend, or for that matter, to put you on the defensive—"

"Defensive? Me? Why should I feel defensive? You've only denied me the sacraments and belittled my job. And it's not even 10:30 yet!"

Ravelo adjusted his glasses. "You were raised Catholic?"

Missy nodded but couldn't look him in the face. The priest's unblinking gaze felt like ice cream melting—sort of sad, but inevitable.

"I do not wish to exclude anyone from the divine mystery," Ravelo said. "But the divine mystery begins and ends in the person of Jesus. It would be pointless and disingenuous to serve and be served something you have not first believed."

Whatever. They were straying. Missy wanted to stay focused.

"If it's all right with you, the theology will have to wait for another day. Luther Sanchez is my main concern right now. I've got some pressing concerns related to Luther that I can't do a thing about until you start talking."

"I'm trying to tell you that I have reservations about participating. . . ."

"I know! But I can't help that! I'm sorry if you have some hyper-idealized view of the world, but the reality is that bad stuff happens to good people and bad people and my job is to report it."

She managed to stare Ravelo full in the face during this monologue, without blinking or blushing—realizing for the first time in definable terms that her skills were reactive rather than proactive—and was so proud of herself in the process that she spilled her purse all over the floor. Floundering, she grabbed her reporter's pad and began flipping pages.

"I've been researching this case. Did you know, for instance, that Luther underwent government-approved hypnosis therapy for almost two full years while in prison?"

Ravelo shrugged. "So?"

"So why would the United States government spend a dollar more than they needed to on a convicted felon, much less a monster like Luther?"

"You're sure it wasn't state money? Or even district money?"

"Positive. In fact, the money was earmarked for Luther alone. No one else was involved. It wasn't a program with a control group. And there were three people assigned to him, not just one."

Ravelo frowned, thought a moment. He didn't like any of this, but the burden of his conversation with Luther felt more tedious to bear now than the effort of involvement. "OK, let's make a deal. I'll cooperate as much as I can on one condition: You don't print a word until you have the whole story. No series. No piecemeal. No weekly updates. If there's any truth to be told, it doesn't need to be sensationalized by the media with a lot of bells and whistles."

Missy shook her head stubbornly. "I can't make that deal. I don't have the authority."

"It's your decision. Those are the terms."

Missy resorted to smugness. "You're assuming that what you have to offer carries that much weight?"

Ravelo said, "No, no. That's assuming there is anything to investigate, period. *With* me, *without* me. Period."

"But there is! I can feel it."

"Fine, make the call. Are you prepared to be proven wrong?"

Missy was quick. "More prepared than you, it would seem."

Ravelo didn't answer. Missy studied him for a moment. He seemed implacable. "It's a deal," she said. "What have you got?"

Ravelo produced the wrinkled scrap of paper with Luther's last message. "Only this," he said.

Missy looked at the cryptic message with a puzzled expression. "What's it mean?"

"You tell me. He acted like it meant something. Or that I should be able to figure it out. Anyway, when he saw the lady from the CIA—"

"It was a she?"

Ravelo nodded. "Decker. Susan Decker, I believe. Seemed pretty antsy to me. Tried to push the warden around. Bad idea."

"Why was she there? Do you have a clue?"

"No. But she did talk to me, all concerned about what Luther told me. Only problem was, Luther didn't tell me anything at all. He was vague and bizarre and tortured."

"Sounds like my last boyfriend," Missy offered.

Ravelo continued. "I can only remember one thing he said, something really strange: We were talking about original sin and he said his sin was *chemical.* He said 'the magic was put inside him.' I have no idea what that means. Isn't that odd?"

Missy scribbled frantically, nodding her head. "Go on, go on."

"That's it."

"You're on record, you know."

Ravelo squirmed in his chair. "I know."

Missy asked, "Why would this Decker character be so interested in Luther?"

Ravelo reached for his guitar. Music always helped him relax, so he strummed a few simple chords. "Well, it certainly wasn't personal interest; that much was obvious. Professional, I'd say, though that still doesn't answer your question. Maybe it was a final follow-up. If what you're saying about the hypnosis thing is true, maybe the government just wanted to do a final analysis on the money they'd invested. Maybe it's standard procedure."

"Not a chance," Missy countered. "I know how to spot a worm in an apple. And I've studied Luther Sanchez for over four years now. I was the one who wrote the lead every day for three months surrounding his trial and incarceration. No way this was standard procedure."

"Well then, there's all kinds of other explanations. Maybe Luther was being studied as a part of some national effort to better understand the pathology of serial killers. You know, study one, understand another. An ounce of prevention—"

"—is worth a pound of schlock. It just doesn't wash." Missy began chewing on the eraser tip of her pencil. "Last year, a colleague of mine did an investigative piece on Gulf War veterans and Gulf War syndrome. Apparently one of the symptoms many veterans share is selective memory loss. My friend tried to find a connection between the syndrome symptoms and documentable military research into posthypnotic suggestion as a way to program aggression and block pain . . . or the memory of pain."

Ravelo pulled on his earlobe. "In my humble opinion, you're really reaching."

"Am I?" Missy started shifting positions in her chair. She was getting excited. "Because I also remember reading about some classified intelligence research from the fifties and sixties along the same line. Mind-control stuff. Really scary. I wonder if Luther is connected to any of that? Next-generation government stuff."

Ravelo smacked his lips, dropped his chin. "Umm, a serial killer?"

"OK, indirectly. Who knows? Maybe he's a research effort gone wrong."

"Research effort? How about a human being? That is what we call them still, isn't it? And do you really believe our government would so flagrantly violate one of its own citizens for research purposes?"

Missy almost guffawed. "We are talking about the same government here, aren't we? The grand U.S. of A.?"

"All right then, naiveté aside, we're also still talking about a serial killer! And about a major security breach. Susan Decker was a piece of tin foil in a microwave in that prison. She stood out like a sore thumb. Someone's bound to talk."

"Like you?"

"Like me. Right. It just doesn't make sense. It had to be routine! If all this stuff you're talking about is even remotely true, the government wouldn't risk exposure over a highly visible criminal element like Luther Sanchez. And besides, where is even the hint of a connection? Luther had no military background. So you've read a couple of interesting stories. That doesn't mean the pieces fit."

"But if Luther was a failed guinea pig, what better way to eliminate the evidence than to allow the court system to legally do it for you?"

Now Ravelo had to laugh. "I've got to hand it to you, Ms. Jenkins, when you conspire you do it on a grand scale! The man killed thirteen people by hammering them in the head! He chose a life of crime!"

"No, no!" Missy raised a finger. "The sin was put inside him! Remember? Isn't that what he said? Do you remember the interview with Karen van Meer?"

Ravelo nodded. "I watched."

"Do you remember what he said? I wrote it down. Amazing stuff." Missy flipped a half dozen pages, brushed a thin strand of hair out of her eyes. "Listen. This is Luther: 'I was dead before I was born,' he said. 'The man made sure of that . . . Now I lay me down to sleep, Big Brother's got my soul to keep! The man was there all along . . . *in the womb.*'"

"Sounds like nonsense. And it doesn't correlate to what you said, either. In the womb? How's that military research?"

"Good question," Missy said, reading again Luther's scrawled message: "mustbe102354."

"Just a hunch, I know. But I've learned to chase these rabbits when I see them jump. Thank you for your time, Father Ravelo. Lovely service earlier. I'll be in touch."

A quick handshake and she was out the door.

"That's what Susan Decker said," Ravelo mumbled. "I didn't like it then, either."

Needing a breath of fresh air, Ravelo used the opportunity to stroll around the block. He visited two or three families down the street who were either sick or needing some sort of care. Talked with a couple of bums on the side of the road; prayed for one, gave a five-dollar bill to another. Visited the Silver Star for a quick round of pool and a chat with the fellas. Finally, relieved and clearheaded, he headed back to the office. There was, unfortunately, paperwork to be done.

Ravelo despised paperwork. It had nothing to do with his office or calling.

Mrs. Huggins handed him the morning's paper as he entered; Remming carried it to his office tucked under one arm. Missy's paper, the *Detroit Sentinel.* Remming decided he kind of liked the girl, despite his original misgivings.

He sat down, crossed his legs, flipped the paper open, and slapped it against his bent knee to flatten the crease. There on the front page, in big bold letters, the cover story screamed for attention. But Ravelo didn't know the importance of the story, had no reason to know. So he skimmed the front page, found most of it distasteful, and moved on to the comics, leaving the headline behind—the headline that declared: "Eminent Jewish Scientist Slain Last Night."

⚓ ⚓ ⚓

A similar headline was on page five of the *New York Times.* It was a decent-size story but was tucked away in the bottom left-hand corner; Hank did not notice as he skimmed the paper while downing a cup of thick, black coffee.

"Noted Pharmacologist Brutally Murdered In Detroit."

Hank finished his coffee and shivered. His apartment felt particularly cold and barren this morning. Remming's phone call not five minutes ago had left him chilled to the bone, a coldness more intractable than the simple matter of regulating the thermostat. At the risk of sounding clichéd, *life* felt cold.

Outside, with clouds overhead, the light was indirect and gray. Hank surveyed his apartment. Typically male. A little sloppy. Clothes here and there. The ever-present baseball cap on the worn-out sofa. A poster of Einstein tacked unevenly on one wall that read, "The failure to imagine is greater than the failure to succeed." Dust and dirty underwear and the TV turned to CNN. The place was not aesthetically satisfying or cozy in any sense, other than to say it was home.

Hank had his blossoming career, his computer, his car, his good reputation. He had worked hard for the last eleven years, come to New York, and made it.

So what?

Facing Remming now, knowing what he knew, no longer seemed so thrilling. The achievements of his life evaporated before his eyes like the steam from his half-empty coffeepot. Remming was obviously involved in illegal activity. And the only way Hank knew that for sure was by acting illegally himself: breaking and entering, theft of intellectual property. He hadn't thought it through, hadn't stopped long enough to ask the right questions, get his bearings. At the time it just seemed right. It seemed like the only possibility. What now? Did that implicate Hank? Maybe Hank had even unwittingly run errands for Remming before, illegal errands. Even more, if Hank pushed the envelope any further, what kind of life was he looking at? Would there be any life? If Rosenburg, a valuable member of this Club Cranium thing, was deemed dispensable by the power players, how much less important would Hank be in the eyes of . . . whoever? That creepy woman? The thought of her chilled him even more. And if they—they! Who they?—didn't kill him, then what? Would he just spend his life on the run? He tried not to drift into melodrama, but the realities of his prospects at this point pointed toward a steady nosedive.

The God Spot files were big, heady stuff, with international ramifications if proved to their present conclusions. The need for secrecy seemed obvious enough, but the God Spot seemed to be more than merely classified research. It seemed to mean something to somebody, or some group of somebodies. You don't kill people for a secret unless the secret equates to something extremely precious, like power or wealth.

Or control.

Hank groaned. Couldn't the research be rigged? Fake numbers? Fake data? It was possible, but Hank doubted it. Remming would never be a part of that kind of sham. He was too much of a scientist to willingly falsify his own science.

So what did Remming want to talk about, then? How could he know anything? Surely he couldn't. Surely this was a coincidence.

Yeah, and when was the last time Remming personally requested a secret meeting underneath a bridge?

With that thought, the room grew colder still. What was all this about? God Spot. Serotoxomiasin. What did it mean, Big Picture? He had chosen the Christian faith. But did that make it exclusively right? More to the point, had the Christian "faith" chosen *him*? If this SPoT exerted genuine biological influence, who was to say what the order of things was? Was he born a Christian and just didn't know it for five years before it triggered a chemical reaction in his head that made him cry and feel good? The pineal itself responds to light and darkness, triggering sleep patterns and wakefulness. The pituitary gland triggers growth spurts and sexual maturation at genetically appointed times. SPoT did not sound so different.

Hank didn't know, and at the moment didn't care. He just wanted to be safe. He thought briefly about up and leaving the state, burning his information, the disks and the papers, dropping out of the residency program for a couple of years, maybe even transferring. Anything—just get away. Hide.

He knew that would be foolish. Why did he have to go snooping around in the first place? It *was* stupid and he raged at his stupidity. He glanced at his watch; a little over an hour to come up with a plan. Nothing left to do but ride this storm out. Very carefully. Very cautiously.

He glanced at the papers on his small, two-seat kitchen table. Hundreds of pages . . . the complete file. For the first time, it occurred to Hank that he had a little bit of leverage in this situation. A little bit of leverage that—maybe, just maybe—gave him a big space at the bargaining table.

Don't get cocky, Hank . . . the wiser part of him thought.

Another voice bent on survival replied: *Not cocky. Just a little strategy* . . .

⧈ ⧈ ⧈

At about that same time, Jay Remming was seated in front of a laminar flow hood with his hands in the isolation gloves, decanting the supernatant fluid off of a sample of neural tissue from the brain of a deceased professing Christian.

He was alone. It was early. Only a few lights were on.

He had finally received the cellular sample from Volgaard, who had secured the samples herself from Runwell, though several weeks late (a fact that Remming noted with irritation). After draining the liquid into a vial, he topped it and removed the vial from the sterile hood. Next, he extracted a measured quantity of the sample and placed it in a test tube, then poured it into a clear buffer solution—pH 7.4— swirling it around in his hands.

Remming licked his lips. No one knew what he was up to. He had not discussed these private forays with the rest of his team, much less bothered to report them to Decker. At least not anything extraordinary, though if some generic bit of information useful for the primary thrust of the team's research emerged, that was OK. No, this was for his pleasure—and ego—alone. Always one step up. The relentless pursuit of a distinct and qualitative advantage, however small. Never know when such a thing might come in handy . . . say for an award or something. Not to mention the element of control.

When El-Saludin had downloaded the probable DNA code for STM-55 a few days back, Remming immediately set to work to isolate and confirm the exact chain. He even cleared his schedule for an entire day just to spin formulas and run a few tests. Human DNA is read in triplets, each triplet corresponding to an amino acid, the chain of which forms the basic human building blocks of protein as defined by the genetic code. With the structure identified, Remming and El-Saludin were able to work backward to define the genetic code of serotoxomiasin by isolating the protein and breaking it up into the probable amino acids.

The DNA probe was the key to everything. It was like a single, thin needle in a haystack of infinite variables. Having secured it, Club Cranium could in a matter of days and weeks successfully execute all manner of clinical tests that would otherwise take years of guesswork. The chain had been the top priority of El-Saludin for months. Even so, he was extremely lucky to have hit the target so quickly.

But now, in the lab, this was not official Club Cranium work.

This was play.

More than that, of course. Remming never played. It was one of many open-ended tests Remming wanted to run, much like a tinkering auto mechanic likes to take his favorite roadster out every once and a while and just let her go on the open road, see what she can do after a bit of tweaking here and there.

So he needed to pull another pure sample. That was always the starting point. Another idea. Remming was a man of relentless ideas. He approached his science with the eye of an artist, not a technician. It was his genius.

He placed the mixture inside a high-performance liquid chromatograph and initiated a run. A couple of hours later, the graph reading rolled across the computer monitor. Remming carefully studied the peaks. The dominant peak assured him of the purity of the sample. He collected the peaked sample in a microcentrifuge tube and held the vial up to eye level. He was staring at a purified sample of serotoxomiasin. Pure neurotransmitter. Like a medieval thaumaturge, he stared at his potion with brooding delight. His creative process was in full swing.

What next? What next?

His eyes shifted focus, staring past the vial to the computer monitor on the desk a few feet away where a three-dimensional rendering of the protein structure of the substance he held in his hands revolved in slow motion. He watched the spinning complexity like a choreographer watches ballerinas performing onstage, looking for clues to improve the rhythm and flow of the dance.

Wonder if it has a chiral center? he mused. *Not that it really matters.*

He set the tube aside and rummaged quickly through a closet in the back to find a polarizing refractometer. Certain molecular structures have a symmetric core with mirrored sides, which allows them to rotate light. Others don't. For all practical purposes, a chiral center was medical minutia, but Remming wanted to understand STM-55 in all its complexities, however mundane. Evolutionary theories on the Law of Homochirality demanded that all biologic systems, if they rotate light at all, could rotate one way and one way only. So he dusted the refractometer off, moved it to the table, dropped a single drop of the sample into the machine, and held it up to the light, expecting nothing.

Instead, Remming got religion. Sort of.

"Oh dear God," he breathed.

12

The thin door swished as it opened and closed. From the darkness of the small, velvet-lined inner sanctum, a voice whispered, "Forgive me, Father, for I have sinned."

The voice sounded familiar to Ravelo. He slid open the portal between his chamber and the confessional, exposing the wire-mesh voice plate. The dim outline of a body on the other side was all he could see, all he ever saw, though he had come to know most people by voice alone.

"When was your last confession?"

The person seemed hesitant. "I don't know. Five or six years, I think. I don't know."

It sounded like Ricky Carletti. More accurately, like Ricky Carletti trying hard not to sound like Ricky Carletti.

"Name your sins, my son."

A long, pregnant silence followed. Ravelo felt the struggle in the young man. He inhaled, waiting, smelled the familiar odor of old wood and cushion foam. "The first step to freedom from the bondage of sin is to bring yourself out of the darkness," he encouraged softly. "There is nothing which Christ cannot heal."

"He cannot heal a dead man," Ricky answered, sounding close to tears. "I killed him in cold blood, do you get me? Dead. And I don't even know his name! Rosenthal . . . Rosenburg? He was a fat cat, just walking down the street and I killed him."

Ravelo recoiled, but was doubtful. "You mean . . . ?"

"Dead."

This was no joke. Ricky's voice held no humor, no mockery. The priest sat up in his seat and placed his hands on either side for support. *Dead?* Did Carletti have something to prove? The tears *sounded* real.

"Maybe you didn't kill him," Ravelo said.

"Read the papers!" Ricky shouted angrily. "It's big news!" He rose, mumbled, "I don't have time for this—"

"No, no, don't go!" Ravelo said, leaning closer to the voice plate. "I'm sorry. I just thought that maybe it was an accident."

Ricky settled in, combing his fingers through his hair as if there were answers to find there. "Murder ain't no accident," he said; then, on a dime, his words switched from agony to trembling. "Hey, Father, you can't tell anyone about this, can you? Ain't that in the vows or something?"

"I could," Ravelo said deliberately. "But I don't."

"That's good, that's real good. 'Cause I don't want to do any more than I have to, to stay alive. I don't want to hurt you." His voice began to strain. "I just want to, you know, forget everything! I want to go jump in a lake or something!"

"Have to? What do you mean *have to*? Why did you do it? Did you want to kill?"

"I thought I did. I needed the hit, the rank. I needed the security. Too much talk going around, if you know what I mean."

"Mmm," Ravelo said. "Go on."

"So anyway the boss tells us we got some business with Mother Scratch."

"Mother Scratch?" Ravelo asked.

"You know, the Agency. The Company."

"I don't follow you."

"C-I-A!" Ricky hissed, annoyed. "You figure it out! Hey, Father, wake up over there! Get this, we do contract work for them every now and then. That's how the CIA operates. Most of the stuff you see on TV ain't right. A bunch of suits run the place, but they contract out the scores. You know, no paper trail, cash deal."

"You did a hit for the CIA?" Ravelo choked.

"Shh! You gotta help, Father. What am I going to do? I hated it! I can't do it again! I thought I could, you know, but . . ." His voice trailed off.

"Listen, Ricky—" Ravelo started, then cut short, frozen, hand clamped over his mouth, eyes closed, breath held, hoping the long silence was a blanket big enough to cover his massive *faux pas*.

Not a chance.

Instead, a shocked, angry sucking sound came from the other side of the booth. The door ripped open, followed by a metallic ping and the sound of running feet. Ricky tore out of the confessional, the church, away . . .

"Wait!" Ravelo whispered hoarsely. "It was a mistake. I don't have to know who you are." He opened the door. Nothing. Ricky was long gone. Ravelo clasped his hands together in front of his chest and shook his head irritably.

Stupid, stupid, stupid! Foolish, clumsy, stupid . . .

But understandable. He looked around, down, up at the ceiling, at the stained glass. No one else was in line for confession, thank the Lord. So what was going on? Why would the CIA order a hit on a man in Detroit? Ravelo found the idea deplorable, even unbelievable. But an even better question was why would Ricky lie about it? What was there to gain? He was obviously distraught, maybe even terrified.

Sweet Mary . . . , Ravelo thought. *What is going on?*

He started to head back to his office to ponder when his shoe kicked something on the ground, something metallic that scuttled across the marble floor and bounced off a pew footing. Ravelo bent down and picked up the object, a thick gold ring of fine craftsmanship, albeit a little gaudy. An engraving trailed around the width of the band. Ravelo looked closer, realizing the engraving was some sort of Hebrew script. Bloodstains caked the inside of the ring. Ravelo scanned the ground for anything else. A step or two away, in the direction Ricky had fled, a neatly folded piece of paper lay on the ground. The priest picked it up. The paper was smeared with dark, bloody fingerprints inside and out. On the inside, Ravelo found an address. No name, just an address. He looked at the ring again, then back to the paper, feeling violated, somehow participatory, by holding the items with his own hands.

Fearing the worst, he hurried back to his office, closed the door behind him, and grabbed the phone book. The blaring headline of the newspaper finally caught his eye now. At the very least, Ricky had told the truth about that much. There *had* been a murder. So what was the victim's name for sure? The news account gave his full name: Theodore Samual Rosenburg.

Rosenburg. Rosenburg. He thumbed quickly through the phone book. Q . . . R . . .

There it was. He glanced again at the bloodstained paper. Back to the phone book. Exact same address listing.

Ravelo sat down, grieving. *He finally went and did it,* he thought. *Got the courage to go and throw his whole life away.* He folded the paper again and dropped both it and the ring in a little paper sack in his desk drawer.

God have mercy on him.

§ § §

Hank arrived at the bridge ten minutes late. Tardiness seemed appropriate; he thought it was important not to show fear.

Remming was on time.

"Hello, Hanson," the doctor said sternly, standing beside one of the concrete pylons at the base of the bridge. He wore shirt and tie, every bit the professional even in such sparse surroundings. The two of them faced each other across an uneven clearing of rock and grass, about a dozen yards apart, with the Harlem River to the east and a steep incline of scrub brush and litter piles to the west. Hank had parked his car at the top of that ridge on the side of the road, then climbed down one of several well-worn footpaths. Farther behind Remming, underneath the bridge, Hank saw a handful of shanty lean-tos, with circles of fire stones and crude collections of pots and pans, ratty old blankets, and whatever else the homeless could assemble for their "homes." Trash was all around, in the river, on the ground . . .

Remming glanced at his watch. "You're late."

"I had some things to do. What is all this about?"

Remming smiled his most patronizing smile; Hank shivered. Visible or not, he was very afraid. He hated the feeling of being squeezed. Overhead, the steady rhythm of moving traffic rose and fell with each passing vehicle, almost like a heartbeat.

Thoom . . . Thoom-Thoom . . . Thoom . . .

The sound was hypnotic. The Triborough Bridge extended 125th Street across the sluggish Harlem River and was named, presumably, because it stood at the junction of three of New York's five boroughs: the Bronx to the north, Manhattan to the west, Queens to the east. Hank glanced at the rolling waters, with the sun falling almost flat upon his shoulders, on the dark water like glitter, and a single thought kept repeating through his mind:

I could die right here and no one would know or care.

Thoom-Thoom-Thoom . . . Thoom . . .

"It was a stupid blunder, Hanson. You should have closed the window all the way." Remming's voice rose into his thoughts, dreamlike. Not an accusation. There was no anger. A hint of scorn, yes, but mainly just matter-of-factness. Hank didn't move, didn't twitch.

Remming continued. "I might not have noticed—it was just cracked, after all—except for the unusually cool air."

Hank took a deep breath. "I don't know what you're talking about."

"Don't insult me, Hanson. You were *in* my office last night."

Hank's pulse accelerated to the speed of the passing cars. No need to mess around with this. "What do you want from me?"

The doctor stepped forward, spread his hands wide, inviting. His cool black skin looked like carved mahogany underneath the wrinkle-free white shirt. "First of all, I want you to know that it's not what you think."

"What is? What's not what I think?"

"Fine, fine. Play your little games. But I'm concerned about you, Hanson. Whatever slander you have imagined against me is absolutely false. I thought we discussed this matter the other day. I thought we had reached an understanding. Next thing I know you've broken into my office like a common criminal! Very disturbing behavior. Not appropriate at all for an individual of your stature and prospects."

He implied *much* more than he spoke. Everything began to collide at once inside Hank's mind—past, present, future. For the first time, face-to-face now with Remming, he realized there was no real way he would ever salvage a medical career out of this fiasco. Eleven years of training, gone, just like that. When this was all over, Remming would make sure Hank received an expeditious and humiliating dismissal; or, best-case scenario, he would hold the whole affair over Hank's head—and his practice—as long as he lived. The very idea should have been tragic. It was not. Knowing also that the *worst*-case scenario was someone like that Susan woman popping out from behind a bush with a gun in her hand and an itchy trigger finger transformed Hank's pathos into a tool for survival.

"It sounds like you are threatening me, Dr. Remming."

"Not at all. Not personally, anyway. I just feel you should be made aware of the severity of your actions. The administration at Columbia, much less the medical boards, do not look favorably on subordinate and irresponsible behavior."

"Criminal behavior," Hank replied. He felt reckless—more and more so with each passing minute. Suddenly, he started climbing the embankment. "I feel pretty bad about all this, Dr. Remming. Really bad. You know what? I think I want to confess. And since you obviously want to turn me in, I say let's just go talk to them right now. Would that make you happy? Let's go tell them all about my suspicions. Heck of an idea, considering I have more access to your files than any other medical student. Let's drop this whole affair in their lap and see what comes of it."

"You don't have anything!" Remming barked. "Enough of this charade." He pointed a thin, bony finger at Hanson. They stood maybe fifteen feet apart now. "I am putting you on six weeks academic probation for questionable behavior, effective immediately. When the six weeks is up, your case will be reevaluated. After that time if you, how shall I say it?—show improvement—you will be transferred to Dr. Ziegrib's department for the remainder of your residency. Have I made myself clear?"

Hank lifted his chin. He didn't smile. "I have the files."

Remming shifted from one foot to the other. He lowered his pointing hand. "What did you say?"

"You heard me. I have them. All."

"What files? I don't know what you're talking—"

"You're insulting me now, Dr. Remming. How's this sound: Club Cranium. Serotoxomiasin potentiated tissue. The God SPoT. Any of those ring a bell?"

Remming licked his lips. His brow twitched. "You're bluffing."

"Am I?"

"You logged on to the Internet somehow. You got lucky. A file. A posting."

"Check your MasterCom call log from last night. It'll be there." Hank reached into his back pocket and pulled out a mashed-up square of folded papers. "I brought five or six pages if you have any doubt." He extended the papers in Remming's direction. Remming didn't move.

"What's this all about?" Hank asked, waving the papers.

"You don't know what you're dealing with here, Hanson," Remming said gravely. "Give me the files, turn around, and walk away. This is bigger than both of us."

"You lied," Hank said. "I trusted you once and you lied. Why should I listen to you now?"

"Give me the files, turn around, and walk away. I offer you full reinstatement, no questions asked. Remember your career, Hanson."

"My career?" Hank snorted derisively. "You've got a lot of nerve. Where is that woman anyway? Who is she?" Hank began scanning the ridge line. "Is she here somewhere, ready to launch my career down the same path as Rosenburg's?"

The name punched a button. Remming glanced from side to side, shaken. His tone was urgent. "Why do you think I left so soon last night?" he whispered. "When I saw the window, I knew I had to get Susan out of there. For your sake. I'm telling the truth, Hanson: I did it for you. This is a dangerous game you're playing."

"Game? People have died and you're calling this a game?"

"Rosenburg wasn't my fault."

"Really? I've read the files. Seems like he opposed the direction of the research."

"Dr. Rosenburg could not tolerate the implications. His prejudice and fear interfered with his science. Period."

"And nobody has the right to challenge science—especially *your* science. Am I right, Dr. Remming? Did I get that right?"

"Don't moralize with me, Hanson. Are you blind? Don't you see the implications?"

"I do. I see that Christians are onto something," Hank offered.

Remming wrinkled his face distastefully. "Bah! A genetic coincidence. We're talking about more than religion here. We're talking about the final unraveling of the human mystery!"

"Really? So I suppose you're a believer now?"

"In a religious soul? A religious savior? Don't be a fool, Hanson. This research is poised to do far more: *help man save himself.*" Remming stepped closer. His hands moved expansively. His eyes lit up. "Listen to me. We don't have much time. If we can name and identify the construct of the biological soul and simultaneously free ourselves from the theological rigors of an abstract, religious soul, then we will have—in a stroke—created a level playing field for every person. Do you see? Furthermore, if we can dissect and label the meaningful neurological, genetic, and biochemical components of this biological soul, then we will possess a whole new arsenal of advanced technology to better serve global man. Not just advanced, mind you, but paramount. We will have tapped into the seminal framework of the human constitution. It's the Philosopher's Stone of modern medicine! How do we treat the whole man? How do we find some meaningful synthesis between all the varied disciplines? This research may hold the key! Psychology, theology, medicine, maybe even physics, will all fold into a rational, biological response for the unhealthy people of this world. It will be awesome."

Twelve different kinds of Huxleyan alarms flared at once in Hank's head. He felt as though he stood in a quarantined no-man's zone, with bright red flashing lights and blaring sirens. "Two questions," he said. "Who exactly do you think will control this 'whole new arsenal'? And who determines who is sick?"

"The medical community, just like now."

"Governed by?"

Remming was confused. "Ourselves. What do you mean? Do you doubt the ability of intelligent people to govern themselves?"

"I don't really have an opinion," Hank exclaimed in a voice laden with irony. "But I sure bet Rosenburg would." Remming exhaled deeply, but Hank continued. "You're kidding yourself, Dr. Remming.

This is not about science; this is about power. You just said as much. Do you really believe the medical community will own the rights to this thing once you're done? It's simple. Who's funding the research? The Merideth Institute? They're the owners. Or whoever owns them."

He started to say more but thought better of it and turned to go.

"Hanson!" Remming commanded. "Give me the files. I'm begging. This research will go on with or without you, but you don't stand a chance alone. Trust me on this if nothing else. The research is not evil like you think. But there are people behind the scenes—people I don't even know—who are committed to its completion. Very committed. Think it through, Hanson—"

"I *have* thought it through!" Hank nearly shouted. "A million ways. I've lost sleep. I've been afraid. I'm afraid right now. My whole world has shifted because of this."

"You don't have to be the hero, Hanson," Remming pleaded. "There's nothing here to win. And everything to lose."

Hank laughed bitterly. "Did you know I'm a Christian, Dr. Remming?" He watched the surprise register on the older man's face. "Yep, been one since I was a little boy. Always been a good guy, you know. Did what I needed to do. Tried to obey what I learned at church, even though I went by myself mostly. Never drank or cussed in school." He shook his head. "Now, suddenly, I feel threatened and I don't know why. I have no idea. Can you tell me why I should feel threatened, Dr. Remming? Or how about not? Can you give me some assurances? See, my parents never talked about God much, so I always kept that stuff kind of tucked in my shirt pocket, you know, handy, where I could pull a virtue out when I needed one. Like a calculator— a practical addition to my day, but not much more. All pretty innocuous. Yet here I am. And you can't offer me a thing to make me feel better. You're basically telling me what I thought happened to me twenty-something years ago is really just a biological accident, a flow of chemicals in my brain that makes me think a certain way and feel certain things. Things I always assumed to be from God."

"Hanson, the data is inconclusive—"

"Let me finish!" Hank cried, clenching his fist and pointing. "I want to finish! You see, there's a third possibility. When I first made sense of these files, I felt a surge like I haven't felt in years. I remember thinking, *Now Christians will get some respect.* Now my mom and dad will understand. But I don't know what that means! What am I hoping they'll understand? What does that mean for me? I think that's what bothers me the most. That, and how much I trusted you. Even up until this meeting, I secretly hoped it was all a big mistake."

"Then let it be. You don't have to lose faith over this."

Hank rubbed his eyes. "How can I lose it? I've got nothing *to* lose. It's genetic, remember?"

"Give me the files. Please. I can't help you unless you let me."

"Help me? Did I hear that right? You think you can help me? Do you really think people want a biological messiah, a formula, a set of 1's and 0's?" Hank scowled. "All this talk of souls. You know what I think? I think *your* soul needs a little tinkering. Mine, too. Probably a major overhaul." Hank stared Remming straight in the eye. "But I won't trust my repairs to you."

"They'll stop you," Remming said flatly.

"Maybe. You just let them know I've already made three separate copies of the entire Club Cranium files. Let them know I've stored those copies in three separate places—that's why I was late, by the way; had some driving to do—with dated instructions. Tell them that if anything should happen to me before I figure out what to do, out they come."

Remming watched him climb the embankment. Sweat dampened his forehead. "Where are you going?" he asked.

Hank thought he heard an almost fatherly concern in the older man's voice. He kept climbing. "To the FBI, I think. Give them my copy of the files. Seems like a logical place to start. After that, back to work at the hospital. Which reminds me: In light of all this, you would do well to leave my academic record alone. But do whatever you think is necessary."

When Hank reached the top he turned to face Remming below. "I really don't want to hurt you or your name, Dr. Remming. That's why I'm asking you to bail out now. Cut the cord. You're more right than you know: This *is* bigger than both of us."

He turned and left.

Remming watched until he heard Hank's car start up. You could tell Hank's Duster a mile away. The doctor's jaw was clenched, his face tight, somber. He looked down at his polished black leather shoes, stared and stared, seeing nothing; he kicked a rock, feeling the energy drain from his legs into the dirt. At length, he lifted the flap on his shirt collar and spoke.

"You get all that?"

Susan Decker's voice crackled in his tiny earpiece. "You told him too much. Very foolish."

"I tried to sway him. Nothing more. If he already has the files, it doesn't matter."

"You should have let me take care of him last night. You should have told me."

"I've seen how you take care of people," Remming said irritably. "I shouldn't have told you anything at all, but the project appeared to be compromised."

Susan sniggered. "You really are a prize, Dr. Remming. Somehow you manage to be self-righteous *and* a coward."

"How dare you!"

"See, there you go. You can't pretend to care about this kid and still turn snitch. Don't get me wrong; there would have been hell to pay if you had let this float. You did the right thing for the project. But don't try to snow me. The plain truth is, you want another Nobel for this research. Everything else is posturing."

Obviously, Susan Decker was feeling a whole new level of freedom and candor—a completely unprofessional level of freedom, Remming thought, but what did Susan care about bureaucratic professionalism? Remming curled his fingers, turned a baffled, raging circle, looking for an object to strike. He had never been a violent man nor lacking in poise, but Susan Decker had a real gift. She continued to speak. Helpless, seething, feeling murder course through his blood, he could think of nothing to do but listen.

"I'll meet with you next for our regularly scheduled briefing. Play your cards right here, Doctor. Your margin for error is quickly diminishing."

"What will you do about Hanson?" Remming demanded.

There was a pause. Remming thought he heard the sound of Susan Decker smiling. It was a wicked sound.

"The kid wants to play hardball? No problem. I'll let him think he's hit a home run."

"If you touch him," Remming said menacingly, "so help me . . ."

"There you go again. Don't worry, he's safe—for now. You just concentrate on your research. We need all of your brilliance focused on this project. Hanson Blackaby is mine."

8 8 8

Hank wasn't quite as good as his word. He wasn't really sure he wanted to go to the FBI, or anywhere for that matter; it just seemed like a good idea to *tell* Remming that he would, to mark his territory, maybe even instill a little fear in Remming in the process. If Hank was to stay alive long enough to figure out what to do, the conspirators on the other side of the fence had to be forced to respect his potential range of influence, regardless of tangible evidence.

At least that's what he told himself.

But there is surprisingly little comfort in platitudes when your gut feels perpetually raw, the kind of rawness that comes from feeling as if snipers might be hidden around any and every corner, with long-barreled rifles poised, fingers curled around triggers, and red laser dots focused on your temporal lobe. Fantasy? Hank wasn't so sure. And *that* was the problem.

Semiparalyzed, what Hank mostly did was drive around in a daze for nearly an hour. During that time he checked his rearview mirror probably a hundred times, trying to mark the make and model of the cars behind him and the faces that drove them. But there was no pattern. No one followed.

At last, exhausted, a spark of an idea blinked through his mind, one he had filed away last night, sitting scrunched and terrified beneath Remming's desk. He had not had time to puzzle it through since. Why, Hank wondered, did Remming—quite uncharacteristically—*volunteer* information about the O'Connel lady's death to that woman last night? The case had no relevance that Hank could see. Even more odd, Susan seemed familiar with it.

Hank slammed on the brakes, spun his car around right in the middle of the street, causing tires to screech and horns to honk and a flurry of expletives to fly his way. He thought he might have lost a hubcap; from his rearview mirror he saw one spinning into the gutter. He hardly heard or cared, just punched the accelerator—sometimes a taxi just wouldn't do—swung a hard left, took the on-ramp to the FDR Freeway and headed for Columbia Presbyterian Medical Center, home base for him and Remming. It seemed as good a place as any to start.

"I'd like to see the charts on Mrs. Margaret O'Connel," Hank said to the nurse he knew best on this shift, a young RN named Nellie. Actually, Hank knew most of the ICU nurses by name, young and old. Since neurosurgery was possibly the most delicate juggling act of any major corrective effort, hypersensitive follow-up care was absolutely critical to a successful post-op recovery, especially for the level of operations performed at a research facility with the rank of CPMC.

"Hi, Dr. Blackaby," Nellie replied. She was several years younger than Hank, bright-eyed and willing to flirt. "What was the name again?"

Hank told her. Nellie tapped the name into the computer.

"Hmm, sounds familiar," she said. "But I've been off for the last three days. Oh, here it is . . ." She read the screen, puzzled. "It looks like she passed away, Dr. Blackaby. Yesterday, actually."

"Yes, I know. I'm just trying to round up any loose paperwork that needs to be completed for her files."

"It looks like ours has been processed already. See?" She swiveled the monitor so that Hank could take a look for himself. He dutifully complied but avoided nudging closer to Nellie. Naturally, she scooted closer to him—Hank figured as much; but this was too close, near enough to smell her hair (which smelled great, by the way). Contrary to Kim's jibes, Hank had an all-American libido and a running crush on two or three different nurses, Nellie being chief among them. In fact, if Hank were the type, he could call on the interests of a string of interns and nurses; interested for a variety of reasons, not the least of which was the fact that he was a handsome young doctor. Nevertheless, frustrating though it could be, dating was simply too impractical and complicated at this stage of his career. Especially now, the stakes were too high to be distracted; Hank politely stepped a little to the side to better concentrate.

He scanned Mrs. O'Connel's file for any protuberant data, anything at all that might dovetail into something meaningful or useful; when nothing of merit leaped off the monitor he scanned again for anything innocuous, punching buttons for different screens of data. Nothing much to get excited about.

Except . . .

"Her daughter admitted her," Hank declared. Wasn't a big deal, but the way he said it sounded like *Eureka!* "Says she was with her as of yesterday. Do we know if she's still in the area?"

"So you've resorted to computer dating?" Nellie grinned. "That's too bad. Let's see: Jessica O'Connel . . . Jessica O'Connel." She turned to a coworker. "Hey, there's a note here about a possible autopsy on the O'Connel lady. Has her daughter consented yet? Do we have a number for her?"

The other nurse barely paid attention. "Who knows? Last I heard she was in town for a couple more days. There's a number around here someplace."

Nellie began riffling through two different drawers, then another, then through a stack of scrap paper. "I remember now. Well, not really remember, it just sort of hit me, you know, like when you remember something you didn't even know you knew. That probably sounds silly to you. Anyway, when I got back the girls told me to treat this Jessica girl really nice, as ordered by one Dr. Jay Remming. Apparently he left special instructions to that effect. Sort of surprised the girls, I guess. They said this Jessica was a handful. But you know Dr. Remming."

"Oh, he's full of surprises."

"Here it is!" Nellie beamed, holding up a small yellow writing tablet. "Hotel and phone number. I'll copy it for you."

She bent over and scribbled quickly. Hank allowed himself a brief respite to admire her shapely features. A little bit of nurse's outfit went a long way with Nellie.

"There you go," she said, ripping off the paper and handing it to him. He took it, read Jessica's name, room number, the hotel name and address. And there at the bottom, tucked away for safekeeping, Nellie's name and phone number. He glanced up sheepishly.

"Just in case," she said, grabbing a chart and brushing her shoulder lightly against his on her way to rounds. Hank smelled her hair again. Delicious.

Oh, God, he thought, closing his eyes. *I've waited this long. I'll keep waiting. Just let it be with a girl like her. . . .*

Logic said the next stop should be Kim Yu's. Actually, logic said just the opposite, but Hank didn't know where else to turn. Emotionally, he felt compelled to further warn Kim to play it *extremely* cool for the next few days. So for about five minutes, sitting in his car, he wrestled with the possibilities, caught midstream between the two great antithetical countercurrents, reason and conscience.

Reason lost.

He started the engine and pulled into traffic, careful again that no one followed him. He drove in circles, took a wanderingly indirect route, made sudden turns—just in case. But no one followed.

Hank did not enjoy tight spots, certainly nothing this tight. It wasn't that he was bad under pressure—he was actually pretty good— he just would rather avoid the crunch, make the find and bail out, leaving the cleanup to someone else. It was an acquired right, an expectation culled from years of winning popularity contests, surviving on wits and flashy smiles, not altogether uncommon among the sanguine. Have a little fun, do what you need to do, make your mark, and exit to the left.

Once he arrived at Kim's he bounded up the stairs, glancing once more over his shoulder, just in case. Satisfied, he knocked on the door and entered just like normal, calling out quiet greetings to Kim without waiting for an answer.

He could not have been less prepared, not at all, for what he saw inside.

Kim's apartment had been devastated; not just ransacked, but devastated. The place had always looked more like an experiment in chaos than ordered living, but now—Hank shuddered at the violence done to the room. Furniture was overturned, glass and mirrors were broken, drawers and cabinets thrown open and their contents expunged.

Hank managed about three seconds of shattered, silent numbness before instinct took over, a very simple emotion, fear—a roiling, primal impulse that made him hunker down, cavemanlike, arms spread, ready for action.

"Kim!" he whispered hoarsely. "Kim!"

Kim did not respond. Again, louder, "KIM!" but no answer. Hank knew no answer would come but, like a broken record, it was all he could manage to say. He walked and whispered and an eerie calm hugged the carpet like a fog. The only sound in the whole apartment came from the faucet, flowing with water. Hank picked his way through the living room to the kitchen, looking for clues. He stared at the faucet. Kim must have been snatched right in the middle of whatever he was doing! He turned off the water. Kim's two computers were overturned and the monitors cracked. Papers strewn everywhere.

He groaned out loud, whispered, "The disk . . . gone." Glancing from side to side, guilt rose in his belly. *I can't believe—. I never dreamed . . .*

And then another, louder voice rose up from within.

Get out of there! it shouted. *Run!*

Hank obeyed. Wordlessly he moved to the door, closed it quietly behind him, flew down the stairs, into his car and away. The faster he fled, the faster he wanted to flee. His foot was a lead weight on the gas pedal. He could go no faster, but he wanted to. He wanted to disappear. Anything. Anywhere.

And like a phantom, the fear grew. This *definitely* was not a game.

13

D r. Abu Hasim El-Saludin checked the figures again. And again. And again. When that failed—succeeded actually, in duplicating previous results—he started all over with fresh cell cultures; he ordered new enzymes, amino acids, proteins and growth factors for the lab, erased the data from his computer and notes to eliminate prior prejudice, error, and miscalculation; he contacted Swissprot and Genpept and the European Molecular Biology Laboratory for any additional information on the protein motifs he was dealing with; he ran a full diagnostic on every set of protocols for the lab's HPLC in preparation for a new round of liquid chromatography; he duplicated the grids for a complete battery of electron microscopy; and in general reexamined every facet of the working hypothesis from every possible angle, looking for flaws.

Serotoxomiasin: What was it? That much was simple. Serotoxomiasin was a newly discovered peptide-derived chemical composition, produced by "the spot," that functioned within the neural anatomy as a transmitter. Neurotransmitters were fundamental components of the functionality of the brain. For any given circumstance, a person's thought processes and emotions were regulated and/or determined by the specific neurotransmitters released into the millions of synaptic clefts within the brain. Synapses were like little open circuits, tiny gaps that separated the dense chains of neurons that wired the brain and body together. When circumstances demanded a response—whether that response was as mundane as heading to the fridge for a snack or as impulsive as swerving off the road to avoid a wreck—various neurotransmitters would rush in and flood the gaps of open synapses, closing the circuit and generating a specific electrical impulse that the body translated into action or thought. Some neuro-transmitters were inhibitory, some excitatory, so the nature of the agent (or combination of agents) that closed the circuit determined the personality of the response. The resulting behavior depended only on what was being inhibited or excited—rage, pleasure, urgency, pain, relaxation, fear—and each of those were coded to specific combina-tions of chemical signals.

It was an immense field of study, pharmacology; the connections between neurotransmitters and the messages they carried were brand-new to science, fifty years old at best, and only beginning to be understood. For example, in recent tests conducted by a colleague of El-Saludin's, a gene essential to the production of the neurotransmitter nitric oxide was blocked in male lab rats. The absence of NO correlated to a marked increase in aggression and violent behavior in the rats affected, while the control group showed no changes in behavior what-soever. As such, it appeared that NO affected the emotion-regulating areas of the brain, perhaps by putting the brakes on aggressive male behavior.

But in *his* tests, El-Saludin had found that nearly every time sero-toxomiasin was released in a human brain, trace amounts of nitric oxide were also released, especially in males, while another neuro-transmitter, oxytocin, followed in females. Oxytocin was often called the "cuddle drug." It was the neurotransmitter most often found when a mother and child bonded, or when a woman felt "in love."

El-Saludin found this fascinating; he knew Western feminism would find it inflammatory. The findings would likely be described by extreme feminists as "oppressively patriarchal" and "hopelessly anti-quated," followed by highly publicized castigations of the research team. But El-Saludin knew what he knew. The facts didn't lie. Depending on circumstance, serotoxomiasin triggered additional levels of nitric oxide and oxytocin, respectively, in males and females who professed Christianity. At other times, testosterone or estrogen or vasopressin or acetylcholine or any one of multiple neurotransmitters accompanied serotoxomiasin—again, situation specific, but *only* in Christians, *only* in persons who bore the pineal gland anomaly; also, increased levels of serotonin had been measured across the board. Every human being possessed the other neurotransmitters and secreted them regularly. But Christians, apparently at the behest of serotoxomiasin, benefited from carefully calculated, additional secretions.

These were the indisputable facts Club Cranium had uncovered thus far. Additional correlations almost certainly remained; as yet, no definitive efforts had been made to examine the cognitive psychological effects, only the biological reality. A whole fleet of professional psychiatrists and neurologists and numerous studies would be necessary to trace the specifics in measurable terms. But taken as a whole, the weight of the research suggested to El-Saludin that serotoxomiasin's influence was more complex and far-reaching than previously considered. The evidence also suggested that, when combined with the predilections inherent to serotoxomiasin, the indirect cascade of regulatory efferents could only be called positive in its overall impact on the psyche. It was like a rinse cycle on a dishwasher. Parameters were reset. Synaptic links strengthened. Neural plasticity increased. Anger, melancholy, even blood pressure levels dropped. The mind, literally, was renewed. By serotoxomiasin.

By God.

Abu tried not to think in those terms. *Review, review! No assumptions. Ground Zero.*

What was known about SPoT, the ganglial cluster near the pineal, the source of the serotoxomiasin? The answer was up to Remming and Volgaard—their field. Remming was the one who discovered the presence of SPoT in the first place. Together, using MRI and Positron-Emission Tomography, he and Volgaard had examined the brains of more than two thousand patients. By cross-referencing their data in a quest to better understand neural signaling failures in Alzheimer's patients, a link began to emerge, the link to Christians.

Serendipity, they called it. Abu frowned. Serendipity was a matter of perspective. What was his perspective? In his heart he found doubt and terror and secret hope, nameless as of yet, formless, like a whisper in the dark of night. Hope that he denied vehemently. In his mind, only rage. Abu Hasim El-Saludin was a peaceable man by nature and by choice. Nevertheless, the thought of a God Spot had, in the last few weeks, drawn out an irrational and irrepressible anger.

What was this area of the brain made of? He knew already, had all of Volgaard's data right in front of him. The answer? Nothing extraordinary, really; just normal tissue, smaller than the size of a pea. Small enough to go undetected by more primitive equipment in years past, especially random as it must have seemed to anyone who might have noticed. And since the body made no attempt to reject the cluster as it would something pathological or cancerous, what was there to attract attention? There was no sort of inflammatory infiltration such as perivascular cuffing, glial transformation, or cytophagocytic cellular activity in evidence anywhere. In fact, Abu hearkened back to the images Rosenburg had sent him a few days ago. . . .

"Observe the way the cells seem to connect with . . . the surrounding tissue in a very invasive way. At least it seems invasive. Yet at each synapse there is a cytoplasmic projection from a normal neural cell . . . a groping for connection. It almost appears that this structure is forming a functional neural network. . . ."

A groping for connection. An embracing. El-Saludin stared at the images until his eyes blurred. The surrounding neural tissue was doing anything but rejecting SPoT. Quite the opposite, it almost seemed hungry for it, reaching toward it, clinging. Abu sighed, placed his palms on his closed eyes and rubbed fiercely. He turned to his computer, logged on to the Internet, typed in an address:

http://columbia.edu/cpmc/research/neurological/private/cc/stm55

Club Cranium's welcome screen appeared. He typed in the password, "Olympus," moving quickly to Remming's latest postings:

". . . SPoT is directing a functional reorientation of the local environment akin to the morphological changes that occur when neural schema form (i.e., memory acquisition, etc.). Quite simply, SPoT is reprogramming its local environment and it is doing so with the full consent of the surrounding tissue. How is this being accomplished? I cannot say. But I intend to focus my energies in determining both how it happens, and whether or not there are any negative consequences to this activity. . . ."

So SPoT was, in essence, procreating neural pathways, pathways that serotoxomiasin capitalized on with increased secretion levels and wider gateways to cortical functions. El-Saludin had already established that receptors for serotoxomiasin were all over the brain—in everyone, even unbelievers. Terminals were especially dense in the "higher" regions of the brain, those areas responsible for emotional and rational processes and sensory valuation, such as the prefrontal cortex, thalamus, hypothalamus, amygdala, pituitary and multiple related substructures. Areas like the cerebellum, pons, temporal lobe, and the nonlimbic portions of the basal ganglia—regions related to motor skills and simple cognition—were least saturated with receptors, sometimes even blank. But in those areas where receptors were present, the sensitivity and depth of the relay processes were extremely sophisticated.

Why?! How? And why was it only in Christians? Abu gnashed his teeth. The very word *Christian!* He had never hated the taste of the word before, but now . . . now it was sour and repugnant on his lips. He pushed away from his papers and desk, slumped down in his chair.

Where do we go from here? Where can we go? Where can I go?

Nowhere, came the answer. Back to the beginning. That was all he had to hold on to. He had yet to study children or babies to determine whether SPoT was present at birth or if it was introduced at some later stage of development. That was next. That was all.

Even so, what is it?

Abu didn't know, wasn't sure he wanted to know. The answer was a nameless voice in the dark. . . .

"Allah!" he whispered angrily. "Where are you? Why do you feel so far away?"

No reply, only the sudden ringing of the telephone. The sound was harsh in the silence, cold and metallic, mocking. Abu answered.

Remming greeted him with aloof courtesy, as if distracted or tired. "Abu, I'm afraid I have terrible news. I would have tried to reach you earlier but things have been so hectic. . . ."

"What is it, my friend?" Abu answered, glad for the diversion.

Remming took a deep breath. "Dr. Rosenburg is dead."

※ ※ ※

The stack of books piled on the library table was half as tall as Missy. Two stacks, actually. The fruit of long, bleary-eyed labor.

"Can I help you with *anything* else?" the librarian beside her asked, most insincerely, eyeballs sulking over the rim of his wire-frame spectacles. "We closed five minutes ago, you know."

Missy shook her head. The man had been pleasant to begin with; now he walked away exasperated. Missy had put him through the paces. She had spent the last four hours looking up everything she could think of; only problem was, for all her demands she didn't actually know what she was looking for.

No matter. She was done now, at least for tonight. Rising, she gathered a stack of books under each arm and headed for the checkout desk. The same librarian regarded her with a baleful expression from behind the counter.

"There is a twelve-book limit, you know."

"Twelve? Oh, no-no-no! That won't do. I need all these. All of them. I'm a journalist."

Silently, the man pointed to a large sign overhead. The sign read in big, bold letters: "Twelve-book limit. No exceptions."

"You can't be serious. I've spent all this time—"

"Rules are rules."

"But I really need the research. For a big story." She started fumbling through her purse for her press pass and ID. "I'm with the *Sentinel.*"

"Look, lady—"

"Why didn't you tell me earlier?" she finally blurted out. "About two hours ago? I need these books. I've had a hard day . . . a hard week actually. And I know *you've* had a hard day. So let's not quibble."

"My day was fine to begin with," the librarian said, lowering his voice. "Pick twelve. Then have a nice evening." He hunched over, one elbow on the counter, resolute.

Indignant, Missy set about narrowing her list of books quite randomly and melodramatically down to twelve, accompanied by much fuming and sighing and rolling of the eyes. Twelve books cut the number by about half and since she used little more than "gut feeling" for most every choice, it was hard to know whether or not she was throwing away exactly what she needed and keeping everything she did not.

Only one way to find out.

She pushed the books across the counter to the librarian. He groused low under his breath, stamping the books one after the other.

"Do you have a supervisor?" Missy asked, arms crossed. "I'd like to speak with him."

The man looked up.

Stamp!

Last book. He pushed the two stacks back to Missy.

"I *am* the supervisor," he replied acridly, then scuffled off to some other part of the library, presumably just to get away from her. Lights began shutting off. Missy huffed, fumbled for her books, and headed for the door.

It was going to be a long evening.

She had been on assignment covering some menial property dispute up around Mount Clemens when she drove by the library in the first place. Inspired, she soon found herself antsy to do a little research once her interviews were finished. Now with every passing mile Missy wished she would have just waited and tried a library a little closer to home. She lived a little north of the Ferndale district, which was just about due north of downtown, so on her way back from Mount Clemens she took I-94 south past Grosse Point Woods, heading west on Highway 102. She pulled into the first ATM she could find at a bank, and grabbed some cash for Chinese carryout, the only sure way to put herself in a better mood. The machine was cantankerous and slow, but eventually spat out a twenty-dollar bill and a receipt that read, "Thank you for choosing Michigan United Savings and Trust." She checked her balance. Not a lot, but more than enough cash to cover a large order of Moo-Goo Gai Pan from Wong's Tiger Lily—with extra water chestnuts—which meant knowingly subjecting herself to fifteen minutes of mouthwatering agony for the remainder of the drive home.

It was a little after nine o'clock by the time she had ordered and was on the road again—a slight detour was required—but it was a beautiful night, with stars high and bright and the pavement greased just slightly by the residue of the quick shower that had pelted Detroit earlier in the afternoon, right about the time Missy arrived at the library. There was little traffic at this time, in this part of town. Streetlights were sparse. The red, yellow, and green traffic signals congealed along the surface of the black asphalt into long, thin knives of color—the blinking silent gods of urban necessity. This was not a bad part of town; neither was it good. Missy watched the drifters on the street, the bums with paper sacks lifted upright to their lips; the working homeless who tried and failed every day to escape. Those who still tried were the recently devastated—that was how you could identify them—for most did not try at all. She drove slow, torturously slow, both for the smell of her food and the pageantry of the night. Countless hazy blue neon beer signs hung from the windows of a dozen different bars, their reflections swirling atop the oil-stained puddles of the gutter system before being devoured by nothing less than an absence of attention.

Missy had covered countless stories in parts like this all over Detroit, where mood was palpable and life unimportant. Ironically, a city's dark side—despair, angst, even habitual crime—when sufficiently filtered for the benefit of the middle and upper class, achieved a sort of literary romance, but only after the "mood" had trickled up a good bit. So for example, the residents of a city like Seattle, while boasting a free-spirited, artistic community, actually celebrated nothing more than the desperation of their youth, all rage and grunge, a generation that felt abandoned, abused, hopeless.

Missy knew better. She had seen the faces of Detroit, the blood, the crack, the children, the underworld of mafia crime and pornography; had seen it enough that she no longer needed to look further than her own mirror to have all the mood she could stomach.

Such was the charm of the big city.

A thousand good stories in the Motor Capital of the world. What Missy needed was a headliner.

Three hours, two chopsticks, and a greasy fork later (the chopsticks just didn't cut it), Missy sat alone in her small one-bedroom apartment, poring over twelve books, countless Internet postings, and another dozen or so periodicals. Every scrap of research, representing a wide, nearly schizophrenic range of hunches, lay strewn about on the carpet, the sofa, the kitchen table. One grand mess.

Her prevailing question was simple: Why was an infamous and much-loathed serial killer on death row undergoing extensive (and expensive) psychohypnotic therapy? And why was the CIA involved?

OK, two questions. Both branched into multiple possibilities.

Missy had already formulated a handful of scenarios, none of which panned out. She considered Ravelo's suggested explanations, too; but, while rooted in common sense, they sounded hollow. Too easy. Not surprisingly, lacking more substantive alternatives, Missy decided to chase the wildest rabbit of the bunch. . . .

There was a sort of logic to it—in the process, if not the final result. Missy had scanned the library's computer holdings for any references to both the CIA and hypnosis and had come up pleasantly surprised with the tally. More than twenty books total, including two compendiums of declassified government materials. Much more info than she expected.

Of the twelve books she had brought home, only four were related to this combination of themes. Four books, five periodicals, and eight or nine Internet files. Missy had never really used the Internet as a research tool before, but the amount of information available was staggering. The web was vast. Everyone—every angle, every agenda—had a voice. Most of it crackpot stuff, Missy figured. But oh my! with the validation of multiple sources, Missy was able to cull some amazing things from the pages. Unbelievable things, really. She had offhandedly mentioned similar readings to Ravelo without truly considering their ramifications. Enough to make the proudest patriot at least a little paranoid.

Apparently, government organizations ranging from NASA to all branches of the Defense Department, including the Central Intelligence Agency, the Defense Advanced Research Projects Agency, and the Office of Naval Intelligence, from about the forties on, had devoted significant resources into understanding . . . well, some really weird stuff. That was the only way to describe it. Stuff like the forced erasure of memory, hypnotic resistance to torture, powerful chemical and neural truth serums, and the limits of posthypnotic suggestion. Which was just the tip of the iceberg. Horrifically, "they" ran batteries of these experiments on college campuses. In prisons. Sometimes in small communities. Always with a perfectly reasonable cover story. "They" also solicited the services of brilliant researchers from major universities, from private CIA-sponsored facilities and independent think tanks, from military institutions such as Camp Lejeune Marine Core Base in North Carolina, the Walter Reed Military Hospital in Maryland, and Fort Detrick, the highly classified top-secret compound positioned within spitting distance of the National Institute of Health in Washington, D.C., just to name a few.

Historically, World War II was the primary provocateur of these clandestine efforts. The government supposedly needed every edge it could muster against the enemy. Thus, the second "War to End All Wars" actually became the first conflict for the human brain as battlefield, with invading forces comprised of white-lab-coated intellectuals, not military green. Among these men were some of the most notable names in psychology and pharmacology at the time. The goal? To modify human perception and behavior through secondary means. Their arsenal ran the gamut, including scopolamine, peyote, barbiturates, mescaline, and marijuana. General William "Wild Bill" Donovan, director of the OSS, tasked his crack team—including Dr. Winifred Overhulser, Dr. Edward Strecker, Harry J. Anslinger, and George White—with finding a "truth drug" for use in interrogating prisoners.

And so it went, page after page. "Wild Bill" spearheaded one of multiple early efforts and, along with another fellow named George Estabrooks, was that proverbial snowball at the top of the mountain, slowly rolling downhill. Other research sought to manipulate and control through the rapid induction of hypnotic states, non-ionizing radiation, microwave induction of intracerebral "voices," electronic stimulation of the brain (with little machines that would be laughable by today's standards if the implications of their limited success were not so terrifying), and a host of even more disturbing technologies. Missy was shocked by what she read. It was like a twisted James Bond spy novel, except that the bad guys with leering smiles were no longer the cherished communist demagogues of the Cold War. No, these demagogues were polished, respectable American professionals— scientists and military leaders, politicians and doctors, supposedly working to protect *us* from the communists.

Unfortunately, the boundaries did not always remain so clear. Civilian casualties—intentional, with full knowledge—and unlicensed research, clearly abusive, autocratic, were well documented. And those were just the cases Missy could get her hands on. To make matters even creepier, the various projects involving mind control—all of them with CIA links to hypnosis research or other related fields—bore arcane code names like any other clandestine operation. There was Project Artichoke and Pandora, Derby Hat, and the infamous MK series: MKDelta, MKSearch, and the most far-reaching of them all, MKUltra.

Missy scanned Martin Lee and Bruce Schlain's book, *Acid Dreams*. She read *Megabrain*, by Michael Hutchison. She pored over a fascinating document labeled *Individual Rights and the Federal Role in Behavior Modification*, officially prepared by the Staff of the Subcommittee on Constitutional Rights of the Committee of the Judiciary, United States Senate. She studied the recorded hearings before the Subcommittee on Health and Scientific Research, which investigated human drug testing and the CIA.

Officially, all research along these lines ended back in the seventies. But inside sources quoted in her books clearly stated otherwise. One, a CIA defector who wrote a scathing exposé of the agency, said flat out that the Senate panel hearings back in the seventies were nothing more than smoke-and-mirrors games involving perjured testimony and disinformation, campaigns designed to diffuse public awareness. By short-circuiting the engine of political oversight and offering tepid apologies to reassure the small minority of public that bothered to tune in, the CIA freed itself and its multiple research sites to fully capitalize on the groundbreaking discoveries made over the previous three decades. In short, the stuff was still happening, despite protests to the contrary, and probably on an incomprehensible scale, considering the explosive advances of modern biology, genetics, and medical technologies in the last ten or twelve years.

Luther must be a part of the present research, somehow. Or at least he was. . . .

So thought Missy. It was a juicy bit of speculation that didn't really have a beginning or an end as of yet, nor for that matter much of a middle. But it stuck with her. A little wobbly, sure, like a tightrope dance over facts and truth, but it *felt* right. Something just felt right. No positive links to Luther. Not even a smidgen of anything that might objectively rank higher than circumstantial gossip, really. But the bulk of the materials splayed out across her apartment was surprisingly thorough. Credible. Well documented. And all the stories overlapped. She wasn't reading the lone ravings of a single madman. If they were madmen at all, they shared a plurality of voice. The main strike against them was not actually the severity of the material, but rather the age. The books were a few years old now—ten or more. Still, at least at one time, they meant something.

What she needed was a local source. A present-day informer. Missy smiled. Maybe the chance was falling upon her to make these stories mean something once again. Something big. She kept reading, making notes, scribbling and brainstorming, cross-referencing, comparing everything she uncovered to what she did and did not know about Luther. Some of it just didn't match, no matter how hard she tried to make it. But more important . . .

Some of it did.

Half an hour later, Missy could hardly stay awake. It was about one o'clock. She had already set aside the books and files and magazines and slumped down on the sofa with the half-light of a single lamp to see by. Now all she did was stare, bleary-eyed, at the scrap of paper Luther had entrusted to Father Ravelo. And he to her. The numbers were so jumbled and disparate it was hard to believe they meant anything at all.

102354. 102354.

mustbe102354.

What must be? What was it? A birthday? A historical event? A lottery number?

It could be anything! Anything! No. Must be one thing. Must be what?

Maybe a license plate? Missy thought sleepily. *Or maybe a date.*

October 23, 1954.

Fifty-four.

Fifty-four.

Maybe Luther had been trying to point Ravelo to some of the very research she had been studying. It was definitely the right time frame.

Maybe something happened on that particular date that would later have affected him.

In the womb, Luther had said. *The man was there all along, in the womb.*

Maybe it was a clue.

Maybe not.

Missy had found nothing that mentioned that date specifically. Of course, neither had she checked out nearly all of the sources she had located. Regardless, it was too late to ponder these things. Her thinking was blurry, her eyelids felt like lead weights. She tried in vain to focus. All that remained for contemplation was the lingering smell of the Moo-Goo Gai Pan, the onions and cabbage and chicken. She could concentrate on nothing but the rich aroma of the food. She stared again at the scrap of paper . . .

mustbe102354

. . . and fell asleep with the sorrowful images of the city wrangling through her brain, of the library and the gaudy colors along the drive home, and of the many wandering bodies drifting up and down the street. Her last cogent thought: *What—who—must be?*

She awoke to the crash of thunder with a single thought:

The bank! It's the bank!

Michigan United Savings and Trust.

Of course! It was so simple! Missy lay on the couch for a moment or two, eyes wide, paralyzed by her own epiphany. Then, prodded by the next blast of lightning, she sprang out of the sofa, scrambled to her feet, using her fingers like a comb on the tangles of her fine, limp hair, flapping her hands with excitement. She glanced at the clock on the wall: a little after seven o'clock. The bank opened at 7:30. Or was it 8:00? Missy didn't care.

Outside, the full force of spring was sweeping up from the south and west, but only in the most technical sense. While the sky erupted from the horizon with the flash and vigor of the times, rolling overhead like a giant crag of black granite, the smell of the weather was winter stale, lacking the freshness and vitality and that certain sense of *esprit de corps* that heralds the breathless hope of green grass and blue skies. Instead, this storm was just wetness and noise and sheets of slate gray. The rain falling against Missy's windows was cheerless. Umbrellas lined the sidewalk below, bobbing and weaving, but even the brightest of them lacked color. And climbing up from the concrete floor of the city, all eyes and no mouth, the stone and brick buildings and glass-faced skyscrapers of Detroit appeared dark and somber against the backdrop of the rumbling storm.

It was, in short, another dreary northern morning.

Not dreary enough to dampen Missy's spirits, however. She was busy tearing off the clothes she had fallen asleep in, throwing on a different pair of pants and shirt. She spent five minutes in front of the bathroom mirror freshening up, gargling mouthwash, scrubbing her face, etc. No makeup; Missy rarely used makeup—just a little bit of eyeliner and pale-colored lipstick. She made sure she looked presentable, then grabbed a Pop-Tart and her car keys and—

Had another brainstorm. The simplest, easiest way to see if she was right. Missy grabbed the phone book out of the drawer by her telephone, opened it up to the white pages, thumbed through the alphabet . . . H-I-J-K-L-M . . . down, down, next page, there!

Michigan United Savings and Trust.

Sixteen locations in the greater metropolitan area. She scanned them all. Sure enough, the ninth location listed was at *Barlow and East 102*! Probably the very one she had used last night. Missy clapped her hand over her mouth.

This had to be it. It had to be. Michigan United Savings and Trust, Barlow and East 102, number 354. But what was "354"? Missy couldn't slow down long enough to think about it. Probably some sort of account number or safety deposit box ID at that location. It didn't matter; she would find out when she got there.

Giddy, she headed out the door.

14

I'm sorry, ma'am," the teller said. "I don't see a Mrs. Ellen Sanchez on any of our forms. You're not on our authorized access card, either. For whatever reason, your husband did not include you."

Missy feigned shock. She was a decent actress when she needed to be. "Oh, of course he did! There must be some mistake. I came here with him myself. Of course I was handling some other paperwork if I recall correctly. . . . Could you just check your files again please?"

The teller was a younger lady, sweet, bordering on naive by Missy's reckoning. She clicked on the keyboard a few times and stared at her monitor. Clicked again and stared. Missy drummed the countertop lightly, trying to appear frumpy and unorganized, which wasn't too much of a stretch.

"I'm really sorry, Mrs. Sanchez, but you aren't showing up on the approved list." She scanned one more screen. "It looks like it wouldn't matter anyway. The account has been closed."

"Closed?" Missy asked. "What do you mean?"

"The latest information I have here says a Dr. Buck Keegan came and emptied out box number 354 two days ago. Your husband's account is no longer active. I'm sorry, but there is nothing I can do." She smiled sympathetically.

Doctor? Missy thought, maintaining a pasty show of teeth. Behind her lips those same teeth were grinding. So close! She was so close! She looked around. The bank was not too busy yet, so . . .

"Buck?" she blurted out suddenly. "You mean Bucky? I had no idea he was even alive anymore. Well, I declare! I haven't seen Bucky in what? Four, five years? He had cancer, you know, several years ago." Missy leaned over the counter, dropped her voice to a whisper. "Testicular cancer, I think. Horrible. Just horrible."

She gave the teller a knowing glance. The poor woman looked nervously from side to side to see if anyone else was listening. This was not the usual exchange between customer and provider.

"And as if things couldn't get any worse, his wife left him for it," Missy added ruefully.

Apparently born with a heart full of goodness, the bank lady recoiled at the thought of such a heartless wife. Missy pressed in. "Took the kids, too. The house. The cars. Even the dog. Just left poor old Buck with a few clothes and a stray cat."

It was all a lie, of course, but the teller—bless her gracious young soul—was moved just the same. She put a hand to her mouth, stared at Missy, waiting for more. Missy said, "I guess he must still be living down in West Bend. It's terrible to lose touch like that. I just feel awful! Back when Luther and I were having problems, Buck stuck with us. And then we just let him drop out of sight with that cancer and all. Last I heard he went to find healing in nature or something. Then I thought he died. . . ."

She turned to go, letting her story drift off into silence. The teller stood like a statue behind her, unspeaking. After two or three steps, Missy whirled about, bright-eyed with hope. "You wouldn't happen to have a phone number for him, would you? In your files? He should still be in West Bend. . . ."

She was freewheeling it in grand style now. Completely flustered, the teller looked again at the computer. "Umm—" *Click, click.* "We don't have a listing in West Bend. The latest address we show is in New Hudson—"

"New Hudson!" Missy declared, thumping the countertop. "Why sure! That was Buck's summer home way back when. Do you have a phone number there?"

"I'm really sorry. I'd like to help you, but I shouldn't be giving out this information at all."

Missy was agreeable. "Oh, sure. I don't want to get you in trouble or anything. Thanks so much. I'll just be on my way."

"Ma'am," the teller muttered as Missy turned to go. Her voice faltered. "Are you *the* Luther Sanchez's wife?"

Missy looked blank faced. "You mean the killer?" she cried. "Heavens, no!"

"I'm sorry. That was rude of me. So sorry. Have a nice day."

Missy left the building. *Very nice,* she thought. *Once I make it to New Hudson.*

⊗ ⊗ ⊗

"There is no God but Allah" came the familiar greeting from the man in the middle of the swath of burnished yellow sunlight. He sat with legs crossed on an ornamental rug in the center of a vast, domed room located along the eastern face of the mosque. The chamber dome was white marble, polished to a sheen, etched with long, flowing passages from the Koran; the walls and ceiling were intricate webs of colored tile. Along the eastern wall towered four open-air columns, beyond which could be seen the older sections of the city of Cairo. It was a lovely place, with a serenity matched only by the wrinkled smile on the older man's face.

"No God but Allah," answered Abu Hasim El-Saludin. "And Mohammed is his prophet. How are you today, Yassef?"

The older man nodded pleasantly and beckoned Abu to come closer. Yassef Adonijah was a holy man and longtime friend of Abu's. Abu glided toward the center of the room and took his place on the rug beside the man, reclining on one elbow. He closed his eyes and soaked in the warmth.

"You are troubled, my friend," Yassef declared at length, regarding Abu with care.

"No, no. Just relaxing."

"If you wish."

Abu opened one eye, turned it toward the priest. "You think otherwise?"

"I see your heart in the falseness of your smile. You are hiding."

Abu stared into the cloudless sky, feeling the hot sun grow heavy against his skin. Thankfully, Yassef did not press the issue. He wasn't truly a priest, at least not in the Western sense of the word, since Islam did not make provision for a formal priesthood. Rather, he was the chief *Imam* of this ancient Egyptian mosque, the man privileged to lead the people in daily prayers—the chief officer of worship. He was also a professor of high rank at the ancient University of Al-Azhar, the theological center of Islamic intellectualism.

El-Saludin began to smooth out the wrinkles in his robe. "You are my friend, are you not, Yassef Adonijah?"

"I am."

"Why? Why are you my friend? What of the Jews? And the Christians and pagans? Are they my friends?"

Yassef tugged at the long, graying hairs of his beard. His answer was simple. "They are the children of Allah. All of creation is the breath of Allah."

"So we are brothers, the pagan and I?"

"The pagan is doomed to hell. Though he is Allah's child, he has cursed the holy name of Allah."

"And the Christian?"

Yassef answered slowly. "Allah spoke to them once, but they failed to heed his commands. They ignored the prophets. So he sent Mohammed as the final messenger. In the span of history, there has always been truth. But there is truth and then there is Truth. We are graced by Allah with Truth. All else is superstition."

Abu sat up straight, fixing the holy man with hungry, needy eyes. "Restore me, Yassef. I beg of you, give me the Truth of Allah."

Yassef smiled. "I am honored to serve you in such a way as this," he said. And then from memory he began to recite long passages of the holy book, letting his gravelly voice drone like the sound of crickets at night when the moon is low:

> *Blessed be Allah, and Mohammed!*
> *Thy servant and messenger, the unlettered prophet!*
> *Why do you weep, oh people of Allah*
> *Or give salt to your eyes?*

Wherever there is ruin, there is hope for a treasure
Why do you not seek the treasure of Allah in the wasted heart?
And if he closes before you all the ways and passes
He will show a hidden way which nobody knows. . . .

Abu listened. He listened closely. But his heart was not lifted.

☷ ☷ ☷

"Thanks for listening, Father," the elderly woman said, rising.

Ravelo had been doing anything but listening. He had heard all the words and nodded and managed to tap the eraser of his pencil on the desktop repeatedly when such a response seemed appropriate. He had even focused his eyes in the right direction and at the right depth. But ninety-five percent of Ravelo's brain activity was concentrated about four levels below the state of conscious participation. In the basement of his subconscious, the priest was riddle hunting.

Briefly, he surfaced.

The lady made some other small gesture, said something affectionate or grateful. He smiled politely, watched her gain her balance, bid him good day, and shuffle for the door, her small purse hanging from the hook of one finger. He knew her name. She was a dear old woman. A dear old woman. Mrs . . . Something.

She came in once a week. Just to talk. About anything. She was a widow. Four children and a gaggle of grandchildren and great-grandchildren. She was the kind of proud senior who didn't like to be helped out of her chair or treated in a manner befitting her age, which had taken Ravelo a few sessions to fully understand. Ravelo really *did* know her well. And he usually listened respectfully. At the moment he couldn't remember her name if his life depended on it.

All he could think about—present tense and past (as in all day today and all of yesterday and all throughout Mrs. What's-Her-Face's monologue)—was Ricky Carletti. Did Ricky actually murder Dr. T. Samual Rosenburg? It was difficult for Ravelo to believe otherwise, what with the ring and the address and all. But what was this line about the CIA requesting the hit? What would the CIA have against

Rosenburg? And why resort to murder? Even more, why employ the mafia to do their dirty work?

Too many loose ends, Ravelo thought. *Too much of a stretch.*

It wasn't the first time he had reached that conclusion. The priest had mentally reviewed this information dozens of times: this angle, that angle, every angle, skeptical to the core. Nonetheless, he could not dismiss the obvious: a bloody ring, a bloody piece of paper, a dead Jewish man.

Oh yes, and a confession.

That part made Ravelo angry, even a little afraid. What was he supposed to do with this confession? He was bound by a solemn oath. To turn state's evidence against a confessor using that person's voluntary admission of sin would violate not only his priestly office but also the gift of trust implicit in an individual's pursuit of redemption. The confessional relationship was not just theology or history; it was *tradition.* And tradition was not a thing to be taken lightly.

Slow down, Ravelo thought tersely. *The pope's not going to phone me some Friday night and scold me in Latin. I'm not the first priest this has happened to. It's nothing new. Quit whining. . . .*

Maybe it had happened to others, but never to him. Ravelo wanted no part of bad faith. Neither did he want a dead man on his conscience. He knew he needed to get involved—the police still had no significant leads according to the news. But how?

No easy answers there. Could he balance the act of confession with the need for justice? Sort of have his cake and at least nibble a bite or two? Maybe there was a way to point the police in the right direction without actually involving Carletti.

Not a chance with fingerprints, blood types, DNA testing . . .

Carletti had a record. And once the police sniffed his lead they wouldn't give a flip about clerical immunity or time-honored traditions. Ravelo might even be forced to testify at Ricky's trial. Talk about bad press for the church! After that scandal, parishioners all over Detroit would find confession about as appealing as ritual scarring.

What's more, if Ravelo ratted and Carletti was ever caught, it would be his word that put him behind bars, no matter how obtuse or hypothetical Ravelo made his report to the authorities. Angrily, he

thumped his desk with his fist. At his core, Ravelo was far more interested in spiritual purification than legal entanglement.

This is simply beyond the scope of my office. . . .

Lacking any better direction, he gathered his overcoat and hat,
headed out the door, got in his car, and headed for 321 West Lafayette
to try to catch Missy Jenkins at the *Detroit Sentinel.* It wasn't a great
idea, not even a good one. It was simply the only idea he had.

The *Sentinel* was nothing more than a thinly disguised excuse for
a rat maze, as Ravelo soon found out. Cubicle after cubicle was packed
into a littered, paper-strewn tangle of people hunched over clattering
keyboards or poring over the latest wire feeds—graphic designers, pho-
tographers, writers, editors—people on phones, shouting, demanding,
coaxing; one grand discombobulated mess. The whole affair called to
mind some spontaneous act of creation: organic, fluid, explosive,
extracting a random sort of order from the gurgling fount of absolute
chaos, though never in convincing fashion. Nevertheless, between the
lights and vast computer network, the broad, wall-size assignment
boards and the whole row of clocks with numerous global time zones,
Ravelo was duly impressed. The office re-created itself each moment
on little more than the momentum of the previous moment.

As instructed by the lady at the front desk, Ravelo adjusted his
bearings and began wading through the morass of chin-high partitions
in the direction of Missy's "office." People to his left and right wheeled
their chairs from one cubicle to the next, double-checking facts or jaw-
ing with colleagues. The diversity of the staff was striking: young and
old; bearded hippies; fresh-faced shirt-and-tie types; black, white,
Hispanic, Asian; women in dresses or ragged blue jeans or, occasionally,
a little slip of a skirt that could hardly pass for business attire.

Amazing! Ravelo instantly loved them all, even the angry and ugly
ones. It seemed a shame for such beautiful people to waste themselves
on something as ignoble as the modern American press. With a little
help he found Missy's cubicle; it was empty. He turned to the nearest
person.

"Umm, excuse me, do you know where I could find Ms. Jenkins?"

The woman he directed this question to was maybe thirty, maybe
forty, with a big poof of black coiffed hair and heavy eyeliner, hearkening

back in style to the days of disco. She was on the phone, actually, but paused long enough to answer, "Not in. She'll be back."

She quickly resumed talking but, when Ravelo did not move, turned to him again, mouth slightly open in a semipolite "Can't-you-figure-it-out?" manner and pointed to a chair cramped in the corner of Missy's already overcrowded five-by-five.

"Have a seat."

Ravelo obeyed. He sat and sat and sat, but Missy did not return. Fifteen minutes passed, then twenty. Finally, he asked the lady again (she was no longer on the phone), "Do you know approximately when Ms. Jenkins will return?"

The lady chewed on a piece of gum, rolled her eyes, did not look up. "Soon."

So Ravelo folded his hands in his lap and waited a little longer as the morning idled by. People marched along in the hall beside him in a steady stream, some of them running, most of them carrying fistfuls of papers in their hands, or maybe photo proofs or galley sheets. Several writers seemed to be clustered in the wing surrounding Missy's office because Ravelo heard a constant stream of story chatter: this lead, that case, this scoop, that headline. *What about the jumper? . . . how about this quote? . . . what's the kicker for page one? . . . fingerprints all over the window . . . bumped me to seven, can you believe it? . . . lousy lead, change it! . . . too much rambling . . . tone it down a bit. . . .* Scandals in City Hall, pollution in the Detroit River, a drive-by shooting in the parking lot of Fretter's, some humongous sale at Hudson's, arson, rape, a smattering of international affairs, and some high-profile local divorce summed up the day's fare. Ravelo tuned most of it out, which was about as easy to do as ignoring a machine gun fired from the room next to you. Still, he tried.

A couple of friendly types drifted by, asking if they could help. He told them he was waiting for Missy. Their answer was universally the same: "Oh, she should be back any minute."

In fact, it was a minute later. Many minutes. Almost another hour of minutes from the time he'd arrived.

§ § §

In New York City, the phone rang in Jay Remming's office. His slender, dark-skinned hand darted for the receiver.

"Remming."

Jay Remming, M.D., Ph.D., had been poring over the God Spot data stored on his system—the very data Hank had stolen. Classified material. He wanted to know exactly what Hank had landed.

To which the answer was, basically everything.

No, no. Not everything, Remming realized. *Almost* everything. Still, it was a disaster in the making. That was when the phone rang. At first, no one responded to his greeting.

"Hello?" Remming said again.

"Your security measures leave much to be desired," replied a thick, murky voice from the other end of the line. Remming did not recognize the voice.

"Who is this?" he demanded.

"Who I am is not important. What you do is what I am. That's my job. Do you understand?" It was a powerful, hypnotic voice—impossibly contrived, as if passing through some sort of digital warping filter that lowered the tenor of the voice into subwoofer levels and gave it just enough scratch to possess menace. Nearly monotone, emotionless, the voice nonetheless possessed a rhythm as affecting as a heartbeat, like the steady thumping of a bass guitar.

But it was not contrived. The voice was disturbingly real. Remming heard the slightly labored breath behind every word. Probably a two-pack-a-day chain-smoker of twenty years or more.

"You must have the wrong number," he said and quickly hung up.

Three seconds passed. Five seconds.

R-I-I-I-I-N-G-G-G!

Remming answered. "What do you want?"

"First, don't *ever* do that again."

Remming closed his eyes, took a deep breath; he did not try to hide his irritation when he said, "I don't have time for games! Tell me who you are. And what you want."

The monotone voice throbbed. "Oh, I disagree. Apparently this is nothing *but* a game to you or you would not have been so sloppy. But to the first question, I am a messenger. As for the second, I want the very simplest of things. I want some assurance that the recent crisis—debacle, really—has been brought under the severe hand of your control. I want some assurance that the significant resources we have contributed will be quickly brought to fruition. I want some assurance that additional leaks have been unilaterally eliminated not just from the realm of possibility, but even from the realm of conceptualization. I ask for nothing you are not amply capable of providing. Merely assurance."

Remming had dealt with strong-arm tactics from politicians and three-star generals numerous times before. If he could tolerate ilk like Susan Decker, he could manage any situation. But today he was on edge and *this* man almost pushed too far. His patience for condescension had long ago run out. He was sick and tired of the arbitrary orders of others, of shoulder gazing, of academic philistines constantly challenging the direction and authority of his work, and of nonacademic autocrats like Susan Decker and this guy, Monitor Whatever, individuals who most likely barely escaped high school chemistry with a B– deigning to instruct him as he pioneered methodologies too advanced even for the journals. Most of all, he was tired of orders and those who presumed to be order givers, of which there seemed to be a preponderance lately. Nevertheless, Remming was no fool. He had no idea who this person was or whom he represented, but he was obviously part of the loop, so he picked his words carefully.

"This is a highly unorthodox method of—"

"Assurances, Dr. Remming."

"Who do you represent?" Remming cried. "What is your name? Your superior's name?"

The voice whispered, "Assurances."

"Fine. I assure you."

"Good," the man answered. "That is all I needed. No need for conflict. We are on the same side, Dr. Remming."

"No!" Remming said with force. "I am not on any side. I am a scientist. I don't even know who you are."

The meaty voice grew scornful. "Come now, Dr. Remming. A man of your sophistication is not persuaded by such naiveté, is he? We *all* take sides. You should know better than anyone that the ivory tower of scientific neutrality has collapsed, if indeed it ever existed."

Remming's eyes narrowed. "Are you challenging my integrity?"

"No, no. Just dabbling, speculating."

"Rambling."

"Probably. Call me philosophically challenged, if you like. Or maybe you are the challenged one? Because I know quite well that the modern world has passed and the postmodern world does not tolerate the vacuum of indifference. Every decision we make constitutes an allegiance of sorts. Nevertheless, think what you will."

The voice trailed off into silence, tempting Remming to refute the accusation. Instead, he did nothing, rubbed his eyes, waited, grinding his molars together like a dog on a leash. Which, at that moment, seemed a fitting metaphor. In the end he could not restrain himself from one brief stab.

"Don't you people already have one mole assigned to this post?"

The man breathed heavily into the phone. At length he murmured, "I had thought our long correspondence would breed more respect for those I represent. I see now that is not the case."

Remming rolled his eyes, pulled the phone away from his ear, and glanced wearily around the room. Games! All these games! He pressed the flat of his thumb against the space between his eyes, boring against the bone of his brow, bringing focus, focus, measure by measure. He wanted to shout, to wrangle something. Instead, focus . . .

"Monitor Nine," he breathed, as realization came. "Of course."

The man seemed pleased.

"Well met, Dr. Remming! We speak face-to-face for the first time."

"Not quite."

"Near enough, I think."

"Do you have another name?" Remming asked. "A real name? Or shall I call you Mr. Nine?"

"You shall not *call* me at all; therefore you have no need of my name. Monitor Nine will do."

Whatever. The cloak-and-dagger routine felt strained and unnecessary. But no doubt, GA had its reasons. And since it was their money financing this campaign . . .

Monitor Nine continued. "We have need of you at a priority facility in Central America. On the bookshelf behind you; are you looking?"

Remming turned, unsure. "Yes."

"Remove the volume of Blake's collected works. The large one, red sleeve, in the middle. Blake is your favorite poet, is he not?"

Remming raised a wary finger to the spine of the heavy book and removed it from the shelf. "Blake was a dreamer," he said simply.

"*Is* a dreamer, don't you think?"

"The man is dead."

"Ah, so we've drifted into cynicism at last," Monitor Nine said, clucking his tongue. His voice rolled on, ponderous and deliberate, like a muddy river winding lazily through valley after valley on its way to the ocean. "It wasn't always this way, was it? If I recall correctly, you yourself said Blake's poetry was for you an eternal thing, that 'sorrow and vision and metaphor, in the skilled hands of genius, become dreamlike with life, like the thoughts of gods to mortal men.'"

Wary, but remembering, Remming said. "The *New Yorker* interview?"

"May 1989. A rare bit of poetry yourself if I do say so, Dr. Remming. Of course, those were better times. How is Anna now? And young Josh?"

Remming was not smiling. "So I have a fan."

Monitor Nine chuckled, a very unpleasant sound. "Oh, most certainly. We are all terribly impressed with you. But back to business! On page 205 you'll find a first-class ticket to Mexico City. Barring unforeseen difficulties, your colleagues, Dr. Volgaard and Dr. El-Saludin, will rendezvous with you at the site. Our schedules have compressed, Dr. Remming. Time is of the essence—"

"This is ridiculous. I'm not just going to jump on some plane without a few answers first! What is going on? Hello?"

The line was dead. Fuming, Remming turned to page 205. An envelope fell to the floor. He stooped to pick it up, opened the flap. Inside: a first-class ticket. JFK International. Flight 344, departing at 7:35 p.m., Gate 29.

Tonight.

For the first time, Remming was afraid.

15

I need more support!" Susan Decker growled. Her grip on the phone was viselike. "Don't hang me out to dry, Nix! Surveillance is nil. I can't manage both of these at once. And Blackaby has the files."

Nix was dismissive. "He's bluffing."

Susan swore, pounded the table. "Shut up and listen to me! My career is on the line if either of these assignments goes south. Now maybe that's what you want . . . maybe that's why you assigned them to me in the first place, but you're dumber than I thought if you think I'm just going to roll over and play dead!"

"You are way out of line, Agent Decker! Your career is on the line? How about my head on the chopping block because of your sloppy vigilante tactics!"

"I did what I had to do," Decker said. Then she snickered. "How it affected you is just a bonus."

"You had no authority to move on Rosenburg and you know it!" Nix shouted into the receiver, red-faced. "Rosenburg has personal friends at the Agency, friends of high rank! And for the last three days they've been closer to me than a bad case of gas demanding the immediate termination of your career with the CIA!"

"Calmly now. This isn't a secured line." Then she softened a little. "They wanted results; I gave them to them. It's that simple."

"No, it's not that simple. Do you know that the only thing keeping you afloat right now is me? For some reason which completely escapes me at the moment, I've told them repeatedly that you're the best we've got. But you're walking a razor-thin line and I'm not climbing the ladder again to steady you. You want to self-destruct, fine. Just go through the proper channels along the way."

Both of them fell into steaming silence after that. Nix was Greek. He lost his cool all the time. On the other end of the line, Decker twirled a pencil between her fingers, eyes narrowed, hungry for more. Time passed. The tension eased, but only a little.

"The O'Connel case will blow over," Nix said at length. "It's not a priority right now. You just need to focus on the SPoT project and make sure this hotshot Blackaby doesn't cause any more problems. Got that?"

"No, I don't *get* that. This is not a good time to ignore Seventeen. Call it a gut feeling, but I think we need to keep an eye on her. She's feisty. This whole thing could blow up in our faces any minute."

"It blew up when you got trigger happy," Nix replied evenly. "And because you took your eye off the big ball—Remming. Leave the little ball alone."

Decker pulled her lips back, exposing long rows of perfectly white teeth. In contrast, her tone grew ever sweeter, softer, like silk on naked skin. "You're making a big mistake, Nix. Big. This is a critical time. She's one of the few normal ones left."

"I have taken your remarks under advisement. Now, will that—"

"I want it in the files," Decker said.

"What?"

"I want you to post my opposition to this decision in my file."

"Fine."

"Fine."

"Consider it done."

Decker laughed, taunting. "You know, none of this surprises me. I didn't really expect you to have the guts to make an executive decision on this scale."

"Agent Decker, I advise you to retract that statement immediately. I'm *this* close to marking your permanent record with insubordination."

Insubordination? Decker mused, but she didn't react, didn't utter a word, didn't even breathe. She just waited, knowing the silence worked in her favor, knowing Nix squirmed whenever someone was quiet. Still, she was on the losing end; she knew that fact all too well and it enraged her. Silence was her *only* weapon. Starting with "Hello," this whole conversation had gone from bad to worse. But there were reasons. . . .

"Insubordination?" she finally said, amused at the taste of the word. "Or insu-*bed*-ination? Tell me, Nix. Just because you've clawed your way to the top, does that mean you can keep shafting the people you shafted to get there?"

Nix ground his teeth together. It was a long, boring story, but Decker could tell he was nervous, as if discussing this subject were the same as announcing it over the Agency's intercom. "I did everything I could to rectify that situation and you know it, Susan."

"Of course, darling! Meanwhile, I'm withdrawn from my post in France, reprimanded, then assigned to this shtick, shuffling paperwork and logging the work habits and personal quirks of a bunch of research blunders born in 1969. And you're promoted to the supervising post I was due for. But you say you've rectified the situation? Good, I feel so much better."

"Not blunders," Nix corrected.

"Study group, whatever. They're freaks."

"*Classified* research. Don't you see? Remming's SPoT project is the direct inheritor of these prior efforts. That's why you're following both, the old and the new. It's a promotion, really. We have orders from the highest levels to assure the success of this research. You were specifically requested for this post."

Decker smirked. "Don't patronize me, Nix. Just give me the manpower I need."

"I have," Nix said. "You."

Decker cursed pure vitriol. Nix continued. "You've got me curious. If you hate this assignment so much, why bother?"

Decker had long prepared for that question. She drew her answer out long and slow for maximum effect. "Because I know what a promise from you is worth, Nix. And I refuse to be your fall guy ever again in this lifetime. *And* because I like to do things right. Something you wouldn't understand."

Which brought playtime to a close. "I'm sorry for the bad blood between us, Agent Decker. I truly am. The whole affair, no pun intended, was a mistake on both our parts. But the present situation is very simple. You have your orders and I have mine. *Kapiche?*"

"And you want me to ignore Seventeen?"

"I promise you, we will resume tracking Jessica later."

"It's a mistake."

"It's a fact! Every department of this agency has been pared to the bone by budget cuts! I'm running this operation on rubber bands and Twinkies, and rumor has it more cuts are coming. You do the math. That leaves me with just rubber bands. So I'm telling you for the last time: We do *not* have the manpower to divert. In fact, if you must know, there is talk of scrapping all domestic projects over fifteen years old. Across the board. Chop! But Remming's project is Level Three. It's active and highly classified. That means job security for you, Decker, if you can get your act together and knock that chip off your shoulder! Do you hear what I'm telling you?"

He waited for a response.

"Loud and clear," Decker replied.

"I'll tell you one other thing and this one's off the record. Call it guilt, penance, call it professional objectivity—call it whatever you want. But in spite of everything, in spite of how mad I am right now and how big of a mess you've made up to this point, you stick with the big dog on this and pull it off and you can write your own ticket."

"Just one agent," Decker whispered, begging. "Just for a couple days. That's all I need."

"If I had a one-handed blind man to spare, he would be yours! But I don't. Deal with it."

Click.

Decker hung up the phone, stared into the shell of her hotel room, her makeshift office, her life. The PC laptop on the rumpled sheets of her bed flickered green and blue with some annoying screen saver. The interior of the room smelled stale. The drapes were dingy.

She hated Nix. She had loved him once. For six months they had a secret, whirlwind office romance that spanned two continents and several conveniently arranged "business" meetings in America and

Europe. Then a position came open that they both wanted. Things got tangled. Decker yielded for his sake. Things got more tangled. And then Nix's first duty was to overhaul his department and bring some of the more unruly operatives under tow. Specifically cited: Agent Susan Decker.

It was not a pretty picture.

Five minutes later she was on the phone again.

A pleasant-sounding man answered. She said, "Jack, I need a favor."

"Name it. Are you in town?"

"For a few days. Listen, can you give me some space? Clear out an office for me? Nothing special, just enough to look official."

"Why? What's the game?"

"I can't say."

Jack retreated. "I don't know, Susan. Why not go through the proper channels?"

Decker forgave him for that. "I don't have time," she said. "The Agency would stonewall me. It's official business, Jack. All aboveboard. I just need a place to shack up until my hunch is proved. Two or three days, tops."

Still, Jack hesitated.

"You owe me," Susan reminded him, using a flirtatiously high falsetto voice.

Jack sighed.

❁ ❁ ❁

At a quarter to eleven, Ravelo reached for his hat, vaguely annoyed, more due to his lack of options than to Missy's failure to materialize. He had been sitting in her office for almost an hour, thinking she would return any minute, any minute, wondering what the heck to tell her when she finally rounded the corner. An hour later, he still didn't know. He even tried not thinking of anything, just sitting.

No luck.

Too distracted to return to the church and too antsy to wait any longer for Missy, besides finding it too noisy in the office for genuine con-templation, Ravelo donned his hat and overcoat and aimed for the exit.

But as he passed by a knot of cubicles a few feet from Missy's, an interesting bit of conversation caught his attention. A reporter was on the phone hammering away at a police detective.

". . . do I look like I was born yesterday, Boxer?" the reporter was asking, pencil tucked behind his ear. He was jabbing a finger at a pad of paper in front of him. "You're telling me you people didn't even know Rosenburg was affiliated with the Institute of Global Relations? Uh-huh . . . uh-huh. OK, so I guess you want me to run a quote from your precinct saying you boneheads didn't know about IGR. . . . What do you mean, how did I know? I found it out from the widow, for crying out loud! The same person you probably found out from. Let's cut it, Boxer. We're friends, right? Why are you holding your cards to your chest so tight? Just toss me a scrap or something. Give me something to chew on. I'm dying here. . . ."

Ravelo was all ears. He pressed his back against the wall outside the reporter's cubicle, tried to look uninvolved. But he listened.

"Yeah," the reported said, scribbling. "Yeah . . . oh, did he now?"

Ravelo desperately wanted to peek around the corner to see what he was writing. He felt a brief, quick pang, wondering if he was doing something illegal. All the same, he couldn't have been peeled away from that spot with a crowbar.

"So where's ground floor?" the reporter asked.

A short pause.

"What do you mean, you don't know? Are you saying you don't have a single possible motive? This man was known around the world in some circles!"

A longer pause. Then a chortling, incredulous explosion of air.

"Geez, you all are lost! The sixties? I mean I know he was controversial and all. But why wait thirty-some years? Why now?"

Ravelo's eyes darted back and forth, processing, trying to find a link himself. The reporter mumbled something. Then all of a sudden:

"Now we're getting somewhere! Oh yeah, that's good! Now this is recent, right? And how many? Just the four of them. Are you sure? Probably not just playing poker, either, huh. . . . Who? Rumor! I don't care about rumor, are we talking about *the* Dr. Jay Remming. Uh-huh. OK. Probably some big stuff. Anything else?" Ravelo could almost hear the reporter rolling his eyes when he finally said, "I should have expected as much. Is it even possible to find out, you think? Sounds pretty high level to me."

Ravelo glanced at his watch. Where was Missy?

"So you gonna go on record with me here, Boxer?" the reporter asked, grinning. "Didn't figure you would. Sure, fine. No comment. Boy, you all are just about as dead in the water as a belly-up fish." He laughed. "Gotta run, man. Got an eleven-o'clocker. Sorry, I'll get back with you."

Ravelo heard the receiver smack against the phone, heard the reporter fumbling for car keys. The priest nervously spun on one heel and began strolling down the hall at a brisk pace. Within moments a tall, lanky man in blue jeans and a sport coat passed him at a trot. Ravelo kept walking, but slowed his pace, waiting until the man was gone for sure. Then he turned and slipped quickly into his office, scanning the pad of paper for information. Not much there. He hurried down the line.

Wait a minute. . . .

One interesting tidbit: Security clearance *through the CIA* was required for admission into the Institute of Global Relations. Mother of God! That made at least one CIA connection. Still, Ravelo had to remind himself that such a connection may well have been nothing more than a formality and did not constitute a relationship or significant involvement one way or another; circumstantial evidence at best. He scanned for more. Nothing on any mafia ties or bad debts, just some sketchy information on that part about controversy in the sixties. Apparently the reporter thought there was something significant about Rosenburg being stationed at a military base in North Carolina in the late sixties and early seventies; beyond that there were only a few other random facts, possibly meaningful to someone, but not to him.

Ravelo slipped out of the office, thankful now for the beehive quality of the newsroom where he was just another drone for all anyone cared. Scooting down the hall—for a moment, if only a brief moment—he found a tiny bit of thrill in the hunt, in the tangle of facts and rumor, the known and the unknown and all the subtle shades of truth in between. It was a rare moment of diversion for the priest and he allowed himself to enjoy it without guilt. He had found a little nook between the rock and the hard place and he intended to stay there for a bit.

Then a voice greeted him.

"Father Ravelo, hi. I was just at the church looking for you. You won't believe what I've found!"

At long last, Missy Jenkins.

"Listen to this," Missy chirped, pleased as punch with herself. And then she laid out the whole scoop of what she had been doing since last night and where she had been earlier this morning: the bank. The recently closed safety deposit box. Dr. Buck Keegan. The materials on mind-control research sponsored by the CIA, the military, and other government agencies. She speculated a few connections to Luther Sanchez and then popped a bright-eyed question.

"So what do you think?"

Father Ravelo had listened carefully. They had moved back into her office and he was wishing fervently for a door or some semblance of privacy when she turned the conversation to him.

"Well," he said, pondering. A good bit of the thrill he had felt just moments earlier was still present, but the weight of the decisions before him had begun to press in again. "Forty-eight hours ago I would have dismissed all of this as rubbish. Now . . . ?"

"Now?" Missy said eagerly.

Ravelo shifted his weight uncomfortably. "Do you have someplace else we could talk? A conference room? Something with four walls and a doorknob?"

Missy glanced over her shoulder. "Oh, no one is listening. It's a code-of-honor thing."

"Uh-huh," Ravelo said doubtfully. He locked eyes with Missy. "If I take you into my confidence, I must have every assurance that the information I share goes no farther than you and me."

Missy grew serious. "Sure, Father."

"No, no, not 'sure, Father.' I want you to understand something, Ms. Jenkins. In light of recent events, I feel compelled to contribute to this investigation. But to do so I must break faith in a way that I find unconscionable and extremely distasteful. Do you follow me?"

Missy said, "I'll take it to the grave until you tell me otherwise, Father."

Ravelo studied her face, taking the measure of her word, her worth. In every respect the priest was a thoroughly uninspiring man to look at, but when he turned his gaze upon Missy, she realized that he *knew* her. The chasm between them in the span of his glance was deeper than she could manage. Dispirited, she said, "I've given you everything I've got, Father. I can't convince you any other way."

"No, you can't. But I trust you."

That meant something to Missy. If there was ever a secret she kept, this would be it. And so Ravelo began his tale, in whispered tones, glancing frequently at the hallway where he himself had easily overheard another man's tale. He told Missy of Ricky Carletti's confession— though he did not mention Ricky by name. He told her of the ring and the scrap of paper and the blood. He told her what he'd overheard the other reporter discussing, the brief mention of a CIA connection through IGR, something about controversy during Rosenburg's military duty at Camp Lejeune in the late sixties. Missy hardly breathed until the very end.

"Wow, this looks big."

"It certainly is shaping up that way, at least circumstantially. But we have almost nothing concrete. And I will not go to the authorities with the intent of using a man's confession against him. So where does that leave us?"

"Very confused," Missy mumbled, running her fingers through her stringy, unkempt hair. "Why would the CIA order a hit on a noted Jewish scientist they themselves granted high-level security clearance to?"

"And why use the mafia?" Ravelo echoed.

Missy snorted. "That part is easy. The CIA has a documentable track record a mile long of shady deals and paying mercenaries to do their dirty work. It's *de facto*. See, Father, you've got the wrong idea. I did, too, until some of this reading. The CIA, by design, is primarily staffed with historians, administrators, and thinkers. When action is required, they subcontract those assignments to a select skill base, usually former military. But that really just depends. Look at Cuba during the Kennedy administration. It's well known that the CIA paid the mafia to orchestrate an assassination attempt on Fidel Castro. No surprises there."

Ravelo frowned, removed his glasses, wiped his eyes. His stomach rumbled hungrily. "Perhaps. But I still don't see how it all fits together."

"Me, either," Missy said, reaching for the phone. "But maybe we can find out."

About fifteen or twenty phone calls later, they knew no more than they did before. Missy had called an acquaintance at the Department of Corrections first and simply asked what reason the DOC wanted to give the taxpayers of Michigan for funding a two-year hypnosis therapy program for a convicted criminal like Luther Sanchez. The man, quite confounded by such a report, declared that he had no idea what Missy was talking about and that she was "off her rocker" for even thinking the DOC would waste its time with "sewage like Luther." Missy said she had proof that Luther received extensive therapy and the man, further confused, could only tell her that if any such program had been in effect, "it wasn't funded by us."

Fair enough. So Missy called the office of the state's internal auditor. Whew! That buck was passed so many times it never landed. Each person Missy talked to was openly grateful to funnel Missy farther down the pike to someone else. It didn't take long for Missy to realize they were in the dark. Which most likely meant it wasn't a state operation.

The Detroit office of the honorable U.S. Senator Jane Lyderman was another story. The senator was in Washington, D.C., but her senior staff assistant happened to be in the office. The assistant fielded Missy's call with all the bluster and political arrogance of a seasoned pro. But when Missy popped her question the woman balked and hemmed-hawed around so much, Missy knew she had hit a button. The assistant knew *something*; Missy just couldn't pry it loose.

". . . well then, maybe you would know why a representative of the Central Intelligence Agency was on location giving orders at the time of Luther's execution?" Missy had asked.

Boy, that had been a prize winner! The assistant immediately launched into an extemporaneous speech about what a great job Jane Lyderman was doing for the state and how the press needed to recognize the limits of an open democracy and how glad she was personally that Luther Sanchez had gotten what he deserved and how the government had acted responsibly throughout the whole process. Blah, blah, blah . . .

So on and on it went. This wasn't the first time Missy had called several of these leads; in some cases it wasn't even the second or the third. Part of Missy's approach to journalism was to create such a fatalistic dread at the sound of her voice that potential sources would gladly yield just to gain peace of mind. She was relentless, knitting together the various strands of conjecture and speculation into a quilted whole. She called the local branches of the FBI, the CIA, several local psychiatrists (just in case they had participated); she called the sheriff's office, the warden's office, the Justice Department, the Attorney General's office. Ravelo was amazed at her tenacity and perseverance, setback after setback. She asked the various individuals if they had any knowledge or reason why the CIA might have had a problem with Dr. T. Samual Rosenburg. She asked about Rosenburg's rumored, unspecified collaboration with other scientists, including Jay Remming. She asked about currently sponsored investigations into the nature of mind control. She came at it from every angle, almost shamelessly. She was laughed at, hung up on, immediately transferred and cursed. Big time.

Last, she called the governor's office. It was a last-ditch effort, but it paid off . . . sort of. Missy had gone to college with a girl who now served as secretary to the governor's chief of staff. They first exchanged pleasantries and chatted for a bit. Then, expecting little, Missy launched a fresh volley of questions. The girl knew nothing. Just as she figured.

"Well, that's all right," Missy said. "I'll talk with you again soon, OK? Good to talk to you—"

"Wait a minute!" the girl said suddenly. "I just remembered something. Oh no, never mind, it's probably nothing. . . ."

"What?" Missy implored. "Tell me!"

"Well, I remember now; I wasn't here at the time, mind you, but I remember my boss talking about how Luther was almost granted a stay of execution at the last minute. Did you know that?"

Missy was stunned. "No. Why?" Nothing along those lines had

ever been leaked, much less reported. For all anyone knew or cared, Luther was a goner from the start.

"Well, what you said sparked my memory. A close friend of the governor called him *that* night and . . . am I getting the governor in trouble here?"

"No, no," Missy assured her. "This has nothing to do with the governor."

"OK, but don't quote me just the same, OK?"

"Sure . . ."

The girl's voice dropped in volume. "So anyway, the governor gets a call the night of the execution and he has a long conversation with this dear old friend. They were army buddies or something. After the phone call, the governor spends some time in his private study reviewing the case against Luther one final time. Believe it or not, word was he was within an inch of releasing the man. Only reason he didn't was because of the political pressure. You know, looking soft on crime. But I think by the time that phone call was over, he wanted to release Luther. He was looking for a way."

"Why?" Missy asked. "What changed? Every statement the man ever made about Luther was aggressively pro-punishment. What gives?"

"I'm sure I don't know. But I bet Dr. Rosenburg could tell you."

"What are you talking about?"

"He's the guy that called. The friend."

Missy almost dropped the phone. "Sam Rosenburg?" she asked. "Did you know he was dead?"

"No!" the girl exclaimed.

"But you're sure it was him?"

"I'm just telling you what the boss said. Look, I probably need to go. . . ."

And that was the end of that, for in fact the girl knew nothing else of value, though Missy pressed her for more. Still, that little tidbit seemed worth its weight in gold. When Missy hung up, she briefed Ravelo on the findings, such as they were. Both of them agreed that the story was definitely worth pursuing, though Ravelo said he felt more and more like the blind men with the elephant.

"All these parts feel so different."

Missy didn't even hear him. She was already thumbing frantically through one phone book, then another, looking for a New Hudson listing. When her brain went on overdrive, it actively blocked all interference. She picked up the receiver, dialed a number. A man answered.

"Dr. Buck Keegan, please," Missy said sweetly.

16

If madness and fear were two faces of the same beast, then Hank Blackaby felt sure he was approaching madness. Between Remming's threats, Kim's molested apartment, rumors of dead men, and the sheer weight of the research he had stolen, Hank found his thoughts increasingly motivated by the primal subconscious demands of one thing and one thing only: survival.

Get the heck out of Dodge. . . .

Unfortunately, it wasn't that simple. Hank's swashbuckling cyber-banditry came at a price, packaged within his conscience as a severe sense of responsibility. He had no idea what to do with what he knew. He just knew he had to do *something*.

But maybe that "something" really was as simple as turning everything he had over to the authorities, as he had suggested to Remming. Hank knew the significance of his stolen treasure, that Christians might be biologically marked, divinely marked—either from birth or at "conversion" or whatever. Those facts alone were enough to shell-shock the world's citizens, the majority of whom were not Christians. But it was what Hank did not know about the research—such as who was sponsoring it and why; how this information would be used—that most frightened him. He simply did not feel equipped to proceed, much less to risk his life for value x, the great unknown.

One thing was for certain, the kind of provisions attached to this research, the secrecy, the CIA involvement, the murder of one of the top researchers, all suggested an MO entirely different from the polite neutrality of "For research purposes only." In Hank's gut, after reading the numerous communiqués by Monitor Nine and reviewing the harsh disputes between the various members of Club Cranium, the SPoT project felt . . . well, *oily.* Dark and malevolent. Slick. Flammable. It struck Hank as a tool, a tool of precisely positioned, scientifically validated information, honed to a remarkably sharp and offensive point, like a sword. And whoever held that sword held power.

We will possess a whole new arsenal of advanced technology to better serve global man, Remming had said.

Serve or control? Hank wondered.

Over the years it seemed Remming had convinced himself that personal ambiguity equaled moral neutrality. The very idea infuriated Hank to no end. Worse than Remming's ethical ambivalence was his own lack of courage. Up until that day under the bridge, Hank had always backed away from calling the cards. So which was the greater evil: to lack conviction or to possess it and remain silent?

Water under the bridge. Hank *had* spoken, finally, and felt relieved. Now that he wasn't furious or afraid or awed by the man, what remained was pity. Hank understood—probably better than most—the darker side of Dr. Jay Remming. When audiences of hundreds or thousands packed in to see him, Hank knew it was the image of the man they pursued.

The irony, however, was that Remming had come to believe in the sincerity of his own detachment. Not only believed, but enlarged it to a Platonic ideal, which, as far as Hank was concerned, proved quite nicely that superior intellect and self-deceit were not mutually exclusive. Intellect was no guarantee of rigid self-awareness. And deceit, by definition, was a thing to be *missed,* an existential blind spot, a consequence of being human. Jay Remming lived as proof of both, especially when he played aloof to a world that fawned over him. High-powered assemblies, awards, new research—these were the only family he could claim, but they surely made for poor consolation in the absence of Josh and Anna and his other children.

Hank realized in that moment that Remming was also a victim. He was two people, shielded by a facade of magnificent proportions, a facade that could no longer be excused as mere eccentricity. So . . . which man to blame, which part of the image? Hank did not know. He only knew with sudden clarity how dangerous the duality had become.

If every life had its price, Remming's was expensive indeed.

As far as his own was concerned, Hank decided that (no matter how afraid or nervous he was) life was only going to get worse with each passing hour and minute and day that he remained in stasis. He had gotten a fair bit of sleep last night—dreamless, thankfully—though he had woken up twice all of a sudden, thinking someone was breaking through his apartment door. Still, he felt rested. All he needed now was a plan, a certain sense of personal fortitude, and a little bit of luck. A whole lot of luck, actually, which made Hank grin dourly. Of these three things—plan, fortitude, and luck—the only thing he seemed to possess was luck. And at present, most of his luck was bad.

So, what to do? More investigation, that was sure. Every one of the messages from Monitor Nine to Remming was on Merideth Institute letterhead, so Hank figured it was time to visit Conspiracy Central— anonymously, of course, though he felt quite safe. Since no one knew what he looked like—as far as he knew—Hank couldn't imagine a less anticipated plan of action than marching through the front door of the lion's den. He could give them a call, or swing by their offices, pick up some literature. Also, he thought he should try to contact this Jessica O'Connel. Her mother's death seemed to be related to Remming's activities, or Susan Decker wouldn't have asked Remming about her. Since Jessica was still in town, she might be able to fill in some of Hank's blank spots.

He reached for his backpack, crammed full of the SPoT files he had printed and the two extra disks from Kim, and pulled out the piece of paper Nellie had given him, the one with the name of Jessica's hotel.

Let's hope my luck begins to change, he thought.

"Jessica O'Connel," he repeated, a little louder this time, leaning over the green marbled countertop of the front desk. "Room 247."

The desk clerk checked his computer again. "Ah, there it is. If you'll hold for a minute I'll check for messages."

Hank turned around. The Columbian was a nice hotel, situated northeast of the Morningside campus a few blocks, surrounded by large broad-leafed elms and gnarled oak trees. The marble floors, broad windows, spit-shined plant leaves, and smartly dressed bellboys were typical of Big Apple class and money. It took Hank about two seconds to figure out Jessica O'Connel had some serious green at her disposal.

"I'm sorry, sir," the desk clerk said after riffling through the drop boxes. He was reading a piece of hotel stationery. "Ms. O'Connel left word that she will not be back until later this evening. She did not specify a time. May I leave her a message? Your name?"

"No, no. That's all right. I'll check back."

The clerk, smartly dressed in navy coat and tie, cleared his throat, the kind of noise you make when you need to sound polite. "It would be better if you could just leave your name. We have strict security here at the Columbian. I will be glad to forward the message to Ms. O'Connel."

Hank headed for the door.

"I'll check back. Thanks."

While there was still a little daylight, now seemed as good a time as any to check out the mighty financier of Project God Spot: the Merideth Institute.

On second thought, just as he exited the hotel, Hank decided he'd better *call* MI first, just in case this was not an open-door kind of institution. He didn't want to go ringing on doorbells looking like a fool. So he stopped at a pay phone and dialed the number on the letterhead. Almost immediately, three loud tones sounded in his ear, followed by a nasally Bronx accent: "We're sorry, the number you have dialed has been disconnected or is no longer in service. Please check the number and try your call again."

His quarter and dime cycled through—*cha-ching!*—and dropped into the change return. Hank reread the number, plugged the coins back in, and dialed the number again. 555-4397.

Same song, second verse. Nobody was home.

Puzzled, Hank called information, told the lady he wanted to know if the Merideth Institute had a new number, or if their number was now unlisted for some reason. What borough? Hank studied the letterhead, found the street address. Manhattan. 1590 Broadway.

"Manhattan. 1590 Broadway."

"No listing available, sir," the operator replied.

"How do you mean?" Hank asked. "Do you mean the number is unlisted?"

"I show no Merideth Institute, sir. Not in Manhattan. Would you like for me to search under a different name?"

"No," Hank mumbled. He wondered if maybe MI had recently moved their offices. "Can you search the other boroughs?"

"I'm sorry, you'll have to change area codes."

"Yeah, yeah," Hank said, hanging up. He tried them all. New York City was so stinking big it took three area codes to cover the phone bill: 212, 718, and 917, with two additional area codes proposed to handle the load. Sure enough, there were four or five listings of a "Merideth Institute" or something similar, but none of them panned out. One of them was a technical trade academy. Another, Meridian Institute, was an amateur cartographer society. But no Merideth Institute, think tank and biomedical philanthropist.

Hank called his apartment, punched in his code, hoping for a message from Kim on his answering machine. No go. Although he hadn't been paged, he would need to get back to rounds soon, so he called the hospital to check on patients and work out any conflicts. The nurse he spoke with clicked a few keys, paused, reading the screen. Her confusion was apparent.

"You aren't scheduled for any rounds, Dr. Blackaby. I don't know why. But I do have a note here that says you need to call Mrs. Sassanelli in Dr. Remming's office. That's all. Sorry."

Immediately, Hank dialed the office. Mrs. Sassanelli answered sweetly.

"Neurological Engineering, Jay Remming's office?"

"This is Dr. Blackaby. I got a message from Nursing saying I'm not scheduled for any rounds."

"Yep," Mrs. Sassanelli said cheerfully. "Dr. Remming instructed me to remove you from all rounds and transfer your patients to other residents. Aren't you the lucky one?"

"Permanently?" Hank said in disbelief.

"Don't know. He didn't mention any time frame."

"When did this happen?"

"Yesterday afternoon. At least that's when he told me."

Hank stepped back, staring bug-eyed at the phone as if it were an impossible riddle. He was at a complete loss. When he put the phone back to his ear, Mrs. Sassanelli had grown concerned.

"Is this bad? Have the two of you not talked about this?"

"We've talked," Hank said and hung up.

Fuming, he got in the car and started driving.

One central fact regarding doorbells: To ring one, there must be a door.

When Hank finally tracked down 1590 Broadway in mid-Manhattan, he realized, dumbfounded, that he could go no farther. His proverbial "door" had not only slammed in his face, it had been removed from the hinges of possibility. Pulling his car over to the curb, he stared at the street signs again, the buildings, checked the letterhead again, then back to the buildings.

Fifteen-ninety Broadway did not exist.

He had been plodding south on Broadway for some time, having just passed 47th. Scanning every building on the west side, the 1580s had come and gone, and now here was 1592, a massive building that took up the entire block. Where the MI headquarters should have been, there was nothing.

Hank's eyes darted back and forth over the surface of the dashboard. Somebody was yanking his chain. Maybe it was Remming. For that matter, maybe Remming's chain was being yanked, too. Hank knew Remming didn't care where his funding came from. He had told Hank as much. As long as it was green and traded hands well, it worked for him.

But there was nothing simple about deception on this scale. As Hank stared just beyond the hood of his car, where traffic lights flashed and people scurried past yellow taxi cabs between streets, he realized with dread how enmeshed he had become.

The Merideth Institute was obviously a sham operation, a cover for something much larger and almost certainly more sinister. Otherwise, why the elaborate measures? Why bother?

He revved up his engine and pulled back into traffic. *My luck is definitely not improving,* he thought.

€ € €

"Where is Dr. Remming?" Jessica demanded, red hair flying. No one bothered to answer. For the last hour and a half she had been given the runaround par excellence. None of the nurses knew the answers to her questions and the other doctors deferred, almost pitifully, to Dr. Remming, since Mrs. O'Connel had been his patient. That phrase . . . they kept using it over and over again. Such blatant Hippocratic patrimony enraged Jessica.

His patient? How about *her* mother!

Like an Andy Rooney editorial on *60 Minutes,* she quietly launched into a mental tirade against the smugness of the medical establishment, the only niche in America's free-market system that remained impervious to the concept of customer service.

Who holds the trump card in a doctor-patient relationship? Jessica argued, as if she stood before a jury demanding a verdict.

The doctor! The hospital! came the resounding cry.

Healing was not even fortunate enough to be classified as a luxury. It was a privilege based on need.

And doctors knew it.

So the other physicians on staff politely offered vague reassurances but stubbornly refused to address her specific concerns. In reality, they did not know the answers to her questions, but were too arrogant to admit such a thing; Jessica wouldn't have believed them anyway.

Thinking to achieve swift retribution, she had stormed the administrative offices. But CPMC was big—one of the largest and oldest and most prestigious medical communities in the nation, if not the world. Theirs was a carefully calculated bureaucratic machine, with prodigious gears and ponderously slow-turning cranks and levers—safeguards and procedures constructed in principle on behalf of the patient, but often running counterprogressive to the patient's actual needs.

In short, Jessica got nowhere fast. The chief of staff was on vacation and the hospital administrator's staff was more adroit at bouncing her between offices than a Korean Ping-Pong champion on game day.

Meanwhile, Remming was nowhere to be found.

"Where is Dr. Remming!" she fairly shouted again, since nobody answered her the first time.

Nellie was on duty. She pulled Jessica aside, said, "Ms. O'Connel, *please* lower your voice. We are trying to do everything we can to help you, but you must understand, we have other patients to deal with. I am deeply sorry for your mother's death, but her case no longer belongs in ICU. It moved from ICU to Patient Accounts as soon as she passed away. There's not much more we can do and you are beginning to disturb the other families."

"Dr. Remming told me to meet him here at six o'clock," Jessica said, pointing to the floor beneath her feet. "He said he was working on things. Now, as soon as you connect me to Remming, I'll gladly move on."

"We have paged Dr. Remming and phoned his office and phoned his home. He has not answered any of these. Someone mentioned the possibility that he might have been called away on sudden business, which is not unusual at all. Dr. Remming is very famous and very busy. All we can ask is that you be patient with us. We really don't know anything else to tell you."

"The truth! Tell me the truth."

"You should just go back to your hotel for the evening and give our business office a call in the morning. Have you been there yet?"

"Have I been there?" Jessica said so forcefully she started to cough. "I've been all over this hospital. I came back here because this is where I started."

"Well, I'm sorry, but I'm going to have to ask you to leave ICU. Someone will call you—"

Jessica latched onto Nellie's arm and squeezed painfully hard. The nurse tried to squirm away. Jessica took a deep breath. "I know that this is not your responsibility. I understand that this is Dr. Remming's case. But I have been given no assurance that any progress has been made. None!" Jessica looked Nellie in the eye. "My mother is dead, Nurse. All of sudden, within a couple of months, an otherwise healthy woman is dead. I simply want to know why."

Nellie didn't say anything, just nodded, though she was plenty mad. She went over to the computer, typed in a few characters, and waited. "This is all I can do," she said crisply. "Then I'll have to ask you to leave or I'll call security." She typed some more, staring at the monitor. Then more typing. Before long, the skin above her brow knotted. She mumbled, "That's odd. . . ."

"What? What's odd?"

Nellie touched the screen. "Your mother's files have been removed. She's no longer in the database."

"And that's not normal procedure when a patient dies?"

"Well, yes, it is. Usually. But research physicians like Remming often leave patient information in the system until a case is permanently closed, which may be days or weeks after that patient has died."

Jessica tucked a loose strand of hair behind her ear. "Remming told me he wanted to move her to . . . Irving? The Irving Center, does that sound familiar?"

Nellie nodded. "The Irving Center for Clinical Studies, that's what I figured. But I don't see her anywhere. Not at Irving. Not anywhere."

The youngest O'Connel daughter fixed Nellie with hard eyes. "I need you to do something for me, Nurse. You tell whoever needs to be told that I want an autopsy performed immediately to determine cause of death. I don't care if Remming is here to do it or not. I want some answers and I want them now. Do we understand each other?"

Nellie opened her mouth to reply, but another nurse cut her short. "Sounds to me like you should take that up with your sister," the nurse said curtly, passing between the two women. "She's already said *no* autopsy."

"My sister?" Jessica asked.

The nurse stared at her, annoyed. "I can't remember her name," the woman snapped.

"Elizabeth."

"Right. Said she flew in from North Carolina. She's still out in the waiting room, I think. Seems to me it would be best to get your family lined up before you go barking at us, Ms. O'Connel."

Jessica marched directly to the waiting area. Half a dozen people lounged in uncomfortable chairs, staring at the television; another two or three sat on a sofa, reading a newspaper, worry on their faces. None of them were Elizabeth or looked remotely like Elizabeth. Jessica peered down the adjoining hallways, first one and then the other, frowning.

Something was very wrong.

She could *feel* it. She knew Elizabeth wouldn't—couldn't—be in the waiting room—or anywhere near New York City for that matter—because Jessica had yet to actually speak to her, to tell her Mom was dead. The phone lines around Maple Hill were still down, which was odd, since the Weather Channel showed bright, sunny skies all over the Southeast; Jessica had made numerous attempts to reach her sister, even checking with the phone company to see if there was a way to break through. They tried. Not a chance.

Which meant that, barring some extreme miracle of psychic energy, Elizabeth knew nothing. Yet someone *posing* as Elizabeth did.

She returned to the nurses' station and waited until Nellie wasn't busy.

"I couldn't find her," she said. "Maybe I'll check down in the cafeteria, though." She turned, stopped abruptly. Nellie stared at her. "I hate to say it," Jessica said sheepishly, "but I think I may need your help. Elizabeth changes hair color more often than . . . this probably sounds silly, doesn't it? . . . but I haven't seen her in so long and so—I guess I was wondering—is her hair still dark brown?"

"Blonde," Nellie answered. "Really blonde."

Jessica began to shuffle off. Nellie said, "Did Dr. Blackaby ever find you?"

"Dr. Who?"

"Blackaby. He's Dr. Remming's chief resident. He was looking for you."

"Nope, never found me."

"Look him up," Nellie said, "maybe he can help." After which she grabbed a chart and continued with her rounds. Jessica watched her walk away. Blonde, huh? Definitely not Elizabeth. And what was this about Dr. Remming's assistant snooping around after her? Jessica set off, chewing on her bottom lip. Tomorrow, she decided, there *would* be an autopsy.

Or there would be hell to pay.

It was late in the evening when she finally returned to the Columbian. To calm her nerves after leaving the hospital, she had stopped for dinner and coffee at the Hungarian Pastry Shop, then allowed herself the pleasure of a leisurely drive up Riverside until she came within sight of the sports complex, with the huge, familiar blue Columbia "C" painted on the face of one of the Bronx cliffs.

The doorman greeted her with a tip of his hat. Jessica flashed a quick, polite smile, then aimed straight for the elevator. Few people could be seen in the darkened lobby, but soft piano music and steady chatter drifted in from the lounge and bar area in the adjacent room. Jessica pressed the "up" arrow on the elevator buttons. Her back was to the front desk, which was on the opposite side of the lobby. From that direction she heard a cautious voice call to her.

"Ms. O'Connel? Jessica O'Connel?"

Jessica wheeled around. From the central lobby, near the black leather couches and glass-top table, a man walked toward her. Something about him seemed incredibly intense, his posture, his manner, and with him, strangely, the entire mood of the hotel. As he walked, his hand was outstretched, inquiring; the effect on Jessica was magnetic, completely unprecedented. Every part of her being funneled into a magnificent, sensual focus. It was frightening, so immediate, so silly. So unnecessary. Like shooting a roman candle across a snowy field on a dark, starless night and watching the frost glitter with phosphor hues. No, more like peering through one of those little toy prism kaleidoscope things, where everything glows in multiple colors. Jessica *knew* she didn't know him. She could just tell, even though the chandelier lights overhead were dim. Nevertheless, something about him rooted her to the ground. And with the fluttering came dread.

I don't want this, she thought. *I don't. I can't. . . .*

The desk clerk, apparently, *did* know him, for he seemed both surprised and disturbed at his presence. As from a great distance, and very slowly, Jessica saw the clerk pointing, heard him say, "I'm sorry, sir, but I told you very plainly to leave. We do not allow loitering in this establishment."

Still the man came. Unswerving, he continued his walk toward Jessica. She still couldn't see his face; most of the light was behind him, but he was extremely well built. For some reason she began to feel afraid and glanced to each side to see if there were any security guards nearby. The desk clerk came around the end of the main desk and began a quick stride toward both of them. His voice grew more authoritarian.

"Sir, I must ask you to leave immediately!"

Jessica glanced up at the elevator lights. Fifth floor, fourth floor. . . . It was taking a long time to descend. The man walking toward her spoke again, softly. He did not sound threatening.

"Ms. O'Connel?"

The desk clerk caught the man by the arm, right as his face emerged into the light—sandy blond hair, square jaw, light blue eyes. He smiled warmly. Jessica felt her heart start to pound.

"I'm Dr. Hanson Blackaby. I think we need to talk."

Jessica exhaled deeply. What had just happened? She knew arousal and she knew dread, but neither had ever caused a room to spin. It was almost mystical.

"Yes, I think we do."

The desk clerk was by now strung tighter than a treble clef piano string. He eyed Hank suspiciously. "I'm terribly sorry, Ms. O'Connel. This man has come in two or three times today asking for you, but he refuses to give us his name." The clerk's head snapped to the left to address Hank. "Sir, our stringent security policies are a courtesy for our guests. Now we have asked you to leave. Please do so now unless you are a guest of Ms. O'Connel's." He turned to Jessica again. "Are you all right, madam?"

From habit, Jessica replied with mischief in her voice. "I don't know. Do I look all right to you?"

Hank murmured something low and approving, virtually ignoring the clerk. "Umm, can we just talk, please?"

Jessica dismissed the clerk with a wave. His eyebrows shot up, surprised and disapproving. He lingered a moment longer, then left. As if at a memory, Jessica smiled. She had prepared for this meeting, had gotten all worked up with facts and frustration, and was ready to press forward until she got some answers. She was determined to be strong and not weak, for the sake of her self-esteem. But now, her hands trembled and her anger fled. When she looked at the face of the man before her, all that was left was a smile.

"Dr. Blackaby—"

"Call me Hank," Hank said kindly. But he also seemed businesslike, in control. Jessica wondered if he had felt anything. Was it just her? It was too intense for only her.

She moved to insulate herself. "Yes, well, Dr. Blackaby—Hank, I'm very frustrated with events surrounding my mother's death. And I want some answers."

So it all returned. The elevator light behind Jessica blinked. The doors slid open.

Hank said, "I want to help you. That's why I'm here."

"Why *are* you here?" Jessica wondered aloud, suddenly bold. "Especially like this. Sneaking in. It seems extremely unprofessional."

"Forgive me if it is. But to be honest, I need your help, too."

"You need my help?"

"Probably more than you need mine." Hank glanced over his shoulder. "I don't think anyone is watching us right now—I've learned to be pretty careful over the last couple of days. But I think we should continue this in private just the same. For safety."

Sounded like a really bad pickup line to Jessica. "I have no idea what you are talking about."

"I can tell you more, but later. Let's just get out of here for now. How about a cup of coffee, my treat?"

He started to move, guiding her by the arm to the front door. Jessica pulled free.

"What are you doing?" she said.

"Please," he whispered. "Trust me. That's all I can say. I don't think you are in any danger, but you might be. I just don't know. I don't want to take any chances."

"Why can't we talk right here?"

"Please, talk quieter! Ask yourself this: Doesn't your mother's case seem more than a little odd?" He took a step forward. "I've looked over the files, Ms. O'Connel. I want to help. But you have to trust me long enough to tell me your story and let me tell you mine. But only in private. I won't talk out here and that's all there is to it."

Slowly, carefully, he extended his hand to her. Jessica put her hands on her hips. Behind her, the elevator chimed again; the doors began to close. She moved but not toward him. And she didn't take his hand. Instead, she held the doors open with the flat of her hand.

"You can come up to my room," she said, stepping behind the double doors. "I think this is ludicrous, but we ought to be safe there."

Inside the elevator, Hank stared straight ahead, heart pounding. He could think of absolutely nothing to say. Nothing that even registered on any scale of intelligibility. Everything in his mouth was stupid, slow, absurd. Vaguely he remembered how Remming insisted on last-name-only relationships, clearly defined boundaries, professional propriety, yadda, yadda. At the moment Hank felt fortunate to have his mouth closed and unslobbering.

So beautiful; the face, the smile, the curves . . .

He started to say something anyway, something very dumb, literally catching the words with his hand over his mouth—thank goodness!— but then, having no other recourse, found himself waxing his front teeth with his index finger once or twice, hoping it looked natural.

This is stupid. . . . He put his hand down. Kind of bounced up and down on the balls of his feet. They had not yet traveled the length of a single floor.

Jessica said nothing. Why didn't she say something? He was grateful she did not.

Hank had expected many things. Anger. Tears. Frustration. A married woman. A husband. A dog, for crying out loud. Rage. Anything.

Anything but this.

"You're pretty young to be a specialist, aren't you?" Jessica finally asked as the elevator reached the midpoint of its slow, whirring climb.

"Not really. Not for a resident."

She did not reply, did not smile, still trying to sort through the confusion of the last ten minutes. When the elevator bell rang again and the double doors slid open, she stepped off, wordless, motioning Hank to follow.

Yet in spite of her reserve and Hank's single-mindedness, a hotel room was a bad place for Jessica to try to sort things out. Inside her room, familiar patterns began to emerge. She fought hard for indifference. All she wanted was to simply uncover the truth, be forceful and obtain answers. Yet one fact remained obvious to the habits of her flesh: Signals had been exchanged in the lobby. Plenty of signals, powerful and spontaneous, beyond even those she was familiar with. Despite *his* apparent reticence, she fully expected Hank to step up to the plate any moment and try to hit a home run. It was what a boy did in a situation like this in New York City late at night in a hotel room with a young woman who has invited you up to "chat," although you are a virtual stranger. She waited grimly for that moment, hated it, wanted it, relied on it. The stress of the last few days had steadily mounted without reprieve. The nothingness of her and her mother's life together felt more than ever like a cracking scab.

And here was Hank. Boy of the moment.

Jessica thought to resist, thought a great many things all at once, but she only knew two ways to relate to a man: antagonize him, such as in court, or use him to satisfy her guilt. She did not know how simply to *be* with a man. Her father had not given her time to learn.

". . . your mother's chart is very difficult for me to follow," Hank was saying, trying to fill the silence. He seemed either unaware or inoculated to her struggle. "It doesn't make any sense. I want to figure this out, but that means we may have to talk about the last few days. If you're not up to it, we can do it later."

Jessica took a step closer. Insatiable hunger compelled her. It was beyond her. She needed sex. "No. I know. The last few days *have* been difficult," she purred, "but I want to keep going."

"Are you sure?"

"Yes."

She stood close to Hank, very close, eyes wide, waiting. And right there, Hank did an amazing thing. With her warm breath on his face and a dreadful desire in her eyes, which anyone could have read as "Take me!" Hank stepped away, sat down, and began talking about her mother's case! Just like that. Didn't even acknowledge or mention her come-on. He started at ground zero with the hard facts and quantifiable data. All professionalism and decorum. And they went from there.

Dazed, Jessica found herself sitting and listening.

Then, before long, a question. From Jessica. And Hank answered, as best he could. Then another question and another answer. As the evening progressed and the two grew more comfortable, Hank's tongue loosened even more, so that before it was over he had told Jessica everything—everything about Club Cranium, the CIA, the Merideth Institute. He showed her the files—a stupid thing to do really, but he didn't care. He needed an outlet. He explained the data, its implications . . . everything. In the process, the earlier moments were forgotten, or at least suffused by the present. Jessica was thoroughly engrossed. When her turn came, she angrily recounted the strange events leading up to her mother's death.

Both tales left the other breathless and uncertain, and more than a little afraid. For Jessica especially, the freshness of the pain seemed overwhelming at times. Hank sensed this. Along the way he talked little of the bigger picture until it seemed Jessica was ready to take another step. Then deftly, patiently, he worked her through the details, never pushing too fast or too far. They worked the story over from a half dozen different directions, and then reworked it, until another strange thing happened.

Jessica burst out laughing. Loud. Uncontrollable.

"What?" Hank said, confused. But Jessica only laughed louder.

"What? What did I say?"

Jessica tried to regain her composure. She took a deep breath, straightened her back. "You said . . . you said—gosh pot! Not god spot, *gosh pot!*" And then she exploded in laughter again, this time so hard that stuff came out of her nose.

And *that* was funny. And it was very late. So they both laughed, Jessica *and* Hank, laughed and laughed; hysterics, to be sure—the pressure and the late hour and the raw emotion—but the sound of the laughter extended a certain, necessary healing grace to both. During the last hour, quite unrealized, they talked only of each other, learning a few of the little details of the other's life—where they were from, why they did what they did—the small snippets of personal history and desire that make a person knowable. By anyone's definition, it would be called flirting. At odd times both would fall silent or make a nervous gesture, afraid that the other knew what they were thinking, of the memory of the lobby, the initial meeting, the breathlessness . . .

But Hank was witty and gentle and never pushed too far, though it was his nature to do so; Jessica, brilliant, passionate, volatile, was so full of life Hank found himself simply staring at times, unable to speak. Neither cared anymore to hide the fact that there was electricity between them. It was transparently obvious. They both knew it. And all the while, Jessica quietly marveled that they were not in bed together.

They talked until 4:00 a.m.—like teenagers on a weekend—and then, overcome, slept like babies. Hank crashed on the floor, feeling warm and comfortable. He had done well, maintaining a reasonable distance so that she would not doubt his professional integrity; the important issues regarding her mother had been breached, if not resolved, and he had piqued her curiosity by not responding to her cues. Deftness and respect were vital; he himself was likely in personal danger, while Jessica remained vulnerable to the pain of her mother's death. On top of which it seemed obvious that she *was* interested in him at some level.

A good start? He thought so. Jessica was beautiful and alluring; given his position he couldn't help but feel protective. Also troubled. Jessica moved fast.

Slow down and get a grip, Hank. She's from Oregon.

It was true. They would have *maybe* three or four days together. On business. Nevertheless, Hank couldn't shake the feeling that tomorrow or the day after might just be a truly grand day . . . if he could just thread the needle of the God Spot mystery, uncover the conspiracy, expose the files, save Jessica . . . and rescue the planet. All in a day's work, since Hank, it seemed, was the self-appointed hero of the hour. Not a job he relished.

Tonight, the hero took the floor. Jessica took the bed.

His last words were, "Tomorrow I'll try to get my own room."

17

The humidity was stifling.

Remming patted his forehead with a handkerchief. Again. He was decidedly uncomfortable. His navy blue Armani clung to his wet skin so badly, and had for so long, that he no longer bothered picking the wrinkles loose. Behind him, the steady *whumpa-whumpa-whumpa* of the helicopter effectively drowned out the possibility of any other noise, much less focused thought.

He stood alone for a few moments, tie and jacket flapping wildly. Beyond, to the west, the airfield was fairly well lit, even though the night was well advanced. Outside the perimeter of lights were only stars and darkness. Finally, a vehicle rounded a corner of that darkness, merging with visibility, headlights bobbing over the rough terrain. On its rubber heels, dimly seen, came a bulging cloud of heavy gray dust. Remming watched as the brakes locked and the vehicle skidded to a halt. Out jumped a man in military green fatigues and UN blue helmet.

"Sorry, sir!" the man shouted, cupping his hand to his mouth. By his stripes, he was a colonel. "Had a flat about four or five miles back." He took a moment to eyeball Remming. "You look pretty rough, sir. If you don't mind me saying."

Remming didn't reply. He didn't have the will to raise his voice over the roar of the beating chopper blades. He just held out his hands and gave the man his bags.

"I'm Colonel Netterson! I know it's late, so we'll just be off if that's all right with you!"

Remming nodded, glancing past the man to the hangar and surrounding complex. It *was* late; he *was* tired. The night had been long, the travel rough, the airports a nightmare. In Mexico City, he was met at the boarding gate by a pair of flat-faced suits, presumably CIA. But who could say? The men quietly passed along new instructions, then promptly disappeared—instructions that Remming found completely unsuitable. He was supposed to transfer to a C-135 for the remainder of the flight to Guatemala, along with various other military hardware and personnel. The presumption of such an itinerary was almost beyond comprehension, but it also puzzled Remming.

Why military involvement?

He never got the answer. The C-135 was fortuitously grounded due to mechanical failure, so an alternative private escort was arranged, and that quite speedily. Remming didn't even make a phone call; the same pair of suits breezed in and out, unannounced, uninvited, with new information. Still, two more hours were wasted at the airport, sipping tequila, muscles cramping. At about midnight, the private escort arrived. From there, a turbulent ride to Ilopango Internationale in El Salvador, then a twenty-minute jeep ride to another army base, whether U.S. or Salvadoran, he couldn't tell. Then another transfer to another military vehicle, this time a helicopter, which angled swiftly north and west, flying low to the ground, disappearing into the deep night sky, taking Remming on a thirty-minute flight toward, as far as he could tell, nowhere.

Now, here stood Colonel Netterson, his fourth military escort. At . . . what time was it?

He might have cared—might even have been alarmed—but he was simply too bone tired. Unspeaking, he sank gratefully into the seat of Netterson's Hummer. The colonel glanced briefly at his ward, then plunged the vehicle into gear. Within seconds they were wheeling down a rough, narrow path, rarely traveled. The headlights fanned out brightly but revealed little. On both sides of the winding dirt road, the thick tangle of vines and trees and undergrowth seemed to be groping in and up and out, alive, clogging vision, containing movement, hiding secrets. From every direction came the sounds of night birds and locusts and frogs, the rustling of leaves in the breeze high above, and other unidentifiable noises. Remming tried to sleep. He could not. In spite of his weariness, he found himself growing increasingly alarmed. He couldn't tell where he was or where he was going, but he had the distinct impression of moving deeper and deeper into the heart of the jungle.

Only he had no idea why.

Why had his presence been requested here? Obviously, it had something to do with STM-55 research, but what? Nothing Monitor Nine had said offered the slightest clue. Remming could not help sliding inexorably into a rootless, gut-level abstraction of paranoia. Not because of the thinly veiled security measures or even the location. He had been a part of plenty of high-level operations. It was the implications of the security and location for *this* operation that frightened him.

Whose control? Hank had asked him, point-blank. *Whose authority?*

Remming shrugged these thoughts away, in part because the narrow road had suddenly opened into a wide field, with pavement and barracks and other facilities.

Right in the middle of nowhere.

The jeep aimed for one of the barracks and skidded to a halt. Colonel Netterson jumped out, grabbed Remming's bags, said, "Follow me, sir."

He showed Remming to a room, sparsely furnished but private—like a threadbare Motel 6 room cut in half—in a small suite adjoining the barracks. There appeared to be half a dozen or more such rooms down this hallway. It was dark. Colonel Netterson opened the door to Remming's room, flipped on a lamp in the corner, said, "I believe you are scheduled for a briefing tomorrow morning at seven hundred hours. I'll be back at that time to assist you and show you to the briefing room."

He nodded curtly and left. Heavy lidded, sagging, Remming glanced left and right, looking for something that was not there. From his suit pocket he withdrew his ever-present mini tape recorder, hoping to leave a few preliminary thoughts on tape. Holding the small, thin player to his mouth, all he could say was, "I can't imagine where this is leading. Very skeptical of the nature of this operation. Very tired, as well . . ."

He took the time to remove his clothes, but not to fold them or arrange them as he normally would. Instead his slim body simply collapsed on the bed.

Soon, he was asleep.

The next day roared in bright and early, to the high-throttled tune of a jeep engine right outside Remming's window. A moment or two later, Colonel Netterson knocked on Remming's door, 6:45 sharp, half expecting the Nobel laureate to be still in bed. Though groggy and somewhat disoriented, Remming nevertheless was upright, sitting in a chair, awake and properly dressed and ready to go.

"Good morning, sir," Netterson said crisply as Remming opened the door.

"Yes, yes. Let's just dispense with all that right now, shall we?"

He brushed past the colonel, stepped into the hallway, turned, came suddenly face-to-face with Dr. Selma Volgaard. She neither smiled nor frowned, nor seemed surprised for that matter. Her face was expressionless, except for the tightly pursed lips, her trademark. Behind her wire-frame spectacles, her bright eyes gleamed with an almost secret joy at the sight of Remming. She extended her hand.

"Good morning, Dr. Remming."

Remming nodded casually, took her hand. "A fine morning indeed, Dr. Volgaard."

"So far. At least inside."

Remming's eyebrows folded together. "I'm sorry?"

Volgaard clicked her tongue. "I feel we will think otherwise, outside—when bugs and heat consume us."

The three strode outside—almost immediately beginning to perspire—but Remming got his first look at the grounds. The camp appeared to be small, but well fortified: L-shaped, with a small, unpaved airstrip running the length of the L-barracks. Munitions, officers' quarters, radar tower, and other facilities were clustered at the end of the strip, and on all sides, dense jungle forest. Around the perimeter, Remming spied the gleaming metal web of the security fence, with teams of rifled guards posted at the west and north gates, which appeared to be the only entrances to the compound. Or exits.

In fact, the more Remming looked, the more guards he noticed. As well as an eerie absence of activity. No training exercises, no shelling or cannon fire from the jungle, no marching troops or drill sergeants. Just guards. At every door on every building. Guards in the radar tower with binoculars and long-barreled sharpshooters. And all of them wore UN blue.

This was a United Nations operation.

He easily hid his surprise but out of the corner of his eye watched Volgaard for a reaction to the grounds. To anything. She did nothing but squint her eyes in the bright morning light.

"You appear to be a prophetess," Remming said, swatting a fly on the nape of his neck. "Have you been here long?"

Volgaard wrinkled her nose. "Yesterday, like yourself. Though earlier. Much earlier. When *normal* people arrive."

Satisfied, Remming climbed into the jeep.

"Let's get a move on it, Colonel."

ⷙ ⷙ ⷙ

Abu arrived at the mosque late in the afternoon, searching for the holy man, Yassef Adonijah. He found him, as usual, in prayer.

"I'm troubled, Yassef," Abu said softly.

Yassef rose. Together, they slipped into the convulsive market streets of old Cairo, all clamor and odor, pressed flesh, where the two could instantly go unnoticed save for the keen eyes of the brightly colored birds, which tittered at them from the cages of various vendors as they passed by. Here, like spilled wine, life ran rampant in all its extremes. Some children laughed and played. Others, toothless and weak, begged for food. Veiled women passed by like ghosts, whispering with one another, eyes downcast, while man and animal baked in the sun, wandering from shade to shade—shade cast by awnings, canopies, buildings, trees, like islands in a river of light. Unceasingly, the merchants rhythmically called out to the steady influx of tourists from America, Japan, and Europe, inviting them to come see their wares: baskets and bracelets, gold, macramé, rugs and other artifacts.

"Speak and I will listen," Yassef said at last, hands clasped behind his back. He did not glance to the right or the left.

"I don't even know how to start," Abu replied.

"Don't know? Or afraid?"

"Both. *Salat,* my prayers . . . they have grown empty to me."

Yassef was unfazed. "That is not so rare, Abu."

"It has never happened before. Always, I have been faithful."

"And still are! It is the act—the devotion—which matters. You must trust Allah."

They kept walking. Yassef continued. "What do we know from the *Sharia,* the way of Allah? What do we know from the holy Koran? There are five pillars, are there not? *Shahada,* which you have done, giving faith to Allah and Mohammed as his prophet; *salat,* five times daily; *zakat* and *sawm,* alms and fasting, and the *hajj*—"

"—to Mecca. *All* these things I have done. Since I was a child. I have made the pilgrimage three times."

Yassef's creased, sun-leathered face solemnly regarded Abu's, searching for his heart. His reply was monotone. "There is nothing more, Abu. Be at peace."

"Nothing at all?"

"There is submission and obedience. What else do you hope for?"

Abu could only whisper. "Hope itself. *Life.*"

Yassef's voice grew more stern. "Life is in Allah. Life *is* Allah. Give yourself to alms and prayer, Abu. Give yourself—"

"It's not enough!" Abu said, smacking his hands together, surprising even himself. "It has never been enough. It can't possibly be enough! Gibran says, '*He who wears his morality but as his best garment were better naked.*' Yassef, I am naked! I am a wretched man! How can my prayers and alms appease the glory of Allah?"

Yassef stopped moving, became rigid. In his eyes—neither angry, nor empathetic—there was nonetheless the gray, flinty color of displeasure. "You are a good man, Abu Hasim El-Saludin. So I will warn you: Be careful."

"Don't tell me that, Yassef," Abu replied evenly, face pointed forward. "I don't think I can afford to be careful. I have gone too far. Seen too much of late. My research—I can't explain it. I don't know how to. But I can tell you this: I wrestle daily with fear."

"This is nothing. Fear is not unnamable. Everything has a name."

"That's just it! This is not a name you wish to hear. It is not even a name I wish to speak."

"Then let it die. Be at peace."

"It's not that easy. This name, this phantom, it has made a direct challenge upon my life. I don't think I can settle on any peace that fails to answer it directly. I think such a peace would be unlawful."

"Allah—blessed be his name—is the only law," Yassef said warily.

"Yes. But isn't it also unlawful to fear Truth? Allah is not afraid of Truth is he?"

In the presence of a holy man the question ignited in the air, leaving a trail of silence and awe behind. That such a thought would even be given voice! Abu felt Yassef's eyes upon him. Shame prevented the scientist from returning the Imam's glance. When Yassef spoke again his voice was cold, like a stone in winter. "You are being a fool, Abu."

"Maybe."

"No. Listen. The fool laughs at the possibility of heresy. The wise man grows silent and afraid."

Abu glanced up. The cultural stigma of a word like "heresy" meant little to him at this point. Still, he was surprised that Yassef would employ such strong language. He drew courage from the danger of the word, found Yassef's eyes, saw there the low gray tone, the stern position of his mouth, his muscles. He knew he should not push further. Still . . .

"Do you think I am laughing?" Abu asked.

"I think you are speaking when you should be silent."

"I am terrified of words."

"And still you speak. And think of moving, moving in one direction or another. You should be still."

"Stillness is a grave. I must *know*."

"You must obey!" Yassef barked. "All else is heresy. Do you presume that Allah—blessed be his name—owes you an explanation?"

Abu opened his mouth to speak. Yassef cut him short. "It is not wrong to journey, Abu. Only be careful where your next step falls. I will say no more to you."

The holy man turned on his heel and briskly strode away. Abu watched him disappear into the crowd. Inside his belly, the void grew.

He approached tentatively, almost afraid.

"Yes, hello?" the blind man said, sensing in the gentle shift of the air the nearness of another. "Alms for the poor?"

Abu took a step back, thought for a moment of turning, leaving, but the blind man urged him to stay.

"No alms?" The man held out a little copper bowl with a few coins in it. "Alms for the poor?"

The beggar was not Egyptian. From India, maybe, by his accent, though his Arabic was flawless. Abu felt silly. The old man retracted his bowl and instead extended his right hand in Abu's direction.

"No matter. At least sit for a moment, friend. Join me here in the shade where it is cool."

Abu nudged closer. The old man had found a perfect little nook on the northwest face of a building. Overhead, a second-story balcony offered moderate coverage from all but the most blowing rains, which were rare enough in their own right. To the east, some kind soul had strung up a line and thrown an old canvas over it for a windbreak. Beyond the old man, to the south and west, the open street thronged with people buying fresh vegetables and fruit. Occasionally, vendors would throw him foodstuffs that were near to rotten. Free meals.

"Come, come! Let's talk. What is your name? I can't see, you know," he said. "You must help me. Give me your hand."

Abu put out his hand. The old man took it, rubbing the skin between his palms, kissing the knuckles. It was a lavish and completely unnecessary greeting. Abu watched him closely. He was thin, missing three teeth, maybe more; his hair, though streaked with gray and dust filled, was otherwise well-groomed. In fact, while Abu expected the man to smell foul, he appeared clean in every respect, except for his tattered robe and unshaven face.

"You are well taught," the beggar offered, looking toward El-Saludin with clouded white eyes.

Abu almost laughed. "Are they that smooth?"

"No, no! They are a man's hands. Only not a man who digs ditches."

"You are a politician. My hands are shamefully smooth."

The beggar grinned a huge, flattered grin. "Will you tell me your name?"

"Abu Hasim El-Saludin," the scientist said, taking a seat beside the man.

"You may call me Jawahar."

The two men sat in silence. Abu watched as waves of heat rose from the dust and concrete like the folds of a curtain, wondering what to say, why he was there. Jawahar's head cocked to one side, as if listening to a faraway birdcall. He did not move. The sounds of the city rumbled on around them—cars and construction work and office machines and livestock—heedless of their conversation, of their very existence, of the tangible presence of destiny between two such people.

Abu chose the moment, swallowed, mumbled, "This may sound strange. But I think there is much I need to learn. From you. Much you can teach me." Jawahar cocked his head again, this time toward Abu. He waited for Abu to continue. Abu said, "I have been watching you, off and on, for many days now."

Jawahar nodded, as if this did not surprise him in the least. *Strange* . . . Abu figured the beggar had not heard right or that he was confused. Then the old man said something even more strange, softly, barely above a whisper.

"If I greet you in the name of my God, will you hurt me?"

It was a timid question, spoken with real fear. Abu was taken aback. "No, of course not."

"I must ask, because I have been beaten many times."

"I won't hurt you."

Jawahar turned his face toward the clouds. His thin gray whiskers looked like gray soap foam on his face.

"You want to know how I can live like this? Right? How I can endure? How I can still smile?"

He waited patiently, made Abu reply, himself a beggar, "Yes . . ."

"It is because I see the beauty of God everywhere, better even than you, though you have eyes. There is great contentment in my knowing."

"But how do you know?"

"It's not so hard. Why is that so hard? In the silence, I hear. In the darkness, I see. I experience. I taste. I smell. The world is more than a blessing for God. It is an expression of his love for man. Look around. It is the life of God you seek."

"I want to understand."

"Then *listen!* God is always speaking. Always calling the seeker to be found."

"I don't know how," Abu whispered, as if in thirst. "I need proof."

The old man almost laughed. "That is your problem! You are *too* well learned! You want to understand the immensity of God here, in this spot"—he pointed a bony finger at Abu's forehead—"while I have received the mystery of him here"—he clutched at his belly with both hands. "What is the size of the human heart? It is the size of a hundred stars! But what is the size of your head?" He held up his hands again, measured Abu's face. "About this big. Do you see? You fear what you cannot understand. I fear *what I can.*"

"Tell me more. . . ."

"There is little more to say. We are both paupers, you and I. But I have tasted grace, like honey. And that has made the difference."

And then Abu grew suddenly nervous, as if the man in one breath had peeled back his chest and exposed a lie. He shifted the conversation. "Do you have family?"

The old man shook his head. "None living."

"How did you come to be here? Where are you from?"

"Questions, questions! Now I will test you. I am from Pakistan. But do you know what the name means?"

"Land of the Pure," Abu replied, pleased at the memory.

"Good! Very good. But I will tell you my simple story. I came from Pakistan to Egypt in 1948 with my wife and child, hoping to find opportunity. We were very poor. My wife had relatives here. Then the rioting began in '51. My wife and son were killed by a pipe bomb. I lost my sight. Since then"—he spread his arms—"I beg."

Abu watched the beggar closely for sleight of hand, artificiality.

"You are on a good road, Abu Hasim El-Saludin," Jawahar said matter-of-factly, which also surprised Abu. "I can tell you are searching. Only be brave. Take the next step. What have you to lose?"

"My soul," came the impulsive reply. "My history."

"What you lose you shall recover a hundredfold."

"How can you be sure?"

And now Jawahar's eyes widened with something very near to delight. If there had been color, Abu was sure they would have sparkled.

"Because I greet you in the name of *my* God, *Jesus.*"

He did not shout. He did not need to. Abu nearly fell over just the same. Not because the beggar's declaration came as a surprise, but because what should have been a pronouncement of death sounded in his ears to be sweet—indeed, like honey—with life. He had secretly, fearfully, hopefully, wondered that the beggar would say as much. Now that he had, he felt the inward loop connecting. He did not know what else to speak or do, or even think. He touched the old man's face, leaned over and kissed it.

The beggar smiled. "Take the name to the land of a hundred stars."

Abu rose and walked away.

He had thought to meander at first, allow things to soak, to sort. But with his dawning sense of—what, enlightenment? No, more like *enlargement*—came an increased urgency and suspicion of all things pertaining to the research. Seized by a new and sudden courage, he returned immediately to his office and began making phone calls. He did not want to contact Remming. Remming would do nothing but coax and cajole and appease Abu with political double-talk. Abu didn't want Remming to even smell his own doubt until he had either confirmed it or released it on his own terms. So he called the American Embassy in Egypt. First, he was, as expected, shuffled here and there, person to person. The embassy claimed absolutely no knowledge of any brain-related research similar to what Abu described. Undaunted, he called the office of an American congressman in Washington, D.C., and then another, and then three different senators, including the powerful chair of the Appropriations Committee. Of course, he never actually spoke with an elected official, only underlings. Every time, same story, same answer: "We have no knowledge"; "We'll look into it"; and miscellaneous other assurances that American dollars were not being spent on anything so ludicrous.

"I don't need your assurance as to the existence of the project," Abu finally told one irritably. "I am already participating. What I want to know is why. What is the agenda?"

At which point the line promptly went dead.

So he called a few more places, asked a few more questions, generally nosing around, growing angrier, more resolved, as each door slammed shut, until finally he arrived at the Office of Science and Technology at Columbia University, knowing of no other place to turn. He had spent over three hours on the phone so far. It was half past nine.

"I'm sorry," a sweet voice said. "You probably need to speak with our administrator about this."

"Then put him on, please."

"He's in a meeting right now."

Abu's eyelids flickered with annoyance. "And what is your administrator's name?"

"Dr. Byron Jackson, Interim Vice-Provost for Research."

"You tell Mr. Jackson—right now!—you tell him that I am prepared to go to the American press with documented and damaging evidence involving faculty at Columbia unless he speaks to me immediately. Do you understand me?"

"I'm sorry, sir. He's in a meeting—"

"No, no, no. I am not interested in your apologies, young lady. Maybe Mr. Jackson is sitting in the Oval Office having tea with the President. I don't care. Page him if necessary. Call his cell phone. But get him on the phone. Now, do you understand?"

"Hold please."

Nearly five minutes later, she returned to the line. "Where can he reach you, Mr. Saludin?"

Abu gave her the phone number, said, "I will expect his call in ten minutes," and hung up the phone.

Three minutes later the phone rang.

"Yes?"

"Dr. Saludin? Byron Jackson from the OSTD at Columbia University."

A polite enough greeting—edgy, but restrained. Abu breathed deep, leaned back in his chair. "Dr. Jackson, I apologize for the urgency and rudeness of my call. However, I am in a difficult position and need direct answers."

"I'm not sure I know what you are talking about, Dr. Saludin. And I'm in quite a bind myself here since you have pulled me from an important meeting. So why don't you get to the point?"

"Precisely what I wish to do. You see, I am a colleague of Dr. Jay Remming. . . ."

Abu said this meaningfully, hoping to prod the answers loose without accusation or implication. He was, after all, a scholar, not a tabloid journalist.

Jackson wasn't biting. "Yes? And?"

"And I need some answers."

The other man snorted impatiently. "I don't have time for games, Dr. Saludin. And I don't appreciate your strong-arm tactics to get me on the phone. Dr. Remming has many colleagues. Get to the bottom line."

"Fine, yes. Maybe a few other key phrases will jog your memory. I, along with Dr. Remming and T. Samual Rosenburg and a Dr. Selma Volgaard"—Abu thought he heard Jackson swallow but couldn't be sure—"have been working for several months now on a highly classi-fied project. We have semi-jokingly referred to it as the God Spot, but the official title is Pineal Body Anomaly/STM-55. Does any of this—what is the phrase?—'ring a bell,' Dr. Jackson?"

Dr. Jackson swallowed again, more loudly. His voice grew flatter, softer. "Go on."

"I have worked on this project from the beginning for the love of the science, and maybe also for the fame it offered, if the truth be told. This is to my shame. I will not now increase my shame with silence, since I have begun to grow highly suspicious of the motivation behind this research."

Dr. Jackson tried to reassert himself. "I really don't know what you are talking about." The declaration was spoken more emphatically than necessary and seemed insincere at best.

"Come now, Dr. Jackson. I suspect not many people at Columbia know what is going on. But you are surely one of them. Who is the funding coming from? Even more, what do they intend to do with the findings?" Sitting calmly in the half-light of his office lamp, Abu could almost *feel* the single bead of sweat rolling down Jackson's temple. It was quiet. "Please understand," Abu continued. "I will be impressed by nothing less than your absolute forthrightness. Since I no longer wish to become famous by the success of a manipulative, politicized science, I feel a great freedom to do whatever is necessary to purify my conscience of any involvement thus far."

"Let me reassure you, Dr. Saludin—"

"Yes, reassure me."

"—this office has nothing to do with the specific oversight or funding of the various projects our esteemed faculty engage in. We facilitate their success after the fact, not before. The research program at Columbia is very large and very diverse, spanning many disciplines and fields of study. We have an unblemished record and reputation—"

"I am not accusing *you* of wrongdoing, sir."

"*Thank God*—" Then, coughing, "I mean, of course."

"But you are being disingenuous just the same."

"I don't know the answers you are asking for," Jackson whispered.

"So it seems. Before I go, though, I wonder if you could help me on another matter. I am from Egypt. I have only visited America on four or five occasions. Do you think the American press would be interested in my story? I have much to give them—what is it called?— *hard* evidence? Do you think this would please them?"

"I *don't know* the answers you are asking for," Jackson whispered again, his voice cracking. "You will ruin me if you press forward with this. Me and many other innocent people."

"I will ruin my soul if I do not," Abu declared. And then, as if a cartoon light bulb appeared above his head, "Thank you. Yes, thank you, Dr. Jackson. You have helped me make up my mind. I think the *New York Times* would be a good place to start. . . ."

Jackson nearly spat. "Rumors! That's all I've heard!"

"Really? Share them."

"Not even rumors. Rumors of rumors. I don't know anything to tell. Dr. Remming and I rarely correspond. All I can tell you is that he is a man of considerable influence on this campus. No one checks up on Remming. His research is allowed *carte blanche,* sometimes with a wink and a nod if necessary. Ninety-five percent is legit and well documented, even a matter of public record. But he has big connections:

the military, CIA, United Nations. You know—*big* stuff. Top-level clearance. He helped them with the Gulf War, I think."

"Is STM-55 a part of that?" Abu demanded, swooping in. "Is it an operation of your government?"

"I don't know! I swear I've never even heard of STM-55 until now. But I wouldn't be surprised. I wouldn't be surprised at all." He sighed. "If that's what you want me to say, I've said it, but I'll never speak of this again with you. Do you understand? I must go. Good-bye."

The phone clicked; the line went dead. Abu folded his arms behind his head, leaned back in his chair, closed his eyes, thinking. The great cacophony of recent events began to coalesce into some semblance of preservability. A recent memory surfaced, like a bubble slipping free of a rock on the bottom of a lake, rising slowly, slowly, erupting on the surface, silently rippling outward.

"Greetings in the name of my God. . . ."

Whose God? Whose? It wasn't his God! Yet if ever he needed guidance, assurance, peace, it was now. Now, when he had done so much wrong, labored for so much foolishness. Where to turn?

What to do? Abu wondered. *I cannot continue as I am.*

And he knew this to be true of both himself and his research. The simplicity of the revelation shocked him, pierced his heart, answered his self-aggrandizing pity with the cool sobriety of purpose, adding color to the paleness of his doubt. It was a moment of divine intent.

". . . in the name of my God . . . Jesus."

There lay all the answer he needed. Finally, he did not resist.

☗ ☗ ☗

My, what a difference a single night can make!

"Wake up," Jessica muttered irritably, perched on the edge of the bed, looking down at the patch of carpet Hank occupied. She said it again. Squinting, Hank stirred, sat up. Pressed against his skin all night, his clothes were a road map of wrinkles. Jessica half smiled, a perfunctory gesture at best. Her face and voice were still sleepy, her eyes heavy lidded, iguanalike.

She rose, threw open the window curtain, stood there, staring out. Light filled the room.

Hank wiped his eyes. With the noonish sunlight tangling in her hair, turning to apricot flame, Hank was transfixed. He tried not to stare, tried to look away, but found himself warmly appreciative and, quite simply, unable to do otherwise. He would need the better part of half a day to really get a clue. Now, however, he found the red-haired woman before him utterly and completely beautiful, dreamlike.

His watching did not go over well.

First of all, Jessica had not slept well. Second, she was not a good morning person. Third and most important, she had no intention of allowing last night's strange wave of emotion to repeat itself. She recalled all too clearly how giddy she was, how she nearly—(though she could hardly stand to think the word)—*swooned*. The memory made her feel foolish and ashamed. Even worse, it made her feel vulnerable, which she hated. If Hank wanted sex, fine. That was one thing. She could tolerate the immediate and singular connection: bing-bang-boom, don't call me too soon. Just don't start to dress it up with sentiment, with the pretense of significance.

So over the course of the night, since she was awake much of it anyway, wielding trial logic and long, protracted mental arguments, she convinced herself that her reaction was nothing more extraordinary than the usual Freudian release of pent-up emotions. Perfectly natural. She had gone to therapy enough to know that casual sex was her "coping mechanism." Thus, her unusual attraction to Hank was nothing spectacular. Any more than Tony. Or Grady. Or any of the others. After that, she was able to fall asleep.

She awoke with the same certainty. This was not the time or place for romance . . . certainly not that starry-eyed brand of Harlequin tripe that turns a woman into putty in the strong hands of her mysterious new lover. Jessica rolled her eyes at the very thought. What a load! Watching Hank stare at her, Jessica felt scornful. Who did he think he was impressing with his Mr. Stare-at-her-until-she-melts gaze?! A thousand cutting remarks sprang to mind, but she checked them. He wasn't slobbering, at least.

She rose, strode into the bathroom, turned on the water. Enough! Now was the time only for answers and information. She and Hank had barely scratched the surface last night and Jessica was determined not to leave New York City until the issue of her mother was *fully* resolved. Call it penance, if necessary. Whatever. But Hank was a useful ally.

As she washed her face, she realized in terms more cold and clear than the water on her skin that last night was a hundred million miles away from reality. Freshly scrubbed, she took a seat on her knees on the floor in front of him, still wearing her pajamas: a pair of boxer shorts and an oversize T-shirt. Her plan was to simply keep him at hand's length until his interest turned elsewhere—as she had time and again with other men—until she found out what she needed to know.

But when she spoke—completely unwilled—a coy, mischievous look crept over her face, like an eleven-year-old girl sneaking lipstick from her mother's purse to use for flirting with the new boy across the street. She buried it quickly in a cough.

"We should probably come up with a plan for the day, don't you think?"

Somehow Hank knew her struggle, the fight within her, but missed the point. He figured she was still just sleepy, or playing hard to get. And that only made her more cute.

"Well, we've got to work through some things. I'm still very confused about your mother's situation, but I'm suspecting more and more that it overlaps somehow with the God Spot, since Remming had his hands in both and seemed hesitant to talk too much about your mother's case."

"And because of the strange questions he asked," Jessica reminded.

"Right. I don't know how the two connect, though. Even more pressing for me is to figure out what to do with these files. There are probably people out there looking for me right now. And I don't like always looking over my shoulder."

Jessica waited for more. "So . . . ?"

Hank switched gears. It was hard to get excited about saving the world with those luscious lips only about eighteen inches from his. Maybe another day or two in hiding would help calm the waters. "I think I need to lay low for a day or so. Maybe you should, too, if only to get some rest and a fresh perspective. I know a cozy little place overlooking the bay. How's that for a plan? And then dinner?"

Jessica's eyes withered. "And then we get back to reality. Listen, I don't want there to be any misperceptions."

Hank raised an eyebrow. "I don't think there are."

"Good. So what do you intend to do about this stuff?"

"Stuff?"

"What we've been talking about. My mother. Your weird brain stuff. We don't have time to lay around navel-gazing. You said it yourself, the two may be connected. Even if they aren't, something's not square."

Hank didn't reply. In fact, he hardly heard her words, though she sure looked cute saying them. All he wanted to do was kiss her. Just one kiss. He almost did, right there, right there; no words, just— whoops!—right on the lips. But . . .

That was earlier this morning, when he was still sleepy and easily confused. Since then, the two had shared breakfast, a rather sullen affair thanks to Jessica. They had talked politics sitting on a park bench. That conversation had turned sour as well. Jessica was a card-carrying liberal, a political mechanic looking for somebody else's flat tire to fix. Everything amounted to a cause to champion, a disease to cure, an opportunity for interference. Hank's Teutonic self-reliance naturally recoiled. Curiosity was one thing that he possessed in abundance. Suspicion was another. You could go so far with suspicion and safely stop. In fact, suspicion was a fine method of self-preservation. But Jessica's radical brand of self-indulgent activism . . . well, that was another matter entirely. Someone could get hurt.

Probably him. He said as much.

No, Jessica thought secretly. But she was thinking of deeper things. *Probably me.*

They continued talking all morning, strictly business; kept right on through lunch. Hank tried to treat Jessica to a nice little French bistro, but she would have none of it and paid her own way. Smacking on a platter of croissant finger foods, neither could formulate how everything fit together, but both agreed something was horribly wrong—a fact that seemed clearer in daylight—that maybe everything *was* connected. Since their politics had run afoul, Jessica asked Hank again, for the fifth or sixth time, what he planned to do; he had ducked the question all day.

As he took a bite of a small croissant stuffed with smoked trout and some kind of mustard sauce, Hank thought for a moment. "What do you think I should do?"

"Not a chance. You first."

"I get the feeling this is a test."

"Nope. I just think you should have a plan. You can't wing this anymore."

"Believe me, I've been racking my brain. You know what I told Remming? I told Remming I was going to take everything to the FBI. That was my plan."

"But . . . ?"

"I've reconsidered."

"Reconsidered?" Jessica said doubtfully.

"I got to thinking. If the CIA is on the uptake, how can I be sure I'm giving the stuff to someone clean at the FBI?"

Jessica smirked, but not so much at him. "Not everyone is crooked, Hank. I've got friends at the FBI in Oregon. They're decent people."

"That doesn't necessarily prove anything."

"No, but you've got to start somewhere."

Hank was dismissive. "Even if I manage to give everything to the right grunt, let's say he's a good man—"

"Person."

"Whatever. That person's boss or their boss's boss may *not* be clean, whether it's with the CIA or not. I just don't much trust the government, you know?"

"It's a minefield. That's why I went with defense instead of prosecution. All the political back-scratching disgusts me."

"Exactly."

"Which is all fine and good. But suspicions of collusion between the CIA and FBI may be borrowing a bit much from the Oliver Stone playbook. You have no legitimate reason to suspect anything on that level. The two don't overlap. One is generally internal investigation, the other external operations."

In the back of his mind, from a casual distance, Hank realized he and Jessica were finally having a nice, normal conversation. The first so far today. He said, "I want to get rid of this stuff. Believe me, I want to unload and move on."

"Yeah, but don't you want to nail these guys first?"

"Of course I do. Given the choice, though, I'd rather stay alive."

Jessica shook her head emphatically. "If 'they' wanted you dead, we wouldn't be talking right now."

"Maybe, maybe not. Point is, I didn't mean to *start* anything. I'm not a crusader and never wanted to be. I'm a doctor, for crying out loud. I was just trying to hack for fun. And then it grew. I should have stopped, but I kept digging. And the hole kept getting deeper and deeper. Now it's way too big—which may be my fault—but I'm done. I want my career. I want my practice. I want to move on."

"I can't believe what I'm hearing," Jessica said slowly, still shaking her head. "I didn't expect this from you."

"What?"

"Cowardice. You seemed more determined to me. Last night. Your stories."

Cowardice? The word didn't bother Hank as much as it could have. He had seen Kim's place and heard about Rosenburg. He understood the danger, whether Jessica did or not. But he was curious. "Determined how? From the hacking and stuff?"

"Partly. But the hacking and investigation *came* from somewhere. From passion and commitment, I thought. Not just from playing around. I love fire in the belly."

Do you, now? Hank thought. *Interesting.* He picked up a stalk of celery stuffed with some sort of cream cheese, waving it in front of his face. "See, I'm not pretending to know what to do. I just know I don't trust these people. At some level, they all become the same. If that's true, then doing nothing may be better than doing the wrong thing."

"That dog won't hunt and you know it."

"I said *if.* And no, I really don't."

Jessica was incredulous. "Yes you do! You've got to know better."

"So I should take it to the FBI? That simple?"

"I'm not saying it's a perfect option, but it's the best you've got. The rest stink."

"Yeah? What about the cops?"

"In New York City? And you were concerned about corruption?"

"Federal marshals?"

"Maybe. The FBI makes more sense, though."

Hank shrugged, kept eating. Jessica sipped her drink. "I could keep it all hidden in a safe somewhere and wait until everything blows over. I might have a better idea by then."

"Yes and by then it might be too late. Besides, how long do you think you could hold out? What good will that possibly do in the end?"

"Well, for starters," he replied, licking his fingers, "I get to not be dead."

No laughter. Jessica didn't buy into the melodrama of the joke, nor the joke of the melodrama. So, after wiping a bit of mustard off his bottom lip with his napkin, Hank changed directions. "My grandfather was part Native American. Have I told you that already?"

Jessica shook her head.

Hank smiled at the memory. "One thirty-second or something. Not much. He was actually a nasal-nosed Vermont Yankee. The important thing to me was that he *looked* kind of Indian. And he talked like one. Had that wise sort of sensibility about him. He died a few years back—I think six now—but I remember him so clearly. Big guy, gray hair, larger than life. He seemed so earthy, like a tree stump or something, rooted, unmovable. I remember how anytime I used to go at someone or get out of sorts he would stop me and lay his hands on my shoulders—he had big, leathery hands—and say, 'Don't criticize your brother—'"

"'Until you've walked a mile in his moccasins,'" Jessica finished.

Hank shook his head patiently. "No, no. Basically it was 'Don't fault someone for faulting you.' Now get this, because if I remember right, Jesus said pretty much the same thing a long time before my grandfather. I can't remember where—somewhere in the Bible—it's been a while, but—"

"Hank, listen."

"No, please, *you* listen. I'm not going to blame you for disagreeing with me. But I can't let that affect me, either. I imagine if I were you and not me it might seem that easy to me, also. But I *am* me. I know what the last few days have been like. I can't convince you of how close I've come to being"—he held up his fingers like quotation marks—"'eliminated.' And I won't even try. But plain and simple, I'm in over my head. And right now, getting out as quick and easy as possible sounds real nice."

"You're right: I don't and cannot understand. You have single-handedly uncovered a major international medical junta. Do you realize that? *Major.* And now you're just going to brush it off, no big deal, better to move on and forget about it. I've got my career and all. Well, know what I think? I think it's an excuse and I don't get it. Who cares what Jesus said? If you do nothing else, at the very least give the stuff to the FBI."

Hank held up both hands, pushing back slightly from the table. "What are you doing, Jessica?" he asked. "Why are you so gung-ho about this? It has nothing to do with you, really."

Jessica leaned over, locked eyes with Hank. If anything, she seemed energized by his question, not deterred. "The truth is *always* worth it." She didn't elaborate, didn't soften her voice; after a moment, she added, "My mother is dead. You yourself said this seems related. If it is related in the slightest, I want somebody to pay."

So now we get to it, Hank thought, though he couldn't blame her. In fact, still reeling from her first response, he hardly processed the revenge thing. *The truth is always worth it . . . always worth it.* The words hit him full in the chest; even more, the passion behind the words. He could do nothing but stare. At Jessica. Everything about her—body language, intonation, the set of her face—was pledged to those words. They meant something. Each one was a well-placed hand grenade lobbed into the superficiality of Hank's house-of-cards life. Left among the rubble, he could do little more than marvel and try to rationalize his own naked guilt. When was the last time he had felt that passionate about something? Not occupationally, but in *principle.*

Bound by honor.

In that moment, Jessica *became* beautiful to Hank. Not attractive. Beautiful.

The conversation fell to silence, both brooding over their food, staring at their hands, the silverware—anything but each other. Jessica knew she had given a part of herself away; surprisingly, Hank didn't capitalize on it. Instead, licking his fingers, he wondered aloud, almost philosophically, "Just give it to 'em, huh? Just hand everything over to the FBI? Isn't that turning and walking away just as much as doing nothing?"

No reply at first. Jessica glanced to the street, watching traffic and passersby. Then a devilish smile began to crease her lips. "What if we play the game on our terms? Let's give the files to the FBI. You can tell them you're out of the game. That way, just in case they *are* dirty, they'll still leave you alone." She crossed her fingers. "Meanwhile, we'll keep a copy of the files to work from."

"Work from?" Hank replied darkly. This didn't sound good.

"Hank, the only way you'll ever be free is to finish this thing. The FBI *may* be able to do it for you. They are certainly the best place to start. But you've got to hedge your bets. For your own sake. You're on the inside and they aren't. Who do you think has the best chance of figuring this out?"

"Why not just leak it all to the press? That was my last great hope."

"Leak what? You've got a bunch of data but no real cohesion or evidence. If the press tried to chase this down at this stage, Remming and Columbia or the CIA or whoever else could frame a reasonable denial. And you'd be the goat."

Hank searched for a quick retort. He had none. He did not trust the FBI. But, as earlier, when he had first conceived the idea of giving the data to them, he knew he had little choice. For her part, Jessica had simply played the role of his personal attorney, cutting through the details with cold logic.

He still didn't like it.

"I'll think about it," he said.

Most of the rest of the afternoon was spent meandering through Greenwich Village drinking cappuccino out of Styrofoam cups. Conversation was steady and reasonably pleasant, a definite improvement over the morning's fare. Somehow, during lunch, they turned a corner together. Not toward romance by any means. Certain topics were simply too hot, mostly concerning politics. Whenever they bumped into one, the exchange that followed was much like pulling teeth with a pair of salad spoons: painful and clumsy.

Yet if not toward romance, then certainly toward trust, or something very near to it. Also to some degree of mutual acceptance. They differed, and that was OK. Hank was not in any hurry and he made sure Jessica understood the same, through distance and honesty and careful attention to details . . . for her sake and his. Because, in truth, the *only* relationship they really had was much closer to doctor-patient than anything else. In spite of the chemistry. He knew she felt something, even now, but neither of them knew how to proceed. Too volatile, those feelings.

At least they could be friends. Jessica did seem much warmer, looser, freer toward him. More responsive. She smiled. They laughed. Whatever battles she had waged last night and this morning did not resurface for the rest of the day, which rolled leisurely along, in spite of their troubles.

In fact, like a gift, both forgot for a while, maybe only five minutes, all their problems.

As the afternoon wore on, two facts became irrepressibly clear to Hank, who tried to ignore both. First, friends or not, he could not stand near Jessica without every cell on the surface of his skin tingling. She was an electric spark. He would have died for any one of the dozen little smiles that he himself created.

Second, forgetfulness never lasted long. In between every step, or at least every other step, deep inside where conversations are not crafted of words but certainties, Hank knew that it would be a terrible mistake to give the files to the FBI.

Two things. No, make that three.

Tomorrow morning, for Jessica, he knew he would do one more thing, the very thing he should not: give everything to the FBI.

§ § §

Abu arrived home at half past ten, curious and alive, yet feeling strangely vulnerable to the possibility of exposure—mainly political, but sadly, Abu realized, also cultural. In spite of this he also felt peace—a strange, surreal peace that nicely counterbalanced his bug-in-a-jar premonitions. His experience with the truth of Christ, though profound, was largely circumspect in nature; transforming, yes, but not in a theological sense, since Abu knew very little Christian theology.

He knew Christian history, but that, too, was incidental. Rather, his experience was one of almost pure spirit, translating downward not so much into an emotional release as a physical rejuvenation of sensual proportions, with an extra measure of rational clarity thrown in to boot. As a result, things made a little more sense, seemed a little sharper in focus, made his pulse a little quicker with possibility and vigor.

That was the positive. On the flip side, his life was still a tangled mess. The reality of Christ had not eliminated his present distress. Abu had chosen his path and taken the next step. There would almost certainly be repercussions. For one, what would his family think? His wife? His children?

Even more important, it was at this point that the "path" grew ambiguous again. What to do next? How? Where? He made his way through his home, searching for his wife, hearing her voice from the living room. As he walked in she was hanging up the phone. Her face was pale.

"What is it?" Abu asked.

"Abu, what is going on?"

"What do you mean?"

"Someone from the university called. They said they were given instructions regarding a flight you are to take immediately to a research facility in Guatemala."

Abu raised an eyebrow, was otherwise blank. *Guatemala?*

"Who called? What do you mean?"

"They said it was related to your brain research. It sounded very serious, Abu. They said you are to go immediately. Your flight leaves in less than an hour."

Abu reached out his hand. "But why are you distressed?"

The small woman took a step closer, laid her head on Abu's chest. "What is in Guatemala? You have told me nothing."

"It is because I have no idea myself. I was sworn to secrecy on my research, but this is the first I have heard of Guatemala."

Saludin's wife touched the back of his neck with her hand, feeling his hair between her fingers. Her voice was soft but heavy. "Before I even answered the phone, I felt sorrow in my heart. I don't want you to go."

But to Abu the path had become clear again.

"I think I must," he said. "But first, there is something wonderful I need to tell you."

18

A winding dirt road framed with grass and heather and abundant pine trees made the final leg of the journey to New Hudson a picture of pastoral bliss. Buck Keegan did not live in the town proper, nor truly did he live just outside the small farming community. Keegan lived in what would generously qualify as the "boonies," on a sprawling tangle of pasture and meadow and freshwater streams, bordered on all sides by Montana-esque skies.

It took Missy and Ravelo several tries to find the place. Few of the townspeople knew Keegan personally, though most seemed familiar with Ranch-K. The drive, uneventful and quiet, induced a state of lassitude in Ravelo about the halfway mark, so with the holy man out of pocket, Missy felt comfortable laying a heavy foot on the pedal. They made good time.

South here, east there, down a dirt road and then another, then a small circle of wood, painted green, burned skillfully with the letter *K*, and a final winding stretch of worn path through a line of trees that looked to be a windbreak.

"I think we've found our doctor," Ravelo mumbled, not quite fully awake.

The exterior of Keegan's ranch home was simple, delightful, and thoroughly fitted to the location. The home was primitive in every respect—or at least maintained the look of primitivity—except for the patently modern forest green standing-seam metal roof. Constructed of hand-planed log beams, placed and mortared with precision, Keegan's home overlooked a small pond and was surrounded on three sides by a well-maintained perimeter of freshly tended grass and landscaping. Beyond the perimeter and fence line, all else was left to grow wild and the bleating of goats or sheep could be heard from the direction of the vaguely wooded southward pastures. A tractor was parked by a small barn out back.

The reporter and the priest approached the front door, but before they could even knock, the front door swung wide, and a simple, handsome, leathered face peered out from behind the metal lacing of the screen door.

"You must be the lady from the *Sentinel*," Keegan said. His pebble brown hair needed cutting, or combing, or both, and his denim shirt needed washing. Or ironing. Or both. But his smile was warm enough. Kind of. Maybe more like academically tolerant. It was the kind of smile that immediately begged a question, a "Welcome!" and a "Why?" and a "Who cares?" all wrapped up into one fleeting movement of the lips—fleeting because Keegan did not try to hold on to his smiles.

He threw the screen door open. "Come on in."

With blue jeans and horn-rimmed glasses, hands folded leisurely in his pockets, mud on his boots, Keegan looked like a cross between an older Buddy Holly and younger Jack Kerouac, like a farmer-philosopher who knew more secrets than the dirt under his fingernails, not because he was old but because he noticed things. There was a raw, teeming intellect in his eyes that seemed intensely focused, ever on the verge of announcement, yet by design, never announced. Missy guessed he was thirty-seven. Maybe thirty-eight.

"My name's Ravelo," Father Ravelo said, extending his hand. Keegan pumped it twice and let go.

"And I'm Missy Jenkins."

More handshakes. Keegan motioned for them to sit, which they did, around a sturdy, beautiful oak table.

"I'm not usually given to entertaining," Keegan said. "I have nothing to offer you. Water maybe?"

Both said no. Missy let her eyes wander for a moment. The home was large and almost completely open, floored in hardwood, sparsely furnished except for an occasional plant or wood carving or area rug or painting—usually reflecting an impeccable but simple taste. One could move with generous provision from the wide-open den to the kitchen to quiet dining by the fireplace without a partitioning wall in sight. Other rooms seemed to be farther back, but overhead, the high-vaulted ceiling and massive cedar beams made the Keegan home a spacious, inviting retreat. And clean. Missy couldn't see a mote of dust in the air. She looked again at Keegan for clues. He was disheveled and relaxed, poised but hardly stiff. There was no ring on his finger. He appeared to be completely alone.

"Would you mind?" he asked suddenly, gliding to a shelf full of books, in the middle of which rested an impressive stereo system. It was then that Missy noticed the complete lack of modern accoutrements—no television, no computer, no microwave, only the stereo and literally half a wall full of CDs. Probably four or five hundred total.

"The one luxury I cannot seem to sacrifice," he said, pushing a button. A moment or two later, from all directions, the intimate piano musings of David Lantz filled the air.

"Dr. Keegan—"

The doctor did not turn around, did not respond. He held up two fingers over his shoulder, signaling a call for silence. The music stirred. He swayed for a moment, closed his eyes, feeling.

"Music," he breathed at length. "Do you feel that? The world could not go on without it."

Ravelo decided then and there that he liked this Buck Keegan fellow. Missy did not gravitate to eccentricity. All she could think was, *No wonder the guy's single.*

The spell of the music passed. Keegan rejoined them at the table, grousing. "So, the rags want to do a little token story on alternative medicine, huh?" Surprised, Father Ravelo—ever the quick one—shot Missy an immediate and disapproving glare. Missy shrugged, unperturbed by the moral contrivances of angling for a story. Regardless, Keegan didn't notice. His brief monologue continued, mildly barbed and patronizing. "Hit a dry spot in the otherwise pressing editorial season? Or just trying to capitalize on the New Age craze? Maybe the *Sentinel* hopes to take the highbrow approach, appearing objective."

Odd . . . and a chip on his shoulder. *Great,* Missy thought.

"Sounds like you've had run-ins with the press before," she murmured as politely as possible, scrounging for the reporter's tablet buried somewhere in her massive purse.

Keegan snorted, wagged his head. "That's the only thing *anyone* has with the press: head-on collisions. Normally in the form of invasion of privacy, libel, irresponsibility. You name it."

Yes, Ravelo liked this fellow more and more.

Missy veneered her irritation with curiosity. "So if you knew I was with the *Sentinel* . . . ?"

To which the doctor only smiled another enigmatic smile, the complex sort of facial expression the queen of England might use when she shakes hands with strangers in a crowd, pretending she gives a rip. "I suppose I'm a glutton for punishment."

"I doubt it," Missy said. "More likely an opportunist."

It was a game. "Ah, so here we go. Enlighten me."

"I did some checking," Missy replied flatly. "You were a fairly controversial figure in the early eighties, got burned for prescribing marijuana for medicinal purposes at your clinic in Colorado, did a little jail time, license suspended, moved here in '91, took up herbalism and other natural healing methods. Nothing much since."

Keegan's eyes narrowed. "Nothing much."

"Except that I checked with your agent from your last book in 1987. Amazingly enough, she referred me in a whisper to your *current* publishing house. Apparently you have a new book coming out next year? Maybe a groundbreaking new study on aroma therapy or something? I really don't know. My guess is you probably figured this interview would be a good way to generate some advance buzz."

Ravelo cocked his head to look again at Missy, sizing her up in a fresh way. Keegan, too, leaned forward, wolfish. "You accuse me of staging a completely self-serving event, even though you *know* that when the final story runs you will horribly misquote me, almost with intent, to give your story the angle you have *predetermined* it should have." He smiled again. "Nothing personal, you realize."

"Of course. Nothing personal."

Ravelo rubbed his eyes. This was not at all what he had planned. He did not know Missy well, was actually quite impressed with this latest display, but he could tell she was starting to vibrate. Keegan, however, cool, unflappable, arrogant, was being led down a rabbit trail that would likely lead to a quick eviction for the intrepid duo when the truth was unmasked. And that would be the last of the only piece of relevant information they had yet uncovered. Ravelo decided to intervene.

"Dr. Keegan, I must apologize. My reporter friend may be working on more than one story, I don't know. I am here for one reason and one reason only. I'm sure you've heard about Luther Sanchez's recent execution?"

He hadn't, that much was obvious. The news took a moment to register. Keegan sat back in his chair, put both hands behind his head, and cursed softly.

"Ms. Jenkins and I have been collaborating on certain statements made by Luther Sanchez before his execution. I was the attending priest at his last rites. There are several extremely suspicious elements surrounding not so much his death as the life that led to his death."

"I see," said Keegan, but his eyes were a million miles away.

"Does this surprise you?"

Keegan tugged at his ear, wiped his beardless face. "Hard as it may be to believe, I actually hadn't heard a thing. I haven't read a newspaper in probably six months. And"—he waved—"no television."

"But you did know him?" Missy asked.

"Yes, yes." He focused on Missy. "That's really why you're here, isn't it?"

Caught, Missy lowered her eyes. She didn't like feeling caught.

"Who is the self-serving one now, Ms. Jenkins?"

Again, Father Ravelo intervened. "This whole situation has been handled a little unevenly, I think. And I personally want to apologize for that. But you must understand, you are the only link we have uncovered—"

"Link?"

"Personal. Professional. We don't know. We don't know what kind of relationship you had with him. We just know there was one. You're the only one we've been able to find."

"I think the two of you should leave."

Ravelo extended his hands. "Please, Dr. Keegan."

"No, I think you should. I did know Luther. Briefly. But I would be of no help to you, I'm sure."

Missy pressed in. "You seem sad that he's dead. Why, if you barely knew him?"

"I said briefly. I did not say barely." He rose stiffly, headed for the door, opened it wide. "Please, go."

Missy looked to Ravelo. He, too, was surprised at the reaction. But with little recourse, they both rose and headed for the door. Dr. Keegan said nothing as they passed by.

"I'm sorry for the misunderstanding," Ravelo said. But his face was on Missy. "We should have been more forthcoming."

"We are all users in one way or another," Keegan replied. "Good-bye."

Before he could close the door, Missy made a sudden and obvious connection. She blurted out, "I just have one question. How could you have possibly not known about Luther's death when you personally cleared out his safety deposit box?"

Dr. Keegan looked puzzled. "Box?"

No one said a word.

Three hours later, the three remained deep in discussion around the kitchen table, papers spread all about, on the floor, the table, the sofa. Although it was apparent that someone other than the real Dr. Buck Keegan had reclaimed the contents of the box, Keegan himself kept a meticulous catalog of all his files, with duplicates of everything carefully stored on the premises.

He told a simple story: Six years ago, a young Latino named Luther Sanchez had shown up at his home late one evening, afraid, begging for help. Luther was on the run for some petty stuff and admitted as much. He told Keegan he was "going crazy" and knew he would do something terrible if Keegan couldn't help him. According to Keegan, Luther said he had tried all the normal treatments, drugs, psychotherapy, etc., and nothing worked. He had "voices" and urges and compelling needs beyond his ability to control or silence.

He said it had been like that since he was a little kid. The voices. The agony. The rage. He behaved violently as a kid, in strange ways, ways he could not control. He tortured bugs and small animals. Not just typical little-boy stuff, either. Much more imaginative and cruel.

He would drive a long thin sewing needle through the thorax of a grasshopper or spider and then put a match to the other end of the needle, heating it slowly, so that the insect burned alive for several minutes from the inside out. He was four years old when he first did that. He did it to a mouse when he was seven. When the mouse died too quickly, robbing him of the pleasure of its writhing, squealing body, he took the mouse and, in a rage, threw it repeatedly against a wall. His mother found him an hour later still throwing the body, although by then all that was left was the split, bloodstained hide. His appetite for punishment—for himself and others—was insatiable. During his teenage years, the only thing that kept him from killing was that he was stoned. Addiction for Luther was a gift. The numbness was as good as answered prayers. So at eleven, when an older acquaintance—Luther had no friends—gave him a hit of crack, he was voracious and grateful. Started right off on the heavy stuff. For the next eight years Luther rarely came down. He was constantly in jail for theft, assault, or something, but was never tried as an adult and so moved from probation to probation. His mother died of cancer when he was seventeen, at which point he was placed in foster care. By eighteen he had been in and out of twenty-three foster homes. In the twenty-fourth, the father tried to sexually abuse him. Luther killed the man. It was judged an act of self-defense, but Luther was sentenced to seven years for manslaughter. He served three and was out on parole. He tried to make it on his own, but six months out, things were getting worse even faster than before.

Luther had told Keegan he averaged maybe two to three hours of sleep a night because of the voices. Sometimes they whispered. Sometimes they screamed. They demanded and directed, like ravenous spirits of hunger. He didn't care about sex, because the voices said sex was wrong, but all of his prime male energy demanded aggressive release. He was bright, at least above average, but with a sick sense of humor. Yet he could be surprisingly gentle. On two occasions Keegan had been present when the voices came, and on both Luther seemed relieved when they grew quiet again. Both times, he wept.

Unfortunately, the voices were rarely quiet. The rage rarely slept. Everywhere he went, Luther saw a need for punishment. Someone, something *needed* punishment. Those were the things the voices demanded, randomly. In the quiet moments, Luther knew better, knew something was terribly wrong. He tried physicians; he stole money to pay for counseling and treatment. He even went to church once or twice. Nothing worked. So he wandered—ran actually, here, there, all over the country, looking for escape. He tried to kill himself twice, failed both times.

And then he showed up at Buck Keegan's. Right before the killing spree began. The spree that earned him the nickname "Bone Crusher" by the FBI, which launched a nationwide manhunt for him. Before his capture, Luther Sanchez was number four on the Ten Most Wanted list.

"Were you able to help him at all?" Missy asked.

"Not in the slightest. Which puzzled me, since I have quite a record for breakthrough treatments with nonresponsive patients. Luther's psychosis was profound, beyond the pale. I've seen dementia, neurosis, schizophrenia. I've seen cancer of every stripe, leukemia, Hodgkin's, Parkinson's, spinal damage. You name it, I've worked with it *and* on it. That's my field, on the edge, with all manner of biological and biochemical aberrations. Usually, I can customize a regiment of therapies, both conventional, and wholistic and experimental—when necessary—to achieve at least a measure of success. Most of the time it's not so much a matter of combating disease, which is what conventional medicine does, but of renewal, of restoring the body's natural sufficiency for the task at hand, enabling one's own system to rise to the challenge and win the day. But with Luther"—he spread his hands—"nothing. It almost seemed . . . I don't know."

"What?" Ravelo said gently. "Tell us what it seemed."

"I just don't know. My approach has always been to treat the source, not the symptoms. To get at the root of a problem. But with Luther that seemed impossible. It went too deep. Luther's psychosis was not a matter of chemical imbalances in the brain. And I'll have you know, I wasn't a fool. I got help. I worked with colleagues I trust and respect, preeminent in their field. No one had a clue. Luther's levels were well within quote 'normal' ranges. He was as sane as you and I. Mostly."

"But not entirely."

"It was genetic, I think. Unnaturally so. Manipulated. It made me angry. Luther was obviously in torment. We had been trying different

approaches for weeks and getting nowhere. He was increasingly frustrated, increasingly fragile. I feared for myself at times, even more for
Luther. So I started snooping around. That's how I came up with all this
stuff. And now I'm convinced, even more since you've arrived. . . ."

"Convinced of what?"

Dr. Keegan hunched forward in his chair, took a deep, hard
breath. He seemed more comfortable looking at Ravelo than Missy,
but uncomfortable just the same, as if the words he spoke were taste-
less plastic. "Luther Sanchez was a guinea pig. Someone messed him
up early, early on. I don't know how—at least I didn't in time to help
him. But I'm convinced Luther might have been a normal child if it
weren't for this." He reached over to a stack of papers about two inches
thick, a stack he had hovered over protectively until now. Missy and
Ravelo had read through dozens of other pages, many of them too
technical to decipher. Missy glanced at this new stack eagerly. The
human drama of this story was horrific; still, she could not get past the
magnitude of the story as "scoop." It was a return to glory. She was
already writing headlines.

Hesitantly, almost fearfully, Keegan slid the stack of papers forward to the middle of the table. On the top page was an embossed and
very official-looking seal. Someone had stamped "Declassified" in red
ink twice, partially obscuring the document title. Missy looked closer,
salivating:

Counterinsurgent Measures
A Summary Report on Experimental Procedures
Sample G: Project Pacifist, 1968, 1970, 1971
Department of Defense
Classification: Extreme, Level 4
Unauthorized communication strictly prohibited

Missy reached for the tome, felt the crisp, raised seal, like braille,
with wonder. Ravelo calmly laid his hand on hers.

"Tell us what this is," he said to Keegan.

It's gold, Missy thought.

"It's a lot of strings I had to pull, a lot of favors I had to call in. I had
researched for weeks and come up with zilch. This file was officially

declassified in 1988. Even so, they have ways of hiding the fact that a thing is available."

"They? The government?" Missy asked.

"Of course the government!" Keegan said, annoyed to have to connect the dots. "Who else would have a stake in this? Bunch of rats."

Missy pulled the stack closer, began to read, page by page. Ravelo removed his glasses and held them up to the light, put them to his shirt, held them up again, looking for smears and lint. The clarity in the room was sobering. Even without knowing what the document said, the moment felt *authentic*.

In the silence, Missy read. Two pages, three. Ravelo felt sorrow in the moment—sorrow and heaviness. He returned again and again in his mind to the memory of Luther sitting before him in his cell, seemingly insane, frightened to die, yet strangely comforted by the thought of death. He recalled the raging, scornful hope of grace in Luther's pockmarked face, against all odds, as Ravelo offered last rites. The hope against hope, which is the truest, best kind. Ravelo wondered if he had said everything he should have in that moment. Keegan rose and paced, staring at the floor.

"Oh, my God," Missy breathed once. Ravelo glanced up. Missy kept reading.

"Oh, my God!" she said again.

Keegan stepped forward, pained. "Take it with you. All of it."

Missy looked up with a kind of terror in her eyes.

"Did this really happen? Are you sure this is real?"

"Just take it. It's all real. I don't want it anymore."

Missy made the connection. "*This* is what was in the safety deposit box. You left it for him."

Keegan lowered his head, ran his fingers through his hair. He had invested much in Luther Sanchez. "By the time I finally got hold of most of this, he was gone. I think he had begun the killing. When I heard of his capture years later, I made copies of everything and put it in the box. For when he got out. *If* he got out."

And then the unspoken truth hit them all at the same time. Whoever *had* emptied the box in Keegan's name did not want anyone else to know about Project Pacifist.

"Are you sure?" Ravelo said. "Are you sure you want us to have it?"

Keegan nodded. "I don't want it anymore. I've carried it long enough. If you can take it and do something good with it, then . . ."

"We'll try," Missy said. "Every now and then we score a big one."

Together, she and Ravelo gathered their things and left. As they walked in silence to the car, they heard behind them the sorrow of the Pachelbel Canon lifting into the crisp afternoon air.

❧ ❧ ❧

"Just a formality, sir. Try not to blink."

The pulsing blue light scanned vertically first, then horizontally across the surface of Remming's eye. Colonel Netterson watched alertly, waiting for confirmation. Remming *didn't* blink. He didn't tremble. He had done this sort of thing before. But his mind raced just the same.

What is happening?

When he arose this morning, he had expected nothing of this magnitude.

From the barracks, Colonel Netterson had escorted Volgaard and him by jeep down another dirt road, one Remming hadn't noticed before, cleverly concealed behind the barracks at the rear of the compound. They spent another fifteen minutes bumping and jostling through more jungle. As they traveled, the terrain grew notably and steadily more mountainous. Remming had absolutely no sense of direction by now, but he was wise to the heavy canopy of tree cover shadowing the road. Whatever this operation was about, it was intended to be hard to find from ground *and* sky.

"I don't suppose you are allowed to say what part of Guatemala we are in?" he asked Colonel Netterson.

The colonel shook his head. "No, sir. I'm not."

Remming glanced all around, at the foliage, the towering hardwood, the dense underbrush, the occasional blur of birds and vermin. He directed his thoughts to Volgaard. "Obviously we're on the outskirts of the highlands, but I suspect we're a long way from Guatemala City. Still, it doesn't make much sense that we weren't routed through the capital. I wasn't. Were you?"

Volgaard shook her head. The roar of the engine was loud.

Before long they arrived at another security post. A high chain link fence, topped with barbed wire, intersected the road all of a sudden, right as the jeep rounded the base of a craggy, moss-covered hill. The fence stretched up the length of the hill in one direction and cut an electric metal path through nearly impassable jungle in the other. In the middle was a gate, offset by a larger than usual checkpoint and a sizable security force, all in blue helmets. Remming counted nearly twenty standing at attention with weapons at the ready. The smell of jungle and jeep exhaust mingled.

At this first checkpoint they had to submit to a fingerprint analysis. Inside the small station were a single computer, some heavy cabling, and a little box with a square glass surface. Once they were approved, the guards parted, the gates opened, and a long, straight dirt road stretched about a hundred yards to a sturdy, boxlike brick building, about the size of a small house. Outside were more guards. Inside, steel and brick. The three of them faced a heavy steel door, no glass, at the end of a short, empty hall. Here, mounted on the wall, was the retinal scanner, and to the side a display panel with digits zero to nine, red and green lights and a small audio speaker.

Remming passed. The red light turned green.

Volgaard passed. The red light turned green.

Colonel Netterson pressed a quick seven-digit access code. The heavy steel door made a deep, ponderous whirring sound as several unseen channel locks mechanically retracted. A buzzer sounded. Colonel Netterson pulled the door open, motioning for Remming and Volgaard to enter. They stepped through into a short antechamber. At the other end was a wire-caged elevator. Colonel Netterson did not follow.

"You'll be debriefed at the bottom. Good day, Dr. Remming. Good day, Dr. Volgaard." He turned crisply on his heel, marched back to the jeep.

Remming was nothing less than stunned. Over and over in his mind he tried to calculate the cost of this endeavor. Surely this was not an exclusive operation . . . surely the base was built years ago, was used by some other organization . . . maybe left abandoned for years . . . only now to be used again. . . .

Volgaard headed toward the elevator, undeterred. Remming followed. They stepped inside, wordless, pulled the industrial door down, looked for buttons. There was only one. Volgaard pressed it. Down.

The elevator descended almost immediately. Down, down, still down. Many times, Remming expected it to stop. It did not. The elevator was broad, designed to carry maybe thirty to forty at a shot; semidark, lit only by the light of a single bulb. Remming glanced at Volgaard. The Swede's expression was inscrutable.

Remming almost asked a question, almost said, "What do you think this is all about?"

He was too proud. He did not want to be the one to ask.

He didn't need to. After what Remming guessed to be the equivalent of ten, maybe fifteen floors, the elevator glided smoothly to a stop. Before Remming could reach for the rope, a man on the other side pulled the doors open. Behind him was a white room, full of light. The man's face was shadowed, but seemed incredibly familiar. Somewhere, somehow . . .

"Stewart!" Volgaard said, pleased.

Even more, *she was not surprised,* Remming realized. In fact, all of a sudden Selma Volgaard was downright warm, affectionate . . . even sensual. At least as much as she could be, which was kind of like describing a shark in maternal terms. But sure enough, the Swede stepped forward, tiptoed—all Remming could see was the back of the knot of hair bunned on her head—and *kissed* the man on the lips slowly.

The shadowed man responded in kind, touching her face with pleasure. Then he extended his hand to Remming. He was alone.

"Dr. Remming, hello. I don't know if you remember me: Stewart Newman, Project Director for Genetics Advancement at the World Health Organization."

19

Remming could do nothing but stare as they shook hands. Stewart Newman drew him into the small antechamber at the base of the elevator. The room was all white—white like the color of thin skim milk; octagonal, featureless, except for a flat set of windowless double doors at the opposite end. Cagelike, absent of voice, echo, or movement, the room could easily have been an ancient whitewashed burial chamber, or a secret shrine for initiates. It was perfectly still. He heard his own breath, felt his own sweat, compacted by the weight of eighty feet of layered earth and rock and grass above. He was an invader here; the silence proved it. Mounting dread tingled in his fingertips, his nose, in the warm juices of his belly. Newman offered no primer, just let Remming squirm, which Remming refused to do. He was no fool. Obviously, Newman was attached to his funding, which meant WHO was attached. The "why" would be just a matter of time, so in the meantime it was best he kept a level head.

You are in control. They need you.

He surveyed the man and woman before him, the room itself, with clinical, unemotional curiosity, revealing nothing. If he was in for a surprise—and obviously he was—he refused to play the pawn for any man.

You're missing the point, a smarter, more honest voice whispered in his mind. *You have already been played.*

"You must forgive the security measures, Dr. Remming," Newman said at length. "Of course, I'm sure you probably suspected as much from the funding you've received. It's all come together rather nicely, but routine precautions are still very necessary to ensure the viability of a project of this nature. The last thing we want is a high profile, so secrecy is essential. Beyond that, I'm not sure where to begin. So let me just say I'm thrilled you can be here with us. As I told you in Geneva, I really am a great admirer of your work."

"Flattered," Remming replied with a cool, patient smile, but his eyes were on Volgaard, who had intertwined her left arm through Newman's. He saw no need to hide his distaste for her duplicity. "Has this been going on long?"

Volgaard arched one eyebrow, disaffected. "Long enough."

In the whiteness of the room, Remming stood like an angled line of protest. Emotionless, he replied, "I'm disappointed. I had thought more highly of your professionalism. I see now my respect was misplaced."

Before Volgaard could respond, Newman cut in. "Now, now, Dr. Remming, let's not be hasty. I admit this all must surely come as something of an unfair surprise, but I really think you will be quite pleased when all is said and done. Try to reserve judgment."

"Pleased?"

"Thrilled, actually. I am, anyway. We are seeing impressive advances, some of unimaginable magnitude." He turned, reaching for the handle of the door behind him. "Come and see!"

And Remming saw.

He saw a Level Four biohazard unit. He saw decontamination suits and pressurization chambers. He saw an impressive underground network of hallways and rooms, of white-coated scientists milling purposefully about with charts and clipboards or huddled in units in zero-bacterial laboratories, poring over samples, wearing masks, and mixing the brownish yellow, the clear, the pale blue contents of tubes and vials of various measurements. He saw an electron microscope, a spectrometer, a Cray workstation, numerous computer terminals wired together . . .

Everything—the entire operation—was about the God Spot. Everything. Full board. Prodded by Newman, he looked at a few of the charts, studied the numbers from the ganglial tissue DNA analysis, the neural pathways. This was *his* data! Remming had expected . . . well, he didn't know what he had expected. Maybe new insights, new ground, additional components. But everything looked to be merely an extension of *his* research. Somehow, Stewart Newman had taken his research—the research of the Club Cranium team—and, by the looks of it, gone absolutely insane. With WHO's money. And WHO's blessing.

Yet he had no idea how insane.

"So are you the Merideth Institute?" he asked. "Have I been transmitting to *you* all along?"

Newman brushed his concern aside. "Time for questions later."

The floor beneath him was spit-shine bright, the air sterile and dry. Every now and then a crackling voice would offer directives over the intercom system mounted in the ceiling, calling the "Blue Team" to Sector Five or security to Sector One or Dr. Such-and-Such to Operations, or Testing, or Research. Newman guided them through the Research wing first, followed by Operations. Remming was amazed and terrified at the size and scope of this underground facility. It was massive, stretching on for probably fifty yards in each direction. Meanwhile, Newman rambled on and on excitedly about this or that, pointing out the multiple focus labs, with doors labeled plain and to the point: Rational Processes, Sensory Valuations, Synapses and Pathways, Pineal Body, STM-55, Synthetics, Antibodies, Code, and so on. It was a carefully orchestrated, fully staffed scientific assembly line.

At the Synthetics focus lab, Newman procured a syringe from one of the lab techs, a young woman, pierced a sealed, rubber-capped pharmaceutical of some type and withdrew 5 cc of clear green solution.

"They call this lab 'The Brewery,'" Newman joked, motioning with a tilt of his head to the small handful of scientists in the room. Then he spoke louder, commanding attention. "Ladies and gentlemen, I'd like for you to meet the esteemed Dr. Jay Remming."

A few looked up from their microscopes or turned from conversation; all recognized the tall, thin black man immediately. They smiled appreciatively. Two even applauded. Remming did nothing to acknowledge their praise. Instead, he began to feel more and more sick to his stomach. Newman thrust the syringe toward him.

"This is our latest attempt to create a synthetic form of serotoxomiasin," he said. "We're still in early development, but the results are promising." He pointed to two or three other flasks, held each one up in turn. "These are variants of the base you hold in your hand. They're scheduled for testing later this week."

Testing? he wondered with alarm. *How do you test this?*

Then Volgaard spoke. "The Antibodies lab is working on the exact opposite. Possibly a retrovirus that attacks the pineal body anomaly or a vaccine that can be given *in vitro*. I think they're also close to a chemotherapy derivative as well." Her accent remained harsh as ever, and clipped, but she spoke as easily as if she had spilled milk on the funnies in the Sunday paper.

Remming held up the syringe to examine its contents. *In vitro? Attack?*

"Be careful not to stick yourself!" Newman warned. Then he grinned mischievously. "Wouldn't want you to become a 'believer' right on the spot now, would we?"

Like a reckless train jumping its tracks, Remming attempted to formulate possibilities on the fly, using great cosmic leaps of intuition, fear, hope, dread, reason. Nothing panned out. Since the time Monitor Nine had called two days ago, everything had felt dreamlike, drugged, impossible to coalesce. And now, here he was, underground in a military research compound, surrounded on all sides by the absurd and intimidating implications of his own research. It would have seemed laughable if it were not so frighteningly real. Elsewhere, he would have immediately and openly challenged a man like Stewart Newman. Here, he felt trapped, by the weight of the earth, his own seclusion, his reputation—after all, the people here were applauding *him*—and the numbing possibility that this massive operation might not tolerate his small-voiced resistance. So he fell upon himself, within himself, collapsing inside over and over again with every step in search of something solid, something knowable to stand on.

Pointless. There was nothing.

They left Synthetics, clattered farther down the hall. Volgaard absorbed the entire production with equanimity. No doubt she had visited the facility before, maybe on numerous occasions. Which only reinforced the obvious: the haunting voice of pride whispered in his ears, louder and louder, clearer and clearer: *Who's the pawn now? Who's the pawn now?* It was a question to which he had no answer. The sound of it berated, accused, and mocked.

The mighty Jay Remming! Nobel laureate! Fool and pawn!

"So this whole operation," he said at last, to quiet the accusations against his spirit, "is funded by the World Health Organization?"

Newman nodded, pleased. "It is our most auspicious and far-reaching biological program to date."

"Why?" Remming asked, baffled. "To what end?"

Before Newman could answer, they reached the end of another hallway. Military men wearing helmets, bearing semiautomatic AK-47s, stood at attention, guarding another, smaller elevator.

My soul, Remming thought. *How big is this?*

The guards saluted, parted, allowing the three of them to step through. Newman pulled the elevator door down. There were only two buttons, up and down. He pressed down. The elevator sank another ten feet and stopped. Newman opened the door, motioning for Remming to enter first.

Nothing could have prepared the man for what he saw next.

§ § §

Abu Hasim El-Saludin watched the wispy, thin trailers of clouds streaming by his window as though they were part of a long, flowing beard hanging from an old man's face. Though he—and the other 200-plus passengers aboard the 767—were cruising midway over the Atlantic at an altitude of about 38,000 feet, his spirit soared higher still. True, he was filled with a deep-seated sense of personal resolve; that alone filled him with courage. He knew what must be done, that God Spot research must be openly challenged and stopped. He knew this. And that was good. But of far more significance, he literally felt as if he had been untethered—like a falcon, after years of service to a hunter, set free. From the moment the beggar spoke to him the name of Jesus, he had felt the cords around his ankles breaking loose. The name was the name. The name was life. As a child he had known the name according to the teachings of Islam, that Jesus was a prophet second only to Mohammed, that Jesus was a teacher, on and on.

Now he simply knew Jesus.

All night, since boarding the plane, he had whispered the name over and over again, each breath tasting like nectar. As he had recklessly told his wife and daughter, something wonderful had happened. While afraid, both women were too caught up in Abu's joy to fear the heresy of his words. He had quoted the poetry of Kahlil Gibran to them, words he had learned and read as a child:

The freest song comes not through bars and wires. And he to whom worshipping is a window, to open but also to shut, has not yet visited the house of his soul whose windows are from dawn to dawn.

And then he had danced. The three of them had danced together. In spite of their fear. In spite of the uncertainty. The grace of this new life was not lost on Abu, that his Muslim family would respond so. Small miracles. It was blissful, absurd, liberating. Now, sitting on the plane between an overweight French businessman and a young Nigerian woman, he gazed with wonder down at the small new book in his hands, feeling all windows thrown open. It would have been impossible to find this book at an airport in Egypt. But his flight from Cairo had connected in London. There he purchased a small, inexpensive English version of the New Testament. Not the Koran. *The Holy Bible,* it declared in plain sans serif characters on the front cover. He thumbed through the pages, his eyes, his spirit, devouring all.

On page 134, something leaped out at him. He could not help but think of the old beggar as he read from the Gospel of John, chapter 9: *"One thing I know, that, whereas I was blind, now I see."*

Yes, yes! To see! *Now I see!* He thumbed forward several pages, clumsy, giddy. There it was again. The words almost seemed fluorescent.

"For now we see in a mirror dimly, but then face to face; now I know in part, but then I shall know fully just as I also have been fully known. . . ."

Abu folded the book, leaned back, closed his eyes.

Just as I also have been fully known . . .

The world, as far as Abu Hasim El-Saludin knew, was just beginning.

❧ ❧ ❧

". . . and over here is our surgical unit," Stewart Newman said proudly as they stepped into a small dark room, labeled on the door as RC Observation.

Jay Remming closed his eyes, wanting to look away, couldn't. From the elevator on, every step of Level Two had grown worse and worse. If Level One was a mad scientist's dream, Level Two was a shop of horrors. Remming was not a man of weak constitution, but here he felt he might physically retch at any moment. Nevertheless, he looked, compelled by the sheer force of his own implacable curiosity. On the other side of the Plexiglas observation panel, Newman was pointing to a massive team of blue-masked neurosurgeons working simultaneously on two men, one Hispanic, one black, both roughly mid-thirties. The reality of the scenario was jarring: two subjects; ten, maybe fifteen surgeons; multiple nurses and assistants; a highly theoretical operation, which, responsibly understood, should be at least a decade away from trials. Based on limited research. His research. *His.*

Helpless, Remming fixated on how well equipped the surgical unit was, with vascular ultrasound, surgical microscopes, endoscopic instruments, and neuroendoscope. Also, immaculately maintained, the stainless-steel tables, instrument tray, crash cart, and cement floor were all polished to a shine. There was nothing gruesome about the place, no rusty implements, nothing careless. It was, in fact, faultless science. The men on the table appeared to be conscious, though mildly sluggish; their exposed skulls were speckled with electrodes. Remming's eyes flicked nervously to the monitor to observe the beta, theta, and alpha waves.

"As you can see, Dr. Remming, these subjects have undergone surgical exploration on the occipital lobe through an incision on the posterior aspect of the skull, through a window in the occipital bone. The occipital lobe and cerebellum have been retracted to allow an allograft of the pineal gland anomaly from the subject on the left to the non-affected subject on the right. . . ."

With what felt like a bruised ear, Remming listened to Newman's litany of the operation in all its unholy magnificence. The scale and audacity were astonishing: The surgical team was attempting a complete SPoT transplant from the brain of a Christian to the brain of an unbeliever. He dug his fingernails into the palm of his hand, took a deep breath, said nothing; could not help but draw out, like squirming snakes, the long tangle of moral implications. Safe in New York, he had the freedom to dismiss the simplicity of Hanson Blackaby's dissent as naive, lacking sophistication and vision. Here, underground, in secret, the cold reality smelled like two men with holes in their head. He wondered what the survival rate was. Still, none of the doctors looked like Shelly's Frankenstein, much less demons or ogres. The normalcy of it all, the casual air, made Remming's head ache. All he could do was internalize the dissonance. *Not just lab work . . . beyond their depth . . . the fools! . . . don't know enough . . . not nearly enough for invasive procedures . . . years down the road . . . what is happening here?*

Just then, Newman pressed the button of the small telecom speaker on the wall. "Status?" he queried. One of the surgeons rose from the huddle, glancing toward the Plexiglas. The sound of his voice crackled through the speaker in reply.

"The graft is complete. Looks to be our most thoroughly received yet. We're closing."

"Good. I want twenty-four-hour monitors on both."

Newman stepped back, smiling, but Remming reached over and punched the button himself. "How much tissue was sacrificed?" he asked bluntly.

The same man turned again, holding up his hands. The fingers of his gloves were bright red.

"About six percent, I'd say. Not too bad."

Remming let go of the button. Behind the glass, he bristled. "Six percent!" he hissed at Newman. "Do you realize what that means? It's intolerable. That patient could lose all primary visual capacity. And worse."

Newman's smile faded to a puzzled half-frown. He held his hands palm up, as if waiting for the punch line. He didn't know how to respond.

Remming pressed his point angrily: "You've just tried to graft a little-known brain anomaly from a carrier to a noncarrier with little knowledge of the consequences, based on preliminary and incomplete research."

"No, no. How else can we learn until we try? He may even lose some fine and involuntary muscle coordination. It is precisely the consequences we hope to quantify. I will admit the process is distasteful. And, to be honest with you, I despise some of the barbarisms of surgical and theoretical research. But I can assure you, these are some of the finest neurosurgeons in all of Central and South America. We've spared no expense."

"I don't care about the doctors!" Remming bellowed, his dark eyes flashing. "Who gave you the authority to treat these people like cattle? For that matter, to perform this procedure at all? WHO doesn't have that kind of authority under its United Nations charter. I've worked for them. I know. So under what auspices do you work? And why this secrecy? If that man's estimate is true, he just performed butchery, not brain surgery."

Again, Newman was calm, apologetic. "I'm afraid that's where you misunderstand our purpose, Dr. Remming. These men aren't patients, they're *subjects*. There's a difference."

"Volunteers?"

Newman pressed his lips together in a patronizing show of patience. But his answer surprised Remming. "Yes, actually. But that's really not the point. Actually, Dr. Remming, I had thought to see more sophistication in you. More appreciation for our achievements." He pointed to the table on the right. "Subject A is from California. He was scheduled to be executed two months ago. Been in prison for over ten years. Claims to have had a big religious experience about two years ago. Sure enough, he's got the spot. And that man"—he pointed to the patient on the left—"is one of society's castoffs. He's from the slums of Brazil, has AIDS, is a drug addict and a homosexual. We think his lack of immune system may offer certain advantages for graft receptivity."

Remming couldn't stand it any longer. Physically, he lost all capacity for restraint and diplomacy. His voice dropped about thirty degrees, slipping into a subterranean level of humus and rage. Fixing his eyes on Stewart Newman—flicking once or twice to Dr. Volgaard—he said, "I don't care who you are; you are so far beyond the scope of international charters, scientific responsibility, and an operative moral code I shall see to it that your license is revoked forever, wherever you got it from. Do you hear me? I don't care who you are."

He waited defiantly for a reply.

Newman did not offer one. He regarded Remming with open eyes, pondering, considering, sliding the tip of his tongue back and forth along the bottom of his teeth.

Volgaard whispered, "You have no idea who you're talking to so foolishly, Dr. Remming. I suspect you will live to regret those words."

But Newman waved his arms. "No, no. Nonsense! All this bickering. We just need more dialogue. As I sit here and think, I must admit this would come as a shock to *any* reasonable man." He hugged Volgaard to his side. She responded to his touch but stared with open antipathy at Remming. "I personally just need to try to communicate everything a little clearer. Come, Dr. Remming. The tour is not yet over."

He didn't wait for a reply but strolled off with Volgaard at his side. Remming hesitated, fearful, disgusted. He glanced again at the two "subjects" on the other side of the Plexiglas window.

This is not my research! he thought angrily. *Not this. Not my fault.*

The echo of the protest inside his head rang hollow. With no other choice, he followed Newman.

He wished he hadn't. With an increasing sense of reckless showmanship, Newman escorted him past two or three more laboratories and then to a row of small rooms filled with human subjects. Many of the subjects looked healthy, though afraid. Some appeared incapacitated—lying on the floor or in bed, shaking, weeping, laughing hysterically. Others were disfigured or confined to wheelchairs, slobber dripping from their mouths. Nurses and staff attendants moved dutifully throughout the room, assisting as needed with variously prescribed oral or intravenous drugs, calming some, disciplining others. Heavyset guards armed with billy clubs were posted outside each of these rooms.

"It's difficult to make this appear as civilized as it actually is. For all intents and purposes this level is little more than an asylum, which, as you know, can be a very messy place. For example, these people—"

He pointed through the window of the last room in the hallway. Inside a woman was shrieking; two male nurse were forcibly restraining her. "These people have yet to be treated in any way. They were *brought* to us in this condition by family members."

Remming glanced through the iron-barred glass for only a moment. "Why are you showing me this?"

"I want you to see that we treat these people with professionalism," Newman said earnestly. "They receive the care here they need, medical attention, all with the utmost sense of respect. This is not Dachau— not even close, regardless of what you may be thinking. We are an enlightened people seeking further enlightenment. We have a rigorous screening process for all our subjects. In fact, you might be surprised to know that all of them come willingly. And most are dying already from one thing or another."

Remming snorted. "And so you just help them along?"

"These people are the rejects of society: the criminally insane, the drug addicts, the prostitutes, the condemned. We offer them a sizable fee to allow us to test certain procedures on them. They are able to send a portion of the money to their families right away, and, if all goes well, they are free to leave with the balance in hand. They know in advance the risks and sign consent forms, which we have on file. It was difficult at first, but now most of the people come to *us*. We do not have to go to them. Do you know how? Nothing aggressive. We post fliers in the slums of cities in neighboring nations. That is all. These people are desperate. They have nothing to lose."

Remming was not fooled. He did not need to look hard to see that most of these people, having once arrived, probably never left. Newman did not invite further debate. They set off again, and as they walked, Remming noted that on this level they only occasionally passed other staff or personnel—maybe a janitor or security guard, all with the appropriate ID tags. Most of the scientists and doctors were upstairs. Finally, they turned right down another hall, pausing in front of a glass window to observe another, smaller lab where four beds were lined up side by side. One of the beds was empty, the other three, occupied. Two men and a woman. Their eyes were covered with thick strips of gauze and tape. An IV drip flowed into each of their arms. One of them spoke softly a streaming nonstop flow of gibberish, in

Spanish, though it was hard to tell for sure. The other two seemed to be constantly swallowing at nothing but air. Every now and then the woman would claw at her face and scream. The door to the room bore a simple sign: *STM-55 Synthetics Trials.*

"Nonaffected subjects, injected somehow with an artificial form of the neurotransmitter?" Remming murmured painfully.

"Yes. But this was one of our most aggressive treatments. Other trials have yielded more stable, though less noticeable results."

"What happened to the fourth?"

Newman sighed. "Unfortunately, she died."

"How many have died so far?"

"All told? Thirty-six. That includes all experiments, both ways, invasive and noninvasive."

The number was staggering. Remming was not surprised.

"And how many have survived?"

"Nine. Mostly ruined, though. They will never function normally again. But we are making great progress. Six of our nine survivors have come from the latest round of tests alone. We're advancing very rapidly. I expect the casualties and severe damage will be almost completely eliminated within a matter of months as we narrow our focus down to two or three of the most promising directions."

Directions?

Something, deep inside . . . As Remming stared at the stammering woman, the gulping men, he felt himself drowning. *Directions?!* It all began to break loose. Terrible guilt. *What could possibly be promising in any of this?* Violently, he doubled over. A spasm gripped his stomach in waves. Suddenly, he vomited. He could not restrain himself, did not even feel it coming. Dr. Volgaard smiled faintly at the sight. Newman simply watched, waited, mildly irritated. Remming felt shame. He did not want to rise. The vomit smelled like vinegar. From where he knelt on the tiled floor he whispered, "I have a hard time believing very many Christians volunteer for these tests."

Newman tried to help him stand, but Remming jerked his arm away. Dr. Volgaard walked a little bit ahead to another telecom speaker and paged for a cleanup crew. When he finally rose, they continued walking with little discussion. Remming trembled.

Newman pondered the question dispassionately. "That is a little trickier, I will agree. We have had a few, such as the man from death row you saw earlier. He was all too happy to risk it."

"Which means you pulled some strings with the State Department, the Department of Justice, the Attorney General's office . . ."

Newman's eyes twinkled. "A few. Anyway, to answer your question, some impoverished locals come and volunteer, thinking they may have the spot because they never miss a Mass. Most don't. Then again, others do. Five thousand American dollars is a fortune down here. All told, I would say we have only had the privilege of examining less than a dozen professing Christians. By that I mean the real thing, at least biologically. So we are very careful in how we treat them. Only three of them have died."

"How do you know the others weren't 'real'?"

Newman patted Remming on the back. "You should know. The credit goes to you and your team. Now that we know what we're looking for and where, we are able to prescan candidates to determine viability. And as you have so ably proven—though we are still baffled as to why—only genuine Christians have it. At first we were skeptical of the certainty of that premise, but it has proven true time and time again. We have found a discernible difference in the psychological profile of those who simply attach the name 'Christian' to themselves and those who claim a genuine experience. We've even brought on a full-time psychiatrist to assist with our evaluations. It's absolutely fascinating to ponder the evolutionary ramifications of the anomaly. Of course, only children and fetal studies can confirm our assumptions. But that process remains several months away."

Children? Fetal studies?

Newman's sense of equilibrium bordered on grotesque. He sounded so *detached* from the pathos and humanity of the situation. Not jaded. Jaded implied an emotional connection at some level or at some point in time. No, Newman was severely indifferent. Here in Guatemala, by whatever means, for whatever purpose, was a huge lab, well stocked with cunningly bribed human lab rats, degenerates and misfits, the kind that no one would miss or care about if their brains were literally fried inside out. Easily discarded. After all, they had signed consent forms. And that made it fine for Stewart Newman.

"And your *assumption*?" Remming asked, patting his lips with his handkerchief to relieve himself of the taste of his own bile. "About the origin of the spot?"

Newman whipped his head to look at Remming. His surprise was obvious. "Present at birth, of course. It's really the only possibility."

Volgaard answered the unasked question. "Dr. Remming has left open the possibility that it occurs later."

"Later? You can't be serious. When?" He held up his fingers like quotation marks. "At 'salvation'?"

Remming's dark skin flushed. Nobody had *ever* laughed at his theories to his face. "I don't claim to know for sure," he said. "I wait until the facts prove themselves. It's called science."

Newman rolled his eyes. He had by now grown very bored with the man's perpetual state of reservation. Not even a "Thank you" for all his hard work. So, shamed already as Remming was, Newman decided now was as good a time as any to lay a couple more of his cards on the table. "You know, Dr. Remming, I have gone to great pains to encourage you with the fruit of your own labors in this place. We need your passion and brilliance to advance. But I don't mind telling you, I grow frustrated with your impudence."

"If that is my only offense against you," Remming said evenly, "then I shall try harder: You completely disgust me. This whole operation is a travesty of science."

Newman glanced left and right wildly. "You hypocritical son-of-a—! Open your eyes and look around! You're so bloated with this false ideal of objective methodology that you miss the obvious, which is right in front of you. It has *always* been right in front of you!"

"And what is that?"

Newman pressed in. "What the world needs! What is *real*."

"You fool! You've shown me nothing real! How can we know what is real?"

"You tell me how. Then I shall tell you."

Remming was immediate. "Through rigorous, open-minded, objective analysis."

"No!" Newman cried. "That's old school! In the new science, reality must *precede* objectivity. And reality is, by definition, established on prejudice. Only when we admit our prejudice can we make room for an authentic objectivity."

"So honest prejudice sets us free? Is that what you say is in front of me?"

"Bull's-eye!" Newman said, reaching forward and pressing his forefinger between Remming's eyes. Remming calmly put up his hand, pushed Newman's hand away from his face, but his blood pressure shot off the charts. Newman smirked. "You've consistently chosen to hide behind the mask of 'Science,' thinking somehow that made you an objective observer rather than active participant. But that's a lie. It's cloak-and-dagger, smoke-and-mirrors. You're a player. We all are. I just happen to pull bigger strings than you do."

The fact that anyone, peer or otherwise, would speak to him in this manner was maddening to Remming, almost beyond comprehension. For the very same reason, it was also very frightening. Anyone else he might have truly thought a fool. But Remming knew the only reason Stewart Newman would talk to him so candidly, so condescendingly, was not because he was a fool, but because *he had the authority to do so.*

"Is that why you've brought me here?" he asked. "To play out your own failure to achieve my success in the medical community with a script of dramatic one-liners? Are you trying to exact some sort of juvenile revenge? If so, I'm done. I'm through. Let me go."

Newman was not through. He laughed even more scornfully. "Brilliant, Dr. Remming! Brilliant as usual. I would expect nothing less. Just don't think you can claim absolution now. Blind, stupid, or self-deceived, I really don't care. I don't need to. You're in too deep to have a say anymore. I don't just own your research. I own *you.* Think about that next time you address me. I'm tired of playing baby-sitter to your vanity and empty moral presumption."

He swiveled on one heel and marched away, heels clattering on the floor. Volgaard did not follow but pulled back, staring hard at Remming. Her skin was tight, grinless, her eyes narrow.

"We hoped for best in all this," she said plainly. "With you. Hope for best, fear for worst. You are a marvelous man, Dr. Remming. I urge you to reconsider your words and attitude. It would be foolish to ignore the opportunity before you."

"And what is that?"

"A place in history! Your work in this is big. It is—how do you say?—colossal. You scorn it to your shame. Newman considers you a part of the team. But he does what he has to. The high ground you think you stand on is not so high. You do not understand. You do not know what you think you know."

"I am a scientist."

"Yes. I see that." Volgaard smiled. It was, in some measure, an invitation to reconciliation. "I am one, too."

"No. You are a girlfriend."

The smile instantly faded.

"We have a meeting scheduled for tomorrow morning, 7:00 A.M. Feel free to examine more of this place until then. You may yet come to understand that we are about to change history here."

"How?" Remming asked, exasperated.

Her answer chilled him. "By changing man."

20

L isten to this, listen to this!" Missy squealed. "This is unbelievable!" Ravelo waited patiently. For the trip back to Detroit he had switched with Missy and taken the driver's seat. He already regretted it. Surely it would have been easier to maintain sanity in the car if he were the one riffling through the information. But he was not. So, as they drove, Missy eagerly pored over the many, many papers, photocopies, medical studies, journal reports and, of course, declassified government documents from Dr. Keegan's private cache. Every time she found something, they would converse for a while, followed by a few moments of more reading, more silence. Then, with no warning, randomly and unpredictably, she would hit a twenty-four-carat nugget and let out a squeal, piercing the comfortable, thoughtless hum of Remming's autopilot mode like a splash of cold water after a nap in a warm hammock. The original sense of fear and awe in Missy had given way to two primary response modes: one, anger; two, the thrill of the chase. But Ravelo was different. He was a pace runner, not a sprinter, both by disposition and breadth of perspective. He possessed a more seasoned view of life, having a history in ministry that brought understanding beyond Missy's grasp, even though, admittedly, her journalistic career had exposed her to much he would never see. Just the same, he was deeply disturbed by what she had found so far. Something rumbling in his spirit told him a very great evil was at work here.

"Whaja find?" he asked. Every time he had asked that so far, the story had grown worse and worse.

"Well, it wasn't just the children who suffered. A follow-up study performed by a congressional oversight committee a couple of years after declassification shows, and I quote, 'a startling failure ratio in the health of all mothers affected by Project Pacifist.'"

Project Pacifist . . .

That was the real kicker. Ravelo reached up behind his glasses with one finger and rubbed his left eyeball vigorously. He asked for more, for the whole story, not just bits and pieces.

Missy gave it to him.

In the early sixties, it seemed, the government had grown increasingly suspicious of what it perceived to be a rising tide of youthful rebellion. In this breeding ground of anarchistic sentiment, the government gave its bean counters the task of estimating the cost of mounting social upheaval. By 1963 no fewer than seven national think tanks and a variety of other federal agencies were working on this "problem" with fervor. Governors from all fifty states were called together to discuss the implications for state and local economies. All was done in secret, of course. The government did not want it to be known that it considered *anything* a threat. And, in point of fact, the documents made clear that on a federal level, the government never truly feared an overthrow or viewed widespread rebellion of an organized fashion as a realistic concern.

But the issues were more complex than the fear of simple revolution. Indirect, but carrying tremendous overhead, was the possibility that the international community might lose confidence in the United States based on wrong perceptions of civil and social turmoil. This was regarded as a legitimate threat to national security given the general dissonance of the times and the political and military tension of the Cold War.

So the bean counters counted. They measured "hard factors" such as cost and time for a projected series of increasingly degrading scenarios—scenarios that would require federal resources for such things as deployment of the National Guard, crisis management, possibly regional and/or statewide periods of martial law, subsequent legislative intervention to manage the various crises, which incurred the judiciary cost of a swelling penal system. Not to mention the impact of such unrest on business and industry, etc.

They also evaluated and estimated social conditions, "soft factors," which tended to heavily emphasize a theorized deflation of respect among the international community regarding America's ability to manage its own household, much less lead the world. In an age of imminent nuclear engagement, these fears took on an exaggerated reality.

Right or wrong, paranoid or not, the multiplied sum of the cost was staggering. So the starched-collar boys in Washington responded with a series of initiatives based on research from the forties and fifties—*Bluebird, MKUltra,* and the like. Sure enough, the very research Missy had already uncovered (which was the first of her squeals). Drawing on this raft of highly questionable mind-control attempts, the government formulated a strand of new research, unveiled in a handful of specifically targeted programs, the last and most audacious being code-named Project Pacifist.

Ravelo licked his lips. Even the name was distasteful. Being something of a child of the sixties and seventies himself, he knew the familiar stirrings of the revolutionary spirit, albeit in a domesticated (and hopefully greatly redeemed) fashion at this point in life. Jesus, Ravelo knew, was anything but a pacifist. To label the Messiah with such a simple word would be to reduce the larger message of who he was, which was in fact a full-scale assault from the Father-heart of God on the powers of darkness present in a fallen world. Within that greatly purchased freedom, life was meant to be lived with a capital *L,* surrounded by mystery and a holy lust for the full joy of everything Jesus died for. Life abundant. It was easy for Ravelo to despise "life-as-usual"; for that matter, church-as-usual, and the sugarcoated conventionality of society-as-usual, which he considered to be nothing more than a clever mask for oppression, complacency, and moral smugness to be legislated by the ruling elite in public but rarely practiced in private. So a name like Project Pacifist—by implication "keep the kids neat and tidy, nothing unseemly, no loose ends, let's all be respectable!"—could do nothing but rub him the wrong way intellectually.

As Missy continued to read, Ravelo found himself rubbed the wrong way in *every* way. All of the programs were offensive, but some of the earlier efforts seemed almost trivial by way of comparison, such as measuring the effects of certain emotional suppressants. Who really believed the government hadn't done that sort of thing before? Heck, a multibillion-dollar and perfectly legal pharmaceuticals industry had grown up around it. Subsequent testing grew more determined, less concerned with hairsplitting ethics, or for that matter, constitutional guarantees of individual rights. Some of these were aimed at halting aggressive tendencies through posthypnotic suggestion or chemical means (both legal and illegal, such as increased levels of nitric oxide or marijuana derivatives). Still others were designed to artificially stimulate reason rather than emotion as a primary response by accentuating certain cortical functions.

Project Pacifist had the most lofty and frightening goal: to biologically engineer a radical moral response *in utero*—a "compelling inclination for good" and a "natural preference for socially accepted standards" according to the papers—that would see adolescents safely through the turbulence and rebellion of their youth and turn them into "productive adult citizens." Thankfully, due to the scope of the project, the initial effort was limited to an extremely small sample—twenty children in one small community. The strategy was simple: purposefully alter the chemical balance of the amniotic fluid during a woman's pregnancy in an attempt to "chaperon" brain development, much in the same way the brain itself regulates behavior by inhibiting and exciting. In other words, at key developmental points—with injections occurring twice during fetal gestation, once six months after birth and a final treatment at age two—nurture certain regions of cerebral growth and retard others. Although procedurally primitive (being more akin to neutralizing an alkaline battery than practicing neural science) the premise was quite advanced, considering the period's limited grasp of neurology.

And shockingly bold.

Early results showed promise, but the promise quickly unraveled. Of the twenty children originally involved, two were born with mild retardation, one serious. From the remaining seventeen—otherwise normal, healthy children—a curious commonality emerged: a telling streak of severity in their personality that erupted in furious full bloom rather than unfolding over time. Though the tendencies varied in "symptom" and manifested idiosyncratically, they were obviously pre-toddler. Unusually so. For example, one little girl absolutely refused to eat her peas until they were lined up in perfectly even rows, with uniform distribution. This, at age two. Worse, she had a different set of rules for different-colored foods and another for different shapes—i.e., cubed carrots versus rounded peas—that she refused to deviate from. Her parents had to guess until they got it right or she wouldn't eat. By twenty months, another little girl became fixated on various sounds, beginning with the sound of a running faucet, and would literally become inconsolable for hours if she could not properly mimic the tenor and texture of the sound. One little boy screamed every night—which local physicians attributed to severe colic—until the parents by chance repainted his room in a deeper shade of blue. Not a different *color*, but a deeper shade of the *same* color. Thereafter, he slept fine. Independent of each other, the quirks could easily have been dismissed. But taken as a whole, the pattern was grossly disturbing. It was as if each of the children's brains *did* respond to the treatment, but chaotically. Wires that were meant to operate independently of each other almost seemed to get fused together.

Of course, the families were completely unaware at all times. The mothers were told the shots were a new kind of influenza vaccine. That was the cover. The mothers died; the children lived—all without ever knowing.

"God forgive us," Ravelo murmured, genuflecting. "This is sick."

Even Missy no longer seemed so thrilled. Her squeals had gradually come to sound more and more like moans. "Why was this ever allowed?" she asked. "I mean, this is America, for heaven's sake!"

Ravelo waved her to silence. "Keep going. Keep going."

She thumbed through two or three more pages, scanning quickly. She didn't get far.

"Oh my!"

"What?" Ravelo asked.

"Oh, man! Wait, wait, let me read."

"Read it aloud."

"No, wait . . ."

And so he waited. Finally, she stopped, took a deep breath.

"You'll never guess," she said.

"Guess what? Tell me!"

"No. Guess."

"I don't know!"

Missy shook her head. "Dr. Theodore Samual Rosenburg was the lead scientist for Project Pacifist. He oversaw the entire operation from nearby Camp Lejeune. You don't think his murder could be related, do you?"

"To this? Why?"

"I don't know. Just kind of coincidental, don't you think?"

Ravelo didn't think. Anymore, he didn't know what to think. He pointed, grunted. "More."

So she read. She read how Project Pacifist treatments caused rapid infertility in every mother but one. How for all twenty families, these Project Pacifist kids were the last kids they ever had. How Project Pacifist testing was cut short by a change in presidential administrations in the early seventies, but that monitoring of the twenty children who were involved had continued in the years since, enough to clearly define the profound impact of the test as the eccentricities of each child took further shape in childhood, deepened through adolescence, and continued unabated into adulthood. In the last recorded tally, of seventeen children, two had become monks—one Buddhist and one Catholic; another had dropped out of school and moved to Calcutta to join Mother Teresa's Missionaries of Charity at the age of seventeen; four had been driven to violent criminal extremes—not just theft or assault, but aberrant, serial crimes—Luther's name was among them; two pursued medicine, one became a ferocious lawyer, three were actively involved in cults, one gave his life to Greenpeace, and the last two, together, moved from city to city as vagrants for the sole purpose of pursuing the pleasures of deviant sex in each city's underground community—gay or straight, they didn't care. In the years since, three more of the original twenty had died, two suicides and one execution—Luther Sanchez. Only one marriage out of a total of twelve had survived, and that barely.

Quite a tally for only seventeen kids.

Before Missy could finish, Ravelo, normally a measured, affable man, was seething. "Luther never had a chance. He knew exactly what he was talking about."

"It would appear that way," Missy whispered. She had never uncovered anything of this magnitude. "What are we supposed to do with this? It's big. Huge."

"Run it!" Ravelo declared. "Run it all. You pull back the rug and show the world the dirt."

"I will. You know I will. But there has to be a process. Corroboration. Verification. This is going to be page one for the nation, not just Detroit."

Ravelo didn't care about the details. He was remembering.

"It's more than me," Luther had told him on the last day of his life. *"More than me."*

The priest felt sick to his stomach. He didn't know what Missy saw in this. Scandal. Fame. Headlines. All he could see were the faces of the *people.* The mothers and fathers. The children. People he didn't even know, could only imagine. Normal people. Trusting people. Most eerie was the fact that this was not history. These people were living in the present. Damaged goods, in one sense—purposefully abused apart from their own consent, unaware of the reason for their own condition. The report made clear from repeated surveillance the reality of their tortured lives, the pursuit of the unattainable that characterized each one. In a flash Ravelo realized the irony—with it, his stomach dropped through the floor of the car to the whirling asphalt beneath. The goal of moral magnification *had been* hideously realized. Each child *had become* something, polarized morally. Only they were not made moral, as hoped.

God knew their names.

Vengeance is mine. . . .

"Read me their names," Ravelo asked softly. Naming a thing makes it real. It was so in the Garden. The first thing Adam did, had to do, was name the animals. Otherwise, what were they? *These* were people. Souls. Both living and dead. Beloved of God. Ravelo wanted to hear their names. Missy flipped back to the front of the report where the names were listed and read, slowly, each one.

She read names that rang with hope and promise. Steven Bricard, Cheri Tank, Luther Sanchez, Ronald Matheson, Alex Ryan, John Williams, Patricia Sherman . . .

She read all of the names. Not just because Father Ravelo had asked her to, but because the sound of the names was strangely reassuring. There was humanity here, which only compounded the tragedy, to be sure, but also gave Missy a stake, a connection, one she realized she did not want to lose in pursuit of a snappy lead line. The reading of the names was sobering. And for this story, sober was good. So she read. But even more, she listened. Each name was *somebody's* own story.

Number Three had a story. Number Twelve. Number Fourteen. But Missy didn't know one from the other. She didn't know that Number Seventeen, Jessica O'Connel—whose hometown of Maple Hill, North Carolina, was the site of Project Pacifist—was conspiring right now in New York City with a young neurosurgeon to uncover a scandal of far greater import, a scandal that stood as the direct inheritor of the legacy of Project Pacifist. She could not have known that Number Seventeen was part of this story in any way.

But she was.

Missy and Ravelo parted, neither really knowing what to say. Both agreed they should meet again, soon; both wanted to pursue unnamed ends regarding Luther's case. Ravelo headed to his parish to pray. In situations like this, his spirit weary and burdened, prayer was all he really trusted. He would probably spend all night in prayer, and tomorrow fasting.

Not so for Missy. In fact, when her collared confidant told her what he planned, the very idea seemed strange and purposeless. Instead, she headed straight to her office, hoping for some serious connect time on the Net. God may or may not have known about this particular situation, she thought, but someone somewhere on the Internet probably did.

It was late by the time she arrived at the *Sentinel.* The editorial offices were nearly empty, though a few intrepid reporters could be seen burning the keys to meet deadline. Missy didn't even bother to say "hi," just quietly ducked into her cubicle, leaned way back in her chair, and closed her eyes.

Please let me find something. Anything.

It was a prayer, of course, silent, reflexive, the kind we all make without really thinking about who our thoughts are directed to. The irony was lost in the fuzz of her brain. She hit the power switch. The computer loaded, the screen began to glow. She launched Netscape, went to Yahoo first. Typed: "Project Pacifist, mind control, counter-insurgent, federal programs, declassified projects." Hit return. Waited.

The search engine returned 1,078 hits.

Too much. Her search parameters were intentionally broad. Each hit only meant the engine had found one of the terms, not necessarily all of them in relationship. The phrase "mind control" alone was prob-ably responsible for more than half the hits. She narrowed her search to include some Boolean links between "Project Pacifist" and the other phrases. Hit return. Waited.

The screen flickered. A new message appeared: "Search returned no articles."

Zero? How could that be? Missy frowned. While it was a big deal for her to be in possession of secretive materials, unknown to the broader public, and to have formed a direct link between those materials, Luther Sanchez, and others, it seemed doubtful that she and Buck Keegan were the only private citizens on the uptake. Surely Project Pacifist was not unknown in other circles . . . the kind of circles that traversed the Internet, that gloated over Deepthroat-style informants, rumor, and chronic intrigue. At the very least she expected a handful of references to the project, however vague. Nothing hard, just a brief, whispered mention or two. She searched again. Same thing. Searched again, this time only for "Project Pacifist," no other requirements.

Zip. "Search returned no articles."

Missy grew perplexed. While hidden from the general populace, a declassified federal program like Project Pacifist was what Net fanatics thrived on. She changed directions, growing more determined, search-ing in other locations, through API archives, alternate search engines like WebCrawler and Lycos, even a couple of the premium databases the *Sentinel* subscribed to. She plugged in every keyword she could think of related to Project Pacifist. Dozens, even hundreds of hits pur-ported to reveal alleged, controversial, and often unsubstantiated mind-control experiments. She read all of them that looked promising and, just to be sure, many that didn't. Nothing, anywhere, ever men-tioned the one elusive phrase, Project Pacifist.

After three hours of trying, Missy wiped her eyes, turned off the power, and headed home.

Cruising down the freeway, the incandescent streetlights, neon signs, and billboards all turned fluid, flushed from the perimeters of her vision like seven colors of paint thrown up against a wall, running slowly down, intermingling, becoming one. On the radio, REM sang about losing their religion. Missy wondered if she was losing her soul. Her consuming passion was solving the riddle of Luther Sanchez, or so she had believed. Yet something itched, something rubbed rough. Unasked, unnamed, it scratched her conscience like a wool sweater against chapped winter skin. Polite questions wouldn't do. Worse, Missy suspected the answer would leave her naked.

She ignored the unasked, kept driving. All that mattered was that the truth be made known.

Bone tired, she climbed the two flights of stairs to her apartment; airy, sticky thoughts wrapped themselves like cotton candy around the weariness in her arms and legs and eyes. She fumbled for her keys, found the right one, stuck it in the door, turned the knob, stepped inside. Her hand groped for the light switch.

Before she could find it, from the darkness, a gloved hand shot over her mouth, spun her into a viselike embrace, arms locked at her chest. Missy froze in terror. A split second later she tried to scream. The hand was clamped too tightly over her mouth, muffling her cries.

"Shut up! Shut up!" an older male voice whispered harshly in her ear. "I won't hurt you. Just shut up."

Oh please, Missy silently screamed. *No, no . . .*

The man remained behind her, one arm across her chest, pinning her arms, the other over her mouth, twisting her neck to one side. He was strong but not overpowering. Missy could squirm a little. What she couldn't do was see. Her assailant must have turned the venetian blinds while waiting, because the pale orange luminescence that normally siphoned into her apartment from the parking lot outside was swallowed by a flat gray-black that seemed to suffocate both sight and sound. Forcefully, Missy stilled herself, enough to let the man know she had stopped struggling.

If he relaxed an inch, she was going to go for his groin with her doubled fist and then run screaming. He didn't relax.

"Did you talk to Keegan?" the man asked.

Keegan? Keegan? Is that what this was about? Missy almost felt relieved until her thoughts caught up to her in a rush of terror. When they did, she grew even more afraid . . . . coldly afraid. After all, she couldn't be sure what the correct answer was. The one this man wanted.

"Answer me! Tell me the truth."

She couldn't speak, just nodded her head.

She felt the man's breath on her neck, could feel his heart pounding on her back. He was nervous. Her answer only made him more so.

"You're getting too close," he said tersely. "You've got to be more careful from here on out. Recon will soon be viable. It's in beta stage now. There's not much time."

Missy struggled to speak. The man relaxed his hand, but only a little, just enough for her to mumble through his fingers.

"What's recon? That's a spy term. What is this all about? Why am I getting too close? Who are you?"

Missy could have sworn the man chuckled softly in response. "Who, what, why. The basics of reporting. Good. Keep that up. But you've got to get smarter. You can't afford to be careless, not even a little. The truth is not a commodity. It is a prize. People trade commodities. They buy and sell them. But they kill for prizes."

Missy whispered, "Please, what is the truth? Tell me."

"That's not for me to say. But it *is* findable. It's out there. Avoid tunnel vision."

"What do you mean? I've checked all around and can't find anything. I'm going to call the FBI and check with the federal archives tomorrow, but—"

The man grew angry. "Think! Why can't you find anything?"

"Please don't hurt me! I'm trying . . . I haven't had enough time."

"Time is what you are wasting. It's all been buried. Again."

"Are you talking about Project Pacifist? I've got information. Surely I can get more."

"Reclassified."

"No, declassified."

"*Re*classified," the man emphasized. "Two years ago. You can't get your hands on jack through the normal channels. You're lucky to have what you've got." His laugh returned, more gentle, more bitter. "You've got to think bigger. Bigger than 'Pacifist.' If you haven't got recon, you haven't got the story. You can't afford tunnel vision."

"But if I don't call—"

"If you *do* call, they'll know you're looking." He was getting angry.

"Then tell me more," Missy said urgently. "I don't know what to do. I need help."

"You are at the beginning. You have the list."

"The list? What list? I need more!"

The man shuffled closer to the door. "Be a reporter. Get the story, then get the word out. I tried myself. Quietly. A note on the Internet. Nobody cares. But they might listen to you."

"You aren't making sense. Why not just call me?"

"Because then I couldn't give you this." He stuffed something into her hand. Felt like a file folder.

"Be a reporter," he snipped. "It's what you do. You're good at it."

Missy grew desperate. "How can I reach you? Who are you? How do you know about all this?"

"Don't follow me; don't look for me. I won't be there." In one rough motion, the man shoved Missy forward into the darkness, turned and slipped outside. Missy tripped over a thin cord the man had spread across the path. She fell, hit the ground hard. As quick as she could regain her senses, she jumped to her feet, turned on the light. The man was gone. She stuck her head out the door, ran to both sides of the stairwell, then down the stairs. Nothing. No car leaving. No fleeing shadow. Nothing. She never saw his face.

Cursing, she went back upstairs, turned on more lights, opened the folder. Inside were a half dozen aerial photos of densely wooded terrain. Satellite shots.

The first zoomed in on what seemed to be some sort of small military base with a couple of tiny jeeps and a few tiny soldiers at their posts. No action, but one of the soldiers was circled. The photo right after zoomed in on that soldier, standing near what Missy assumed was a gate. His blue helmet was circled in thick red magic marker.

United Nations?

The other photos panned out, revealing more of the terrain, which was far too thick to differentiate, especially with Missy's untrained eye. She wouldn't have even noticed the thin, broken dirt road snaking through the trees if it, too, had not been highlighted. The final photo zoomed in tight again. Another thick magic marker circle, this time around a small nondescript building in the middle of nowhere, guarded by more tiny soldiers with rifles. The thin road leading up to it came from the direction of the base.

Underneath the image was typed data, most of it blackline censored. One phrase remained unmarked, which Missy could read:

Proposed Research Site, Guatemala Highlands.

"Oh no," she whispered. "It's happening again."

21

In a somewhat apocryphal story regarding Einstein, the old master was said to have expounded on his famous theory thus: "If you lay your hand on a burning stove for two seconds, it feels like ten minutes. But when you sit by a beautiful woman for ten minutes, it will likely feel like two seconds. *That's* relativity."

If relativity also meant ups and downs, a complete lack of certainty, and the extremes of both delight and annoyance, then Hank's experience of late had proved truly relative. His "ten minutes" with the ravishingly beautiful Jessica O'Connel felt like ten years one moment, ten seconds the next. Every impression was an extreme. If the choice were between a rusty ice pick stabbed in his leg or being locked in a room alone with her and a copy of the *National Review,* Hank would gladly reach for the hydrogen peroxide and brace himself for a bloodletting. Though both quickly learned to avoid politics like the plague, in his mind Hank had already played out a dozen darkly comic scenarios, Hollywood-style, where he went laughingly mad during one of their discussions and threw himself into the nearest body of water he could find; or maybe ripped open a tube of Tums and ate every piece, mouth foaming, in the middle of a crowded restaurant; this, after each disastrous attempt to traverse something as simple as, oh, say, Ronald Reagan.

Yet he could not help his fascination with her. If the question was turned to a choice between listening to her laugh or cry and tell stories of her passion for the less fortunate—if the choice was between that and a fame-bringing medical discovery, and if the two choices were mutually exclusive, Hank was not so sure he wouldn't choose the pleasures of Jessica's company. She was brilliant, pale like ivory, and lovely, and when she smiled, other lights grew dim. Yet she was so much more. Something deep inside him felt shaped with her name. Even when her bare Southern-tinged voice cut like a whip, he heard, behind the barbs, the music of her soul. It made no sense, like a cruel divine joke. Why not Nellie? That seemed so much easier, nicer. But when he and Jessica headed in separate directions, or when he could glimpse her from a distance, or think of speaking with her, those feelings grudgingly gave way to the most exquisite ache. Simply put, the intrigue of Jessica O'Connel was greater than the eccentricities. Sum versus parts.

Worse yet, some of the annoying parts were starting to get cute. Relative, indeed.

Such a time came when Hank mentioned returning to his apartment to grab a couple of changes of clothes. They were in Hank's car, on their way back to the Columbian. Jessica asked about Kim's molested apartment with more than a hint of concern in her voice. It was a casual betrayal of emotion; the rawness was plain, if not severe. But she quickly covered so that Hank wasn't sure in the end if she feared for him or for herself or was simply being polite.

When they arrived at the hotel, Hank felt that he should walk Jessica to the front door, whether it offended her or not. So he did and she didn't argue. Standing at the entrance in the cool evening air, each lingered, unwilling to walk away from the other. Just in case he was considering the idea, Jessica sternly informed Hank that he should not spend the night at his apartment. Might not be safe, she said. Hank agreed, but did not think it was appropriate to spend another night in Jessica's room, either. She offered to register a second room in her own name. He could pay her back later. Fine. Thanks.

"I'll see you in a bit," Hank said, turning.

A couple of hours. No big deal. He would be careful.

Jessica walked inside the hotel, didn't look back as Hank climbed inside his Duster. Safely inside, though, she watched through the glass as he drove away.

It took Hank longer than two hours. He had to gather a few things: clothes and all the money bills he could find; had to grab his Powerbook and a few toiletries; still needed to hide one of his two remaining disk copies, which he buried in his bedroom in an envelope at the bottom of a tin full of loose change. The last he would keep on his person until he knew what to do—though he already knew the answer. So he sneaked in quietly, did his business, and left just as quietly, hoping all was well. It seemed so. The air was warm—Hank had left his thermostat running—placid and stale.

Translation: undisturbed.

Let's keep it that way, he thought, closing the door quietly, firmly behind him.

Back at the hotel, he rapped lightly on Jessica's door, got the key from her, said good night. He felt relieved to be there. Couldn't tell how she felt. No late-night conversation this time around. They were both tired. Hank curled up in his bed and was fast asleep.

"Hey, I'm off," he declared the next morning, knocking on her door.

She opened, sleepy eyed, waving him in. Hank used her mirror to cinch the tie around his neck while she dressed in the bathroom.

He spoke louder so she could hear him. "When can we speak again? Your call."

Jessica opened the door, wiping her mouth with a white hotel towel. She wore pants, a loose-fitting sweater, cream flats, no jewelry. Her hair was a mess . . . a beautiful red mess. She emerged from the bathroom, grabbed her purse, waved something at Hank. "I'm going to call this number. It's worth a shot."

"The one the nurse in ICU left for you?"

"Mmm. From my 'sister.'"

"Good luck. How about we meet back here at two o'clock?"

"That should work. Where are you going?"

Hank rummaged through his duffel bag, pretending to look for something, stalling; finally he reached for his briefcase, which held all of the files he had stolen from Remming and downloaded off the Net.

"The FBI, of course. That's the plan."

Jessica took a deep breath. "Are you sure. What made you decide?"

Hank stepped closer. They stood face-to-face.

"You did."

Jessica stepped back. "Don't say that. That's not fair."

"Jessica, I'm not going to lie to you; I've got a hole in my gut about this. But I've got to do something. You helped me see that. So I'm doing this for you, whether I think it's right or not because you've made me want to do the right thing. I'm just not sure this is it." Closing the door behind him, he called out, "I'll see you later, then."

Jessica did not reply.

"Later," he said again, more softly, from the other side. Ducking his head, he set off down the hallway.

The elevator doors were nearly closed before Jessica caught up to him. She shoved her hand in, forced them back open, stepped hurriedly inside. She was obviously nervous, maybe even annoyed. Hank stood alone in the elevator, right in the middle, hands in the pockets of his khaki pants. He was dressed casual, in a denim shirt, tie, and Doc Martins. Jessica thought he looked like a little boy with his head down. Was he pouting about something? Or simply leary of the plan? He glanced up, but it took a second or two to register her presence.

When he did, he smiled. "Came to see me off? Or did I forget something?"

Jessica fudged and fidgeted, but her eyes were locked on his. This was *not* what she wanted to do—not her idea of distance and control. Not at all. But when she heard Hank say good-bye, when he left her room, when the door closed, the thought occurred to her that she might never see him again. Absurd as the idea was, it terrified her so much that her next conscious thought was of rushing into the hall, semipanicked, feeling again the memory of their initial encounter from the lobby stirring in her breast. Now she stood before him, breathless, embarrassed. More than a little peppered that she felt anything at all.

Better just to get it over with.

She leaned forward awkwardly, whispered, "You forgot this," and kissed Hank lightly on the cheek. She thought to pull away then, but, surprisingly, her lips lingered a moment more, just an extra moment, so that Hank could feel her breath on his skin . . . so that Jessica could feel the warmth in his flesh. The moment was quick and ungainly, at the same time, seemed to last for a delicious month. She immediately regretted it.

"Be careful. Just in case you're right," she said quietly into Hank's ear, then stepped back, right as the doors closed again. This time *her* head was lowered to hide her blushing cheeks, yet she glanced up just in time to see Hank, droll, open-mouthed, confused.

That, of course, made it worthwhile. The doors closed. Jessica couldn't help but giggle.

Standing on the sidewalk, staring up at 26 Federal Plaza Building as the yellow taxi at his heels jerked, cut sharply into traffic, then went careening down the street, Hank felt very small. On Broadway, north of City Hall, this part of New York City was as crowded as any other. Maybe more so. A constant stream of jostling bodies filed past him like salmon swimming upstream, both ways. The air was chill. Most people wore overcoats, sweaters, but some wore short sleeves. Others carried umbrellas. In New York, an umbrella was always a good idea this time of year.

Spring was in boisterous full bloom and the fever was everywhere. With the weather clean and crisp, the sky above the officed towers of glass and rock looked like a screen of cobalt blue smeared with white. Odors amalgamated: asphalt, paint, exhaust fumes, a dozen different kinds of prepared foods, flowers from the lady at the corner and perfume from those passing by, all rolled into one potent, nearly surreal aroma. Unmoving, Hank stood on the corner for about five minutes, abruptly doubting everything. Like a Freudian watch—passing one way and then the next, feeding his indecision—people filed by at the periphery of his vision: silver-haired, clean-shaven Wall Street types; plain-clothed housewives on their way to market with kids in tow; red or navy crisply suited businesswomen; goateed, baggy-pantsed wannabe artists; testosterone man-boys with bulging flesh and muscle shirts; sauntering, tight-shirted or short-skirted, braless women, the kind who claimed liberation but dressed dependent on a man's gawking attention.

Hank squeezed the handle of his briefcase tighter. He really had no choice. This was the only logical solution. Sure, stuff would hit the fan.

Very likely what Hank was about to do would mean Remming's career, maybe even his own. Who knew? But what else could he do? He doubted Kim Yu would want another crack at this, if he could even find him.

If he was even alive.

No, no, no! Rationally, Hank knew it didn't make sense to jump to such extreme conclusions. For all he knew, Kim had been contacted, maybe threatened, and had bailed to try to cover his tracks. And Jessica was right, too: If they really wanted *him* they probably would have gotten him by now. Which only confused the issue, because the facts didn't quite add up. Why would they trash Kim but leave him alone? Hank was pretty bright and had been careful to watch his backside, but surely they could have tracked him if they really wanted to. He wondered if he was overreacting.

Yet he vividly remembered how cold his blood ran when Remming and that woman talked about killing Rosenburg. She didn't sound as though she was kidding. Either way, Hank didn't want to find out.

What to do? He would rather not have his face or name associated with any of this—the research or the snitching. For a brief, commanding moment he seriously contemplated putting all the files in a plain manila envelope, sealing it anonymously, dropping it inside the front door and disappearing. Quick and dirty. Done deal. No more pressure or responsibility.

No guarantee the right people would see it or take it seriously, either.

So he steeled himself for the task. He had made this bed, snooping around where others had warned him off, and now he had to lie in it. He took one step forward, then another. By the time he reached the front doors, Hank had convinced himself that this was the right thing to do, the courageous thing, to face up to one's own mistakes, no matter what it cost him. After all, the situation was complex. No answer was perfectly right. As Jessica said, this answer just happened to be more right than the others.

He almost believed it. Except that he knew it wasn't true. This, of all plans, was the *easiest* for Hank. And the most foolish.

But why? He asked himself that question as he stood on the smooth, marbled floor before the main information center, a broad, tall counter behind which sat three young ladies. Behind them stood a chisel-faced man in a flat gray suit with an earpiece and walkie-talkie. A handful of other people stood in line with Hank, waiting for assistance. Security guards were posted throughout the spacious central foyer and people in suits were constantly coming or going or crossing from one side of the chamber to the other.

"May I help you?" asked one of the ladies politely. She wore a thin operator's headset, the kind with a wire that curved around her jaw to hold a tiny pea-size microphone right in front of her mouth.

Hank shifted from one foot to the other, lowering his voice. He was still a little nervous from the security check at the entrance, even though they let his briefcase through unopened. "I have some material I need to discuss with someone at the FBI. I don't know who."

"Material?" the woman queried, thumbing through a handful of papers as she spoke. "What is the nature of the material?"

"The nature?"

Distracted, the woman didn't seem to hear him, though she did manage to find whatever it was she was looking for. Hank wiped at his dry lips, thinking how best to answer level one. After all, she would need to know something to be able to route him to the proper office. He leaned forward over the counter and spoke in a whisper. "Just some medical information I've come across at work. Some research I think somebody needs to look at. It's, umm, confidential."

The woman glanced down again, then back at Hank. She seemed unsure but smiled. "Let me get you an ASAC. The FBI is on floor twenty-three. The elevators are right down that hallway. When you get there, take a left. I'll phone Bill Sander and tell him you're coming. Your name, please?"

"Oh, that's not necessary. Thank you."

The woman smiled, touched a button on the switchboard. She spoke softly, a word or two. Hank shuffled off. She never took her eyes off of him.

On the twenty-third floor, the elevator doors opened onto a hallway, the left end of which was a wide, glass-fronted office labeled Special Services. Venetian blinds hung the length of the glass, blocking Hank's view. Feeling conspicuous, he glanced right. The other end of the hallway formed a T with left and right wings. No one passed by. He took a few steps, trying to walk softly (though not sure why), opening the door to Special Services. Inside, a man greeted him from the front desk. Sheets of plastic and masking tape draped the furniture and creased the walls. The thick smell of a fresh coat of paint hung in the air.

"Sorry. We're doing some remodeling. Can I help you?" The man extended his hand.

Hank shook it, read the man's name tag: *Bill Sander, Assistant Special Agent in Charge.*

"The lady at the front desk told me to come up here."

"She phoned," Bill replied, smiling. "What can we do for you, umm—?"

"I'd rather not give my name. Can I speak with your supervisor?"

"She's in a meeting. I can give her whatever you have."

Hank furrowed his brow. Bill said matter-of-factly, "It's not standard policy for me to just pass along everything that comes down the pike, if you know what I mean."

Hank did know. His mother's sense for the out-of-place had flared the moment he stepped inside. He held up his briefcase like show-and-tell. "I work as a resident at a local university. I uncovered some information regarding research improprieties. But I don't feel comfortable passing it along to just anybody, if *you* know what *I* mean."

Bill smiled politely. "Of course." He picked up the phone, dialed a four-digit number.

"Sandy, this is Bill Sander down in Special Services. I've got a gentleman in my office that wishes to speak with Special Agent Nero, but she's out until later this afternoon—" He covered the receiver, looked at Hank. "I didn't really even ask. Would you like to try your luck and come back later?"

Hank shook his head. Bill put his mouth back to the phone. "Yeah, Sandy, you got anybody up there that could help me out? I think it's legit. The assistant director? Yeah, great . . . OK, I'll send him over."

Bill hung up the phone and pointed. "Head down the hallway and take a left. Keep going until you can't go any farther, then take another left. You're looking for Jack Henigan's offices. He's the Assistant

Director in Charge. Depending on what you've got, he can probably help you."

"Thanks," Hank said. He followed directions, ending up in front of a set of double glass doors. The office inside was much larger than Special Services, appearing to be actually a cluster of several offices, with half a dozen cubicles in the front section alone. Taking a deep breath, Hank mustered his confidence, stepped inside. A man noticed him. Another suit. They all looked alike.

"Can I help you?"

"Bill Sanders sent me."

"Sander," the man corrected.

"Right."

The FBI man touched his tongue to the back of his teeth. "No 's' at the end. *Sander.*"

Very slowly, Hank said, "OK . . ."

"Come this way." The man led Hank through one of the back doors, down another hallway, to what was apparently a waiting area, with four or five chairs. "Wait here, please. Someone will be with you shortly."

Hank sat. Ten minutes passed. Twenty. He squirmed. Thirty. He began to argue with himself. This didn't *feel* easy, he reasoned. Easy was dropping and running, not looking strangers in the eye. Yet, pithy one-liners and all, his sense of reason could not match the tangy certitude of guilt. Otherwise, why bother to argue with yourself? So here it was: Jay Remming, one of the most respected scientists in the world, had taken Hank under his wing. He had trusted him. Now Hank was about to turn him in without even attempting to act on a better plan, a plan that might help save Remming from himself. The pressure a man like Remming must be under was enormous. Hank, of all people, knew this well. If all Remming made was one wrong decision, it would be a miracle. Yet Hank was going to nab him for the first known offense.

A word drifted into Hank's mind. A simple, single word. *Grace. Grace . . .*

Not a usual part of his vocabulary. But that was the issue. Grace. Ironically, Hank, the one who supposedly knew grace—a man who claimed the grace of God had touched him, changed him—was ready to throw the whole shtick out to see justice achieved. Or was that it? Was it that simple? Hank rubbed the back of his neck, closed his eyes. He knew the irony was actually much deeper. He could forgive Remming and show a little mercy. But at what cost? What if he did and then Remming went and scientifically redefined the parameters of his faith—the faith of all 'believers'—according to the strictures of simple chemistry? What did that leave Hank actually believing? He knew his faith was real. OK, not powerful, but it meant something. He had told Remming basically the same thing underneath the bridge. Maybe it was nothing but a running residual from childhood, moral overspill, little more . . . *but real, nonetheless.*

Hardly compelling. So why did he think it was real at all?

Which begged the question: *What* was real? Define real. Define what.

Intellectually, anyone's faith-based assertion of realness was extreme, whether for its audacity or its foolishness. Faith was an intangible. Which meant . . .

Slam!

Hank quickly and instinctively welded that mental door shut, unwilling to give such sophism even a chance. Instead he forced himself to downshift to anything else handy . . . the copy of *Newsweek* on the end table beside him. He had to. Like a crazy aunt hidden in the basement of some ultradysfunctional family, Hank's introspection was likely to turn up all manner of unwelcome theological issues—issues he was ill equipped to deal with. Which, of course, was precisely the reason he did *not* want these small-voiced thoughts exposed to the logic and process of conscious thought. Ever since he first grasped the implications of the God Spot research, especially after his talk with Remming, he had labored to keep them *sub rosa.* Most of all to himself. But the whole affair would no longer suffer the quiet burial plot Hank had assigned it in his subconscious. What about legitimate doubts? Even more, what about reasonable questions? Sitting in the numbing offices of the FBI in New York City, the *real* question finally surfaced, rising like a monster in a child's dreams and, at last, demanding an answer:

Was his, Hanson Blackaby's, faith just a clump of nerves in his brain?

Hank screwed his eyes shut against the torrent of thoughts that came rushing through the hole of that dike. Was he born with it? Genetically predisposed to it? Just waiting for a certain flavored name, a name given by a little boy in a park twenty years ago? Did his faith—emotion, practice, foundation—hinge on some sort of Jungian synchronicity, a matter of timing, where chemicals and hormones and gray matter collided with circumstance to achieve mythical self-realization; a sort of spiritual gumball machine—put your quarter in the slot and out comes a ready-made, premade Christian?

If not that boy in the park, then who? And what name? What other God? Why only Christians?

Is it all just a formality? The sinner's prayer? The feelings . . .

A sucker born every minute, said W. C. Fields. Was that it? Blessed, hopeful, genetically induced "believers"? The very word would become an instant self-parody. Believe in what? A spot in the brain that causes one to think they believe?

A warm male voice interrupted his thoughts. "Hi there, I'm the A.D., Jack Henigan." The voice came from over his left shoulder. Startled, Hank bolted out of his seat, grateful for the diversion. He extended his hand. Jack took it in a firm grip and shook. "I understand you don't want to divulge your name?"

"No, sir."

"That's fine, fine. Why don't you come with me?"

Hank followed Jack through another door; past, presumably, Jack's personal secretary, who was talking on the phone in a shrill, nasally voice that literally caused the hair on Hank's arms to stand up, then finally to a spacious office with leather seats, a window view, and rows of books lining two walls. Jack motioned for Hank to sit and then closed the door behind him. The door closed with a tight seal and a click. Instantly, the room grew quiet. The few sounds outside the office, including, mercifully, the secretary, disappeared. Hank glanced at his watch. Forty-five minutes had passed. It was now or never. Now *more than ever,* thanks to forty-five minutes alone with his thoughts, he felt an indefinable sense of unease. Giving the files away was easy, he knew now, because it cost him nothing. And, thanks to his suspicious nature, Hank fundamentally mistrusted the very people he was about to give his life to.

More important, give Remming's life to.

But Jack was pleasant enough, seemed like a real human being, not a robot. He looked to be in his early sixties, probably three weeks from retirement, a little heavy around the middle, solid jowls, a ready smile. As he sipped at a cup of steaming coffee on his desk and leaned back in his chair, he grinned ruefully. "I used to only drink a cup of coffee in the morning. One cup. But then they made these federal buildings smoke-free and, well . . ." He let the thought trail away. "What can I do for you, son?"

Hank set his briefcase on his lap, rolled the combination, popped the top. "You should know right off that I'm very uncomfortable with what I'm doing. I simply don't know where else to turn."

"Of course."

"I'm a research student. A few days ago I uncovered some research at the university which I suspect to be illegal in nature and/or illegally funded. I was able to obtain copies of the files related to this research."

Jack asked the obvious. "How?"

"I'd rather not say, sir."

Jack raised an eyebrow. "I think before you go any further, you should know something. This field office is home to the Computer Crime Squad. We're the regional Bureau office for investigating illegal computer intrusions all over the northeastern United States. Now . . . care to continue?"

Even though he could feel the heat in his face, Hank managed to shrug nonchalantly. "You decide what's worth prosecuting here." He pulled out a thick stack of papers, laid them on Jack's desk. "This is pretty much everything. Some of the names involved are big names you will probably recognize. You must understand, I wouldn't resort to measures like this if I wasn't truly concerned."

"Of course," Jack said again. He thumbed through a couple of pages, offering only a cursory glance. "Are you sure this is what you want to do?" he asked. For a moment, the way he asked, Hank thought Jack could have been his father, any father. He stared hard at Hank, whose answer was soft:

"This is too big for me."

Again, Jack nodded. He turned to his computer, pecked a couple of keys and looked at the monitor. He was in no hurry. After a minute or two he said, "Would you wait outside for just a moment?"

Hank rose, left the room, sat down in a chair beside the secretary's desk. From the blinking lights, Hank guessed the secretary was juggling three concurrent calls on her five-line phone—the fifth was marked "Reserved"—moving at about ninety miles an hour. Needless to say, she didn't bother to speak to Hank, or, for that matter, even look at him. Her desk was carnage, strewn about with computer disks, pens, pencils, precarious stacks of papers and folders, two coffee mugs, and about a dozen paper clips. Listening to her speak, looking at her desk, Hank couldn't believe this woman had ever managed to become a secretary, especially since her voice had all the charm and comfort of fingernails on a chalkboard.

Crooking the phone in her neck, the secretary jumped to her feet and scurried over to one of several tall filing cabinets lining the far wall.

"Uh-huh," she said. "Uh-huh."

Her bifocals hung from the tip of her nose, defying gravity as she scanned the contents of an open drawer and retrieved a folder.

Hank didn't bother listening to her conversation. In fact, he tried to tune her out. His stomach was still in knots over what he was about to do. If he hadn't been so distracted he might have been able to catch the coffee mug the secretary's stretched phone cord dragged over the edge of her desk, which, though more than half empty, still had enough cold coffee in it to make a mess. The mug hit the thin carpet with a dull thud, splattering black liquid at Hank's feet.

Time for a vacation, Hank surmised.

Frazzled as she was, the secretary, still on the phone, now started fussing over him and the spill. Hank looked around for a roll of paper towels or something he could use to soak up the coffee but couldn't see anything. He wouldn't have had the time, anyway; the secretary was a whirlwind of activity. As she bent down to retrieve the mug, she knocked off a small stack of papers, which, as is the way of such mishaps, landed straight in the middle of the coffee puddle.

Time for a vacation . . . today.

Amazingly, none of this seemed to bother the woman. She wasn't on the verge of tears. Frazzled, maybe, but not worried. This seemed to be just another day at the office. She moved from crisis to crisis with relative calm like a mother moves from one crying child to the next. Oh, here's a problem . . . and now this? Fine, what next . . . ?

Hank reached for the soggy, brown-stained papers, picked them up individually, letting the coffee drip off. Most appeared to be official office memos. Hank was intrigued. The top one read:

"Attn: All staff. Remodeling efforts will continue through the end of summer, possibly into fall. The schedule for each floor and wing will be posted as necessary . . ." Blah blah blah.

Generic administrative kind of stuff. Nothing spooky. Another one caught Hank's eye. "Attn: All second-floor personnel. Clear line 27 for S.D. All protocols observed. Receive as—"

Jack's office doorknob rattled. Startled, Hank glanced up as the older man swung the door wide. The secretary snatched the pile of letters from Hank's hands, blotted them with a tissue and moved off to the next task.

"I've glanced over your materials. Very interesting. We have special agents assigned to this sort of thing. Can you wait another ten to fifteen minutes?"

Hank shrugged his shoulders, nodded.

"Good. I've called one of our best to come take a look." Jack patted his shoulder, then stepped back inside his office and closed the door. Fifteen minutes, he said. It did not take long for Hank to figure out that time was relative for the government, as well. Half an hour later, he was still waiting. Then, without notice, the front door opened and a cold, leggy blonde strolled through, dressed to kill. She glanced at Hank briefly, then marched unannounced into Jack's office. A moment later, both Jack and the woman stood before him. Hank rose from his seat.

"This is Special Agent Decker," Jack said, holding his hand palm up toward the woman. "She'll be handling your case from this point on."

Hank glanced at the woman's name tag, nodded deferentially, but countered, "Not *my* case. That's why I'm giving it to you guys."

"What's your name?" Decker asked.

Hank thought something sounded very familiar in the tenor of her voice. "I'd rather not say," he stated firmly. "And I'd rather you not try to find out when I'm gone, either. I know you probably can pretty easily once you look through the files and start tracking names. But I'd rather you not try."

"Are there any other copies of these files?"

Hank shook his head. "No."

Odd. He could not understand why he felt so cold all of a sudden, why his heart was pounding. He was almost done, finished, free! Special Agent Decker was unnerving. Her eyes. The way she just watched him, without emotion. And her voice. Or maybe it was the way she talked. What was it? . . .

"Do you have any electronic copies, such as computer disks?" Decker asked.

"I had almost forgotten." He reached inside his briefcase and retrieved a computer disk, placed it in her outstretched hand. She regarded it with one eyebrow raised.

"Is that all?"

"Yes."

"Are you certain?"

What do you mean, am I certain? Hank wondered. *Why would you doubt me?* He did not feel good about this. Less and less the more Decker talked.

He also didn't care. He simply wanted to be done. His answer: "Yes."

"Good. Jack briefed me by phone on your files. I suspect there's nothing to it, but we'll look closer."

"You don't need me for anything else, then?" Hank queried.

Decker glanced at Jack. Jack said, "I don't think so. Here's my card if you need to reach me. Decker, do you have a card?"

She didn't even check. "No."

"Please don't contact me," Hank said, but he took Jack's card just the same. "I want to be done with this."

Decker folded her arms as she watched him leave. She smiled. *Perfect.*

When Hank strolled through the double doors of the Columbian into the sunlit lobby at twenty past two, he found Jessica standing at the far end with her back to the door, biting her fingernails.

"Jessica?" he murmured softly, coming up behind her.

Without turning, Jessica knew him. His voice felt good and comfortable, like rain in the summertime. She had not been idle while Hank was away, having spent the whole morning and afternoon alone with her thoughts. A person with courage to truly be *alone* with their thoughts can emerge reborn.

"It's seventeen minutes past two, you know," she said, trying to sound stern. It didn't work. During her time alone, her instinct for withdrawal had succumbed to something—something more than relief. Something nearer to the plain stretch of desire. To give in to the unknown.

To the possibility.

The possibility of what? Relationship was the only answer. Something real and honest. She remained face forward, her back to Hank. On the speakers overhead, Billy Joel softly sang, "She's Always a Woman to Me."

Not yet. Not ready.

"Sorry, red tape," Hank explained. "The government. What can I say?"

Say anything! she thought. *Anything . . .*

"How long have you been waiting?" Hank asked.

"Not long."

Not true. Since 1:30. When two o'clock came and went, fear came and stayed. She wasn't equipped to deal with this. She had not come to New York for her mother to die. Nor to uncork her fermenting mix of personal demons.

But oh! If she knew anything, she knew she wanted more. The elusive. The denied.

Something about you, Hank.

Was it the goodness he had patiently proved, the way he had earned her trust? Maybe. Even more meaningful and immediate was the sense of his nearness. When Hank was gone, fears came. Jessica spent the first half of the morning worrying for his safety and the second half hating herself for it. Then a moment of honesty, a question. Which was a greater waste of energy: the hating or the wanting?

Seemed pretty simple.

She turned slowly to look into his face. Her eyes were dry, but Hank could tell something was stirring in her soul. "Is everything all right?" he asked.

Everything inside her screamed, *Hang on!*

Instead, she let go.

"It's starting to get better. Much better."

They ate a late lunch together in the hotel bar and grill. Jessica sipped iced tea and munched distractedly at a chef salad, minus cheese and olives. Hank downed a burger and fries. Jessica recounted her day. Her plan had been to pose as a nurse and try to schedule an appointment to meet with the impostor Elizabeth. But when she called the hotel number, she got cold feet and couldn't follow through, fearing exposure if "Elizabeth" were to ask anything medical that she couldn't answer. She thought it wiser to let Hank call, and so spent most of the morning and afternoon reading, doing a little bit of office work on her laptop, waiting for him, though she omitted the latter in the telling.

Hank agreed that she had done the right thing. He felt better making the call as well. If the whole thing went belly-up, as it well might, Hank didn't want Jessica's emotional state regarding her mother further bruised by anything said during the conversation.

Talk turned to other things. It was pleasant again, much like yesterday afternoon, and Hank enjoyed every minute of it. Slowly but surely, they were building something. From time to time, Jessica would draw away. She didn't even ask about the FBI drop-off. But her tone and body language were hemispheres apart from yesterday morning and growing consistently warmer. Every time her eyes met his, every time she smiled, his world changed colors.

Hank knew he could love this woman. He knew it.

They talked of family. Jessica told stories of her mom. Hank listened, relishing his new freedom from the pressure and burden of the god spot files, though the drop-off still gnawed at him. Of more immediate concern, he wondered how he would integrate himself back into the system at Columbia. Branded by what he knew, he was now a stranger, an outsider. The otherwise legitimate educational process stood tainted in his mind. More to the point, Remming had flexed his considerable muscle and removed Hank from active patient involvement. Hank assumed the suspension to be temporary, but what if it wasn't? What would become of him?

"What do you believe about God?" he asked suddenly, his blue eyes growing distant. Jessica was taken aback.

"I believe there *is* one, if that's what you mean," she said. "I couldn't comprehend justice the way I do without a God."

"But is there more? What's he like?"

"You assume he's a he?" Jessica grinned.

"Don't you?"

Jessica had hoped for humor. She put down her fork, thought for a moment. "I have a hard time thinking about God at all. It's hard to explain."

Hank was searching for firm footing himself. How could he begin to help her?

"I don't remember my father very well," Jessica said, watching him. "But I've seen lots of pictures. You have his eyes. I like that."

The waiter came by, refilled their glasses, left the ticket. Hank paid for his. Jessica paid for hers. Neither fussed. Together they strolled back into the lobby.

"I think it's time I get to know your sister a little better, don't you?"

"High time."

"Got the number?"

"Of course. Here—" She reached into her purse, handed Hank the paper with the phone number. "You know, whoever this is doesn't know Elizabeth very well."

"How so?"

"Well, she didn't bother to do her homework."

Hank nodded. "Doesn't surprise me. Five mistakes in every crime, you know. It's a statistical fact."

Jessica laughed. "Well, Mr. Trebeck, how did you know that?"

"I don't know. I read it. Point is, they always screw up. Someone, somewhere does something stupid. That's how they get caught."

"Well, this is mistake number one. Elizabeth's a Motel 6 kind of girl. She would never stay at the Plaza."

Hank read the number on the paper: 555-1627. He said, "I'll go call. Can you wait here?"

"Sure."

He turned, never took a step. His feet froze. Something clicked in his brain.

Jessica said, "What's wrong?"

Hank read the number again. And again. He felt his stomach fall to the floor. 555-1627. He felt sick.

It can't be. It can't be. . . .

"Oh, God," he whispered. "Wait here."

Of course she didn't. Both ran to the phone. Hank plunked two coins in the slot, dialed the number. His fingers trembled.

"What's wrong?" she asked. Hank held up a finger so he could hear the receiver better. His chest hammered. He took a deep breath.

The phone rang twice, then a lady answered. More like a voice. An unmistakable, shrill voice. A voice Hank had heard just a few hours earlier in the day when he had read a coffee-stained memo knocked to the floor: *"All second-floor personnel. Clear line 27 for S.D. All protocols observed. Receive as—"*

"—Plaza Hotel. May I help you?"

Hank closed his eyes, feeling nauseous. Wordless, he hung up the phone, reached into his pocket for Jack Henigan's business card, which only confirmed the obvious.

Jack Henigan, Federal Bureau of Investigation, 555-1626.

"Hank, what is wrong?" Jessica whispered. "You're frightening me."

"You said the woman posing as your sister was a blonde, right?" he demanded.

"That's what the nurse said. Very blonde."

Hank ran his finger through his hair. "Everything is wrong. Absolutely everything."

22

Remming had the afternoon to cool off, get wise, which he did in part. An operation of this magnitude was not to be trifled with—not when you were the sole voice of dissent and eighty feet underground. In every other top-level project he had participated in, the objective had either been transparently benign, or, if hostile, at least clearly defined and meriting hostility. Such as in the case of war. Here, the objective remained cloaked in secrecy, which only lent further suspicion to the whole, which appeared to be anything but benign.

"To change man," Volgaard had said.

Not a new revelation. Remming had said basically the same thing to Hank, under the bridge. Though in his own mind it had not sounded so sinister, nor so fraught with peril.

Change how? And why? Those were the real questions.

Answers only Newman could give, but not what Remming wanted. More than anything, Remming wanted to rail against Stewart Newman for unprofessional conduct, breach of ethics, fraud, not to mention scientific crimes against humanity. What he realized he *could* do—all he could do—was observe, try to return to a place of neutrality, and get out alive. As simple and cowardly as that. Remming didn't even bother to convince himself of loftier virtue. Fact was, he hated cowards and had always thought himself something of an intrepid frontiersman. But here, for the first time in years, Jay Remming was truly afraid. At this point in the game, valuable or not, Remming had to be viewed more as an expendable threat than an ally, all because he had blown his cool earlier.

Not only was he afraid, he also had to face up to some hard facts: The STM-55 research of his team had been sabotaged from within and without. From the inside, Volgaard was probably on the take the whole time. And Remming, foolishly, had given the Merideth Institute the key to the front door from the outside. That was the real kicker. Private research efforts operated on funding from little-known foundations, charitable organizations, high-risk investment groups, think tanks, and paramilitary organizations all the time. He himself had overseen at least a dozen or more such efforts in the last decade. It simply wasn't unusual—especially when the project involved cutting-edge science and preeminent names—to prefer a don't-ask-don't-tell policy as far as the money trail was concerned, or to operate through back doors, legal loopholes, vagaries, and confidential liaisons such as Monitor Nine (though most at least had a face and a normal name). Looking back, Remming could recognize some foolish choices along the way. But the world of high-tech science was a highly competitive field. In the early stages of the discovery, with the wonder of the pineal gland anomaly still fresh and the threat of another scientist somewhere else beating him to the punch being very real—and with funds limited and time of the essence—the motivation for an otherwise unholy alliance could be easily rationalized. Not to mention the lure of another Nobel. After all, this was literally the scientific find of the century. What to do? Put a few "feelers" out through the right channels, wink at your university's supervisory board, and wait for the telephone to ring.

When it rang for Remming, after three torturous months, an unknown humanitarian organization—or as they preferred to be called, a "global intervention group"—was on the other end. Said their name was the Merideth Institute. Frankly, by that point, Remming didn't care if it was the Andy Griffith Club. He was all too glad to take their money with few questions asked. Only one stipulation. The research was *his*. Fine, they said. That was before Monitor Nine. Before the ramifications of the early findings became clear. Before the validations mounted in staggering fashion. Yet the very next day after the approval of additional funds, Remming had assembled his team of four and they began.

Now this. Radical and invasive experimentation on humans. It was too much.

He decided to make the most of his time, patrolling the halls, stopping at each lab, each testing room, each monitoring station, each surgical and postop ward. He looked over page after page of complex data, growing ever more amazed and terrified at the scope of the research, the enormous resources and equipment and personnel that had been funneled into this facility. It was unparalleled in his experience. He glanced around, at the lights, the long hallways. The physical space itself must be some sort of renovated command bunker, possibly funded by the CIA during the guerrilla wars that had plagued Central America for decades. But for its present use, everything—the whole project—must have mobilized quickly, in record time, since his own research had barely begun to reach maturity.

Hours passed, moving from lab to lab. No one challenged him or questioned him. He had been given *carte blanche* by Newman, so he decided to talk with the physicians and lab technicians personally, hoping to draw out what they did, or, more important, didn't know. Many were transparently nervous or awed at his presence. Yet in time, the real stories emerged. Various ones told him of dramatic transfigurations of the subjects in both personality and conscience. Notably, not all the treatments were as extreme, nor as permanent, as the surgeries. Many were clinical trials involving drug treatments. One man, a kleptomaniac, had been released after an initial treatment and had not stolen anything in three weeks since taking a daily dose of a synthetic STM-55 base derivative. Another described a woman with severe insomnia who had slept like a baby every night for more than two months. A formerly suicidal manic-depressive was holding a steady job and doing volunteer work. Secondary indications were also good: Blood pressures often dropped; CBC numbers improved; some people even modified their diets.

The failings of these reports were not lost on Remming. Trial samples were small, follow-ups fairly subjective, and treatment schedules woefully short-term. And the variations of experience were far too erratic to quantify. Yet hard numbers were available in chemical analysis, blood samples, and gene surveys. Moreover the stories, however subjective, displayed an obvious pattern too striking to ignore. In spite of his revulsion, Remming was awed.

This could change the world! So much here. Bigger than . . . bigger than steroids. Bigger than the polio vaccine and penicillin combined. Maybe even bigger than gene sequencing itself! Prozac will be forgotten . . .

One of the physicians he interviewed voiced pretty much the same sentiment.

"The research is young, you understand. But in essence, we're talking about global behavior modification. Affecting an entire person with a single drug. Light-years ahead of present pharmacology."

Yet for all the positive stories, there were multiplied more on the negative side. These usually involved Christians, mostly extremely poor and uneducated, who were treated with various forms of serotoxomiasin inhibitors, restrictors, or, in some cases, antibodies designed to target the gray matter of the God Spot itself. For the sake of objectivity, screenings were done prior to experimentation to secure only psychologically stable case studies. Yet these same subjects drifted into everything ranging from lying and laziness to explosive bursts of anger to self-mutilation or sexual addictions of every flavor and degree. A few cases stood out. One otherwise peaceable man began to use incredibly offensive racial slurs regarding the ethnicity of his own wife. In another instance, within seventy-two hours of a single treatment, two of the antibody subjects had committed violent crimes, one rape and one armed robbery.

The stories were as shocking as the images Remming had been force-fed all day. In a room designed to serve as an intensive care unit lay the two men from the transplant operation. Two nurses were on duty—also, interestingly, the psychiatrist. Remming quizzed the attending nurse on their conditions. She said the black man, the Christian transplanter, was in system shock, a common occurrence, and that, yes, early indicators seemed to point to total blindness in one eye and some form of muscle paralysis in the other. The transplant recipient, on the other hand, was in stable condition, vitals were good, and he had already asked for a drink of water. Based on prior medical information, his white blood count was the highest it had been in three years, and his mood was good.

"We've seen this happen before," the psychiatrist added. "Problems crop up later, maybe a week, maybe less. They always do. But initial receptivity is amazing. The recipient seems to literally soak the graft in like a sponge. It will seem like a perfect match. Afterward, in follow-up sessions, they test out as happier, more adjusted, more at peace. I mean, this guy was a wretch when he came here. Look at him now."

Remming did look. The man lay in bed, propped up against a couple of pillows. He was hooked up to all kinds of tubes and wires, surrounded by monitors. He was awake. He glanced over at the nurse, smiled.

"What goes wrong?" Remming asked. He already knew. Their approach was skewed. They didn't have the whole riddle solved, but they thought they did.

"Don't know. Only that the system eventually rejects the graft. The body and personality short-circuit. They may go mad; they may have a massive brain hemorrhage. Or cardiac arrest. Hard to say. We need better recon."

Strike one, Remming thought. "And the donor?"

"That's what I mean. The lucky ones die. That's got to change."

"And the rest?"

"Most experience severe psychosis. Some become vegetables."

Remming asked, "How many donors have been studied in this way?"

The psychiatrist reflected a moment. "I don't know. Maybe thirty. Maybe forty."

Either way, a lot more than twelve, Remming thought, recalling Newman's assurances.

"Do you have a surviving recipient that is in good condition?"

"As a matter of fact we do," the psychiatrist replied. "I'll take you to her."

Together, they visited Maria, a young and heavyset woman, sitting alone in a four-by-eight room, furnished nicely with a TV, soft bed, pictures on the wall, and a sink. She was connected to a monitor, but otherwise had plenty of mobility and seemed in good health. The psychiatrist had already informed Remming of the woman's past: a street prostitute, mother of two, she had sold her own seven-year-old girl to a man once to get the extra money she needed for drugs. Remming entered the room alone. The woman sat on her bed, reading a book. She was Latino, but spoke decent English.

"Is it time for another examination?" she asked.

"No, no. I'm Dr. Remming. I just want to talk to you. If that's all right?"

Maria shrugged. "What about?"

"About you. About how you feel."

The woman smiled warmly. "I feel great."

"What's different, Maria?"

Maria put her magazine down, hugged her arms to herself. "I don't know, really. I know I hated myself before eight days ago."

"When they operated on you?"

Maria nodded. "But now, I just feel . . . I don't know. I can't explain it."

"Try. Please. It's important."

"Do you have a wife?" Maria asked.

"Once," Remming answered. "Not anymore."

"Did you ever buy her a new dress?"

Remming closed his eyes. *Once.*

Maria said, "When she put it on, what happened to her? Did she look more beautiful?"

Yes, Remming thought, but he said nothing.

"She did, didn't she? Do you know why?"

"No."

"I can tell you, it wasn't the dress. It's what the dress did. It made her *feel* beautiful. That's all I know to say. I feel different."

Interesting, Remming thought for the first time. *Perhaps all chemistries are not d-form specific. Is that even possible? Could that explain the occasional success?* "And what about your life when you leave here? What about your little girls? What about your past?"

Maria covered her eyes with her hand. "I can't think of any of that right now. I don't know those answers. I just want it to be different."

"Will you turn tricks again?"

"No!" Maria whispered fiercely. "I don't care what I've got to do, I'm not going back to that. I'll wash toilets."

"Why didn't you wash toilets before? If it's that easy now, why not then?"

Maria stared hard at the floor, then at Remming. "If you were in my head, you'd know. You could understand then."

Remming thanked her, closed the door behind him. He glanced through the glass window. Maria was reading again.

"She seems genuine," he commented. "But that doesn't prove anything. Any analysis at this stage must be considered short-term and highly subjective."

The psychiatrist agreed. "The only problem is that long-term is simply not an option. She's already lasted longer and done better than anyone yet, but her system is already showing signs of rejecting the transplant."

"Why?" Remming asked. He needed to know how close they were.

"Dunno," the psychiatrist replied. "We're working on that. Best we can figure is the obvious . . . the anomaly didn't come naturally. Despite its beneficence to the system, the system considers it a foreign object, an invasion, and rejects it."

Remming's eyes narrowed pragmatically. *Strike two.*

Later, Remming asked to be taken back to base. Before he left he visited a couple more subjects, with equally disturbing results. Then a fresh-faced private shuttled him back. Sitting in his small room in the half-light of a single lamp, Remming felt the entire burden of what he had seen resting on him alone. This operation could not go unchecked, that much he knew. Inaction was complicity. But exposure at any level would severely implicate him as well. Remming felt trapped. This scandal could be his undoing.

He began undressing, slowly, muscles aching from the rough roads. Thoughts crowded and dispersed, feeling like walls crunching tighter and tighter in his brain. Snaking through his fears, he could not shake the words of the last man he visited before returning to base, a white-haired, sixty-some-year-old, bearded madman. He was an

uneducated, wretchedly poor Christian who had volunteered for the
test so that his granddaughter could afford to go to college in America
with the money he made. Remming was certain the man had no clue
what he had volunteered for. Not really. Probably thought it was just
like a really fancy blood donation or something, rather than a violent
stripping of his soul. The man said the same thing over and over—
moaning, slobbering, nearly incoherent. Except for one phrase. Over
and over again . . .

"Abominacion de desoluciones. Abominacion de desoluciones.
Mucho desoluciones!"

He would say it and weep, then shout it in rage, then whisper it in
fear.

"Abominacion de desoluciones!"

"What does it mean?" Remming asked the psychiatrist.

"Nothing. It's just gibberish. It makes no sense."

"No, it means something . . . he's talking too fast. Abomination
something?"

The psychiatrist sighed, annoyed with the old man and Remming
for paying him any attention. "Abomination of desolations," he said.
"Figure that one out."

Remming removed his jacket and coat. He had to think! This was
beyond the pale, lurking as an international atrocity in the making,
regardless of Newman's civilized rhetoric.

Think! Remming demanded of himself. *Think!*

He knew the research was broad but was pleased to realize it also
lacked depth. A sense of automation—assembly-line thinking—per-
sistently kept the operation overfocused and slightly sterile as a result,
at least in terms of advancing the knowledge base. These were analysts
on a string, not explorers. With only half the equation, they could only
study the effects, not the cause. In fact, causality was a question any
one of Newman's team had yet to truly ask; they assumed conventional
wisdom. Evolutionary theory hardly accommodated the appearance of
"supernatural" consequence. Skeptical himself, Remming reserved
judgment if only because, absurd or not, at this point no better explanation existed. He had glimpsed the unexplainable. While he was just
another blind man groping at an elephant, he maintained two critical

advantages over Newman's research: he suspected he was blind (in more ways than one), and he knew there was more to the elephant than just one part. The part being touched at the moment was sero-toxomiasin. A big part. After all, STM-55 ran the show. But what ran it? And *how* did it run? Not at the receptor level. At the molecular level.

Forget STM-55. He could win a Nobel for what he knew *apart* from serotoxomiasin.

Precious little good it did him now. Whether clever or parsimo-nious (or both) to research in parallel, Jay Remming was little more than an assembly-line puppet himself at this point. He sat down, slipping off his shoes, socks, pants. As he laid aside his suit, an idea literally fell into his lap.

8 8 8

"Do what you do best," the stranger had told her, referencing her job as a reporter. What does a reporter do best? Report? The answer was obvious. An investigative reporter investigates. Tracks leads. *"You have the list,"* he said.

Missy reached for the declassified report, flipped the pages to the names of the children. The morning was bright. She had decided to work at home today.

Might as well start with a few phone calls.

Four and a half hours later she took a break, fixed a peanut butter and jelly sandwich for lunch, and collapsed on the sofa, bleary-eyed. She had started with number one on the list and worked her way through number sixteen. The report did not list phone numbers, only addresses vis-à-vis 1985, which meant Missy had spent most of her time thus far on the Internet tracking down current residences, which also meant she had waded through a lot of duplicates. She simply did not have enough information to be more precise. Names, that was all she had. Names, parents' names, and a point of origin: Maple Hill, North Carolina. In 1985, most of these children were still teenagers, living at home. Now they were adults, scattered here and there. Missy had to start from scratch with each one, call the family home, hope it was still the family home—which three out of four were not—and then track down whatever leads those leads created.

Her results were meager. Every single one of the living test subjects had dispersed, a fact Missy noted, since small towns usually retain at least a few of their children into adulthood. Not Maple Hill. Also, with all of the mothers deceased, the family connection was much harder to track. She had reached a few, three to be exact, but each and every one refused to talk.

Shoulders sagging, Missy downed the last of her sandwich with a swallow of skim milk, rose from the couch and picked up the phone to attempt number seventeen, Jessica O'Connel. She held pen and paper in hand.

"Hello?" a semi-frazzled voice answered, sounding surprised. In the background, Missy heard kids screaming.

"Hello, my name is Missy Jenkins. I'm—"

"How did you get through? Are we connected again?"

"Umm . . . I'm not sure I know what you're talking about."

"Well, what a surprise. I guess we're up and running again. About time. I'm sorry, who are you?"

"Missy Jenkins. I'm looking for a Jessica O'Connel. Does that name sound familiar to you?"

The voice laughed. "I think so. Oh, and sorry about all that. We've been having some unusual phone trouble lately. Eighteen houses on our street and we're the only one with no service for the last couple of days."

"Guess I'm the lucky winner. First one back on line."

"Lucky you. I'm Elizabeth, Jessica's older sister. But she's not here, of course. Hasn't been for years."

Missy sighed with relief. "That's OK! I'm calling from the *Detroit Sentinel*. We're doing a feature piece on—"

"Let me guess," Elizabeth interjected. "Young, successful lawyers?"

Missy didn't miss a beat. "Actually, yes!" she said. She had learned this racket. Reporters had to go with whatever they were given to get what they needed. "How did you know?"

"Jessica's been featured a couple of times already in similar stories. They did a story in *USA Today* a few years back on America's brightest collegiates. That sort of thing."

Elizabeth's manner was passé about the whole thing, but Missy could hear the pride in her voice. "Well, I wasn't given much to work with, if you know what I mean," she said. "My editor just threw this stuff at me and said, 'Do something with this.' So here I am. I knew your sister didn't live in Maple Hill anymore, but I was just trying to get a little background from the family. You know, color, for the article."

"Well, what would you like to know? This used to be our home when we were growing up. My husband and I bought the place from my mother. I've got a lot of memories of Jessica here."

"Well, let's start with the basics." Missy scrambled. *What basics?* "I'm showing that Jessica graduated *magna cum laude*, but I think that's a mistake."

"Of course it is. Jessica was *summa.* Always the best at everything. She was heavily recruited by dozens of high-profile law firms straight out of Cornell."

Missy tried to snake her way forward. "From your perspective, as her sister, did that make her choice hard or easy? The pressure, the attention, the push to be the best?"

"Neither," Elizabeth replied softly. "The issue was really very simple. All Jessica wanted to do was get away. I'm a small-town girl. She definitely is not. Her decision was as easy as picking the farthest-away firm she could find."

"And so she did," Missy agreed cluelessly. "But I guess it's not too bad. Could have been farther."

Silence. Hurt silence, Missy thought. She rolled her eyes. *Gambled and lost.*

"Portland is about as far as you can get from Maple Hill, Ms. Jenkins."

"Of course!" Missy said. "I was thinking of Hawaii, but that doesn't really count."

Portland. Portland! It was all Missy could do not to hang up right then. She quickly shifted gears. "Would it be all right if I called you again if I need more information?"

Elizabeth seemed puzzled. "That was an awfully short interview."

"Just the beginning," Missy said. "This is going to be a huge story."

Immediately, she called information for Portland, got Jessica's home phone number—two Jessica O'Connels were listed—and dialed. The first number was busy. The second rang twice, then changed tone, rang two more times. *Call forwarding.* A female voice answered.

"Kirkland, Stubing, and Minsk. This is Mandy."

Pretty good bet, Missy thought. She did not introduce herself. She simply asked for Jessica. Mandy informed her that Jessica was out of town on vacation. *In Maple Hill?* Missy asked. No, Hamden, in Connecticut, where her mother lived, who apparently was not well.

What about a phone number? Mandy declined at first, but Missy sweetly explained that she was an old friend from Cornell and that she lived just outside of Buffalo and would love to see Jessica if she could; said she had lost contact and had been trying to locate Jessica for several months. Mandy was hesitant but relented after a little more friendly haggling. She gave Missy the number to Jessica's mother's house.

A maid answered. "No, no. Ms. O'Connel has gone to New York with Mrs. O'Connel. Is something wrong? Who is this?"

"Nothing's wrong. I'm just an old friend. Will she be back soon?"

"Don't know. All she left was a note saying they were going to . . ." Missy heard a couple of drawers open and close. "The University of Columbia Hospital."

"Sounds serious. Is her mom OK?"

A pause. "I'm just the maid."

"Of course. Sorry. Listen, I really need to reach Jessica. Did she leave a hotel number or anything?"

"Nothing. This note. That's it."

Missy wiped her eyes, hung up the phone. She was rapidly wearying of the chase but didn't want to give up just yet. She strongly suspected Mrs. O'Connel may have been forced to visit Columbia because of the consequences of her Project Pacifist treatments. She took a deep breath and called information. After about a half-hour of holding, paging, call switching, and attempts at four different numbers for various departments within the CPMC system, she somehow landed at the surgical nursing station, where a tired nurse typed in a few things on the computer system, mumbled a few words, and transferred her to ICU nursing.

A nurse named Nellie answered.

☗ ☗ ☗

Seven A.M. rolled around much too quickly for Jay Remming. It was a wrenching paradox. He wanted more time—more time to think, to plan. Greater still, he wanted to vanish and never return. Instead, he sat now with Stewart Newman, Dr. Selma Volgaard, and a handful of other men and women he didn't recognize—high-ranking military officials, government reps with briefcases, two or three other scientists (maybe?)—in a small rectangular room, completely unadorned except for the polished oak executive table capable of seating twenty, which was full, save for the empty seat near Remming and an empty seat near Newman. Introductions had already been made all the way around. Though the majority of the group was from the United States, there were representatives from Japan, Russia, Germany, Great Britain, and Brazil. At Newman's right hand was a white telephone and a stack of papers. Around the table in front of every seat lay a hardbound ninety-three-page document marked "Classified" and stamped with the seal of the United Nations. No projector, no overhead, no dazzling multimedia display. This was bare bones, not intended to win anybody. Only to inform.

Necessary politics, Remming thought.

He listened as Newman articulated the meaning of the research compound in global terms; listened with hands folded to a peak under his nose, expressionless, silent.

"The World Health Organization," Newman began, "under the auspices of the Regional Office for the Americas and the Pan American Health Organization, and with primary financial backing from the United States government, has been investigating for nearly a decade the specific goal of advancing the human species genetically to better prepare for the volatility of the new millennium. Limited participation and investment is also forthcoming from G7 nations and the developing European Community, though their involvement has been nominal at this stage. Now I don't need to tell you, ladies and gentlemen, that this discussion is highly classified and has been authorized by the Secretary General of the United Nations himself. No breach of confidence will be tolerated. . . ."

Thus, in a relatively abbreviated speech, the rubber finally met the road. Motive and mission. Jay Remming regarded Newman coolly, but hung on every word. He knew he could not afford another confrontation, especially not now. Yet as Newman droned on, his reserve was pressed to the limit. Newman briefed the group on the progress of the discovery of the pineal gland anomaly and its concurrently sophisticated receptor network for serotoxomiasin. In short order he hailed the discovery as the lynchpin for the mounting demands of "global human resource management." Newman coined the phrase to describe the diminishing capacity of regional governments to sufficiently supply the needs of the general population required for a civil society. Previous generations relied on the various tools of social engineering, legal enforcement, political loyalties, institutionalized religion, and other dogmas and programs.

Those tools were no longer adequate, Newman said.

"The facts are incontrovertible. We have numerous studies from a variety of disciplines highlighting megatrends of enormous import for the prominent countries of the world," Newman said. "Not only are historically valid paradigms collapsing, but more and more weight is being placed on their weakening shoulders. In the field of health and medicine, rapid industrialization is leading to new diseases and new illnesses as more and more humans are exposed to untested elements, both artificial and organic. The ozone hole continues to grow. In fact, WHO's Division of Emerging and Communicable Diseases Surveillance and Control Group is predicting a fourfold increase in malignant melanomas alone during the next two decades. TB and other drug-resistant strains of superviruses have been popping up in heavily populated areas at an alarming rate. And substance abuse continues to drain the major economies of the world, in spite of massive and costly educational campaigns." He turned to one of the men in suits. "Charlie?"

Charlie spoke in a gruff, no-frills manner. "You'll see the paperwork in the report. But tightly monitored geological think tanks have predicted with relative certainty at least two major earthquakes in the next fifty years, one in the Pacific Rim and one in the United States, both likely to measure in excess of 8.5 on the Richter scale. I'm not at liberty to divulge the locales, but if our calculations are even close to the mark, I can assure you the tectonic damage will pale in comparison to the economic aftershocks. We feel eighty percent sure we've got another twenty years, minimum, but there is a twenty to thirty percent chance it could happen in the next decade."

A woman sitting beside Charlie spoke. "As everyone knows, both regions contain key financial markets. And earthquakes are only part of the problem. Global weather patterns have grown increasingly erratic. Last year, El Niño amassed damages in the billions of dollars worldwide. Hurricane Mitch killed thousands in Central America. Ignore the people if you want, but industrialized nations have investments to protect. Insurance companies are straining to remain solvent. Japan's major banking centers are saddled with billions in bad debt. The Asian economic crisis is only a small token of this volatility. In the United States, major programs like Social Security are already trying to pick between the least damaging of a dozen different bankruptcy scenarios. Think the global recession is serious? Insiders are quietly telling us that the recent 'crash' was hardly corrective and hardly a crash. The markets remain artificially propped for the sake of investor confidence. We assembled a team of government economists from the G7 nations. Their classified report described Tokyo and New York as 'hairpin triggers.' Depending on the severity, London and Toronto would quickly follow. And I haven't even mentioned Y2K yet. We simply have no way of calculating its repercussions, though we expect the panic pre-2000 might surpass the actual damage of systems failure. But I've read hundreds of reports and I can guarantee you, the entire world is way behind the curve. When this hits, we're all going to feel it."

The room fell silent.

"Pre-2000 panic?" Newman wondered aloud. "Does any nation represented here have a solution? Even close to one?"

No response. The question was rhetorical.

"Are your leaders concerned? You bet they are. Or you wouldn't be here. And not just pre-2000, but post-2000." Newman motioned to a dark-haired bulldog of a man. "Major General Sutton."

The general nodded curtly. "As many of you know, intelligence indicates that both Iraq and Libya are manufacturing biological weapons capable of mass destruction. These weapons can be deployed low-tech and involve odorless, colorless substances, a teaspoon of which could easily kill over a million people. This is fact. Also, the Russian mafia has emerged as a major regional influence. Our intelligence has confirmed that the mafia control as much as half of the dismantled nuclear stockpile of the collapsed Soviet Union. International terrorism and regional peacekeeping missions are *de facto* operations precisely because any one of them could conflagrate. India and Pakistan have the bomb. We have good intelligence that at least a dozen other developing nations are less than five years away from also going nuclear. China, an ally of no one, has an army that is pushing 100 million."

Newman picked up the baton. "Transmittable diseases are on the rise across the board. A Sudanese prince is as likely to contract AIDS as a Nebraska farmer or a French chef. And all of this is just an overview. There are a dozen other war zones we could discuss: political, economic, racial, social, religious, on and on. Yet the one I find most fascinating, most compelling and the most dangerous is this—" He held up a copy of *Time* magazine; the cover showed a massive bank of dark clouds looming on the horizon and read "Millennial Fear: The Facts, Fright & Fatalism." He held up similar covers from other magazines, *Psychology Today, Newsweek, Forbes, Money.* "With the onset of the new millennium, powerful psychological factors are bearing hard on the collective rational and emotional centers of entire nations, particularly Western nations. The effects of this are, quite literally, incalculable. Panic is not too big a word. Not at all. Global panic, mind you."

He took a deep breath and exhaled slowly, glancing from face to face. "Of course this is nothing new—nothing more, really, than a highly speculative, subjective, and superficial overview of our present state of affairs. We've skimmed the surface, with little time for the hard evidence each of you has been so careful to gather. Summaries of all this data are in your briefings. Yet make no mistake: The major governments of the world are paying *close* attention to these trends. You only have to ask your local mayor if his city has a grip on things to realize the need for broad and decisive assistance in human-resource management."

A woman sitting across from Remming said, "These are the realities of modern life, Mr. Newman. From what I can gather, the impact of these 'megatrends' is extremely hard to quantify in meaningful ways. Besides, we've heard alarmist rhetoric before."

"I can only answer from my own perspective. As you say, the effects of these realities are difficult to quantify. Frankly, I'm not worried in the slightest. I think the greatest years in the history of man lie just ahead. So this may or may not satisfy you. But Madam Secretary, what I am trying to say is this . . ." Newman spoke with a flourish. He took a sip of coffee, glanced at Remming. "Humanity is in the birth pangs of the next evolutionary cycle. We could argue the merits of this both pro and con. But according to the dictates of the Secretary of the United Nations, the reality of life on Planet Earth at this stage in her history is best defined by three compelling needs: manageability, adaptability, and compatibility."

Power, Remming translated. He heard Hank's voice echo in his mind. *Control.*

Newman continued. "STM-55 is one small but significant part of a compelling hope, a tool that, once perfected, fully mapped, and made safe, has the potential to contribute significantly to the stated goals of manageability, adaptability, and compatibility."

And so it went. Newman detailed three primary stages of the research: *Determination,* which meant to fully understand the implications of the SPoT and STM-55—the nature of, and genetic reason for, an evolutionary, yet highly selective physical reality; next, *development,* which meant isolating and analyzing those genetic components, tracing the length and breadth of the functional neural network it imposed upon the brain and mapping that network to a grid of specific biological and behavioral responses. The first two stages were nearly complete, Newman told the group.

Strike three, Remming thought fiercely. *Overconfidence. Pride kills.*

Finally, Newman spoke of *implementation,* wherein the results of all development could be translated in meaningful ways to a "composite health program designed to propel the human race forward," meaning genetically, across the board—socially, physically, behaviorally—thereby increasing the chances for survival and diminishing the strain of "global growing pains" predicted by the men and women who had the power to predict such things.

Impressive, vague, philosophical medical rambling.

When Newman reached for a glass of water, Remming asked, "So is the neural network of STM-55 a good thing or a bad thing?"

"Ah, you strike at the heart of a matter, don't you, Dr. Remming?" Newman replied with an evasive smile. "It is too early to tell yet. We simply don't know. My hunch is that it is favorable, though there are some extremely negative qualities affected people seem to carry in common."

"Such as?"

Newman squinted his eyes, wrangling for words. "I should speak with sensitivity. Affected persons—"

"Christians," Remming countered. "That's who you're talking about."

"*Affected persons* have many qualities desirable for the larger population. A generally law-abiding record, a general commitment to the family unit, and, according to some of our latest research, marginally longer life spans."

"But?"

"But they also possess certain bigotries the larger body of humanity finds offensive. Not to mention divided loyalty. They are law-abiding when they agree with the law, but have historically proven to be among the most willing to disagree with laws that run contrary to their belief system."

"And that's bad?"

"In philosophical terms, no, of course not. A democracy in particular thrives on such interaction. But in practical terms, as we look to the immediate future, yes, it is bad. Perhaps *limiting* is a better word. Now, now, don't get me wrong. When laws are bad we should want them changed. But all our best information indicates that the next twenty to thirty years could be some of the most difficult yet for modern societies. Pragmatically speaking, some laws may need to be adverse or inhibitory for the sake of the larger good."

"Inhibitory?"

"I'm not a legislator, but I liken it to grounding a child: It doesn't last forever and it's not really punishment. It just helps pass time through a crisis, forces a little bit of maturity, and hopefully helps avoid subsequent events. The kinds of things the world's governments are predicting may never happen. We may evolve naturally to a more reasonable state of affairs, science may cure AIDS, and the earthquakes might delay a century or two. But if not, if the opposite is the case—and we hope it is not—but *if* it is, you sure don't want a vocal sector of the population loudly opposing the reasonable cause of law and order."

Remming frowned. Newman continued in an offhand fashion. "As to the bigotry, it is well known that affected persons have a much narrower moral tolerance. And breadth."

"What does that mean?" Remming asked.

"I think you know. It wouldn't take long to rattle off a list of 'behaviors' or personality traits considered acceptable to tolerant societies that remain sermon fodder on Sunday morning. Religious morality does not allow science or reason to intrude. Statistically significant differences have been confirmed in numerous internal studies."

"You mean they aren't like us?" another man asked.

Newman answered with a question. "More wars have been fought in the name of religion than all other wars combined. Why is that?"

"Because they aren't like us. That's what you're saying."

Newman shrugged. "I think we are all able to recognize the differences. At least in the extreme cases."

"My mother is a Christian," one woman said tersely. "What are you saying will happen to her?"

Her question broke the dialogue wide open. Yet politely so. Another voice joined in and then another and soon the whole room was abuzz, probing, questioning, debating. Newman tried to answer the flurry while Remming watched, growing ever more troubled. The debate was much too subdued. No one was outraged. He seemed to be the only one—he and one or two dissenters; yet even their concerns were largely cosmetic, including, surprisingly, the woman with the Christian mother. Newman had done a masterful job of alluding to the trouble and alluding to the solution, but defining neither. When had there not been earthquakes and disease?

The rest of the ensuing debate dealt largely in details and cautionary words on process and public relations stuff. Remming wondered how much these people actually understood the research and its implications. Policy makers rarely enjoy details.

Finally, Newman said in a loud voice, "Ladies and gentlemen, please! Please! It goes without saying, but let me state emphatically, we don't want to hurt these people. Or any people, for that matter. We want to help them and allow them to help us. We are simply waging a very necessary battle against our species' self-destructive tendencies, and you have been invited to help move humanity forward in the process. The pineal gland anomaly is the most precise evolutionary insight yet into what we are capable of, both good and bad, profitable and unprofitable. But our research proceeds either way . . . either to encourage serotoxomiasin production in nonaffected persons or inhibit its production in affected persons."

There was a knock on the door to the conference room. Timidly, a young private poked his head in. He apologized, motioned to Newman, held up a phone. "Mr. Newman, you have a call, sir. She says it is urgent."

"Take a message," Newman said, dismissing the man with a wave of his hand.

"She won't tell me her name, sir. She insists on speaking with you."

Every face turned to Newman, who politely excused himself, took the phone in the empty hallway adjoining the conference room.

"Yes, what is it?" he said irritably.

Susan Decker was on the other end. "Stewart, I have good news and bad."

"Make it quick."

"I'll make it however I need to make it," Decker said slowly. "And when I'm done, you'll thank me."

A long stretch of silence followed, just for emphasis. Finally, Newman said, "Go!"

"The good news is that I have recovered all the stolen files from Remming's assistant. It's a done deal. He suspects nothing."

"Excellent," Newman whispered. Indeed, he was pleased. "The bad?"

Decker lowered her voice. "Dr. Saludin has been snooping around. A couple of high-level sources have informed me that he has been demanding answers to some very negative questions. It doesn't sound good. I think he's fallout material."

Newman took a deep breath. "I suspected as much."

"I figured you would know how to deal with it."

"Of course I do. Which reminds me, Decker—"

"Yes?"

"Don't call me here again."

Newman killed the connection with a flick of his finger. He entered the conference room again. The discussion had already resumed in his brief absence. He took his place at the front, began sorting through his papers. Just as he was about to speak, the door opened again and in strode Abu Hasim El-Saludin, grim faced, escorted by a short, thick, swarthy man with a cement-block head and sunglasses, wearing a dark suit and carrying a briefcase.

Newman said, "Dr. Saludin, welcome! We've been expecting you."

Abu glanced around the room casually, nodding in turn as his eyes met others'. He took the empty seat by Remming, shook his hand, smiling with pleasure.

"Good to see you, again, Dr. Remming," Saludin whispered, nodding also to Volgaard across the table. Though Remming had only spoken face-to-face with the Egyptian on a handful of occasions, he saw something in Abu's eyes, a combativeness, which frightened him. He knew why Abu had come.

"Keep a level head, Abu," he whispered solemnly in the man's ear. "This is very, very serious. More serious than either of us knew."

The man who had entered beside Saludin moved with a cocksure swagger, like a stump on legs, to stand near Newman. The two exchanged murmured words, then the short man sat down. Remming caught the man out of the corner of his eye, watching him with something between amusement and malice. The steadiness of the man's gaze, the secretive grin, made Remming's skin crawl. He was an ugly man.

At the same time, Abu turned from Remming, from the warning, to face Newman.

He said aloud, "I know I am late and have missed introductions. I don't really know anyone here. I don't even know you," he motioned to Newman, "though I am told your name is Stewart Newman. But as a member of the primary research team I have grave and growing concerns about the purpose of this research and about the death of Dr. Rosenburg. We are dabbling in unlawful, unethical medicine. I accuse no one. But my heart tells me something is very wrong. So I have come. But not because anyone invited me. I have come for answers."

Instantly, the room grew still, as though all the air had been sucked out. Newman rocked back and forth on his heels. He glanced at his watch.

"Ladies and gentlemen, I think a short recess is in order to collect our thoughts and get a breath of fresh air. Let's plan on reconvening at, say, fourteen hundred hours? We can pursue some actual strategy sessions at that time. I need to have a quick bull session with my esteemed medical team"—he motioned to Volgaard, Remming, Saludin—"and dialogue through some issues. We'll convene back here at fourteen hundred and then get you on your flights back home as scheduled. That's a promise. Thank you."

Nobody moved.

"Thank you," Newman repeated more firmly.

Slowly, a little confused, everyone rose and filed out, except for the three scientists, Newman, and the man beside him. For some reason, Remming's pulse raced. As people jostled past, he reached over, underneath the table, and touched Saludin's leg.

"Don't do this," he whispered. "You have no idea."

Abu met his gaze with unflinching peace, so plain and simple Remming almost recoiled. "If I don't do this, will you?" he asked.

The door closed; the last person drifted away. The sound of their footsteps faded. Newman paced back and forth at the front of the room. Volgaard opened her mouth to speak, thought better of it, looked away.

"Speak plainly," Newman said. "I'm the man who authorized funding for your work. I probably have the answers you need. And believe me, consensus is critical for any team effort. So let's hash out the details. I'm not above inspection."

"That is part of the problem," Abu said, speaking softly. His accent was beautiful. There was nothing threatening about his stance or tone. "Everywhere I turn I seem to be confined to things I already know. All other information is very hush-hush. This makes me nervous, especially for this research. *Especially* for this. I know Dr. Rosenburg had concerns also. And so I wonder, why is he dead? Why? I am not good with these things, but I ask questions and those questions lead to more questions. And in the end, all I can ask is, If there is no secret, then why all the secrecy? I am a lover of truth. Truth never hides. I wish to have nothing to do with hidden agendas."

He turned, looked from face to face, to Remming for support. Remming's expression was one hundred percent blank, registering neither a hint of surprise nor doubt, though in truth he was mortally terrified. The air was electric. Quietly, innocently, Abu Hasim El-Saludin declared the emperor naked of virtue and principle. Volgaard refused to look at either man, or Newman. Newman touched the shoulder of the man beside him. The ugly man calmly reached into his jacket, pulled out a pistol, aimed it at Abu—

"Yes, I will," Abu declared, though no one had asked a question.

—and fired. Point-blank range, as easily as if he were eating a candy bar. Abu didn't flinch or hide. The gun had a silencer, made no noise, just a quick, muffled release. Abu's chest exploded. Blood splattered on the walls, on Remming's jacket and face and hands. The force knocked his body backward. He was dead before he hit the ground.

In a single, hushed moment, all the life Remming had ever possessed drained out of his body through his feet. He sat stunned, could not move. He wanted to howl. He wanted to vomit. He wanted to kill or die or run. But he could not move, could not even think. With the squeeze of a trigger the entire composition of his being had been ripped out of his body, dunked in winter cold and left for dead. He stared at the spot, the blank, empty space, where Abu had sat. Warm red blood trickled down his check, stuck in his eyebrow. He began dabbing absently at it with his handkerchief. Volgaard covered her face with her hands.

"Pity that," Newman said. "He was a brilliant man."

The man beside him shrugged, mumbled something in a voice that was meaty and short on breath, but hypnotic, resonant with dread like low C on a piano. Even in his stupor, Remming knew he had heard that voice only one other time.

"I suppose consensus has been reached," the man said.

Remming moved his lips. "Monitor Nine."

Monitor Nine nodded respectfully, put the gun away. "When is lunch?"

23

W e aren't eating," Newman replied somberly. "None of us will eat today, in honor of Dr. Saludin."

Jay Remming had no strength to eat anyway, couldn't have kept food down if he tried. Warmth and color drained from his face, leaving his smooth dark skin cold. Volgaard stared straight ahead, hard as a rock, refusing to glance his direction, or at the fleshy, lifeless body of Abu Hasim El-Saludin sprawled at his feet. Abu's eyes were open, vacant; his neck bent unnaturally sideways. A sheen of globulous bright red puddled underneath him on the cement floor from the torn flesh of his chest.

Newman clicked his tongue, shook his head. The sadness in his voice was real. "This is not what I wanted. Not at all. A loss for all of us."

"Most of all, him," Volgaard murmured. "And his family."

"They will be well provided for, I promise you. I will see to it personally."

With those words, the simple square room closed in on itself. Windowlesss, with no light from outside, the heaviness inside began to eat the fluorescence, turning the light gray and sickly. Remming breathed deeply the soft air laced with memory and death. Subconsciously, he pushed himself straighter in his chair, resting both arms symmetrically at his sides. With both hands, he nudged the briefing on the table before him so that it ran at a perfect ninety-degree angle to the edge of the table. He needed order.

"Now, Dr. Remming," Newman began, but his voice slurred in Remming's mind as if made from molasses, dripping down from a great, incomprehensible distance. "I'm willing to put our little disputes behind us and move on. Agreed?"

Remming nodded dumbly.

"Good. Your instructions then are as follows: Since your current work environment has been compromised by your assistant, I want you to return to New York, gather all your data and transfer it here, to Guatemala, shifting your base of operation to this facility. First task: coding. We are severely hampered by our limited grasp of the neurotransmitter's DNA. From your reports I gather you are not much closer to an exact sequencing than we are?"

Remming shook his head, lied. "You just killed the only man that might have been close."

"Well then, you will have to do better. A probe will be your chief priority. You will be better equipped here and can assume your rightful place as chief of operations. More to the point, under your direct leadership, I think we will begin to see rapid acceleration in all aspects of the work. And as I'm sure you would agree, our team has made some impressive discoveries of their own."

"I would prefer to remove myself completely. I will give you everything I have."

"That's not acceptab—"

"Please!"

"No, absolutely not!" Newman exclaimed, as if he were addressing a dim-witted child. "You see, Dr. Remming, while we could likely succeed without you eventually, we cannot do so in the required time frame."

Remming shook his head. "What time frame? I don't know what you mean."

By the look on his face, Newman must have thought all Nobel prize winners were idiots.

"Implementation!" he whispered hoarsely, pounding his fist on the table. "Stage Three."

"And what does that look like? What? I deserve to know."

Newman didn't move. Remming held up his hands, like an angry beggar, eyes bulging. A dead man lay at his feet. He had a right to more than generalities.

"The more you know, the more you increase your liability," Newman offered. "Is that what you want?"

"I want the truth!" Remming shouted. Monitor Nine started to rise, bulldog faced. Newman touched his arm; he sat. Volgaard said nothing.

Newman seemed to weigh the risks, finally held up two fingers. "One, we're going to exploit the positive factors—the emotional stability and general health. And two, we're going to neutralize the negative, the religious psychosis and dogmatism."

"I want specifics. What are we talking about? What does 'exploit the positive' mean? Criminal rehabilitation efforts? Like what I've seen here?"

Newman nodded noncommittally.

"And the negative? What's that? Mandatory infant vaccines for all newborn children? Attempt to destroy the receptors for STM-55 in certain select regions before anything can get started?"

Newman shrugged. "Possibly. On a certain level, SPoT is no different than polio. People need to become educated to protect themselves and their family."

Remming felt numb. "How about quarantining Christians? Maybe for the sake of 'public health'?"

"We've converted two dozen closed military bases in the States alone for such a contingency."

"For deprogramming? Surgical removal?"

"We call it Reverse Conversion. Hopefully that won't be necessary."

Necessary or not, memories triggered, blurred by distress: the sign in the surgical unit (what did it say?)—*RC Observation;* vaguely, he also remembered the psychiatrist's curious statement: *"We need better recon. The lucky ones die."*

"Recon," he said. At the time, he had skimmed past it. "Reverse Conversion." Then he understood something more. "You weren't concerned about the implant, were you? It's the removal you want to perfect."

"Both actually. Look at it this way: The role of government is to be prepared for any crisis scenario. If order is collapsing, divisive influences must be contained. Call it damage control, or a national security risk, or whatever you want, but Christians increasingly fit a threatening extremist profile. Our government and many others feel like SPoT may be a key to social stability. I hope you see, Dr. Remming, that we feel a tremendous sense of urgency."

"I see," Remming murmured, eyes glassy. He moved his lips, forming two improbable words, asking a stunned, silent question: "Reverse . . . Conversion?" But Newman could not hear him.

"I'm proud of my team," Newman continued. "They are among the most proficient and technically brilliant in the world. I made sure of it. But *visionary* brilliance, that's another story entirely. Selma will tell you the same."

"It's true, Dr. Remming. Your presence is critical."

Remming wiped his eyes, feeling the cage close shut. "What about my position at the university?"

"A sabbatical has been arranged. Everything has been arranged. The Merideth Institute has been dissolved, the paper trail has been erased, the financial transactions legally buried. At this point, all you've got to do is write the words. We'll carry the tune."

All Remming could do was sit, stare, and blink. Never in his life had he felt so vulnerable, nor so powerless. Newman made him an offer that, literally, he could not refuse. They owned him. No terms to negotiate and he knew it. Sure, the paper trail to the money may have been erased, but not to him. Not a chance.

"When do I leave?"

"Right now. My assistant will escort you to base and then to your flight. You have forty-eight hours to return."

Remming rose to his feet. His legs were shaky, his suit permanently stained. He glanced a final time at Abu's body, then moved to the door, careful not to step in the blood.

"I will want to change clothes."

"Of course."

Monitor Nine rose to follow. Newman pulled the stocky man aside, told him in a low voice, "Do whatever is necessary. Loyalty or silence. Understand?"

Monitor Nine nodded.

⊟ ⊟ ⊟

Hank moaned, his fingers balled up in a fist in his hair. He and Jessica stood by the pay phones in the hotel lobby. "I've got to go to the apartment. My last copy of the disk is there. It's my only hope."

"Hank, it's too risky."

"It's *my* apartment. The deal was they'd leave me alone. I'll be fine."

Anything but fine, he sprinted out the hotel doors, hailed a cab and headed off, seething at the betrayal, the outwitting, the unraveling of his life.

And for what?

When he opened the door to his apartment, he knew the answer. A ruined apartment, that's what. All around, sofa cushions were slashed open, chairs overturned, wall hangings thrown down. Clothes and trash and all manner of stuff—*his* stuff—were strewn everywhere. The scene was immediately reminiscent of Kim's place, only more violent.

Whoever did this wasn't only looking for something. They were making a statement.

Hank ground his molars so tight his jaw throbbed. He would have shouted except for the unwanted attention it would have drawn. *Who? Who would do this?*

We had a deal! he roared silently, followed by the aftershock of realization: Whoever did this wasn't just making a statement, either. They *were* looking for something. He nearly sprinted back to his room, dodging piles and junk, heart sagging.

Please . . .

His bedroom was equally trashed. Every drawer was open. Clothes were scattered like old rags. Clothes . . . and coins. The coin tin was overturned, thrown into the corner by his bed. He picked it up.

Empty, except for a note in 12 point Courier:

"You shouldn't have given the files to the FBI. Wrong move. The only safe way to play the game is to quit the game. NO MORE WARNINGS. Merideth Institute."

Chilled, Hank wanted to shout. But he had no voice.

⊟ ⊟ ⊟

Jessica leaned back in her chair, studying the note. One hand was propped behind her head. Her hair was tied in a ponytail and she had traded her pants and blouse for a pair of old jeans and a sweatshirt. She twitched nervously, working into quite a lather herself, but only incidentally by Hank's tale. Most of her anger was directed toward herself. Still, the note was perplexing.

"The Merideth Institute? I don't get it."

"They wanted their stuff back, I guess."

Jessica wrinkled her nose. "That just doesn't make sense. It's too obvious. What would they have to gain?" She puzzled over the message quietly. "You know what I think? I think it was Decker. And I think she dropped the ball big time."

Hank was all ears. "Go on."

"Well, think about it. It would be a colossal blunder for the Merideth Institute to try to intimidate you at this point and risk further exposure. They could have done that a long time ago. Meanwhile, Agent Decker's pulled off a massive coup by duping us into giving her the files. But she's got to be paranoid. She has no reason to trust you and probably wonders what else you may have up your sleeve."

"She did act paranoid when we met," Hank remembered. "Asked about other copies and then really pressed me. A simple 'no' wasn't good enough."

"See there? She wanted to cover her tracks. So she searched your apartment and left a fake Merideth Institute note for misdirection. It's her cover story. Which might have worked except—"

"We know who she is," Hank said, comprehension dawning. "But she doesn't know we know."

"Exactly. That's where she blew it."

The revelation was complete and satisfying. Both shook their heads, feeling proud at first, then sobered. Decker, the CIA—whoever—was frighteningly committed to securing all loose SPoT data. Figuring out their scheme was small satisfaction. Hank's apartment was still trashed. And they had voluntarily turned everything over to the enemy.

Jessica wiped her eyes. "So, no other backups, you say?"

"None. I thought I had the bases covered. First with Kim, then my place."

"So what you told Remming by the bridge, about three separate copies in three separate places—"

"They've stolen two and we gave them the third. I didn't think it would go this far."

Jessica swallowed hard, took a different tack. Her familiar black cloud began raining down grief and accusation. On her. She wrung her hands, scrambling for dry ground. "We know her name, the agent, right?"

"Remming called her Susan. Must be Susan Decker. They're one and the same."

It was a dead end. Jessica shook her head, frustrated. "Probably doesn't matter. I was wondering about legal recourse, but you haven't got much to go on."

"I've got nothing. This is the CIA, for crying out loud. And the FBI helped them. It's a done deal."

His voice trailed away. Length upon length came the still sound of nothing. Hank heard the stillness first. Jessica heard the pain. Gradually, other sounds surfaced, extracted one at a time from the anterior calm surrounding the lobby. First, the gentle chatter between guests and clerks at the front counter, then the ringing of a cellular phone from the purse of a lady near the elevator; next the occasional, faint crystalline clink of wine glasses from the bar. A man on a sofa nearby bent over a note pad, deep in thought. He held a ballpoint pen in his hand, flicking the top with his thumb.

Chick-click. Click-chick.

Hank, too, bent over, staring at his marbled reflection on the floor of the Columbian, his thoughts black and tangled, like weeds and bracken collecting around the edge of a stagnant pond. He labored for epiphany. Loose, delicate, his ideas fluttered away, rising from the surface of the floating water like wee mosquitoes, never escaping, touching down again, only to be nibbled into obscurity by the raking fish. All about, the restrained ambience beckoned to his sense of clarity, then laughing, chased it away.

"I have absolutely no ideas," he said at length, defeated.

The finality in his voice triggered despair in Jessica. In the span of time it took for Hank to produce that singular thought, Jessica had died a thousand self-executions. She dropped her eyes. "This is all my fault."

Hank tried to be chivalrous, even though he partially agreed. "Don't do that, Jess."

To which Jessica could only think: *Don't do what?* Break a pattern twenty-nine years in the making? The old ways came all too easy. "Everything's ruined," she said matter-of-factly. "You didn't want to do it this way. But then Jessica comes along. Get out of her way! She's got to get involved." Wordless, she added, *hurting others, never yourself.* The scrape of her own thoughts against her soul felt just. She needed to hurt. To be hurt. *What have you lost, Jessica O'Connel? Nothing. What has Hank lost? Maybe everything. You don't deserve his forgiveness.*

"I'm so sorry," she said softly. What good was that? "So sorry."

Hank reached over, touched her hand. "I made the choice, Jess. *I* did. Even if I did it for you, the choice was still mine."

"But maybe you wouldn't have—"

Hank gently interrupted. "Let me tell you something. You need to know that what you said the other day changed my life. That line about truth being worth it. It was wonderful. Luminescent. Do you know why?"

Jessica shook her head.

"Because I could tell it wasn't just a line, it was *you*. It was conviction. It reminded me of everything I love."

Eyes rimmed and turning red, Jessica looked away. Hank pressed on. "I could try to make myself feel better by claiming that some superficial love of truth is what got me into this mess to begin with. But up until you, I would have been playing the martyr with the facts. Then you came along and reminded me that a mess like this is *worth* getting into, regardless of the consequences. You have nothing to apologize for. It was beautiful." He reached up, touched her face, pulled her chin to look at him. "I think *you're* beautiful. Thank you. No apologies."

And now it was Jessica's turn to stare, to have her own house of cards bombarded—not with truth but mercy. The shrapnel of unexpected grace punctured her lungs, took her breath away; she recoiled. The effect was magnetic. She could not look away. Something in

Hank's eyes shone. Something she had never known, always wanted. The lure of his words was a hook and she was a starving fish. When she took the bait, his words enveloped her, washed her, bent down, like a medic over a wounded soldier, bandaging the wounds.

Too much.

She stood, fled. To the elevator. To her room. And wept.

When she returned to the lobby an hour later, Hank was still there. Jessica smiled, feeling light, embarrassed. She did not want to talk about it.

"Later," she said. "Not now."

So they sat together, simply sharing time. And that was fine. After a while the conversation turned to simpler fare. Or at least Jessica tried to make it so. Hank had returned to racking his brain for ideas, answers. She pitched him an invitation.

"The key is to stop trying so hard! Do what I do. Get distracted. Ideas come easier that way."

Did he hear the invitation in her words? Not a bid for sex (miracle of miracles!). Rather, the invitation to knowingly take another step together.

Nope. Hank missed her completely, furrowing his brow, trying harder not to try.

"That's not distraction; that's an aneurysm!" Jessica laughed. "Think about something else. Something different. Here, look up. Look at me."

Staring at Hank—distraught, hair tousled—loosed a murmuring current within her. Maybe it was his eyes. Like her father's. Jessica wanted to protect him, be with him. He was a good, decent man.

Imagine that.

Her unwavering smile held him. Dressed as she was, as if ready to paint a wall with a big roller brush or set to work in a garden, Hank found himself wandering the wide fields of imagined pleasures, beginning with . . . a kiss . . .

Not realizing he did so, Hank leaned closer, maybe only an inch or two. The signal sent sparks up Jessica's spine. Unaware of her own shifting body position, she reflexively drew nearer. The hotel lobby, the world outside—every molecule grew still, anxious.

. . . One kiss. Almost. Hank lifted his hand, touched her face. Her skin felt like rose petals. His brain, his skin, his fingers, everything began to tingle. Jessica closed her eyes. She was beautiful. A beautiful red flame.

When an idea hit him like a sack of rocks.

"Kim. Kim's *computer.*"

He pulled away. Their lips never touched.

"Kim," he told her, as if that should make sense. At the moment nothing made sense to Jessica.

Hank jumped to his feet. "I'm sorry. I'll be back. Wait here."

He scurried out the door.

He opted for a taxi to Kim's. Standing in the street below, Hank felt dread staring up at the dark windows, knowing Kim's apartment lay in ruins.

The door pushed open with ease. Shivering, he took a wary step inside. As soon as he closed the door the flat of a hand connected powerfully with his jaw, throwing him to the floor as easy as a rag doll. A body pounced his own. A heavy body. Hank strained underneath the weight, groaning.

"I'm . . . unarmed," he managed to grunt.

Immediately, the heavy body rose, cursing. Hank recognized his attacker's voice.

"Kim!" he nearly shouted, struggling to his feet. He was dizzy; his jaw ached. "Kim! I didn't know! I thought . . . Why didn't you ever call?"

Kim didn't speak, but turned, stumped to the back room, growling low under his breath. All the window shades and blinds were pulled, leaving the cold room sunless. Three or four candles were lit here and there, in the kitchen, the living room, their luminescent wicks melting and melding shadows from the otherwise dark apartment. As Hank's eyes adjusted, he noticed something strange: floor space. Boxes and boxes were stuffed with all the junk Kim had never bothered to bother with. On the wall, the only poster that remained was Charlie Parker, leaning back with sax pressed to his lips in a flamboyant pose. Underneath, the word "Yardbird" was scrawled in purple. Every other wall was bare.

Quickly, Hank's eyes darted to the corner . . . the important corner.

Kim's computers were gone. Boxed, presumably. Or worse. He rubbed his jaw tenderly.

"Kim!" he called out.

"Shut up!" Kim snapped as he reentered from the rear bedroom carrying things haphazardly in his arms, stuffing them carelessly in whichever box had space. "Shut up and leave."

"I can't. I won't."

"Suit yourself. Just shut up."

"Kim, what's wrong? I need to know what happened to you."

Fast for a big man, Kim twisted his body, leaned forward over a candle, pointing to his face. "This!" he hissed. "This happened to me." Kim's face was laced with minor abrasions. Even in the dim light Hank could see the purple bruises and swelling.

"Kim, I'm so sorry. I had no idea."

"Leave," Kim snarled. "I don't want you here."

"Where then? Where can we meet?"

"Nowhere."

"I need the computer files, Kim. I know the disks are gone, but I thought you might still have the files on your hard drive. It's important."

Gurgling with rage, Kim lunged, wrapping Hank in a huge bear hug that nearly knocked him off his feet again. Hank struggled, but Kim was heavier by at least sixty pounds and had the better position, with Hank's left arm bent painfully behind him. He shoved him toward the door, gingerly reached around, turned the knob, opened, and then shoved Hank out.

"Erased," he whispered, sweat dripping from his battered face. "All erased! Everything. Not just your stuff. Mine too. Now leave me alone. Don't ever come here again. I'll be gone."

"But Kim—"

The door slammed shut.

Hank pounded on the metal frame with his fist, drawing a quick response. Angrily, Kim jerked the door open, his eyes darting back and forth like a frightened bird. Hank had never seen him so nervous or agitated.

"I *need* those files."

"Weren't you listening? They're gone!"

"I don't want us to end like this, Kim. I never wanted this."

Kim clenched his teeth. "They told me they would kill me if they ever caught me speaking to you again. Got that? They told me never to even get close. Is that what you want?"

"No. Of course not."

"Then leave."

"No."

"Hank, leave! My wraithing days are over. They made sure of that, too."

He slammed the door again. Hank left.

§ § §

Jessica fell asleep in her room waiting for Hank. After about an hour or so the phone rang, jerking her to a sitting position. Half conscious, she reached for the receiver. The touch of the cool plastic seemed like a warning. Maybe not such a good idea . . .

Decker? Surely not. But maybe. Things were so convoluted at this point, it was hard to tell. Sluggish as her thoughts were, the possibility made more sense than it should have. Why risk it?

The phone rang again, its third time. Jessica counted the rings. Eight total.

Then silence.

The lurking unknown nearly drove her crazy. What if it was someone from the hospital with information about her mother? Something for Hank? Some danger? What if, if, if? Yet with all these thoughts, her eyes grew heavy once more. Numbingly, sleep overtook her.

In that brief, twilight shard of time, she had a dream. A dream of hands around her neck, throttling the life out of her. An all-too-real dream.

Five minutes later, the phone rang again.

24

When Hank returned about an hour and a half later, Jessica blinked, trying to smile, but her voice trembled. "Someone called. I didn't know what to do. It just rang and rang."

She sat on the bed with her knees pulled to her chest, like the petals of a flower folding at sunset. Even though Hank had his own problems, he forgot them, moving quickly to her side. Yet his face told a more convincing story. Jessica saw the discouragement. She stretched out her hands in invitation, said softly, "No luck, huh?"

Most often when Hank was frustrated he would just clamp down and turn off. Not so with Jessica. Awkwardly, he sat down, reached for her, sliding closer, wrapping his arms around her neck, holding on. She leaned into his embrace, mirroring the creeping touch of his fingers on her shoulders until her own arms were wrapped around him.

"We'll figure this out," he said, squeezing tightly. "Who do you think was calling?"

"Don't know. I tried not to be afraid. I just didn't know what to do."

They sat together for several minutes in silence; on that stiff hotel mattress, in the rough press of warm flesh, both felt small or burdened or powerless in a dozen different ways.

I don't care about the rest, Jessica thought. *Just stay with me.*

As if he heard her thoughts, Hank pulled back—back, not away—enough to face her, quickly put his lips on hers, like melting butter. No gloating. No words. Nothing but a hesitant, childish wish made real,

a well-rubbed coin plunked in a deep fountain, attached to hope, spi-
raling down through unknown waters. His hands moved to the
smooth skin of her cheek. Nothing electric. Just a kiss. Jessica traced
his movement, leaned into him, making her own wish known. It was
a curious moment. Who knows why these things happen? How does
one isolate the beginning of a thing? Love and need are profound com-
panions; so, too, fear and catharsis. Is the leap from one to the other
ever perfectly divisible? So it was in this time that the feathery touch
of their connection took on new shades, exploding inside both of
them with something far more primal, and simultaneously meaningful, being neither merely need nor fear. Their embrace grew more
rough, less planned. They kissed with abandon—hard, hungry.

Jessica began to move farther, unbuttoning her own shirt. It was
what she knew. Sensing this, Hank withdrew, laying his hands on hers.

"Jessica, no," he said gently, smiling, buttoning her shirt back up.
"It's not that I'm not tempted. But there's more for us than this."

She longed for more. "You don't have to be this way . . ."

"I *want* to be this way. If I take this moment and ruin what's
beginning here, I would never forgive myself."

Jessica flushed. The color could not hide beneath her fair skin. In a
fraction of a second, feeling shamed, both mockery and begging rose up,
like twin roads converging on the same bleak horizon. Two choices. All
in the span of a breath.

Both died on her lips. She herself was dumbfounded. She had
offered her body to Hank like a ripe, sweet peach. He had turned
away. *And she let him!* For the first time she could remember, the pleasure and honesty of the moment were its own sense of purity. Before,
the honest thing was to drive hard to the hoop, so to speak, because all
she wanted was release and all the guy wanted was to score. Wham-
bam-leave-me-alone. That was reality.

Now here was Hank, and he spoke of journey, rather than destination. And Jessica gratefully listened.

Something's changing. . . .

Lowering her head, she stirred with memory. A line. A trail of
prose, like bread crumbs, scattered at her feet for no one but her to see.
Unconsciously, she moved her lips, nibbling at each one, tracing the

words without breath, sound. "A little still she strove, and much repented. And whispering 'I will ne're consent'—consented."

Hank heard only the brush of air, knowing thoughts were attached.

"What did you say?"

"Nothing. You amaze me."

Again, he touched her face. The warmth of his hand got into her blood, flowed through her body. He lifted her chin. Bravely, she received his eyes, shame and all.

"Jessica, I kissed you because I wanted to touch your soul. Because I didn't know how to say anything with words. Can you see that?"

She nodded, blinking. She had never given anyone permission to speak so tenderly.

Hank said, "Remember that feeling in the lobby when we first met?"

Jessica smiled in reply.

Hank continued, "I've never felt anything like that before. Never. But it's not the feeling that I want. It's *you*. First and last. Somewhere in between, maybe—"

The phone rang sharply.

Jessica tensed. It rang again. Hank almost didn't answer. He picked up the receiver.

"Hello?"

"Hello. Is there a Jessica O'Connel in the room?"

"Who needs to know?"

"My name is Missy Jenkins. I'm a reporter for the *Detroit Sentinel*. I've tried calling several times already. I'm working on a major story that involves Jessica in ways she may be unaware of. I have information she needs to know."

Sounded doubtful. He put his hand over the receiver to mute his voice. "You don't have any connections in Detroit, do you?"

Jessica shook her head, puzzled.

"I'm sorry, Ms. Jenkins. Jessica's not here. If you have any messages, I'll make sure she gets them."

Missy was adamant. "No! I need to talk to Jessica. This is important."

Hank shrugged, looked at Jessica. Jessica idly popped her knuckles. Her huge eyes vacantly stared at Hank. She took the phone, straightened her back.

"This is Jessica."

Missy told her everything. For the next hour and a half, Jessica's world fell apart. Luther Sanchez. Her other classmates. Names and faces she hadn't thought of for twenty years. Project Pacifist. Her own history. Her mother's illness. Just like all the other mothers. CIA surveillance. Like water, everything Jessica thought she knew of her life began to slip through her fingers. The collaboration of truth was terrifying.

Yet everything made sense, too. Jessica hardly spoke. Only a question here or there. Meanwhile, Missy fired off dozens of questions, taping the whole conversation with Jessica's permission. It was a long, grueling affair. Hank sat on the bed beside her, never uttering a single word. He just held her hand.

"So my mother's death? What was it?"

"They still don't know. The body just gives out. The reports compare it to Lou Gehrig's disease. But they really don't know. For whatever it's worth, your mother lasted the longest."

Jessica asked one last question, based on a rumbling hunch. "You said I've been watched . . . that we've all been watched by the CIA. Do you have names? Agents' names?"

Missy thumbed through her notes. "There's been more than one. I'll tell you the most recent."

Jessica cut her short. "I already know her name. Decker. Susan Decker."

Now it was Missy's turn to be surprised. "How did you know?"

"When the water gets to your ankles," Jessica murmured, "you know the big wave's coming." She glanced at Hank, with a flat voice, said, "We aren't safe yet."

§ § §

They greeted Father Ravelo with a small chorus of "Padre!" when he entered the Silver Star. It had been an unusually long interval since his last visit, and gratifyingly, several had noticed. For his part, Chubs lifted his head, grunted—which passed for hello—said, like clockwork, "Beer, Padre?"

Ravelo smiled. Some things never change. "No thanks. Turns my urine green."

Chubs shook his head as if that made sense and, without asking, served him a hot cup of coffee and a plate of corned-beef hash. Three stools down sat the man Ravelo had come to see, the man who had yet to glance up or acknowledge his presence.

"Hey, Ricky, how's it going?" Ravelo asked.

Ricky ignored him, like a sullen, spoiled child.

Ravelo left it alone, concentrating on his plate of food. Oh, how he loved this place. The smell of the food, the smoke, the grime, the rough-edged brush of humanity. Nothing delicate or pretentious here. He sipped on his coffee and swore even the coffee tasted better at the Silver Star than anywhere he'd ever been. He determined not to miss so many days again.

When he'd finished eating, he played billiards with one of the guys and won. Only one game, though the man demanded a rematch. No, no, he said. Too much at the office to catch up on. His time away with Missy had seriously interrupted his routine. Parishioners were lined up for counseling; he needed to work on next Sunday's homily; folks were sick and needed visiting. And Mrs. Huggins was cracking the whip on a mishmash of chores and duties he needed to be about. Sometimes building the kingdom meant nothing more than keeping the machine greased. In those times, with the proper perspective, the feel of the grease was an almost holy thing.

Before he left, he took time to scribble a note to Ricky. Ravelo had observed the diminutive wise guy from the corner of his eye while playing and eating. Ricky had hardly moved. Ravelo figured he had probably been that way for days.

He walked over to the stool Carletti sat on, folded the note, slid the paper across the bar until it touched his fingers. Ricky didn't budge. He was hunched over, half drunk probably, eyes straight ahead. Ravelo walked away.

When Ricky was sure he was gone, he unfolded the note: "Confessional booth. One hour. Now is the chance for redemption."

Ricky smirked, rolled his eyes. He didn't care if Ravello was the Pope, what did he know about redemption? As if Ricky gave a flip. The mobster took another draught of beer, belched, starting cussing at Chubs, demanding another fill. Chubs ignored him. Ricky didn't care about redemption. He hadn't done anything wrong. Business is business. You get a job, you do a job, you get paid. It wasn't so bad.

He read the note again, cursing. Again and again. Just stared at it until his eyes blurred.

Redemption . . .

He watched the note until the letters began to crawl. *One hour.* And then he stared at the clock.

❦ ❦ ❦

Five minutes after the seat-belt light blinked off, Jay Remming rose casually from his seat in first class and headed to the front of the plane, to the small bathroom behind the curtain near the flight attendants' station. He was on the final leg of his journey home, and for whatever reason, Stewart Newman had decided to fly him commercially, rather than using the egregious military transports Remming had been subjected to for the sake of "secrecy" on the flight to the compound. Remming was careful to move as unobtrusively as possible. He figured Newman had at least one set of eyes on him, though he had looked in vain for the man named Monitor Nine.

Safe inside the bathroom, he closed and locked the door, then reached into his suit jacket and pulled out his mini-cassette recorder. He rewound several minutes worth of tape, then hit play. He heard shuffling feet, the low murmur of many voices. Then his own whispered supplication: "Don't do this. . . . You have no idea."

A pause. Then, pulled back from death, Abu Hasim El-Saludin's voice, frozen in time: "If I don't do this, will you?"

Remming closed his eyes and pounded the flat of his hand against his forehead. He could not rationalize this moment, was even less equipped to process the emotion of it. The rawness simply overwhelmed him. Without knowing it, he touched his face, where Abu's lifeblood had splattered against his flesh. He would never forget.

Turning down the volume a couple of notches he listened, grief stricken, to Newman's voice; then more from Abu. Then, inexplicably, a gunshot. Even expecting it, knowing it would come, Remming jerked, nearly dropped the recorder. His hands shook. He fast-forwarded to the noiseless denouement, when he exited the chambers with orders from Newman to return to New York City, hit stop, moved his thumb over the record button, and took a deep breath.

It all hinged on this.

A few moments later he emerged from the bathroom without flushing the lavatory. The curtain blocked the line of sight, but if anyone was listening, Remming needed them to think he was still busy. Remaining behind the curtain, he motioned to one of the two flight attendants seated nearby.

"I have a very urgent request of you," he stated in a calm, firm voice as she stepped closer. He was sweating. The young woman was inexperienced and immediately grew worried. For all she knew Remming could have been a terrorist about to make his demands. He had that look about him, in his eyes.

"This is not what you think. I just have a favor to ask of you before I go sit down and finish my iced tea." He held up both hands. "Please don't be afraid."

The woman breathed deeply. "What do you need?"

"Do you live in New York City? Are you stationed there?"

The woman shook her head.

Remming asked, "Does this flight have an extensive layover there tonight by any chance?"

Again, no.

"My friend lives there," the stewardess offered hopefully, motioning to the other lady. "Maybe she can help."

The "other" lady stepped forward. She was a little older and more experienced. "Can I help you, sir? You really should return quickly to your seat."

"I have a very urgent request of you after landing in New York City that I am unable to accomplish myself. I understand that may sound strange, but I need you to deliver this to a doctor named Hanson Blackaby at the Columbia-Presbyterian Medical Center at the university. Do you know where that is?"

The woman shrugged noncommittally. Remming held out a small, unmarked manila envelope, folded in half. "There is nothing dangerous in this package, simply some important materials. I cannot explain the nature of this to you right now, but please trust me, this is absolutely urgent. If you knew me at all, you would understand how unorthodox this is for me to even ask something like this of a stranger. Now listen, I want to repeat: You are in no danger. I simply cannot be the one to deliver this. Do you understand?"

The woman shrugged again, noncommittal.

"This isn't a game!" Remming whispered. "Will you do this for me? Can you do it tonight? Tomorrow at the latest?"

The woman hesitated. Remming opened his wallet, took out two hundred dollars, handed it to her. Eyes wide, she took the package. "I'm not going to accept any responsibility for this, you understand?"

Remming handed her another piece of paper. Tiny droplets of sweat streamed from his forehead. "Here's the address and phone number where you should be able to reach Dr. Blackaby. And here's his home address and phone number just in case. You don't have to give any message. Just the package. Thank you."

Patting his skin with his handkerchief, he stepped back inside the bathroom to flush the toilet for noise. Before he swished the curtain open, he splashed a little cool water on his face and patted that away, too. The flight attendant did not move; she put the envelope in her purse, watching Remming warily. Remming adjusted his suit, nodded to her, and then moved back to his seat.

In coach, Monitor Nine lowered his paper once more to casually scan the plane. Behind the first-class curtain sat his ward, Dr. Remming. It was good to keep an alert eye. Remming, he felt sure, would prove to be a slippery one.

He turned the page and kept reading.

❦ ❦ ❦

In the confessional booth, Father Ravelo checked his watch half a dozen times every minute or so. Four different parishioners had passed through since he had returned from the Silver Star, each telling a tale of guilt and grief. Ravelo was excellent in this environment, always ready and joyous to extend the Father's mercy and love. But on this day and at this hour he was somewhat distracted. Every time the small confessor's door opened, his heart strained in hope of hearing Ricky Carletti's voice. Each of the four times so far, when the voice proved otherwise, he had had to carefully mask his disappointment.

He glanced at his watch again. It had been more than an hour, nearly an hour and fifteen minutes.

Father, he prayed. *Have mercy. He's a whelp. A boy-man. A murderer. He's never known love or family. Draw him to yourself, extend to him the hope of his own life. Save him from the pit. . . .*

He waited for another half-hour. Three more parishioners came and went, seeking penitence and finding it. But Ricky never showed. Ravelo exited the confessional booth and wandered around the sanctuary of the church, searching.

Ricky was nowhere to be seen.

☗ ☗ ☗

Jessica's breathing had fallen into a deep, rhythmic pattern of sleep. Hank listened, smiling. It was a sweet sound, a sound he wanted to protect. A sound he knew he wanted to hear every night for the rest of his life. How does such a thing happen? To live twenty or thirty years and then, all of a sudden, want to live an altogether different life? He sat in the small recliner in the hotel room, head laid back, eyes closed, just listening. It was late. One, two in the morning? With the pale light of a single lamp falling on his face and lap, he pulled open the pages of the Gideon Bible he had snatched from the drawer beside the bed. It was the first time he had opened a Bible in, what? Ten years? At least. The binding cracked as he opened the book. Not used much.

He wanted so much to happen in this moment, but knew so little would. These things required time, investment, emotion. Just the same, he hoped. What did he want?

Don't know.

He wanted grace. For the next step. For understanding. For the faith to have faith again. These were hard things. But some part of him deep inside intrinsically understood them to be worth the chase once more. Maybe that, in itself, was the beginning of faith.

He smiled, pleased.

For about twenty minutes he thumbed aimlessly through the pages, feeling both familiar and strange, like a brother-in-law at a family reunion. Finding nothing, frustrated with looking, he folded the book, set it aside, and turned off the light and returned to his own room, closing the door softly behind.

"Good night," he whispered. Jessica slept.

One door down, he crawled into bed with blanket and pillow and closed his eyes. In the darkness, he knew sleep would come quickly. But just before it did—just *as* it did, actually—Hank found himself jerking awake with a stretching thought, a phrase, resonating in his mind, but from *outside* his mind. Strange indeed.

Read again, it said. *Read again.*

Hank felt a rush in that moment. He flipped on the light, flipped open the book, though this one seemed a bit more used, began thumbing through as aimlessly as he had before. Toward the back, he noticed a piece of paper sticking out, a simple marker from some earlier pilgrim. Hank found the marker in 1 John. Apparently someone had found meaning there; a handful of verses were underlined in dull No. 2.

"I have written unto you, fathers, because ye have known him that is from the beginning. I have written unto you, young men, because ye are strong, and the word of God abideth in you, and ye have overcome the wicked one. Love not the world . . . the world passeth away . . . but he that doeth the will of God abideth forever."

Again, Hank smiled, pleased. He, too, found meaning.

25

What do you do the day after your first kiss? First *real* kiss.

If you are Jessica O'Connel, you sleep like a baby.

Like all good things, though, even good sleep must come to an end. And good sleep, however good, is no guarantee of a good attitude upon awakening. Nor are great first kisses. For Jessica, this morning's disposition came tuned to the racket of a jackhammer in the street below, pounding and cracking the cement, harmonized by shouting voices and the hydraulic creak and whoosh of a dump truck or some other piece of road equipment. Followed by the sound of someone—who was that?—rapping loudly on her door. She groaned, pulled the pillow over her head, almost caught another twenty seconds of sleep.

"Jess, let me in!" Hank called.

Half snarling, she crawled out of bed, threw on a robe, swung the door open, and promptly returned to the warm spot on the mattress shaped like her, buried under pillow and covers.

"I'm not getting up yet," came the muffled voice of a sleepy lawyer.

Hank mimicked the metallic tone of a Borg drone—"Resistance is futile, resistance is futile"—and swung the curtains wide. Streamers of light shot into the room, onto the bed, onto which Hank also pounced, sending Jessica bouncing underneath.

No, there would not be another twenty seconds. Jessica sat up in bed, staring at Hank in disgust. "Here's a clue. Think of me as a hibernating she-bear. I wake very slowly and there's not really a good way to go about it, so better just let me do it my own way."

Hank laughed, studying the face of the flame-haired woman he had kissed yesterday. Even makeup free and unfixed, she was alluring, clean, fresh. (Jessica did *not* feel that way.) Her complexion was simple, earthy. Accented with shades of chardonnay, her hair fell off her shoulders like long strands of silk. Her skin beckoned his touch.

"And you told me you weren't a morning person," Hank said softly.

His words trailed off into her wide-mouthed yawn, one of those involuntary full-body muscle stretchers that require the full extension of all arms and legs and the tensing of every body fiber. Dressed in her long sleeper T-shirt, Hank could not help but notice the contours of Jessica's beautiful shape as she arched her back midstretch. The robe prevented him from much more than hints.

"Why don't you go get us some breakfast while I shower and check my calls at the office."

Hank nodded curtly. "Done. Even though it *is* 10:30."

Jessica shook herself awake as Hank left. 10:30? Anybody can be happy at 10:30.

Indeed, she felt lighter and more hopeful than she had in many years. But nothing is free. Here was Hank, and that was good—

Wonderfully good.

—and thanks to Missy Jenkins, Jessica finally could understand the reasons for so much of her life. She also knew the truth of her mother's death. Another good. But there is a burden that comes with ignorance and another that comes with knowing. The truth—the finality of truth surrounding her mother's death—was a heavy, mixed good. Weariness, new and different, but weariness just the same.

Nevertheless, as she showered and got ready, she tried to concentrate on undiluted pleasures. The day was bright, she could bury her mother in peace, and, though she had fought it tooth and nail, the fresh fever of love was here to stay. Wasn't it? How does a person know for sure? She had never fallen in love before. And what of Hank? Jessica felt embarrassed, grateful. Last, puzzled.

What made a man decline the enticements of a willing woman?

Thankfully, her allotted time for vacation wasn't up yet, so she still had a little room to breathe and figure things out, but things were beginning to stack up at the office and would require all of her attention when she returned. Time to breathe or no, she *would* need to return soon. Which complicated things with Hank as well. Jessica determined not to think about those things. Mandy, of course, was handling the office fine. And that was good enough. Time would have to take care of itself.

While Hank fetched breakfast, it occurred to Jessica that she should try Elizabeth again. Maybe the lines were repaired. She dialed, waited, expecting nothing. But on the second ring, her sister's familiar voice answered.

"Elizabeth! I've been trying to reach you. It's me. We need to talk."

So Jessica told her. Not everything. Not the Project Pacifist stuff. That could wait. Better time, better place. And face-to-face. The news of their mother's death was more than enough for one phone call. Also apologies, since the lines were down. But Elizabeth took it well, or seemed to. Jessica wasn't surprised. Her sister was often strong in needful times. The death had happened suddenly, which was shocking, but before Elizabeth left Hamden, she had braced herself for the worst. She knew her mother was badly off. She knew the doctors were baffled. Then when she couldn't get word for several days, she mentally worked through all the scenarios, most of which included her mother dying.

"I'll start arranging the funeral," she said.

Jessica nodded. "I'll make plans for Mom to be transferred."

"It's not Mom, Jess. Not anymore. Don't say that. Now it's just her body."

They talked a bit more and both cried. Even Jessica, surprising herself most of all. Jessica told her she had more she wanted to talk about, but it could wait. They made plans to speak again tomorrow. Jessica would attend the funeral before returning to Oregon. Elizabeth told Jessica she loved her and said good-bye.

Jessica knew her sister would cry for the rest of the day.

A few minutes later Hank returned with jelly-filled donuts and coffee. On the very first bite, he squirted a blob down the front of his shirt. Jessica laughed. So nice to laugh! Hank made her laugh. Hank stripped his shirt right then and there. He was fairly muscled for a doctor, Jessica decided. A nice athletic build. He left quickly, came back with a new shirt.

"I'm going to be leaving in a few days, you know," she said, rising, wrapping her arms around his neck, sucking a spot of jelly off his lower lip.

"Hmm. Where'd the she-bear go?"

"I'm being serious."

"I know. Let's not go there yet."

"OK. What's the agenda for today?"

He kissed her lightly on the lips. "I've been thinking about that. I figure we've got at least a small advantage because this Decker character probably doesn't know that we are together." He motioned to Jessica and himself. "I mean, how could she, right?"

Jessica tracked with him every step. "And remember: It would also seem likely that she does not know that *we know* who she is. Two advantages."

"And one big disadvantage. She holds all the cards. She's got the materials."

"We just play it straight, then. Set up a meeting. Go face-to-face."

"You think?" Hank asked, though he was inclined to agree. Apart from such a move, their options were extremely limited.

"Hank," Jessica said, and there was a flickering, hard spark in her eyes. "I want to meet this woman. I don't know if you can understand, but she's the closest thing I'll ever get to in this whole Project Pacifist thing that has a mouth and a voice. Besides, as far as I'm concerned, she killed my mother. I want her to know I know."

"OK," Hank said slowly. He wanted to nail this thing to the wall, too. But he didn't like the tone in Jessica's voice. "Are you sure that's a good idea? Maybe we should rethink."

"Think about what? Right now we have no leverage. You are the one most at risk here. Unless you get some leverage, they can put their thumb on you anytime they want in the future. Just because you've given them the stuff they want doesn't mean they'll play fair if they ever feel you are a threat, for whatever reason. Think about it. She's already trashed your place."

"OK, but what kind of leverage?"

Jessica held up empty hands. "I have no idea. The only way I can see to get an idea is to arrange a confrontation. It blows our cover, I know, but I'm not sure how long our cover can last anyway."

"But . . . that's not all," Hank said reservedly.

Jessica shrugged. "Missy Jenkins clued me in. I want more. If we can catch Decker by surprise, maybe we can call the shots for a little while."

Or better yet extract some sort of revenge. Nothing criminal, no doubt; Hank really could not imagine how or in what fashion Jessica thought to mollify herself. But on any scale, such desire endangered their ability to think clearly and do what was right. Relieved, Hank realized *that* was the issue for him. What was the right thing to do? Not just the safest or the smartest. The *right* thing. Hank was no fool—there wasn't always a right; but he figured there should at least be a better. In time he would understand that, in a fallen world, the holy thing often proved to be no more certain than the grit of teeth and blind trust.

"I'm beginning to understand some things about myself, Jessica," he began. "I'm beginning to remember who I am. . . ."

Jessica pushed a lock of hair from her eyes, tucked it behind her left ear. She waited for more. Hank waited, too. The room grew sacred with silence. He sat down on the bed and closed his eyes.

"It's like waking up from a dream. I've been pursuing, pursuing. Pushing myself. Doing things. All the time I'm doing something. Most of the time without thinking, without asking the right questions. Even this . . . I wanted to know, so I dug in. Now I think I'm more interested in asking the right questions, even though I'm already in the middle of this. Like, what if I'm here for a reason? See?"

"I have no idea what you're talking about."

"OK, let's come at it this way. The God Spot is as personal to me as Project Pacifist is to you." Jessica raised a curious eyebrow. "I'm part of the study group, Jess. When I was just a kid, I made a decision to believe in a man named Jesus that I'd never met face-to-face except in the eyes of a little retarded boy. All my life I've thought that was a singular event, an individual thing, which is all fine and good. But now I realize how isolated I am from the very community I claim to be a part of.

"See, I've got that thing in my brain"—he jabbed a finger at the base of his skull—"the same thing all this research is about. I've never been tested for it, but I know I have it."

Jessica tried to make a point, but her voice trailed off. "I believe in God. . . ."

"Not really," Hank countered. "You believe in some nebulous idea of universal goodwill. Not the kind of God that would invade and stamp himself upon our very being." He touched Jessica's forehead with his index finger. "Here's what I can't get a handle on: Was my spot there before that decision as a kid, or after? For several days now I've been beating myself up over what that issue of timing means. But it means nothing. That spot doesn't matter at all. What matters is that what I have is real. It affects my life." He glanced up, found her eyes, hoped for connection. "I believe in so much more than I've lived and experienced lately . . . so much more than I've told you about. But I want to start. I've found something in you that I've never thought possible, and it makes me want you with everything I have. Yet I've got to hold out for a better time, a more *right* time, because I believe there is right and wrong. I know all that sounds strange." He struggled for words. "Do you know what I'm saying?"

"No," Jessica sighed. "But I like to hear you talk about it." The picture of his words in her mind was painted in colors she had dreamed of. True colors. Something real. She longed to be awakened herself. "So what if I want the spot?"

What if? Hank hadn't a clue, could do nothing but rub his hands together and look perplexed. He had never considered the possibility. How would that work? Say the sinner's prayer and grow some new brain cells? Repent and receive a neurotransmitter? Seemed unlikely. If Jessica didn't already have the SPoT construct in some latent form, if she wasn't born with the genetics, could she ever get it? Up until now he had only considered the equation from the biological perspective of Christians. The elect. The called.

"The spot itself is not the point," he said weakly. "It's the faith."

"Maybe that's what I want, then," Jessica said agreeably. "Maybe that's what I need."

Hank's head hurt. He had no idea where to go from here—no idea what was real for anyone else, only him. The existential leap. Which was true, but completely untrue. A right answer matched again to the wrong question. Maybe that was part of his discomfort, his urgency for resolution. Millions of others just like him would have the same questions. Millions more like Jessica. Like it or not, Hank *was* a part of something bigger, a family he never knew or cared about, all sharing a link more tangible than creeds and rituals. That family needed him to care.

Not just my faith anymore. Ours. And those to come, whoever they are.

Maybe Jessica. Whether she had the spot or not. He skirted past for now. "Let's go back to the beginning. I was trying to make a point. We've got more to do and we both know it. Confrontation is the only option left. I just want you to know that it needs to be about doing the right thing, not your revenge or my career. You can't carry the burden of your past forever. At some point you have to let it go. I know that may not be fair for me to say right now, all of a sudden, but it's true. Whatever you're thinking with Decker, you have to let it go before we see her or we should not see her at all."

"Maybe seeing her is part of my letting go."

"Maybe. Maybe not."

Jessica frowned. "I don't want to hurt her. Is that what you think?"

"I don't think anything. I just need you to know where I stand before we make a plan."

"OK, but let me tell you where *I* stand." Jessica tried to remain cool, but a bit of Irish anger crackled in her reply. "I *will* talk to her, with or without you. That's all I'll do, but I'll do that much. I want to look at her. She's been watching me for years. You want to talk about what's right? *That's* right. I deserve it."

Calmly, Hank said, "We'll do this together. Let's just play smart and not lose our heads and we may come out on top. Hand me the phone."

"What are you going to do?"

"I'll call her and set up a time to meet."

"That's it? She'll recognize you."

"I'll use a fake voice. I'm good with accents."

"When? Where?"

Hank began to dial. "At the hospital, I suppose. Later today. I don't see any reason to wait."

§ § §

"I don't know, but I think they may be in danger," Missy told Ravelo over the phone. It was midmorning in Detroit and the smell of the office was most easily identified by the smudged stack of preprints from the morning's run, for some reason deposited right beside her cubicle by an absent-minded delivery boy. The smell of the fresh ink combined with the rancid odor of her three-day-old coffee grounds into a sinus-clearing amalgamation worthy of pharmaceutical research.

Affable, but unconvinced, Ravelo said, "Your journalistic hunching is outrunning the facts, Ms. Jenkins. Why would they be in any danger?"

Just then, Jack, the senior news editor, strolled by. He poked his head in, ignoring the fact that Missy was on the phone. "We're hitting crunch time on this Sanchez piece, Jenkins. I got people barking at me to move on."

Missy held up one finger. Jack said, "No, I won't wait! I need something printable quick, with named sources. Too many other fish you need to be frying. We've sung this song before. You've come up with some interesting stuff. But I'm not adding another verse. Got me?"

Missy nodded, stammering an apology to Father Ravelo. Jack held up three fingers. His lips moved. *"Three days."* He wanted the first run by the weekend edition.

"Sounds like you're the one who should be worried, Ms. Jenkins."

"Father, listen. You don't have to believe me, but if you stop and think about it, I've proven myself and my hunches enough that you should. Jessica sounded scared when I told her who the agent was. Actually, she ended up telling me. She already knew. Apparently she's had some other run-ins with this woman while in the Big Apple. Remember Agent Decker? You saw Decker and you said she was scary, right?"

"Chilling."

"Well, there's more. After I unloaded on her, Jessica and some guy named Hank turned around and unloaded big time on me. I mean big time. Makes Project Pacifist look like one of the professor's lab tricks on *Gilligan's Island.* You follow me?"

"No."

"Well, of course not! We can't do this by phone. We need to talk." She lowered her voice. "It's about some heavy-duty brain stuff they're doing on Christians. You need to know about this, Father. It's serious. And that's why I'm afraid for them."

"Christians? What do you mean?"

"I can't talk like this. We don't have time to talk. You got any connections in New York City? I need to get this story from them, but they need some help. Like now. I can feel it in my bones."

"You have yet to convince me, Ms. Jenk—"

"Good grief, Father! Call me Missy, please! You're killing me."

Ravelo spoke very deliberately. "Missy, I *would* like to get together. We need to bring some resolution to this whole affair and move on."

"We can't move on yet! There is no resolution! The story just exploded by a factor of ten!"

"Because of Jessica," Ravelo deadpanned. "And . . . Hank."

"Who happens to be a rising star in neurosurgery—"

"Uh-huh."

"At Columbia University—"

"Uh-huh."

"Under the watchful eye of none other than Dr. Jay Remming himself, who is apparently part of this whole religious-brain-scandal thing."

Here, Ravelo paused. "*The* Jay Remming? Nobel prize winner Jay Remming?"

Missy grinned fiercely behind the receiver. "Uh-huh." She knew she had him.

"Well, I'm not sure of any danger, but I don't like the sound of brain research—"

"On Christians."

"*On* them? What does that mean?"

"It means specifically and purposefully them. There is something genetically unique about the Christian brain, for lack of a better description. Remming discovered it. Then Hank discovered Remming. And Susan Decker's working with Remming to protect the data. Something like that. My little non-Christian brain was short-circuiting before it was all said and done. They didn't want to talk long anyway, but I gave them my number."

"And how did Hank find Jessica?"

"Her mother just died. Typical Project Pacifist thing. She was a patient of Hank and Remming."

"Oh my…" Ravelo's voice trailed away to silence.

"So what are we gonna do? I don't know what we can do. But if they're straight on this, even half straight, we gotta do something! Don't we?"

"We must pray, Ms. Jenkins," Father Ravelo said emphatically. "We must pray. God will show us the way."

Missy almost yawned at the thought. "You said you hung out with a pretty rough crowd, didn't you, Father?"

The priest missed her completely. "Yes."

"Well, I don't know about you, but I'm thinking God might want a little help on this one. Maybe pull a few strings. You know. If he can't, maybe someone he knows could."

By now Ravelo's spirit was too troubled to chatter. "I'll call you later, Ms. Jenkins."

He hung up.

Lunch was quiet and disturbing. *Tests on Christians? What for?* What was this all about? So little to go on, Ravelo knew he should just drop the whole thing. But something in him, that voice he had learned to trust, said he should not drop this.

He left the Silver Star feeling ill at ease, tried to walk it off, but the discomfort only increased. Something was not right here. Something, in fact, was very wrong. Ravelo knew the subtle impressions of the Holy Spirit in his own. He knew he must take this to prayer. But, like Missy, he suspected there may be need for more.

As he passed by a narrow alley a hand reached out, pulling him into the shadows. Ricky Carletti held Ravelo firmly, facing him. Not threatening. More like desperate. Ravelo couldn't see the young man's eyes underneath his black fedora in the shadows, but he could tell by how Ricky chewed on his toothpick that he was agitated. Ricky didn't mean to, but he shook Ravelo as he spoke.

"You said final redemption. *Final* redemption . . . in the note. What does that mean? You think I'm gonna die?"

"We all die, Ricky. That's not what I meant."

"Well, what did you mean? Why final? Ain't I got another chance? This is bull, Father, you know. I didn't do nothing wrong."

"Then why do you feel so bad?" the priest inquired, gently prying free of Carletti's grip on his arms.

"I don't know. I think it just takes some getting used to."

"Wrong. That's the worst thing that can happen, Ricky. You're at a point now where you still know what makes sense. You can grab hold of that or you can throw it in this Dumpster. But if you do that, your whole life goes with it. You'll never know what it's like to feel bad again, because you won't feel anything. Good or bad. It's that simple."

Ricky fidgeted. He was a good six or seven inches shorter than Ravelo. He wanted so much to be a big man. "I got no clue, Father. I got no clue."

"Let's pray, Ricky. How about that? Let's just pray together."

"I ain't saying no prayers, Father! Don't start to push me over. Besides, we ain't even in the church. How can we pray?"

Ravelo held up his hands. "Fine. Sorry. We'll go slower."

The priest pulled off his glasses, cleaned them with his shirt, scratched his chin. This was a fragile moment. Whatever he said next needed to make sense to Ricky. Not too much, not too little. Baby steps.

A thought struck him. A risky thought. Quickly, he slid his glasses over his nose, focusing hard on Carletti. His voice grew severe. He was about to make a deal with the devil and all he could do was hope heaven didn't mind.

"Listen very carefully to me. Are you listening, Ricky?"

Ricky played it cool, chewed his toothpick, shrugged.

"Sometimes the first step is to stop thinking of yourself. Now I've got a big favor to ask of you, but not just for me. I think this may be good for you, too. Will you do me a favor, Ricky?"

The thought of helping the priest put Ricky in a favored position. Kinda cool. Ricky liked that. Caught him off guard.

"Keep going," he said.

So Ravelo told him, in brief, about Jessica and Hank, that they might be in danger. That they couldn't go to the police about this because there was no legitimate suspicion of danger. Besides, they were asking for protection from the CIA. Ravelo wasn't sure of the details, but he felt that something needed to be done. Did Ricky have any friends or associates in New York City? Any contacts in "the family" that could maybe shadow Hank and Jessica for a few days?

"Like guardian angels?" Ricky said wickedly, and his Italian-American accent had never been more thick. Now, it was like he was trying to play the part.

"Like guardian angels," Ravelo repeated.

"This is part of my redemption?" Ricky asked. He saw the irony.

"Perhaps. A small part."

"I ain't so bad after all, am I, Father? You coming to me and all."

"Not so bad, Ricky. But no killing. Absolutely no killing. Do it right. That's part of the deal."

Ricky began to grow cocky. Ravelo felt a quick, painful spasm of doubt, wondering if he was doing the right thing. It was a huge gamble, and Ricky's soul was only part of the stakes. The wise guy stepped out of the shadows, glanced across the alley. No one was around.

"So this is it? This is the favor?"

"Just the beginning. You can't stay in the mob, Ricky. You know that."

"But you need me in the mob now, don't you, Father?"

"I need you to . . . no, *you* need to do something good, where you are, so that you can be free enough to leave it. But make no mistake, you must leave." It made sense to Ravelo, but he wondered if it sounded like a line to Ricky. Truth be told, it sounded like a line to him, too.

But Ricky pursed his lips in thought. "Makes sense. Just not yet."

Ravelo smiled sadly. Ricky wasn't so dumb. "Just not yet."

"I'll see you around, Father."

That was it. Ravelo grew nervous. "Wait! What do you think? Is this going to work?"

Ricky turned, still walking, now with a swagger. "Don't know. I'll need to check with my boys. New York's a long ways away."

Ravelo had to shout for Ricky to hear him. "They're at the hospital at Columbia University! He's a doctor there! Don't you want phone numbers and addresses?"

Ricky called back. "If we can do it, we can find them."

Ravelo did not feel comforted. But he could see Ricky grinning with huge white teeth.

"Don't worry, Father. Your guardian angel's watching out for you."

§ § §

The answering machine beeped four times. Four messages. Hank punched in his code to retrieve his messages, pen and paper in hand. He sat in the hotel room, waiting for Jessica, who was changing her blouse in the bathroom. She said she felt "springish," what with the weather in the city being so unseasonably mild. Together, they had already been to lunch and back and were now waiting only to meet with Susan Decker at six o'clock at the hospital. Everything had gone well. Susan had not recognized Hank's fake accent and had responded well to the ruse in general.

The phone beeped again in Hank's ear. Message number one: static. No message.

Message number two: a friend named Buddy, checking up on Hank—hadn't heard from him in a while. No big deal.

Message number three: static again. No, actually, someone was breathing on the phone but not talking. The person cleared their throat as if they were starting to talk, then hung up.

Message number four: a woman's voice, not one he recognized, saying she had a package for him. The woman sounded a little unsure of her own story:

". . . anyway, this tall black man hands me this package and asks me to deliver it to you, that you would know what to do with it, that he couldn't do it himself. He didn't tell me anything else, but he gave me two hundred dollars so I figured I ought to follow through. He was pretty intense, so it must be important. I don't feel comfortable giving you my phone number, so I'll try you again later."

Puzzled, Hank called back and listened to the message again. He felt his stomach knotting, even though it didn't make sense. The woman was describing Remming; that much was obvious. She must not have known his name. Why would Remming route something to him through a flight attendant? Again, the obvious answer was because he was in some sort of danger, maybe. Hank wondered what he should do. But the two hundred dollars? That was the giveaway. Not Remming's style at all. It smelled like bait. Who would be baiting him? Decker? Why?

He didn't know. All he knew was that, for better or worse, he was not going to tell Jessica any of this.

     ❦ ❦ ❦

A few miles away, only a little earlier that day, Jay Remming woke from a long, exhausted nap on one of the plush sofas in the parlor of his home. His first thought:

Hanson . . .

When he returned from the airport earlier this morning, he had been too exhausted to think about anything, had simply collapsed on the couch just off the entry of his spacious estate and fallen immediately to sleep. But a man of Remming's means had servants. Two, in fact. One lived on the grounds in a small bungalow behind the rear gardens. Another commuted. When the live-in servant saw Remming there, asleep, she laid a blanket over him and set about fixing some broth and tea for when he awoke. It was not an unusual occurrence for Jay Remming to show up late or early or whatever, unannounced and, by now, unmissed even up to a week at a time, but it was fairly rare for him to fall asleep the moment he entered the house.

My, what a house. A small mansion, really. Three stories, eight bedrooms, spiral staircase, walnut and mahogany and Italian marble, Corinthian columns out front, manicured lawn, rolling hills, and the whisper of the wind in the trees all about, located just on the outskirts east of the city on prime real estate in an exclusive and historic development. In years gone by, the home had once been the summer getaway of several of New York's aristocracy, though Remming never bothered to learn their names. The real estate salesman had made a big deal of that part of the home, but history was not one of Remming's fancies.

Poetry, however, was.

In his private study, an entire wall housed his personal collection of the world's greatest poets. And, of course, the track lighting fell most prominently on the complete works—a limited, signed collection—of William Blake. One volume alone was valued at nearly twenty thousand dollars.

It was the kind of building and atmosphere that represented all that Remming had worked so hard to achieve. And failed to maintain. Once it had been more than an achievement; it had been a home. Four children used to tear up and down that curving staircase, completely oblivious to its monetary value. His beautiful wife, Anna, used to glide through this house like a vision from another world, in and out, making sure all was in its place. She knew Remming liked his home to be ordered. Josh—rascally Josh—used to hide behind the columned entrance, waiting to jump out at just the right moment and scare his dad—who would at least act scared—when he came home from the university. Every day! Every day that boy did that for an entire summer.

A long time ago. A different man.

Remming sat up on the couch, glancing left and right. The big house was just big, now. Big like the vacuum of space and just as cold. On the end table beside him he found a cup of warm broth and steaming tea.

Are you even alive, Hanson?

The thought slipped through the cracks into his consciousness like the jolt of a cattle prod, jerking him awake. Surely he was. Why wouldn't he be? He posed no real threat anymore. Besides, he's a smart kid.

Remming rose to his feet, feeling suffocated in his unwashed Brooks Brothers. He peeled off the jacket, turned a hapless circle, unsure where to begin—unsure of anything, really. He laid the jacket over the back of a chair beside the sofa, his agile mind darting a dozen directions. Something, he noticed, was poking out of his jacket, something bothersome, a pulled string on the collar of his suit coat. He leaned over to inspect more closely, tugging gently on the string. It pulled but left a tiny scar in the texture of the fabric. A tiny but noticeable scar.

The string might as well have been pulled from his lungs.

Swift and terrifying, barely controlled rage surfaced. Remming's eyes bulged, his fingers tensed. He seized a deep, measured breath, still staring at the string, as if he could set it on fire with his eyes, cursing it without words, like an Indian shaman might curse a stalk of corn, so that it would wither and die. Rising stiffly, he moved away.

But the four walls closed in on him and he could think of nothing in the midst of everything there was to do. Nothing but the string.

Snakelike, it coiled around his thoughts and bit deep. From several feet away he saw the string jutting defiantly up, a silhouette of unreason, mocking him. Remming dashed back, grabbed hold of the string—he would fix this thing!—pinched it at the base between the finger and thumb of one hand and gave a good, swift pull with the other. Like a Dantean joke, instead of breaking, the string unraveled farther, cutting a deep swath into the fabric of his coat and simultaneously burning a thin line into the tip of his thumb. Enraged, Remming pulled again and again. He growled, bit his teeth, picked up the coat, thrashed about with it, then threw it to the ground, stomping, shouting until he was purple faced and breathless.

But he never cursed.

His servant came running, fear on her face. Remming saw her, barked, "Leave me! Go!"

Terrified, she turned and fled. Remming stomped on his jacket more, picked it up, grabbed hold of the string, several inches long now, and, gurgling, choking on his own bile, bit it in two.

He threw the entire coat into the unlit fireplace and stormed to his study.

An hour later, calm again, Remming opened the bottom drawer of his desk and pulled out cherished faces. There was Anna. Josh. The whole family. The day he sent them into exile, he had taken every photo down and either thrown them away or locked them in storage. A handful of the most precious he kept here, in this drawer. He had not looked at them since Anna left, seven years ago.

Now, unbidden, as unbidden and unwelcome as his anger had been, salty tears burned in his eyes and broke free. He spread the pictures out over his desk and wept.

All of this was gone. Everything. His one possession, a reputation, over the course of the last seventy-two hours had been removed from him. He owned nothing. He possessed much but owned nothing. Stewart Newman would be his master for as long as Stewart Newman wanted to be. That was how the game would be played and Remming could do nothing about it. Even when he was free of the current obligation, he would never be free again. The prestige and ubiquity of his name in the medical community, the very thing he had labored to achieve, now conspired with Newman against him, sealing his fate.

Remming inhaled deeply, wiped his eyes. He needed to pack. He had important files, clothes, all his research, computer files. He had to take it all. Newman would want it all. He would pack here first—was he being watched still? Yes, of course. Every move—then go to his office to gather the remainder of his things.

One thing was worth risking though, watched or not. One phone call. Remming picked up the phone, dialed quickly. He had the number memorized. Jay Remming did not memorize the numbers of very many residents. But this one was different. Had always been different.

Please, Hanson, be there . . .

Hank was not. The answering machine picked up. Remming paused, frozen, cleared his throat . . .

Hung up.

26

The plan was to keep the plan as simple as possible: a meeting after-hours with low traffic, yet enough to eliminate anything rash on Decker's part. Hank had arranged for one of the lab rooms in the William Black Medical Research Building to be used, just a floor or two above Remming's offices, with instructions for the nurses and receptionists on how to direct Decker when she arrived. The ruse was that he was the chief pathologist for the hospital; that for the last three days he had been investigating some artifact they had found in Mrs. O'Connel's blood work; that he had determined, to his own surprise, that it was a rare, federally controlled substance—a regulated toxin, or some other such nonsense—which required documentation from both Jessica and Elizabeth, signatures and such. Also that Jessica had already signed off on these forms. Hank just tried to make it sound convincing for nonmedical ears. For good measure, he also offered again to do an autopsy, pretending to be very intrigued, since the whole ordeal had made for an unusually long internment period and needed some justification. Regardless, after the "release forms," Mrs. O'Connel's body could be transported back to Hamden for burial.

So much for plans.

Hank and Jessica arrived at the empty laboratory well in advance of Decker's planned arrival. Only half the fluorescent tube lights were on, the back half, left by those for whom the workday had already ended. Reaching for the other switches, Hank thought he saw movement out of the corner of his eye. In the shadows by his hand.

Instinctively, he spun—not quickly enough—felt something hard cuff him painfully across the back of the neck. That, and being shoved, falling . . .

"Get in, quick," a familiar voice said. "Don't make a peep."

Before she could react, a hand snaked through the door and pulled Jessica in, too.

"Get over there, together."

Hank struggled to focus his eyes. The first thing he made out in the low light was the Marilyn Monroe hair. The second thing was the 9-mm Decker held in her gloved hands, pointed right at his face.

"Do you think I'm stupid, Hanson Blackaby?" she purred, shifting her weight to one foot so that the curve of her hips jutted out with noticeable sass. Decker *knew* how to wear a black dress. It was classic threaten-and-entice Decker. Hank blinked, still smarting from the blow to the head. Jessica held on to his arm, fearful, but not so fearful that she ever looked away. Her eyes smoldered.

"Ooh, you're a feisty one, aren't you?" Decker snickered. "Glad to have you join our little party, Jessica O'Connel."

"Please, call me Number Seventeen."

A rare bit of surprise crossed Decker's face. "You've done your homework, I see. Impressive."

"Shut up. I want answers."

"Do you, now?"

"Tell me why. Why me? Why would you want to be a part of this—"

Decker rolled her eyes, dismissive. "This isn't where we get all snugly, just us girls, and cry and hug and say we're sorry, is it?" She held up her hand to examine her fingernails, then turned her attention to Hank. "I wonder, Dr. Blackaby, did you think I was a rookie? Fresh out of training? Did you think"—here she adjusted her voice to mimic the British accent Hank had attempted—"that I wouldn't know a fool when I heard one?" She held up a printed sheet of paper. "Or that I wouldn't check the docket of physicians on staff with the name you gave me?"

Decker lowered her weapon, casually pulled a cigarette and a lighter out of her purse, lit it. One long pull, then another. She exhaled out the side of her lips, wasn't nervous in the least. Hank and Jessica stood together, shame faced. There were no windows in this lab, no possibility of anyone seeing them and the walls were thick. Besides, most people had already gone home for the day. *Not quite enough traffic,* Hank decided. Too late.

"What do you want?" he said.

"You're the one throwing the party," the agent replied. "What do *you* want?"

"All right, I'll tell you. I want to know that I'm not going to have to look over my shoulder every night for the rest of my life. I want to know my career is safe. I want to know I'll never hear from you people ever again—"

"You want a lot."

"*And* Ms. O'Connel would like a little respect. Some answers. For heaven's sake, her mother has just died."

"OK," mused Decker coolly. "But let's consider all this in light of what *I* want to know. I want to know why I shouldn't just kill you both and be rid of the trouble of you. No career problems there, eh? And no questions to answer."

Jessica's eyes widened slightly, disbelieving. This was not a part of any scenario she had seriously considered. "The noise," she breathed. "You wouldn't get away with it."

"Quite right." Decker pulled something out of her purse, screwed it onto the end of her firearm. She held the silencer up for them to see. "Now I can." She waved it back and forth in the air, then suddenly jabbed it toward them and said, "Bang!"

Both jumped. Decker dropped her cigarette, stepped on it. She didn't bother to laugh at them. She paced instead.

"I will tell you something about myself: I am a student of strategy. I'm fascinated by it, the issues of control and submission and timing and chance. The randomness. So when I realized that you knew who I was, it added a bit of mystery to the contest."

"A stalemate," Hank said, forcing his heart to slow by sheer will.

"Hardly."

"Mmm, don't be so sure."

"Please! Don't insult me twice."

"Think about it," Hank said. "Do you really think we would risk this if we didn't have a measure of confidence? Or do you take *me* for a fool?"

Beneath a bleached coif of platinum, two eyes narrowed. The strategist was running the numbers. Jessica squeezed Hank's arm, said nothing.

"What have you got?"

"Enough to make it worth your while."

"You're bluffing."

"Am I?"

Which was why they called these confidence games. Who could outmaneuver the other? Hank held his cool, but inside he was screaming for the answer to his own riddle: What did he have that could buy them some time?

"I don't believe you," Decker told him, taking aim with both hands.

"Then finish it!" Hank whispered defiantly, hardly believing his own ears. But he had to be willing to play out his bluff for it to work. "I'll just take it with me." He held up his arms, closed his eyes. Bluff or no, this was real. Hank held no illusions about how real the bullets in her gun were. Ten thousand dreams ripped through his soul in full fluorescent color. He stood on the brink, stared into the face of God.

And knew he was safe.

Decker lowered her weapon. "Start talking."

"How do I know you'll let us go?"

"You don't. Start talking."

"I've got a backup. You asked me about that. Remember?"

"You said no at the time."

"I lied."

Decker regarded Hank with obvious skepticism. "I think you're lying now. Ten seconds for something better or your lady friend here is the first to go."

"How can you do this?" Jessica screamed. "We are American citizens! You are a federal agent! This is completely illegal!"

"Are you so naive? Do you really think we care about you people?" Decker sneered. "We exist to protect the highest common denominator, not the lowest. We safeguard the prime numbers. At this point you all are way too much of a threat to that security. It's that simple. Besides, I've been shafted so many times, I simply don't care. You think I'm playing loose with the rules, but really I'm bucking for a promotion. See, if I can keep this whole thing neat and tidy . . ." Her voice trailed away; she glanced at her watch. "Three seconds."

She took aim, right at Jessica's forehead. Her finger caressed the trigger.

"I've got something from Remming!" Hank blurted out. "I don't know what it is yet . . . it just arrived. Something new."

"Dr. Remming is away. You know that."

"He's back! Some flight attendant contacted me just this morning. On the plane, Dr. Remming gave her a package to deliver to me."

Decker did not lower her weapon, did not let go of the trigger. But she did pause for several moments, studying Hank's face, his eyes, in silence. Her lips were a thin line of thought. "Where is it?" she demanded. "What is it?"

"You wouldn't believe me if I told you. You'll have to see for yourself."

"Don't play games with me, Blackaby!" Decker hissed. "If you're lying . . ."

"I'm not. Take us there. I'll show you. Then we'll never trouble you again. Will we?"

Jessica was sobbing. She shook her head, couldn't speak.

Decker cursed, bit her bottom lip. Another wrinkle, another possible leak. Chafing, she motioned for them to step out the door.

"Nothing fast. Nothing funny. I'm watching every step. Got it?"

"Got it."

They headed out the door.

※ ※ ※

As Hank and Jessica were escorted at gunpoint out the front doors of the William Black Medical Research Building, only a few offices down the hall and a couple of floors lower, Jay Remming frantically logged on to his computer system, keenly aware of his timetable. He popped disk after disk into the hard drive, copying files. He logged on to the mainframe. He grabbed books and folders and nearly completely emptied out his filing cabinet into several cardboard boxes. All the while his eyes darted furtively from the windows to the front door, windows to front door. Despite the mad rush, he was collected again—possibly never more rational in his life. This was now the process and exercise of cold logic, his domain. Nothing emotional anymore. Simply what had to be done.

Ten, maybe fifteen minutes later, most everything was accomplished. Almost everything. He sat down in front of the terminal and began typing furiously, clicking from screen to screen. He hit the delete key several times. Typed in "delete" at other times. He was sweating. So much work, so much time spent here. While the computer crunched along, he leaned back, took a deep breath, trying to consume as much of the moment in one last sweeping glance as he could. For all he knew, Newman might never let him return.

Then he grabbed a couple of boxes and began hauling them to his car.

୫ ୫ ୫

Hank had no idea how near his mentor was. A half minute later and Hank could have helped load his Beamer. All except for Decker. And the gun.

The three made it to the car in short order, offering stiff-lipped smiles to the two people they passed. Decker forced Hank to drive her car, with Jessica in front beside him. To assure Hank's complicity on the ride she kept the gun trained on Jessica, who was nothing if not shell-shocked. Jessica didn't move, didn't twitter, just stared straight ahead, but her lips trembled, and what little color there was in her skin had drained from her face. Hank, on the other hand, kept his eyes on the road and his hands on the wheel, working furiously through his options. None seemed pretty.

The drive from CPMC to Washington Heights wasn't far. Five minutes maybe. When they parked, Hank got out first. Jessica jerkily rose to her feet.

Her green eyes were an open petition of fear and mercy. "I'm so scared," she whispered.

"Shut up," Decker told her from behind, poking Jessica in the ribs with the barrel of her gun. It was mostly evening now; few people could be seen milling about, so the darkness covered such movement well, even though the street was well lit. As he began to climb the stairs, all Hank could do was hope God was watching. Otherwise, things were probably going to get messy really quick.

He took a deep breath, pulled his keys out of his pocket, unlocked the door. The one big flaw to his whole scheme was, of course, that there was no package. Not yet, anyway. He had never returned the lady's call. Kind of hard to get around that little detail.

"Slowly," Decker said. "Very slowly."

He opened the door with Jessica right behind, stepped inside, fumbling for the switch, Decker following. As the lights flared, simultaneously, several things happened—an explosion of bodies and movement. Decker cried out as a fist crashed down on the arm holding her weapon. A muffled shot rang out. The room blurred.

"Down!" someone shouted as her 9-mm discharged, but Hank and Jessica had already been shoved to the ground. Glass broke. There was a scuffle. The lights went off again. Hank heard Decker groan, then cry out again. There were sounds of pummeling, tearing clothes. He started to rise, but a hand clamped over his mouth and pinned him with expert efficiency to the ground. Same for Jessica.

Then, at last, "We got her."

"The spook?" asked the man clamped on Hank.

"Hit the lights."

When the lights came on the first thing Hank saw, the first thing he cared about, was Jessica, eyes rolled to white. She was fine. Then he saw everything else: four other figures in the room, all in black, with black ski masks pulled over their faces. Only one held a gun in his hand and it was pointed at Special Agent Susan Decker, who lay flat on her stomach with a knee in her back and a dishrag stuffed into her mouth. She was moaning, shouting even, but the sound was garbled and weak. The left side of her face was badly bruised, the shoulder of her dress torn. Still, she squirmed and kicked and in her eyes was the buzzing fury of an angry wasp.

One of the men spoke. "I assume you're Hank?"

His voice was nasally and thick, with a heavy Brooklyn accent. Or was that Italian? Hank nodded, speechless. His assailant—or savior, apparently—pulled his mask up to his forehead. He was swarthy, olive skinned, dark haired. Mid-forties. Looked like a plumber, if anything.

"And this must be Jessica. Very nice."

He helped Hank and Jessica stand. "We were afraid we weren't going to find you. Didn't have much time. Then we weren't sure where to position ourselves. Somebody messed up your place pretty good. Guess we just got lucky." He grinned, patted Hank hard on the back. "Guess *you* got lucky."

Dumbfounded, Hank nodded, mouth gaping. The men had cleared a broad path through his wrecked apartment, throwing Hank's belongings into piles so that they could maneuver easily, and setting up a couple of lamps for light. Jessica's knees were wobbly; she worked hard to regain her composure. Tried to, anyway. When her knees buckled again, Hank caught her and held on. She buried her face in his shoulder. The man with the gun gave it to Hank. It was Decker's weapon, Hank realized.

"Tie the spook up," the leader commanded, motioning to Decker. The other three grabbed Decker, cleared some more floor space, and dropped her in one of Hank's kitchen chairs. They frisked her first, then tied her hands and waist and knees to the chair frame with duct tape.

"Who . . . what?" Hank stammered, holding the gun as clumsily as if it were a huge dill pickle he was about to eat. "What just happened?"

"You got friends in Detroit?" the man asked curiously.

"No."

"Well, you do now. My name's Alphonse, but you don't need to remember that. We're just paying back a favor. It won't happen again. See you around, Hank."

Simple as that, the men filed out, disappearing into the darkness. Hank and Jessica stared at the blank face of the closed door for several moments, too stunned to move or speak. Cognizant now, Jessica pulled loose from Hank, took three giant steps toward Decker, drew her hand back and slapped Decker full across the face. Then did it again. So hard her own hand burned and she had to hold it. That done, she collapsed on the ground and wept. Hank moved closer. Decker was seething, but she was also more than afraid. Hank could smell it, knew what it looked like; he had lived it. He, too, wanted to make a point, do something to get Decker's attention, something to humiliate her. Even more, he just wanted to get away.

"Jessica, we should go." He reached down to help her up. She pulled away with one word.

"No."

"Jessica—"

"No! I want those files back! That's what we came for and we aren't leaving without them. Let Decker sweat for a while now!"

Hank bent down, whispered softly so that Decker couldn't hear, "We're lucky to be alive, Jess. You know that. I know that. Let's take the luck we've got and run. We'd be fools to push it now."

"What have we got, Hank?" Jessica demanded, tossing her hair, not caring if Decker heard.

"Well, for starters, we are alive."

"For how long? We've got nothing. As much as I'd like to, we can't kill her, which means she will only come after us again. So what do you want? Without hard evidence, we can't prove anything to anybody who could keep her—them—away."

Hank took a deep breath. "I know you want justice . . ."

"Yes, I want justice! Is that so hard to believe? Look at us, Hank! Look at me! I don't want anyone to ever have to go through what we've gone through. I don't want anyone to have to go through what I've grown up with all my life. It has to stop! All this research, this human guinea-pig testing! It has to stop!"

Hank turned to face Agent Decker. Her eyes were blurry with pain, but it seemed she hurt most when she breathed. He reached over, touched her side. She winced. Probably a bruised rib, maybe even broken. Nothing critical, just painful.

"I don't much care for your remodeling style," he said darkly.

Decker didn't move, didn't even grunt.

"Do you have any idea of the enormity of this research?" he asked her. "The evil that can come from it? It's big. Very big."

This time she gave a muffled reply. Hank pulled the rag from her mouth.

"Bigger than you know."

"Why do you want to be a part of that?"

She told him the truth. "I am a part of nothing else."

"Will you ever let us rest?"

"I would have. Before today I was done with you."

"But not now."

Decker did not reply. Hank stood, gave Jessica the gun.

"Watch her," he said. "Use that if you have to."

"Where are you going?" she asked fearfully.

"Don't answer the door or phone. Keep the shades pulled. I won't be gone long."

After about five minutes of catlike silence, wordless stare-downs, with neither flinching, Jessica said, "Tell me about my mother."

The air was very still. Jessica cleared space off the couch in the living room, several feet away from where Decker sat in the kitchen. She turned out all the other lights except one. Most were broken anyway. Not the lamp on the table behind her. With it she wanted to see Decker, not have Decker see her.

The agent was nonchalant. "What do you want to know?"

"Is there any known cure, anything that could have helped her?"

"No. Your mother lived longer than most."

"What about me? What about the others? Are we going to get sick?"

"The treatment has already affected you in full. Your personalities, drives and passions are, relatively speaking, the only 'symptoms' you should ever have to deal with. But that hasn't proved easy."

"Like my need for justice—"

"And the sex," Decker said wickedly.

Jessica didn't bother to take offense. She grew reflective. "—both come from Project Pacifist."

"Number Seventeen."

"Don't call me that."

"Whatever. Actually, you're one in a million, a classic case. Driven exactly and precisely down the path the government hoped all of you would follow, toward a deep sense of moral order. In many respects you were a success. But the analysts realized something too late. Your sense of moral order emerged from a vacuum. There was no justice in you, just a *need* for it. The repercussions were as destructive as the intended good."

"The sex," Jessica repeated, lowering her eyes.

"Among other things. One drive fueled many others. None were ever satisfied. The guilt . . . I studied you, I know. The others weren't so different."

"And Luther?"

The CIA agent harumphed. "Sanchez? He was *not* a success story. Went crazy. Funny thing, though. He had the highest IQ of all of you. He was a smart one."

Jessica was aghast. She wanted to cry, to scream. To shake Decker so hard she would wake up and care. "You don't feel sorry for anything, do you?"

"Just doing my job," Decker replied evenly.

"No, now you're lying. You've got an angle. This isn't part of the job. Telling me these things. Why are you telling me this?"

Decker shrugged. "If you don't kill me, I'll kill you. Either way, the secret doesn't matter anymore. You all know what's out there. You've won this round."

The light in the room trembled. "A strategist to the end."

"Don't bother getting sentimental. I only said you won *this* round."

So they sat and waited a while longer. No more talking. Jessica checked to make sure that Decker was held securely, that her hands and feet couldn't move or reach anything useful to freedom. The mobsters had tied her up so well that Decker couldn't squirm more than a quarter of an inch. Almost too tight. In spite of herself, Jessica felt sorry for the woman. She was bruised and in pain. She had no soul, no remorse. She was an unfeeling, pitiful thing.

"I can't forgive you. Ever," Jessica told her at length.

Decker snorted. "I didn't ask you to."

"I know, but somehow I think I should. I just can't."

"Oh, please!" Decker sneered, looking away. "Go jump in somebody's bed! It's what you do best in times like this. Do it with Hank."

"I've already tried," Jessica answered. She was remarkably composed now, clear-eyed, wise. "He won't let me."

"Who are you kidding? Can't handle you, maybe! Or doesn't want damaged goods. How about that? Or is he just a freak?"

Something crystalline emerged inside Jessica's breast, something spurred on by Decker's thick-crusted temerity, which produced an altogether different response from any she ever thought possible—an oasis in the mirage of the moment. In a life of twenty-nine years, a little bit more of that life made sense.

"Your research might think so," she said. "He's a Christian."

27

When Hank returned he carried a small duffel bag. He had yet to get used to the look of his ruined apartment.

"What are you going to do?" Jessica asked.

Hank held up two fingers over his lips, approached Decker. "I'll give you one more chance to deal with us."

"Or what?" Decker laughed. "If you had the stomach for killing you would have done it already."

"I want the files."

"No."

Hank reached into the duffel bag and pulled out a long-needled syringe, laid it on the table. Decker's insolence peeled from her face like a thin layer of skin. A caged and wary dread took its place.

"You won't make me talk," she boasted, but her eyes never left the needle.

"Too late. I'm past trying," Hank told her. He pulled out a couple of cotton balls, some rubbing alcohol, and last, a rubber-sealed vial of clear yellow fluid. The vial was labeled, but Decker couldn't read the print.

"Give it up, Dr. Blackaby!" Decker said as authoritatively as possible. "End this charade."

Hank plunged the needle through the seal, began drawing the contents into the syringe. "What's the matter? Don't you want to become a Christian?"

Decker was intelligent. Even so, it took a moment for the meaning to register.

"You're bluffing."

"Am I? Remming's been theorizing different transmission and treatment mechanisms for months. But don't worry, this is one of his latest efforts, from just before he left, actually. The earlier stuff didn't work too good. But that was on monkeys and rats."

Decker grew violent. Her nostrils flared like a wild horse; she began thrashing in her chair so forcefully that it fell over.

"Whatever you try to take from me is the property of the federal government! Do you hear! You'll be a fugitive!"

Jessica still didn't comprehend Hank's plan, but she watched Decker with troubled fascination. The agent lay pinned to the floor by the weight of the chair, cheek flattened against the carpet.

"Just a little random testing," Hank said mildly, waving the needle in front of her eyes like a hypnotist's watch. "Think about Project Pacifist. No different. Well, there is one difference. I'm at least telling you up front."

Decker had neither anger nor wit left. Now she begged. "I'll do anything! You don't know . . . you don't know! Please, I'll get the files. All of them. I wasn't going to kill you. I promise."

Hank took the rag and stuffed it back into Decker's mouth. He was tired of listening to her. "You are not a very nice person, Agent Decker. It would do you good to 'get religion,'" he said, chiding, making quotation marks in the air. "Don't you think?"

Decker's chest heaved from the mounting sense of claustrophobia. Hank patted her head, squirted the air out of the syringe until a little of the honeyed liquid fountained from the tip. "Think. Breathe through your nose." He waited until her breath became more regulated. "If someone didn't know better, they might think you don't like Christians. That's not true, is it?"

He didn't wait for an answer. Instead, he took the cotton ball and alcohol and wiped the skin on the muscle at the back of her arm. Decker kicked once then stopped. No point. She stared straight ahead, vacant-eyed, as if she had resigned herself to the imminent crack of a firing squad. Hank pressed the needle to her skin.

Someone rapped lightly on the door. The sound stopped him.

Hank jumped to his feet, grabbed the gun from Jessica, instructed her to get over by Decker, behind the break in the wall outside the line of vision. All his senses tingled. But when he peeked through the eyehole, he saw only a small woman in her thirties with a package in her hand. Hank closed his eyes, groaning. More than ever, he couldn't help but be suspicious.

"Who is it?" he called out.

"My name's Ellen. The flight attendant. I left word on your answering machine earlier this morning. I have a package for you."

Hank spun in a circle, thinking. It could be a trap. Finally, he said, "Step back two steps. I'm going to unlock the door. You open it, but don't enter. Just drop the package inside and leave."

"Umm, OK."

Hank watched through the hole. She didn't so much step back as shrink back. If she was for real at all, Hank couldn't blame her fear. When she was at a safe distance, he unlocked the door, then stepped back himself and took aim.

"Now?"

"Now," he called out.

The door creaked open, two, maybe three inches. A folded manila envelope fell to the floor. Ellen shoved it in a bit farther with her toe, then quickly closed the door.

"I'm sorry," Hank said, putting his mouth to the surface of the door. "I can't explain. Thank you."

Ellen didn't hang around long enough to say "You're welcome." As soon as she closed the door she was gone. Hank stooped, retrieved the envelope, opened the flap. Trepidation began to form in his belly, streaming out to the palms of his hands, which, buried in the envelope, began to sweat as they clutched and withdrew a single mini-cassette. He glanced wonderingly at Jessica, then popped it into his own recorder and hit play.

There in his apartment, Hank and Jessica and Special Agent Susan Decker, lying on the floor, became privy to the inner workings of that specially summoned task force operating in tandem with an internationally chartered organization to discuss the single greatest effort at social engineering ever contemplated by the human race, on a global scale that was both profound, unprecedented, and frighteningly doable. It took time for the story to unfold. They heard the conversation in the briefing room, with Remming and several other VIPs. Hank thought he heard the phrase "World Health Organization" but missed the rest. He was sure he didn't recognize the majority of the voices, including the leader's. But Decker knew at least one.

Newman.

The voices were slightly muffled; every now and then it sounded like fabric scraping the mic. He heard the presentation, the reserve and criticism in Remming's cautious additions to the dialogue. He heard someone named Charlie speak and another named Major General Sutton. A woman identified the leader as a Mr. Newman. Then he heard a door open, some sort of interruption, the leader guy excusing himself, after which Remming must have fumbled with the tape player, because it shut off unexpectedly and resumed with the leader speaking again after an undetermined interlude. More dialogue. Hank got the whole plan. The scope of the plans for the God Spot was awesome and intimidating but vague. He could do nothing but stare at the turning wheels of the tape, open-mouthed, feeling cold.

After a few more minutes: *"Dr. Saludin, welcome! We've been expecting you."*

The conversation shifted tone, grew tense. Hank tried to make out Remming's whispering, stopped the tape, rewound, listened again. A warning. Everyone leaving. Dr. Saludin and Mr. Newman exchanging words.

Then the unthinkable. A sharp, whispery pop, like the strike of steel cable.

Jessica put a hand to her mouth.

Was that what I think it was? Hank thought. Something hit the floor. What? The conversation on the tape turned abruptly to dreadful silence. Hank *heard* Remming's heart pounding. His own skin grew clammy.

"Pity that," Newman said. *"He was a brilliant man."*

Then he heard Remming press for specifics. He heard Newman

outline mandatory serotoxomiasin vaccines for all newborns, to destroy their capacity to biologically process STM-55 in morally critical brain regions. Then the final volley: Reverse Conversion—surgical removals of SPoT from uncooperative Christians. Hank gulped for air, stopped the tape, set it aside, almost like a dirty thing or a bomb that might explode in his hands. He stood, began to pace back and forth, back and forth, pulling at his hair, moaning. He couldn't help it. All he could think, say, feel, was, "No. No. Please, God, no . . ."

The God Spot was worse and bigger and more terrible than anything he could have ever imagined. And he was a part—maybe in some ways the biggest part right now because he had the power, depending on what happened next, to expose it all.

He knew then, no matter what, that exposure *must* happen. In a moment that goal became his single reason for living. No matter the cost.

Jessica numbly fumbled for the empty package, picked it up, turned it upside down. A small piece of paper floated to the floor. She picked it up, read it, handed it to Hank.

"I think this means something," she said.

Hank read the note, a scrap of a poem torn out of a book:

> *And did the Countenance Divine*
> *Shine forth from upon our clouded hills?*
> *And was Jerusalem builded here*
> *Among these dark Satanic mills?*
> *Bring me my bow of burning gold!*
> *Bring me my arrows of desire!*
> *Bring me my spear! O clouds, unfold!*
> *Bring me my chariot of fire!*

"Blake?" Jessica thought out loud.

Hank didn't care who wrote the poem. He was afraid for what it meant. He turned the paper over. On the back, two simple words. The handwriting, unmistakably, was Jay Remming's:

Forgive me.

Scrawled in fine-tipped black ink. Hank dashed to the phone—

where was the phone? He dug under a pile, tracing the cord from the wall, punched in Remming's home phone, wiping furiously at the skin of his forehead. He wanted to scream. At the back of his throat, fear began to choke him.

No, no!

No answer. The line was dead. Not even a ring. Just a dial tone, then the numbers he punched. Then nothing. He hung up, dialed again, pounding on the phone. Same thing. He tried the office. No answer. Remming's cell phone. Dead air. Hank held the receiver like a hammer and struck his desk, shouting, "No!"

Frightened, Jessica pulled on his shirt sleeve. "Hank? What? Tell me what's happening."

Hank slammed the receiver back onto the phone, hunched over the table, breathing deep gulps as if he were a goldfish in dirty, airless water. The room grew strangely calm.

"Remming's going to kill himself."

⚊ ⚊ ⚊

Remming knew there was no other way.

No one could save him now, least of all himself. The options available to him at this point were statistically insignificant. One thing, the only honorable thing he could do, rather than playing a mouse on a Ferris wheel, would be to command his own fate and destroy the data. All of it. Even his private research into the higher functions of STM-55 over the last several weeks. The only way he knew to secure the destruction completely would be to destroy himself with it. Otherwise he was a living ghost in hiding, a shadowy spectacle to his colleagues, an industry joke, or a dead man walking under Newman's control, forced to replicate his previous successes.

He felt little emotion in the decision, even less sadness. Only that it had come to this. It seemed so wasteful.

Precious little time for reflection, though. As with Hank and Jessica, Remming returned home to the closeup portrait of the barrel of a revolver pointed at his teeth, with Monitor Nine on the other end. The man was a stump. His eyes were shadowed and deep, heavy lidded, banished to ignominy by the bushel of brows that crowned his leather face. Remming found him to be very much like a caricature, a troll, a bridge dweller, pulled from the pages of the Brothers Grimm. Expressionless, Remming knew from experience that the troll was as content to pull the trigger as fix himself a sandwich. Remming had barely stepped through the front door before that deep, murky voice asked, "What were you doing on your computer at the office?"

Remming didn't flinch, granting the man taciturn compliance. "Erasing. So no one else could get at the data while I'm gone."

"What about the project?"

"I made copies."

Monitor Nine pulled back the hammer. "You connected to the mainframe. Why?"

"Deleting the Club Cranium thread. It's not necessary anymore."

Monitor Nine lowered the gun, uncocked his weapon, but his eyes remained fixed on Remming's face.

Remming said, "It's no secret that I want out. I don't want to be here. I don't want you to be here. I want to be free of this whole thing. But I'm not a fool. If you doubt my intentions, go check my car." He motioned with his head. "Loaded and ready to go. Only a few more clothes to pack. Or haven't you been watching me as well as you're supposed to?"

Monitor Nine grunted.

Remming set off upstairs, threw a few clothes in another suitcase. He took his time, but not too much time. He needed this to look as believable as possible. With any luck he could somehow take Monitor Nine with him.

Monitor Nine! The very presence of the man pushed the limits of his self-containment. Remming realized he was throttling the life out of the shirt in his hands. Absurdity and banality began to consume him. What was with the Dick Tracy *nom de plume*?

"What's your real name?" he demanded as he descended the stairs again. "If I'm going to be working with you, I refuse to call you *Monitor Nine*."

"A rose, Dr. Remming. What did the Bard say?"

"You are an illusion. You play a part."

"Illusions sometimes take on a life of their own."

"Bah! I refuse to guess at your riddles. Let's go."

Monitor Nine chuckled. It was a dreadful sound. "'A man must refuse to allow himself to be transformed into an institution.' Do you know who said that, Dr. Remming?"

"No, I do not." They stood facing each other. Remming had finished packing, finished trying to appear busy to avoid interaction. A new thought crossed his mind, one that felt very satisfying. If the man wanted a battle of wits, he would have one.

"Sartre," Monitor Nine muttered. His lips barely parted when he spoke. "A very interesting fellow. He knew something you do not. That the image of a man can become larger than the man himself. At that point, the man isn't a man; he's an object, the slave of himself."

Remming caught the not-so-subtle rebuke. Monitor Nine was preaching. Catlike, he narrowed his eyes, took a step forward.

"So by hiding behind your false image, your false name, you think to protect yourself from the reality of your pitiful little life?"

"There are twelve monitors," Monitor Nine said simply. "I am Monitor Nine."

An evasive, mysterious answer. All working for WHO? Surely not. More likely for the United Nations. Or some other shadow group. Of course it could have been just a ruse. But Monitor Nine seemed content. He wasn't trying to impress.

"Who do you work for?"

"Who do you?"

"I am free." A lie. But he would be free before the night was over. His last breath would be a free breath.

"'Man is condemned to be free,'" said Monitor Nine, expressionless and dark. He holstered his weapon behind his back. "'From the moment he is thrown into the world, he is responsible for everything he does.'"

Remming reached down, picked up his bags. "I'd like to go now."

§ § §

In the darkness of his apartment, Hank lifted Decker's chair to a sitting position. Her hair was a mess, had fallen over her eyes and face.

She was disheveled and still, obviously, in some degree of pain. The tip of the rag dangled from her open mouth.

Hank trembled but was clearheaded. He thought of the tape. "So you use someone. You take their skills and brilliance. But that's not enough. Then you take their life?"

Decker was in no mood for conversation. She, too, was surprised. More like confounded. Not at the killing but at the scope of what she was involved in. Good or bad, she had learned as much from the tape as Hank. Classified projects had various levels of security. Everything was on a need-to-know basis. Previously, she assumed the CIA was calling the shots and WHO and others were maybe doing some of the legwork; as such, she could leverage her position for a good two or three steps up the ladder. But the reality was quite the opposite and far more complex. *She* was the grunt labor. Muscle, not brains. And muscle never got promoted that way. Also, the breadth of the project, the plans being laid, the networking of people, and the nations involved— much less the specifics of the science, the God Spot itself—far exceeded her intuitions.

She had been used once again. In Hank's hands, the needle remained.

"Please don't," she tried to say through the rag, but Hank could not understand her and didn't care to try. A single tear slid down each of her pale-skinned cheeks. As they did, Hank put the needle to her arm, let it slide easily through her skin, then emptied the contents into Decker's bloodstream. All color drained from the woman's face, like someone had pulled a stopper from her leg. She shivered, moaned; her eyes rolled to white. Jessica, too, shivered, watching with dread. Hank held a cotton ball to the entry point, applied pressure for several seconds, then stripped a Band-Aid and put it over the tiny droplet of blood. Decker had a zombielike expression; there was a deadness in her eyes, as if someone had reached down and scooped out her soul with an ice-cream scoop, then plopped it down to melt beside her, unshielded by the mortal coil. Hank saw all this, her own fear. He closed his eyes. The tape, the poem from Remming, having strengthened his resolve, had also quashed his anger.

"The STM-55 DNA substructures are attached to a virus in the serum you've received," he told Decker, reaching into his bag, pulling out another vial of bright blue. He held it up in front of her blurring eyes. "The virus can be neutralized within forty-five minutes by another injection. This. That means you have approximately forty-four minutes to go to your office at the Plaza Hotel, retrieve all the files I delivered to you, and return. Do you understand me?"

Decker said nothing. Hank removed the rag from her mouth.

"You can do this, Agent Decker! It's not too late. This is an extremely stable solution. The virus is well behaved. And I have the necessary antibodies. If you give up now, I can't help you. But if you go and return, you have nothing to fear."

Decker did not respond. Hank leaped to his feet, went to the kitchen, shuffled quickly through the mess of items underneath the kitchen sink. He found a bottle of ammonia, brought it back, opened the lid, and waved the container underneath Decker's nose. She shivered, threw her head back. The fog lifted from her eyes.

"Stop. OK, fine, let me go," she snapped. Hank grabbed a pair of scissors and began cutting the duct tape. Jessica moved to an angle where she could keep the gun trained on Decker. Just in case. But Decker offered no struggle. She wiped at her tears angrily.

"I don't know that I can make it there and back in forty-five minutes."

"That's OK." Hank smiled. He dipped another syringe in the vial of blue, pulled the plunger, squirted some out. He knew she would find a way to make it. "I don't know that it will last much longer than thirty, anyway. Of course it may last an hour. Hard to say."

Decker's eyes bored into his like a lance of smoldering metal. Hank touched his watch. "Time's ticking. . . ."

The agent turned to go. Hank added one final thought. "We'll be watching you. If anyone—anyone, anything; if so much as a stray dog nips at your heels or follows you back here—" He held the syringe over the kitchen sink. "No antidote. The virus will be yours for good. Of course, the virus will run its course and go away. But all that it carries with it stays, in your brain, in your genetic code, forever."

Decker curled her fingers. Furious and afraid, she spun on her heel and stomped out the door. She labored for composure.

But she ran to her car.

28

About three seconds after Susan Decker's exit, both Hank and Jessica cognized everything they had just survived. In the semi-darkness, realization came like a deluge, leaving both chilled. It passed, followed by a hushed calm, then wonder and something near relief. They groped for one another, colliding in a rough embrace.

"I was so afraid," Jessica said. "So afraid."

"It's OK," Hank soothed, running his fingers through her hair. "Everything's all right now."

"Who were those guys? Where did they come from?"

"I have no idea. Probably not the Boy Scouts. It's OK, though. It's only us now."

"No. She's coming back—"

"—on our terms."

Jessica pulled away enough to study Hank's face. "You were amazing," she said. Her admiration was real. "I don't know how you did it. Kept your cool."

"You did pretty good yourself. Ever held a gun before?"

"Never," Jessica told him, with a quirky grin pulling at the corners of her mouth. "Well, once, but—"

She never finished. Hank pulled her face close, kissed her. Long and deep. Kissed her with every fragment of emotion and adrenaline that had hammered his system over the last few hours, all compressed down to the urgent touch of flesh on flesh. Her lips were soft and delicious. Jessica responded warmly, wrapping her arms around Hank's square shoulders. For a brief moment, neither cared about anything except the safety of the darkness and the nearness of the other.

"It's so strange," Jessica murmured, exhaling deeply. "Don't laugh, but I wish I were a painter."

"I'm not laughing."

"I so much want to capture this feeling and don't know how. A thousand words isn't enough, but perhaps colors would do. I see this thing in my mind, how you make me feel, and it's beautiful. Like a Monet, with all the subtle lights and shadows and colors. And everything's blurry up close. But then when I step back and see the whole thing, I want to just sit and soak in it. Do you know what I'm saying?"

Hank kissed her closed eyes, her forehead, her temple. "Yes."

Jessica still searched for words to explain the gentle taste of wonder on her lips. "Do you think you can miss someone you've never met?"

"I guess so. Why?"

The fact that she knew the answer made Jessica smile so brightly the entire room came shimmeringly alive. "I think I've been missing you all my life and I'm just now realizing it."

Hank didn't know what to say. Any word not perfectly weighted would have broken the delicate spell. Uncluttered, enchanted, such moments were not to be trifled with. All he wanted was to hold her. But Jessica, spirited Jessica, grew strangely serious again, as if the key to the one puzzle formed another puzzle in her heart. A cloud passed over her face, the burden of the years, of regrets which did not so easily let go of their hold.

"I've made a lot of mistakes, Hank. I think you know that."

Hank shook his head, glanced out the window shade for Decker; it wasn't yet time.

"Shh. Don't . . ."

"No, I need to talk about this. I want to. I understand more about myself now, but that doesn't change what I've done. I've got a lot of baggage and it'll take time to work through it all. Maybe a lot of time. I can't make any guarantees. I would understand if you wanted to walk away."

Hank touched her face. Didn't she understand? No, of course not. How could she? With eyes rimmed and glittering, even now, still fearing, she stood in that wondrous, dreadful place where a person can balance on only one foot, not yet knowing which way they will fall. Quick emotion rose in Hank. He wanted her to understand. Wisely, however, he shut his mouth, gave her only a single soft kiss on the cheek as an answer. She must fall where she *wanted* to fall. She could not be pushed. He pulled away. "I don't want a China doll, Jessica. I probably did once. Now I'd rather have someone who's on a journey."

Jessica lowered her head. "I'm not sure I can get to where you're going. You have something I don't."

Hank grew insistent. "Look at me." He made her look. When she did, he showed her his heart. "I'll slow down. I'll wait."

Jessica shook her head. It was hard to believe.

Hank continued softly. "You've captured me, Jess. I don't know how or why, not yet. Only that I'd rather walk this with you than without." He stopped short, wondered if he had said too much. "Listen, I can't say for sure that I want to commit my soul to you, Jessica. That's a big thing to me. A big step. But I am willing to share it for a while. I think—no, I know—we'd both be fools not to find out where this leads."

Jessica sniveled, tried to laugh. "Pretty heavy."

"Too much?" he asked.

She shook her head. "No. Just right."

The phone rang. Hank answered it quickly, grateful for the interruption.

"Hello, Dr. Blackaby," Jay Remming said calmly on the other end.

Hank leaped to his feet. "Dr. Remming! Are you all right, sir?"

"Yes, fine. Actually I wanted to inquire as to your condition."

"Sir?"

"Tell me everything, Hanson. We don't have time for anything less."

So Hank told him. About taking the files to Susan Decker. About meeting her and how she trapped them, threatened to kill them. About Jessica's involvement. Last, he sketched out the strange turn of events at the apartment, how they were presently waiting for Decker to return with the files. Remming did not let him finish.

"Listen very carefully to me, Hanson. You have got to get out of there right now."

"Why?"

"Don't argue! We can't discuss details. This line may be tapped. Did you get the package?"

"Yes."

Remming sighed. A great burden lifted. "Then you understand my grief."

Hank lowered his voice respectfully. "Yes. But—"

"No buts. Why are you still there? Why wait for the files?"

"Because I need evidence."

Remming grew irritated. "Did you listen to all of the tape?"

Hank sat down. "We heard the man, Dr. Saludin, die. Other things were happening. I don't know."

Remming was emphatic. "You have got to get out and get out now! Agent Decker will wear a tracer or bring a team with her or something. It's not safe. They will kill you and not think twice. Do you understand me?"

Hank resisted. "What about the files?"

"The files don't matter. Listen to the rest of the tape. Decker probably destroyed those files the day you gave them to her. Think about it, Hanson. I've been feeding them data on a weekly basis for months. I've seen horrors beyond imagination, all based on *my* research. They already possess it all. They just didn't want you to. That was the whole thing."

"So they can't be stopped," Hank breathed solemnly. The line grew silent.

"Oh yes they can," Remming murmured, warlike, proud. Hank understood.

"Dr. Remming—"

"No. No! This is the only way. I am ruined, Hanson. You tried to warn me. Thank you for that. But I am ruined."

Behind Remming's voice, Hank thought he heard the sound of a revving engine or maybe screeching wheels. Remming himself sounded strained, more so as time passed. Hank closed his eyes. He didn't know what to do or say. But he was afraid. It didn't need to end this way.

Remming knew better. "I am not without power. The power to destroy what is not known will devalue the currency of what is known. I have that power. Believe this about me, Hanson: In the end, I have chosen wisely."

Hank could hear the strain in his voice. His words now came in broken, distracted gulps. At length, he said again, "You must . . . get out of there now."

Hank was desperate, "If this god spot means anything, Dr. Remming, it means that people can change. They can be changed."

"Too late for me. Too late. Get out, Hanson! Now! All that matters . . ."

The line went dead. The last thing Hank thought he heard was a gunshot.

⊗ ⊗ ⊗

The alarm clock blinked to 9:32. Fifty-three minutes had passed. No more time left.

Without warning, a crack squad of four armed men burst into the room, literally tearing the door off its hinges. Dressed in noiseless black, all four wore night-vision goggles and carried weapons. Jessica's voice screamed in the darkness. Hidden under a blanket on the couch, she shouted frantically.

"Hank, you're too late! Come and get me! They're here!"

The men pounced like cats. Two fanned quickly through the apartment, angling, almost running, with weapons aloft. The other two fired nearly a dozen silent rounds up and down the blanket. The guns popped softly. Hot shells spewed from the weapons as foam and pillow stuffing sprouted into the air. Strange metallic clangs reverberated from a couple of the rounds, but no blood. Jessica's voice warped, lagged. A moment later, Susan Decker strolled into the room, flipped on the small lamp beside the sofa. She threw back the blanket, swearing. Underneath, atop a pile of pillows, a bullet-pierced answering machine struggled through another round of an endless loop message:

"Hank, you're too late! Come and get me! They're here!"

Then a warbled scream. Then, with the tape dragging and sticking, the machine played the whole thing again.

Swearing more violently, Decker touched the spot on the back of
her arm. She shouted at the men in black. "Abort! They're gone. Abort."

The men filed out, unaffected. Decker strolled into the kitchen,
turned on another light. On the table lay a bottle of aspirin with a
note:

"Take two and call me from heaven. Happy God Spot. H.B."

As Susan Decker fumed, Hank and Jessica, buried in traffic about
ten miles away, laughed and laughed. They hadn't felt mirthful at first,
not at all. At first it was simple urgency: medical stuff and bags and
clothes all thrown together, his computer, a few other belongings. At
first it was terror and flight and the squealing tires of Hank's Duster as
they screamed away from his apartment. For the first fifteen minutes
neither spoke a word. Both barely breathed. Remming had spooked
them. His logic made sense, but more than anything, Hank heard a level
of emotion in his voice like never before. There was a rawness, a dreadful
certainty, that cottoned Hank's mouth dry.

So the laughter began in whispers and weakness. A timid joke,
"Boy, did you see the look on her face! . . ." That sort of thing. Much
shoulder glancing. Sweaty palms. Jessica found herself hunching over,
as if she would quickly need to duck to the floorboard if someone
passed by. Yet as they purposefully lost themselves in traffic, their disposition lightened ever so slightly. And as emotions have a way of
doing, at about the tenth stoplight they hit, thrill and panic smeared
so suddenly and inexplicably that Hank was barely able to keep his left
foot on the brake pedal as he latched onto Jessica's face, tangling his
fingers in her hair, covering her lips with his own. It was a desperate
and grateful affection. She pulled him tighter. For a few, brief seconds
time stood still.

Until the car behind him honked.

The light had turned green. Hank ignored the sound, unwilling to
lose a moment of the connection. When the man honked again,
longer, Jessica couldn't help but giggle, pull away. Her eyes sparkled.

"You don't want to bring all of New York City to a halt, do you?"

"Is that where we are?" Hank grinned.

Jessica rolled her eyes teasingly. Gently, she pushed him away. *Go,* she moved her lips, pointing forward. Hank shifted back into his seat, let go of the brake. The man behind him jerked into the other lane as soon as he had the space. As he sped past, he mouthed curses at Hank through the window, gave him the finger, scowling. Hank just smiled, waved.

From there, the laughter had come easier, mostly at Susan Decker's expense. It was tense but cathartic. After a few minutes, Hank reached into his pocket and pulled out the vial of serum he had injected into Decker's veins. About a third of the yellowish fluid remained.

"Reach into that bag there, please," he said, pointing. "Yeah, there. See that syringe? Hand it to me."

Jessica leaned over mischievously and bit his ear. "What's the password?"

"Hey, careful with the driver!"

Jessica lingered in that position. Her tone grew reflective. "Hank, I don't ever want to be afraid like that again."

"Me neither."

"No, no. It wasn't the gun. I was terrified of the gun. Of everything, actually. But I was *afraid* only because I thought something might happen to you. I've never felt that before."

Hank took her hand. Jessica tried to shrug off the spell but found it difficult.

"This'll cheer you up," Hank said. "Give me that thing."

Jessica forced herself to chime in, play the game. "Password? Magic password?"

"Pretty please?" Hank ventured.

Jessica toyed with him. "No, no. Repeat after me: I, Hanson Blackaby, promise to never do anything stupid ever again, like letting the beautiful stranger I've fallen in love with go to a lab with me when she could get shot and killed there."

Hank burst into laughter. Before Jessica could react, he reached over and snatched the syringe. "Like you even gave me a vote in the matter."

He plunged the needle into the liquid. Jessica watched curiously at first, then in horror as he held the needle above his open mouth and squirted, then swallowed. His face contorted.

"Man, that is nasty stuff!" he groaned, shivering.

"What are you doing!" Jessica cried. "What in the world did you just do!"

Hank grinned a cocky grin, holding up the vial for her to see. "B-12. Nothing but a vitamin."

Jessica squealed with delight. In incalculable fashion compared to only a half-hour earlier, both felt better. Hank felt free, if for no other reason than all options but flight had finally been removed. And Jessica felt, at an indefinable subconscious level, that a new door was opening and an old door was closing. And both the opening and the closing were good.

Hank said, "You know you slipped just a minute ago." He searched her face, framed in shadowed red. "Do you really think I'm falling in love with you?"

Jessica received the question calmly. Inside, her choices distilled to hope and fear. This time, hope won. Easily. Eyes wide open, fixed on Hank, she said, "I think so. I know I am."

Hank barely heard. Suddenly, he jerked the car hard right.

"What?!"

Hank held up two fingers to his lips. Jessica looked, understood. He had swerved into an underground parking lot next to a Greyhound station. They parked, got out, grabbed a few things, locking the doors behind them. When they were a good distance away, Hank said, "Sorry. It's probably not bugged, but who knows? I just realized we ought to bail for a couple of days and lay low. Any ideas?"

"My mother's place in Hamden? It's not far away."

"Hmm. I bet they'd think to look there. What do you think?"

Jessica shrugged.

Hank said, "I've got a friend in Jersey. He's not a relative and has no connections to the hospital. Let's head to his place."

They marched up to the ticket counter, bought tickets. The bus they needed was scheduled to leave in half an hour.

"It's our lucky day," Hank mused.

"Maybe. The question is, how long will our luck hold? Are we safe yet?"

"You mean is it over?"

Jessica nodded.

Hank reached into his jacket pocket and pulled out the miniature cassette Remming had left him. "I have a hunch this will tell us."

☗ ☗ ☗

What a waste . . .

A surprisingly casual and lucid thought, coming from the mind of a man hurtling over curving asphalt at eighty-five miles an hour while behind him a madman had already shot at him twice. Apart from that singular thought, everything else seemed dreamlike. Jay Remming, perhaps one of the most brilliant scientists of the last half century, was about to die. Dreaming or awake, nobody understood that with greater clarity than he.

Indeed, it all seemed like so much folly. Like a bad novel, hand-crafted in gilded leather, with the obvious question: Why? Why bother with all the accoutrements of class and substance when the tale in between is so poorly told and the ending so poverty stricken with futility? Hardly an heirloom or meaty charge to the next generation of dreamers—more like a pitiful curio, the embarrassing purchase of some eccentric antique dealer, ruefully placed on his coffee table to discuss with family and friends in bemusement, or perplexity, or maudlin tones of wistful remembrance.

What a waste . . .

Behind him, Monitor Nine knew the game was afoot and gave full chase. The experience was surreal, almost gothic. They were about forty miles outside of the northern extreme of New York City, heading farther north, up I-684 at first, toward the lush foothills of the Taconic Mountains, then generally north and east on state roads. New York State grew quickly rural outside of its major enterprises, so the roads Remming chose were increasingly winding and undulated and mostly absent of traffic, though they did hurl past one or two autos intermittently. It was dark. It was quiet—except for the contented purr of German engineering humming under the hood of his BMW. Everything was normal except for the speeds, the chase, the rage in the predator, the coolness of the prey. The destination.

When Remming had made it clear that he was not heading to the airport with a couple of quick, unannounced off-ramps, trying to shake his tail, Monitor Nine had aggressively made his displeasure equally clear, and in increasingly threatening fashion. Newman's henchman had revved and honked and tried to pass Remming, as if he could push him from the road and force him to brake. Remming, steady-as-she-goes, constantly blocked his ability to pass. He was calm (relatively speaking) and focused. But the longer the road stretched, the more his translucent sense of tragedy yielded to panic and simple, grim determination.

They were deep into the darkness now and the road grew treacherous at present speeds. So Remming accelerated. Tires squealed. A blast ripped the air. Another gunshot blast, the third. The back shield of glass in Remming's BMW shattered into ten thousand prismatic fragments. Remming instinctively dived to the side, jerking the car slightly with the motion of his hands. He quickly peered over the dashboard and righted himself. Two cars flew past; he narrowly missed one.

Not yet. Not yet . . .

Another jolt rocked the car—his head flew back—this time Monitor Nine ramming him from behind, bumper to bumper. No, this was no dream. And the game was no longer a game. Monitor Nine understood the stakes too well.

Either he didn't want Remming to take his notes with him, or, at this point, he wanted to make sure Remming, in finality, died with his notes.

The two cars played a furious round of cat-and-mouse for several minutes, bobbing, weaving. Veering suddenly, Remming chose one specific road, rubber squalling as he slammed on the brakes and pulled hard to the right, moving deeper into the dark-hilled countryside. He maintained a dogged course. Not random. He knew the destination.

But not yet . . .

He gritted his teeth, breathing harder, hands locked in a death grip on the wheel. Another gunshot, sounding like a cannon. He heard the blast penetrate the metal skin of his trunk. From his rearview mirror he saw Monitor Nine's thick body, half hanging out the window, shotgun in hand, his face hidden in shadows. Remming hunkered down. For the last forty-eight hours, he had wondered incessantly what he would be thinking in these final moments . . . precisely now in fact. He could think of nothing. Only a dim sense of regret. And how proud he had been when his first son was born. And the smell of coffee in the morning, so many years ago, when his wife woke before him just to make him a pot.

And his Nobel.

He realized with a shock he had forgotten the prize, left it at home, sitting on the shelf, collecting dust.

Nothing so foolish as pride. He recalled his own thought in Guatemala. *Pride kills.*

The road opened up just ahead. Remming knew this place. It emerged from his past as if it were steam rising off a hot spring in the winter. (He reached down, pushed the cigarette lighter into its socket to charge.) When he had been a romantic man, he had brought a woman here and asked her to marry him. And she had said yes. How many years ago? Two days, it seemed like. Two days and a lifetime. Nothing romantic about *this* moment, though. Remming, even now, could appreciate the irony. A Shakespearean flourish never hurt any exit.

Quickly, he ripped off the cap to the two-gallon can of gasoline he had placed in the front seat, began madly shaking the fuel over the front and backseat, himself, everything. The air instantly grew heavy with fumes. Two more containers of gasoline lay on the floorboard, front and back.

Up ahead about thirty yards, lost, but known to him, the road curved sharply. Remming couldn't see it yet and didn't have his brights on, but he knew the place, so he rolled down the back window halfway. The gas would need plenty of oxygen. Then he unbuckled his safety belt. Then he turned off his headlamps . . .

And hit the brakes full force.

It was not what he had planned to do; it was in fact his final act of defiance, spontaneous and unscripted. But it worked.

The automobile driven by the man named Monitor Nine slammed into him from behind so hard Remming's neck whiplashed; but both vehicles were propelled forward. The sound of grinding, tearing metal filled the air. Front bumper and rear bumper locked together.

The cigarette lighter popped out. (Nothing was left to chance.)

Remming hit the accelerator again. Monitor Nine was hooked. Remming's fate would be his own.

Another gunshot ripped the air. Remming felt like a baseball bat hit him in the head. He felt blood, saw his life supply splattered in mucky globules on the windshield in front of him. Everything began to grow softly, sickeningly dark.

Bring me my bow of burning gold!
Bring me my arrows of desire!
Bring me my spear! O clouds, unfold!
Bring me my—!

The BMW broke its embankment, plunging over the fifty-foot granite bluff.

The dream now was measured in heartbeats. With his last bit of consciousness, Remming slumped forward, thumbing the lighter loose from its socket.

So beautiful, he thought absurdly, *the darkness. No . . . so cold.*

He was numb. Suspended in midflight, he was half dead already. For a moment he felt relieved. Then came the fear, the final rush, before judgment. His fingers worked the lighter loose. The metal thread tumbled to the floor; the chariot of fire erupted in flames, dragging Monitor Nine, screaming, behind it, down the plummeting cliff side, an orange ball of molten fire, consumed from the inside out.

By the time the two cars collided with the earth, the flames reached to heaven.

On tape, the sound of Remming's voice was haunting. At nearly midnight, Hank and Jessica sat together on the sofa in the living room of his friend's house. The man and his wife had already gone to bed; Hank had asked for some privacy. Though he and Jessica were exhausted, the lure of Remming's final message drove sleep away, at least for him. Jessica curled against his shoulder like a cat by a fireplace, eyes closed, lips barely parted, her chest swelling and deflating in deep, even strokes.

"Hanson, I have urgent information to relay and little time," the message began. Remming sounded cramped, solemn. "By the time you hear this, I will probably have expired. This is to my shame. Follow the course you have chosen and it will, no doubt, lead you to a better circumstance than I now find myself inhabiting.

"You alone will understand the ramifications of what I am about to tell you, so you must take pains to explain it properly to the American press and whomever else you deem appropriate. A massive, well-funded research program is under way under the auspices of the World Health Organization. Somewhere in the mountainous regions of southern Guatemala sits a thoroughly equipped and fully operational laboratory that is highly classified. Their stated purpose is to exploit the pineal gland anomaly for the purpose of, crudely speaking, a better riot-control mousetrap. Actually, I'm talking about mass behavioral modifications as the presumed starting block, with grander schemes to follow." Remming paused, cleared his throat. "Hanson, you should know that people of the Christian faith will shoulder the brunt of the political and social repercussions of these programs, at least for a time. One way or another, they will be exploited, both for the beneficial genetics of STM-55 and, depending on the whims of politics and circumstance, against. Severely, brutally against.

"I don't have much time for details, but in my private research I have uncovered two monumental additions to the present grid of research—factors which have not yet been contemplated or discussed. I saw no evidence that the teams in Guatemala were thinking in these directions. This is strategically significant.

"Hanson, as I'm sure you've read and learned by now, serotoxomiasin, along with its accompanying and highly sophisticated neural delivery mechanism, is the neurotransmitter responsible for massive behavioral changes in Christians. The WHO effort assumes, much like I and my colleagues did for a long while, that the neurotransmitter is the sum total of the effectant system. Instead I have learned that it is barely one-third of the equation! The first third is this: Before anything ever happens, a novel trophic hormone must be released in quantity from the cerebral cortex. I don't know when this happens, but at some stage in the brain's development, it does. Without the trophic hormone, all receptors for serotoxomiasin remain dormant and nonbinding. Of course, as our research has proven, this is the native state in all people, because, amazingly, everyone has the receptors, and thus the potential. But the trophic hormone turns on the switch. We've been operating under the assumption that the *anomaly* was the switch, the SPoT gray matter. But it's just the opposite. *The trophic hormone is the primary trigger which launches the pineal gland anomaly itself.* Prior to the trophic flood, the anomaly is an unrecognizable dot of ten to twenty cells and will remain completely nondescript throughout a person's lifetime. But the trophic flood, like any other trophic hormone—such as those in the pituitary gland which regulate growth patterns and sexual maturation—activates the anomaly, which immediately begins to grow in size and produce trace amounts of serotoxomiasin. Simultaneously, the hormone proceeds to activate every STM-55 receptor throughout the body, allowing the pineal gland anomaly to exert its considerable influence. And not only in the brain, but in all types of tissue, muscle, nerve, etc. I've never seen anything like it. . . ."

In spite of his own fearful predicament, Remming's voice was childlike with awe at the mystery of his own discovery. For just a moment, his voice rose above the constraints of a hushed whisper. Hank, too, was dumbstruck. The wonder of redemption spread before him like a feast—not just a feast of the spirit, but of the frame as well. SPoT didn't turn on a switch; it *was* the switch. The entire STM-55 system, subnetworks and all, lay hopelessly dormant apart from trophic activation. Therefore SPoT could not determine who was a believer and who wasn't; it simply served as evidence. Biologically speaking, a believer was someone who was activated through the trophic flood.

Then, once activated, STM-55 starts shaking and baking. Suppressing and encouraging various behaviors. Amazing! But Remming did not allow him to formulate or ponder long.

"The second third of the equation is the truly amazing part, the part that breaks all the rules! Listen carefully, because you aren't going to believe me. Everything in the human body is constructed with l-form optical isomers. You know that; it's fundamental. *Not serotoxomiasin!* Somehow, the substance of serotoxomiasin is dependent on the *d-form* optical isomer and, in nearly every case, *refused to bind to an l-form.* I discovered this by chance when I looked for chirality. In fact, d-form serotoxomiasin seems to be given precedence in the neurochemical hierarchy, determining uptake and destruction or production and release of otherwise autonomous neurohumoral systems. I suspect this power of suppression is a key to the behavioral influence the transmitter creates. But can you imagine? D-form anything is contrary to rational physiology. The WHO teams aren't even considering it as an option. They would never dream to think in that direction."

Not in a million years, Hank thought. L- and d-forms were like two completely different key shapes to two completely different locks. Everyone knew the right key to the lock of any biological life was l-form. Enter the god spot. *Contrary to our nature. But it works.*

"Let me say it again: The neurotransmitter serotoxomiasin and its receptors are *dextra*rotary form. Do you see? The l-form synthetics the scientists in Guatemala are working on will not bind properly, rendering their influence nil nine out of ten times. No matter how accurate they are with the content, if the direction of the isomers isn't correct, their otherwise flawless antibodies are worthless. And as you well know, we don't have the technology to isolate d-form within a biological entity . . . so even if they figure this out—which they won't—it would be impossible for them to truly replicate the effect of STM-55 on a consistent, measurable level. They're stuck.

"I will concede one thing, however: There must be a few congenital l-form mutations out there, because some of their trials, however barbaric, did yield impressive results. And since serotoxomiasin is a cutting-edge substance, there is a statistically reasonable chance that they will create a sort of dual effect with their synthetics—variations on a theme, perhaps, that could theoretically bind partially to other receptors, especially those for serotonin. But my tests have clearly shown that the native receptors activated by the trophic hormone are specifically d-form, which means serotoxomiasin is itself d-form, which means that in every other case they might as well be reading their formulas backward and upside down. What they've got now is a mixture of dumb luck, coincidence, serendipitous pharmacology, and misdirected causalities. Do you see, Hanson? Look at the research for yourself. Without the knowledge of the trophic hormone and the d-form specification of the neurotransmitter, all they can do is study the natural occurrence, but they cannot trigger such an occurrence themselves, nor can they re-create synthetic variations of the effect because every attempt at mimicry would default to l-form. Even their heinous transplant attempts are two stages too late to be of any benefit, since there is no authentic trophic flood in the native system to turn on receptors."

By now Hank could hear Remming's mounting nervousness. There was a pause in the tape, one deep breath, then another. He felt claustrophobic just listening.

"Having said all this, we still must exercise extreme caution and go on the offensive with what we know. We are not out of the proverbial woods yet. Hanson . . . Dr. Blackaby. As a colleague, as an American citizen . . ." His voice grew weak for just a moment. "As a friend . . . you must turn everything over to the press and the proper authorities, as quickly as possible. I am going to transfer everything—except the latest data on the trophic hormone and the d-form structure of serotoxomiasin, but everything else from Club Cranium from beginning to end—to a new directory on the university's mainframe."

Remming spelled out the new IP address planned for the data, repeated it, paused. All Hank needed was whatever password Remming would decide to assign to the server. The first had been "Olympus."

"Icarus," Remming murmured, anticipating the question. No self-pity in his voice, yet it sounded mournful nonetheless. Remming was a scientist by trade. Yet more than ever before, facing what he faced, he acted from the soul of a poet.

The tape ended with a promise. "I will make sure all hard copies of the data are destroyed. All the files downloaded to the server will self-erase in forty-eight hours. You have that much time, no more. For my sake, I ask one courtesy: that you destroy this tape as well when you have completed your task. All else I take to my own destiny."

The tape clicked off, from static to silence, then suddenly on again.

Remming had a final thought. "I've cleared your record at Columbia. Even if I hadn't, you would succeed as a surgeon, Hanson. Not would. *Will* succeed. I'm sure of it."

Those were the last words of Jay Remming that Hank would ever hear.

29

H ank awoke the next morning still mulling over Remming's final message. Something premonitory deep inside felt that Remming was dead. And though he was sorrowed by the thought, the profundity of the sacrifice forced him back to reality, to the more immediately comprehensible, which was the data itself.

So much for freedom. Yet he mourned Remming's death.

He and Jessica had fallen asleep on the couch, slumped over, loosely entwined; neither had moved an inch all night long. Her nearness was good. So good, in fact, that though his mouth was pasty and his skin felt clogged, the experience of her resting in his arms in the warm morning light was simply too precious to trade for the squeaky pleasure of clean teeth and a hot shower. The time was half past ten o'clock. Hank hadn't slept this long in . . . how long? His friends had both long since gone to work, he was sure. So Hank closed his eyes again, settling in for simple pleasures: lying on the sofa, listening to Jessica breathe—beautiful!—and, of course, the inevitable need—or at the very least temptation—to unravel the mysteries of the faith that defined him and countless millions.

Everything seemed to fit. After a long absence of spiritual definition in his life, Hank looked forward to unpacking the message that had once captured his heart. From what little Remming had shared, much remained to discover about the biological mystery of grace. Nevertheless, from a theological perspective, Hank thought it wise to theorize only what struck him as obvious.

The trophic flood was likely not prenatal but probably occurred at or near the moment of "salvation." Something in the brain was somehow triggered by the act of faith, or so he guessed. But it made sense. Quite the contrary to being a transparent, purely spiritual event, why couldn't the act of spiritual regeneration literally begin a regeneration of the body as well?

Hank had read enough to know that serotoxomiasin was like no other neurotransmitter he had ever studied or encountered, nor was it like any pharmacology yet invented. Its structure and substance were complex; its benefits, broad, deep, spanning the gamut of emotional, physiological, and mental health. Yet herein was divinity most evidenced: no known negative side effects. Aspirin couldn't make such a claim, much less Prozac or Ritalin or AZT. Within the largess and precision of Providence lay a breathtaking pattern of tax-free utility.

But if the trophic flood was beautiful, Remming's claims of optical orientation were mind-boggling. Again, Hank had the barest threads of information, but much of it made sense at first blush. If humanity operated naturally with sin—emerging in thought and behavior from some construct of self-destructive genetics—then it would only make sense that something almost "unnatural" would need to be released into the system to wage war against the "magnetic" attraction of man's inherent tendencies. Sin was a spiritual and psychological reality, Hank knew. It carried a theological definition. But what if it were biological as well? After all, Adam's fall wasn't merely a spiritual death. It was physical, too. What if part of that physical dying involved a reorientation of the genetic code? Why couldn't the stain of sin soak into the human frame so deeply that even brain functions were altered? And why couldn't part of the work of grace be about restoring the brain and other body systems to a previously superior state?

Remming had alluded to the ability of serotoxomiasin to control other transmitters, both for suppression and elevation. That made STM-55 king of the jungle upon activation, the tactical commander in the hierarchy of dominance. On any field of battle, the other soldiers all saluted when the field general arrived, including the lieutenants who had been running the show before his arrival. Everything operated better with the tactical commander in place, made more sense, had more direction. Probably in every person STM-55 began as a nominal influence, but like any other brain function, the more it was used, the stronger it became.

Since the interplay of all the soldiering neurotransmitters were critical determinants of decisions, behaviors, and attitudes—literally fighting for mindshare and reaction—the fact that serotoxomiasin could insert itself into the equation and command an otherwise unachievable, yet natural alternative would be to invert the previous, natural reality of living in a fallen world. Wouldn't it?

Hank breathed a low breath of wonder.

It meant man was being re-created from the inside out.

"And a simple blood screen could tell you," he mused out loud, surprising himself with the thought. Now that they knew what chemistry to look for, a simple blood test could reveal who was a Christian and who was not.

New life. New blood.

The irony was too much for him. He started to laugh. Startled, Jessica stirred from her slumber. "Hmm?"

"Sorry, nothing. Go back to sleep."

Jessica pushed herself up, blinked her eyes. Complete confusion. If it had all come down to that moment; for life or death, she couldn't have said where she was. Bit by bit, glancing all about, she regained her orientation.

"I'm up. I'm up."

"I need to connect to Columbia. I want to download Remming's data."

"I hear a 'but' in there," she murmured, smacking her lips. "Everyone's got a big 'but.'"

Hank held up his hands. "No modem."

Jessica pulled herself to a sitting position, started to get up. Hank grabbed at her shirttail and pulled her backward until she fell into his arms. Blooming love or no, Jessica was still not a morning person.

"Hank, you've got my heart. But you better let go of my shirt."

Hank chuckled. "Ooh! The lawyer speaks."

In spite of a valiant effort, Jessica could not entirely suppress a grin. She broke free of his grip, moved across the room, peeling apart the blinds of a nearby window to stare into a sunny blue sky streaked with ribbons of frothy pearl white.

"I bet your friends have a modem here you could connect with. If we had swung by the hotel, I could have grabbed my Powerbook. It has a modem."

"Did you say Powerbook?"

"Uh-huh."

"Mac? Not PC?"

Jessica nodded. Hank grinned a huge grin. No more confirmation necessary. Here, at last, was love. He climbed to his feet, began scouring about for a computer in the house, found it in a little reading room just off the master bedroom. It was a PC, but it had a modem. Hank could make it work.

He plugged it in, fired up his Powerbook, connected to the Net, and typed in the IP address. Password: "Icarus."

He was in.

Just as Remming said, everything was there, like ripe fruit waiting to be plucked. Hank began an immediate download of the entire site.

The last of the files downloaded just before lunch. Hank strolled into the living room where Jessica waited, reading a book of poetry. She had showered but still wore yesterday's clothes. Regardless, to Hank she looked fresh and wonderful.

"Did you get it?" she asked.

"Yep. All of it. Haven't looked through it yet, but I'm sure everything is there. Dr. Remming is a very thorough man."

"*Was* a thorough man, unfortunately. Take a look."

She motioned to the morning paper, haphazardly strewn, opened to page five on the clear-coated oak coffee table. Hank skimmed, saw. His skin grew chalky. Midway down, a bold headline proclaimed the inevitable: "Renowned Scientist Found Dead In Fireball."

"You were close?"

"No one was close to Jay Remming." He folded the paper, leaned back, covering his face with both hands. No sense of personal loss, just grief for the man.

Jessica tried to change the subject. "I should call Missy Jenkins in Detroit, don't you think?"

Hank mumbled through the palms of his hands. "What about the *Times?*"

"Missy should get first crack. She helped us quite a bit."

"Fair enough."

Jessica pulled her phone out of her purse. She dialed a long string of numbers and waited.

"You know," Hank said presently, "I think maybe I should move the final year of my residency to the University of Oregon. Portland, right? What do you think about that?"

Under the light of Jessica's brightened eyes, the whole room shimmered.

"They've got a pioneering program, I hear."

"And the local attractions . . . hard to beat."

Jessica tossed her hair, teasing him. Hank leaned closer, but she held up one finger, as if to say, *first things first.*

Then she spoke, but not to Hank.

"Missy Jenkins, please."

웅 웅 웅

"Yeah, Missy speaking."

Her tone sounded like the flavor of a shot glass full of vinegar and lime juice. Hardly inviting, but so what? The day had been lousy from the beginning, so everyone could just wallow in it with her. Tomorrow was the deadline for her story—actually, this afternoon by six o'clock, which meant that, practically speaking, she had already missed her big shot. Primary layout for page one was complete. Jack and the other editors had agreed on the major stories. Everything was in place, she wasn't on the short list, and none of her begging made a difference. In fact, begging only worsened the matter, prompting Jack to hurl a few needless insults at her earlier this morning.

Missy still smarted from that exchange.

All of which seemed terribly ironic considering the rash of mysterious and anonymous assailants threatening her life. She had been shot at once and nearly ran off the road twice in the last few days—all for an apparently unimportant story. Objectively speaking, she couldn't fault Jack. Credible journalism requires credible sources. But why the secret little warnings from hired fists over a story that—they must've known—was dead on the vine? She knew the pressure that came with a piece like this. She knew there were forces behind the scenes that had probably whispered her name more than once. She also knew that if they truly wanted her dead, she would *be* dead. Obviously, they hoped to scare her. But Missy Jenkins didn't scare easily. Except when a deadline came and went, and with it, her opportunity not so much for glory anymore (though that would be nice), but more for revenge. For fears and warnings. For the victims.

For Luther Sanchez.

This thing had gotten into her blood. It was personal now.

So it didn't take a fool to understand how even the thought of Jessica O'Connel's voice on the other end of the line could suddenly make everything better. She didn't mince words.

"Got anything for me?"

She could hear Jessica grinning across the miles of phone line. "Only about three hundred pages of data outlining the research into the brain we told you about the other day."

Missy licked her lips. "The god spot."

"Crudely spoken, yes."

"I'll take it all. All of it. The sooner the better."

"Are you sure?" Jessica teased. "Because if you aren't sure, I think we may be able to find someone here in New York—"

"For pete's sake, I'll give up chocolate!" Missy pleaded. She knew Jessica was yanking her chain, but it couldn't hurt to play along. Already, she had scribbled a half dozen lead ideas on her reporter's pad.

"How do you want the stuff?" Jessica asked. "Fax? E-mail?"

"I'll take it in skywriting if I have to. But e-mail would—"

"Hold on," Jessica said, cutting her short. Missy heard another voice in the background but couldn't tell what he was saying. Must be Hank. Jessica returned quickly to the line.

"How about if we just give you an address and a password and let you download it for yourself right off the mainframe?"

Missy's heart skipped a beat. "Nothing would please me more."

8 8 8

"I promise you, please—anything!—I don't feel well at all!"

"I understand," the doctor replied evenly, a young highbrow internist in private practice in Upper Manhattan. There would be no CIA physicians consulted on this matter because there would be no official report. "I believe you, Ms. Decker. But I can't prescribe something for nothing. And right now all I can find is nothing."

Feeling faint, Susan Decker wiped her forehead. She hadn't slept a wink last night, drifting between feverish and weak one moment to chilled and weightless the next. She passed in and out of hysterics. Her tongue itched. Her fingers tingled. Her brain seemed to be swelling. She was sure of it. Of course, the thermometer always showed a rock-solid 98.6. . . .

"I know you can help me!" she demanded. "I'm not one of your pretty little fools! There are broad-spectrum antibiotics you can legally prescribe."

"Listen, if you want, come back in a day or two for more tests. All I can tell you right now is that your blood work is clean, your CBC and chemistry panel are both normal. You have no external indications." He held up his hands. "I'm stumped. Maybe this is an allergy?"

"No!" Decker roared. She felt herself swooning. "If you are too stupid to assist me I'll go somewhere else."

And so she did, storming from the office. Don Quixote chasing the windmills of God.

8 8 8

At the parish for midweek Mass, Father Ravelo had prepared a homily based on Paul's letter to the Ephesians, chapter two, verses eight and nine: "For by grace you have been saved through faith; and that not of yourselves, it is the gift of God; not as a result of works, that no one should boast."

He read the text aloud in his soothing, gentle manner. Before him, the faces he saw, old and young, mostly poor, dressed in plain clothes and weathered skin, appeared to his well-trained eyes to be something very near to angels, the beloved family of Father God. Adjusting his horn-rimmed glasses, the priest took a deep, chesty breath, then folded his hands to a peak at his chest as he let his voice carry out across the parish hall.

"There is something in all of us that yearns to please God. But this desire is often more akin to the need to please ourselves than it is to holiness, for such desire, at its very heart, is deception. It is blind self-will. 'There is none that does good, not even one.' We cannot please God one whit with our foolish attempts to please him. Yet if you are in Christ, his pleasure rests on you in full. Why? How can one thing be a lie and the other be a truth? Because wherever the grace and mercy of God rest, God is pleased. So here is the paradox: When we quit trying to impress God, when we quit trying to win his favor and instead fall on his mercy, suddenly then, in that moment, his mercy and favor will fall on us like warm rain in the summertime. In the goodness of the heart of God, we are granted the very thing we cannot achieve as soon as we are willing to admit in humility that we cannot achieve it.

"Beloved, our earthly father, Adam, was once perfect in form, function, and spiritual faculties. He breathed the grace of God and walked with him in the Garden. His spirit was alive with God. His body was whole—no death, no sickness. His mind was in tune with the thoughts of God. He was God breathed, God minded. And God was pleased." Ravelo smiled wistfully. "Does that sound like you? I know it does not sound like me."

He glanced up from his notes just in time to see the double doors at the back of the sanctuary slowly open. Ricky Carletti slipped through and quickly took a seat on the very last row. His black fedora was pulled low over his eyes. Ravelo smiled again.

"My friends, we underestimate the fall of man. We underestimate the legacy of sin we carry in our being. We think we are only mildly stricken, but our thoughts are desperately wicked. Consider the state of man: wars, sickness, poverty, abuse, selfishness, sorrow. Yet some-how we think in all this we have done little more than lose our car keys. We convince ourselves of our inherent goodness and then go about our lives making all our decisions based on instinctual self-preservation, which only perpetuates the very problems we abhor when multiplied across nations of self-preserving people. We curse the flawed masses and the problems they cause. Yet *we* are *they*. The individual is merely the singular expression and source of mass corruption. It's in our genes. If I were an electrician I'd tell you we're not wired right anymore. The problem is *much* more than cosmetic. A disciplined and self-improved life cannot change the womb from which we emerged."

Ravelo paused, not for effect or dramatic interpretation, but because the reality of his message welled up with fresh revelation for his own life. He was no different, no better, than Ricky Carletti or Luther Sanchez. But there was a difference.

"Ah," he whispered. "But then, into each of our lives, the favor of God in the person of Jesus Christ opens a door. And the light that shines through—like a candle burning in the window of a woodsman's house, far out in the frozen snow, promises to the owner of that house the possibility of warmth and shelter after a hard day of exposure in the wintry cold—so does the light of Christ transform our humble, fallen state into a place where the pleasure of God can rest. Not because of anything we have done or ever could do. But because for one brief moment in history there lived a man, a man like us, but unlike us; a man with the mind of God, as Adam once knew, who did not try to preserve himself, but gave his life for many. And that, my friends, forever and completely, pleased God."

⊗ ⊗ ⊗

In a few days, the whole story would be blown wide open. Missy Jenkins and the *Detroit Sentinel* would make sure of that, with Dr. Hanson Blackaby among the quoted sources, along with multiple references to the Club Cranium files. The story would begin with Luther Sanchez—that was the local touchpoint—but it would go much farther, much deeper, into the echelons of government and power. It would launch from the failed experiments of the sixties, including the infamous Project Pacifist. Though often disjointed, the links from the forcible social engineering and mind-control research of Project

Pacifist, to the much broader and more potent applications of the pineal gland anomaly known as the God SPoT, would be obvious. A foundation was laid thirty years ago, and then built upon in the last three, in secret, but sanctioned nonetheless by the government of the United States itself. No doubt, there would be a congressional over-sight committee assigned to investigate the ensuing scandal. Within days—weeks at the most—the compound in Guatemala would be closed. Maybe closed entirely, or maybe just dismantled with a big enough public spectacle on CNN to appear to be closed, while the powers that be merely shifted operations to another location. The director of Central Intelligence, a Columbia University alum, who pulled the funding strings on behalf of WHO and convinced two key university officials to look the other way, would face prosecution and disgrace. Jay Remming's name would be mentioned frequently, with puzzled speculation as to what he took to his grave. Hank burned the only remaining media that revealed the answer.

Yet before the uncertainties of the not-so-distant future played themselves out, weeks before press briefings, rampant coverage, con-gressional posturing and senatorial tirades, in the jungled foothills of the Guatemalan highlands, research proceeded just as it had for months, delving into the mysteries of the human brain, mapping the resources and effects of STM-55 on the body, mind, and disposition.

And somewhere there, safe for the moment behind steel fences and top-security apparatus, on one of the stainless-steel tables lay the preserved body of a deceased Arab scholar.

Cause of death: a single gunshot to the chest at point-blank range.

The lifeless gray shell of Abu Hasim El-Saludin was surrounded now by a team of physicians who, under orders from Stewart Newman, were searching for something. Something small and innocuous, imperceptible in its early stages, especially if one didn't know what or where to look.

The scientists carved a small hole in the skull. They made precise and delicate incisions. There, tucked away under the frontal lobe, near the pineal gland, the truth was revealed.

Just three short days ago, if the men had looked, the surface of the brain in this region of this man would have been smooth and undisturbed, like most every other brain. But something had happened to Abu Hasim El-Saludin three days ago. He was changed. He became something different, physically and spiritually. And the evidence was plain: a thin layer of cells, discernible only under a microscope at this stage of development, but quantitatively real.

A touch of the divine.